HEART
of EDEN

ALSO BY CAROLINE FYFFE

Colorado Hearts Novels

Heart of Eden

Prairie Hearts Novels

Where the Wind Blows
Before the Larkspur Blooms
West Winds of Wyoming
Under a Falling Star
Whispers on the Wind
Where Wind Meets Wave

The McCutcheon Family Novels

Montana Dawn
Texas Twilight
Mail-Order Brides of the West: Evie
Mail-Order Brides of the West: Heather
Moon Over Montana
Mail-Order Brides of the West: Kathryn
Montana Snowfall
Texas Lonesome
Montana Courage
Montana Promise

HEART
of EDEN

A COLORADO HEARTS NOVEL

Caroline Fyffe

Montlake
Romance

Published by Montlake Romance, Seattle

www.apub.com

Amazon, the Amazon logo, and Montlake Romance are trademarks of Amazon.com, Inc., or its affiliates.

ISBN-13: 9781542048323
ISBN-10: 154204832X

Cover design by Michael Rehder

Map design by Mapping Specialists, Ltd

Printed in the United States of America

Heart of Eden, a story of five sisters finding their way in a brand-new world, is dedicated with much love to my four older sisters: Shelly, Sherry, Jenny, and Mary. I hope it brings smiles, joy, and even a few tears, since the tears make the joy that much sweeter. I love you all.

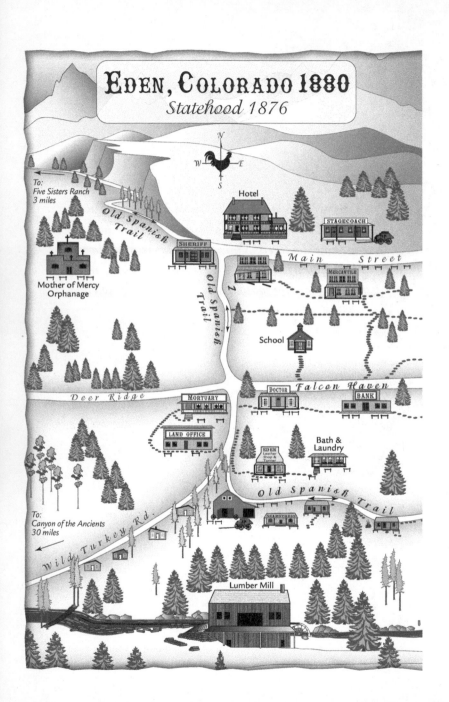

CHAPTER ONE

Eden, Colorado, 1880

From atop a small rise, Blake Harding sat on his horse as he surveyed the north pasture of the Five Sisters Ranch. Large, puffy clouds hung motionless in the indigo sky. If not for the movement of the bald eagle that had appeared from the west, he'd think he was looking at a painting. A crisp breeze ruffled Banjo's mane, and all seemed right with the world.

Everything here and now, anyway.

Blake sighed and relaxed his tense shoulders, letting a hard-earned peace push back the agitation that was never far from his mind. He missed John. For the last eighteen years, his boss had been so much more than his mentor—he'd taken the place of the parents he didn't remember and the brother he'd lost in the Civil War. John Brinkman had been Blake's whole family wrapped up in one honorable man.

From his position on the rise, he spotted Trevor Hill cutting through the herd. The cowboy's lips moved slowly as he spoke to the cattle in an effort not to rile them as they grazed. At the base of the slope, he waved and then loped to the top of the knoll.

"Trevor, what brings you out this way?" Blake called once the ranch hand was within hearing distance. Trevor had worked for the Five Sisters for three years. "Thought you were in Eden today, picking up supplies."

"Was, boss, but came back as soon as Henry gave me this." He held out a folded note.

So it's actually going to happen.

Still not used to the men calling him "boss," Blake took the paper. Henry had sent a telegram two days ago. Upon hearing of their father's death, John's daughters had apparently responded right away. *Imagine that.* He opened the note and scanned the missive, anger twisting his gut. There was only one thing worse than having to contend with John dying—that would be confronting his five selfish, self-centered daughters. Blake stared at the words in front of his face. *Well, miracles do happen.* The Brinkman sisters would be arriving within the month, after all the years John's pleas had fallen upon deaf ears. He fisted the note in his hand.

"Boss . . . ?" Trevor said, a bit cautiously. "They comin' to Eden?"

"Yeah, they are. Too bad it took John dying to get the deed done."

"Why now, do you think?" Trevor lifted his hat and scratched his head, then gazed lovingly up at the morning sun. "Seems a bit late."

"Doesn't take a genius to figure what they're after." He remembered two little girls, two toddlers, and one infant. The eldest, Mavis, had been almost five to his ten the last time he'd seen her.

"Money?"

"What else?"

CHAPTER TWO

———— ~❧⁀❧⁀❧~ ————

Philadelphia, Pennsylvania

B elle Brinkman hurried down the sidewalk toward her older sister's apartment holding the folds of her black mourning dress, lest she catch her toe and fall. The blustery wind pulled persistently at the ribbons that kept her headpiece from tumbling into the rain-soaked street. Lesley had surprised her with the gift last week, and she'd not let it spill into the mud.

She wrinkled her nose at the puddles, horse manure, and garbage that lined the road. Passing the slaughterhouse, she pinched her nose closed. *How I despise this part of town.* She'd begged Mavis not to move there when she and Darvid wed, one year ago last month. Unfortunately, both Mavis and her sister's late husband earned little at the department store, where they worked in accounting. Compassion stirred in Belle's chest for her sister's plight. A month ago, Darvid had taken ill with pneumonia and died—but only after racking up a bill with the doctor to add to their other debts. *Where will Mavis find the money to pay?* As far as Belle knew, she had little put away for emergencies. The pittance Belle had wouldn't go far to help.

Belle sighed, ashamed at how coldhearted she'd become. Instead of thinking of her brother-in-law, who was now gone to his just rewards, she was worried about money. *The lack of money is the root of all evil.*

Appalled at herself, she thought of her mother, dead for fifteen years. "I know, Mother, it's the *love* of money that's the root of all evil, but sometimes it doesn't feel that way at all. Scrimping by gets old." Belle's mother had been the kindest, most loving woman—at least that was what her six-year-old self remembered. Left orphans for all intents and purposes after her death, Belle and her sisters owed everything to Vernon and Velma Crowdaire, friends who took their mother in after she fled their unstable father and the untamed wilderness called Eden. Her mother's death, three years after arriving at the Crowdaires', had been a shock. The couple the girls now called "Aunt and Uncle" took them in permanently, providing room, board, and even the clothes on their backs.

Still, Vernon Crowdaire has no right to make us feel so indebted every second, Belle thought as her disgust for him surfaced. The way he flaunted his generosity like a badge of honor made them all feel like beggars. *It's not right.*

Gathering her skirt again, Belle stepped over a wide puddle and then sidestepped a lump of refuse in her path. The bedroom she shared with her three younger sisters in the Crowdaire home was a bit less crowded since Mavis had married. And two years before that, their guardians had moved to a more upscale area of town as well, giving them a larger bedroom—but still just one. That was something. *I should work on my charity. Not harbor such dislike for Vernon. Try to be more grateful.* She knew she should, but she hadn't after all these years.

As often as the Crowdaires expounded on what good catches she and her sisters were, only Mavis, the eldest, had received an official offer of marriage, and that from a man who had little more than two nickels to rub together. Even though Belle had liked Darvid, she'd been against the marriage from the first, feeling Mavis was settling because of

Velma's constant harping to accept the proposal. It had almost seemed like the Crowdaires wanted Mavis out in order to relieve the burden of expenses. It was understandable, she supposed. They *had* done so much over the years.

In reality, what did Belle or any of her sisters have to offer a husband, besides love? Each year the tiny stipend their guardians gave each girl grew by only a few coins. As soon as they were out of school, each of them had found work to help pay their expenses and supplement their wardrobes. They had all long passed the age where only hand-me-downs would do. Katie was the exception. The youngest Brinkman sister had taken a loan from Uncle Vernon to attend a normal school in Massachusetts and train to become a teacher. She'd graduated three months ago and was in the process of looking for a position.

Finally arriving at the tall brownstone, Belle ascended the crumbling brick steps, opened the door, and proceeded to the first apartment at the back of the lobby. She rapped several times.

"Who's there?"

"It's me. Belle."

Mavis opened the door dressed in widow's attire. Her wavy mahogany hair was swept on top of her head, and she wore the wrist-length gloves she never went without to hide her disfigurement. Her blue, wide-set eyes gave away that she'd been crying, bringing an ache to Belle's heart.

They embraced.

"How're you?" Belle asked, stepping back, knowing well her sister was taking Darvid's death extremely hard.

"Getting by. Everything still seems so surreal." She glanced around the room. "Everywhere I look, I see Darvid's face. I don't know how I'll get through this."

Belle looked her up and down. "Mavis Brinkman Applebee, you're resilient. The strongest woman I know." She laid a gentle hand on her older sister's arm. If she could take away her pain, she would, in a heartbeat. Mavis had always been Belle's best friend. Loyal to a fault.

She glanced at Mavis's left hand, and the abominable gloves hiding her missing pinkie. Belle's guilt was ever present. Before they'd moved from the river area to a nicer neighborhood, Mavis had gotten her hand caught in some tangled fishing line. Cleaning up the litter in the alley beside their uncle's home had been Belle's chore, but she'd put the distasteful task off that day. Mavis, wanting to spare her sister a tongue-lashing from Aunt Velma, had come out to help. A passing carriage caught the line in its spinning wheels. In an instant, Mavis's finger popped off at the knuckle as easily as a pea snaps in half.

Belle would never forget the sound.

Or the look on Mavis's face.

Because of her mutilation, Mavis hid herself away at her accounting job at Thornton House department store. Until Darvid joined. In less than three months, she'd said yes to his proposal—even though she'd confided to Belle that the most she felt for him was a deep, abiding friendship. Darvid was a nice, considerate, mild-mannered man who smiled and laughed at every chance. And indeed, until now, that had seemed enough. Although they'd had little, they'd appeared happy.

"Do you have a moment to talk?" Belle asked.

Mavis closed the door. "All right. My manager has been quite understanding. If we hurry, I won't be too late."

She directed them to the secondhand settee in front of the fireplace, resting her hand over a small tear in its arm as she sat down. "What's on your mind, Belle? I know you don't enjoy coming to this part of town."

"You don't either, if you're honest."

Mavis ignored the comment. "Whatever you have to say must be important."

"Actually, you're right. It *is* important. I've received a telegram from Eden."

Mavis's eyes grew so wide that Belle could almost read her thoughts right through them. *Eden.* Where Mother and Father met and married. Where all five sisters were conceived and born. A place Belle wondered about all the time. Her memories of their departure when she was almost four were foggy. Her clearest image was of Mother stuffing clothes into a large trunk as a man, who must have been Father, stood back, taller than any tree, watching in disbelief. Belle thought she remembered a need to run to him, lay her small hand upon his cheek, but the tears on Mother's face had fastened her feet to the floor. Belle convinced herself that must be a dream, something her mind had conjured up, distorting the truth for want of a father's love. She'd been too young to know the kinds of questions to ask her mother. It was only after Mother died that Uncle Vernon told them—with unseemly glee— that their father had been a violent man, disrespectful and coarse. That their mother fled out of fear of what he might do to her or the children. The story each of the sisters carried inside was that John Brinkman had been a despicable character. And hadn't he proved as much? He'd never come to see them or sought them out in any way. He'd turned his back on his family, pretending they never existed.

No point tiptoeing around the news. "Father has passed."

The color drained from Mavis's face. For a moment, they sat in silence.

"This feels like a pointed arrow through my heart," Mavis whispered. "Somehow, some way, I always believed we'd get a chance to be reunited." She looked at the floor. "I was wrong."

"Oh pooh," Belle said. Mavis was too much of a romantic for her. "Why would you want to? He didn't want us. Why should we despair now?"

Mavis's lips wobbled. "He was our *father.* Regardless of how he treated Mother or us, we should show a little respect."

"He never gave this family a moment's thought. We were *nothing* to him, Mavis. And actually, saying that aloud *does* break my heart." A

9

strange image of a man stirred inside her. His scent, the rumble of his voice—she felt a faint longing for his gentle touch, a kiss good night . . . She blinked and looked away from Mavis's censorious scrutiny.

"When did you receive word?"

"Last week."

Mavis's eyes widened again. "Why didn't you tell me sooner?"

If Belle didn't explain quickly, they'd have an argument on their hands. "I know you don't like being kept in the dark, Mavis, but I was sheltering you. Darvid passed barely a month ago."

"And the others? Do they know?"

Belle nodded. "You've gone through so much. I wanted to spare you for a little while—*we* wanted to spare you. Emma, Lavinia, and Katie agreed." *Well, sort of. Two out of three.* "You'd do exactly the same for one of us. Aren't you glad you've had this week to yourself, without it being more complicated?"

"Father shouldn't be thought of as a complication."

Time to change the subject. "Everyone is packed and ready to travel, as am I. Strangely enough, we've been summoned for the reading of Father's will. Mr. Glass, an attorney in Eden, sent enough fare to cover our travel."

Mavis pushed to her feet, her lips pulled into a frown. Belle knew all too well that her oldest sister didn't like being left out of the decision making. She considered herself substitute mother and protector of them all. But her irritation lasted only a moment. She walked slowly to a window overlooking the gray day outside.

"What happened? Do you know? How did he die?"

"His horse fell, and he broke his leg. Infection set in."

"How horrible."

"I agree. And that's all I know—except that the will can't be read unless all five of us are present."

Mavis turned, a wistful expression on her face. "I remember sitting in tall, green grass with you, Emma, and baby Lavinia. Katie wasn't yet born. Someone was singing. A man's voice. Father must have changed greatly." She slowly shook her head. "I don't think I have the energy to travel west. From what Uncle Vernon has told us, the little Father had has been lost over the years. A broken-down house on a small patch of land with a handful of cattle."

"Then I guess we'll have to go without you." Belle gazed innocently at her hands, folded in her lap. "Though the telegram *did* say we *all* had to be present . . ."

Mavis returned to the sofa. "You can't go without me." Alarm tinged her voice. "Who'll make sure Katie doesn't become turned around in some station and get left behind? And Emma needs her cup of warm milk before bed. You know she can't sleep in a strange place without one. Don't get me started on Lavinia. She's liable to be run over by a team of horses if a pretty bonnet catches her eye. I swear, I don't think I want any children of my own after raising the four of you."

Irritation rippled inside Belle. *Mavis doesn't have to act like she's the only one with a brain in her head.*

"What about me? You're not the only one capable of looking after Katie and the others."

A silly smile pulled at Mavis's lips. "You're right. I meant no offense. I worry, is all. You know you can be impulsive, Belle. When you get angry, you pay little attention to what's happening around you. A train ride has dangers. Bad weather, outlaws, Indians. Snakes!"

Belle shuddered. "That's plenty of peril to worry over." She hesitated. *She's not going to like this.* "The train doesn't go all the way to Eden. We'll have to take a stagecoach from Pueblo for the last three hundred miles."

Mavis's hand flew to her chest. "What about Katie's claustrophobia? No, absolutely not. We'll wire and tell Mr. Glass a trip like this is impossible. He can come to us."

Belle's patience vanished. "For heaven's sake. She can sit by the window or up top with the driver."

"You're heartless, Belle."

"Pack your things. We have tickets for tomorrow and will arrive in Eden in about a week and a half. We'll stay long enough to hear what the lawyer has to say, pay our respects to Father's grave, and get back on the train. Think about it, Mavis. *Why* does the reading have to be so formal?" She lifted a brow and let that thought simmer. "What if Father *did* have at least a little something set aside to leave to us? Any amount will help with Darvid's medical bills, and more. We *must* go."

Mavis's mouth was still set in a stubborn line. "I can't. I'll lose my job. Being a widow, I depend on that income."

"Your manager has already offered you time off, which you didn't take. And he thought very highly of Darvid. He'll understand, I'm sure. Especially when you tell him why you need the time away." Belle stood. "Discoveries await."

"Really, Belle, you sound like a novelist. What about Lesley?" Mavis tipped her head. "I can't imagine your fine young gentleman is just letting you waltz off to Colorado. Not when the two of you are so close to making your relationship binding."

Belle smiled at the mention of her sweetheart. "You're right about that. He's coming with us. To keep us safe. I thought that exceedingly kind."

"You're wiping away my objections like they're ice in the sun," Mavis said, her brow still lined with worry. "And Uncle Vernon? What does he think about the whole situation? He never had one nice thing to say about Eden—or our father."

At the mention of their uncle's name, Belle cut her gaze to the window, squelching her immature desire to make a face. How she loathed that man. "Actually, he's been very strange since the telegram arrived. When I told him we'd been called back to Eden, his face turned white as chalk and he said little, which confounded us because we've all heard him go on and on about Father. Anyway, the next morning, he announced that Aunt Velma would be accompanying him on a long-planned business trip. They packed that day, wished us well, and departed."

Mavis cocked her head, confused. Their aunt and uncle had been orchestrating their lives for years and didn't give power away without a fight. "Not one protest or complaint?"

"No. It was the strangest thing. I'm still trying to figure out why."

"How curious," Mavis whispered. "Where'd they go?"

"I have no idea. Uncle Vernon hadn't mentioned the trip until that moment."

Tired of trying to figure out their guardians' motives, Belle turned her attention to the mysteries ahead. "Even more surprising is that, after all these years of speculating about our past, we'll be on a train to Eden in the morning." She reached down and squeezed Mavis's hands. "No matter what we learn about Father and his brutish ways, it'll be better than always wondering, longing." Belle warmed with the sense of excitement rolling around inside her.

What the future held was anyone's guess. But she was anxious to find out.

CHAPTER THREE

Eden, Colorado

The office above the mercantile was a stuffy tomb. The usual high-mountain September temperatures were ten degrees warmer than normal for this time of year. The voices of the shoppers below rose to barely a murmur over the pounding of Blake's heart. He ran a finger around his snug collar, wishing he could dispose of his black bolo tie. Or better, that he was out riding herd. If he could, he'd reverse time so John had never gone to ride fence the day his horse spooked at a rattlesnake and fell on him.

Word was that John's daughters had arrived the day before. Blake wondered if he'd be able to pick out who was who. He thought he would remember them well enough, despite the growing up they'd all done. Would they remember him? For a few months after losing his own, they'd been family. He hadn't even minded they were all girls. But then they'd left for good, without a single word to him. He'd felt betrayed.

Silly, maybe, for children so young . . .

Going to the window, he pushed the pane up as far as it would go, sucking in what seemed like his last breath of life.

"Relax, Blake," Henry Glass said on a chuckle. "Everything's going to be fine. You look like you're ready to meet the enemy."

Henry might not think so, but Blake wasn't so sure. He'd seen all the nights John had paced the floor, waiting for a reply to any of his letters. Just one damn reply was all he'd dreamed about, year after year, until his colorful heart full of hope was reduced to a dreary brown, dried-out piece of driftwood.

Henry pointed a finger at him and raised a brow. "I'm serious, Blake. John wouldn't want you holding on to any animosity toward his girls. You need to put your personal feelings aside. Get to know them. Forgive them."

"That's all fine and good," Blake responded, thinking his scar was feeling exceptionally tight and angry today. The sensation could happen anytime, making the years-old blemish pinch for no reason whatsoever, except perhaps when his ire had been raised. Blake hated the sensation. The wound began at the bottom of his chin, ran down the left side of his neck, and continued over his left chest muscle. People who didn't know him gawked or turned away in fright. That's why he preferred the wide-open ranges to the confines of town. The fewer people he had to face, the better he liked it. "You're not gonna be the one who has to deal with 'em night and day now, are you, Henry?" Blake shook his head. "No, sir, you're not. It's gonna be me putting out any problem that ruffles their citified feathers. I can just see it now . . ."

"You're being a mite melodramatic, aren't you?"

Blake ignored Henry's comment as he absentmindedly fingered his scar. "Why can't you tell me why I had to come to this? I'm the ranch foreman, not family. The reading of a will should be private." He watched his friend try and ignore his question as he went about straightening his maple-wood desk. "You know what's in it. Hell— you're the author."

Henry shrugged. "You know I can't say."

"I don't expect anything from John." He shot Henry a critical look. "He should have left fate alone after he died and not forced the girls to come to Eden. If they'd wanted to be here, they'd have returned long ago. Maybe I'll ride out before this circus gets started. Look for greener pastures."

Henry let go a long-suffering sigh. "You've been running the ranch with John for years. Now, just because he's passed on, you're going to hand over the reins to five city slickers wearing dresses? I know you better than that. You love that ranch. I don't think *anything* could ever make you ride out of Eden—or off the Five Sisters Ranch."

"Maybe not, but I should. If I knew what was good for me, I'd go right now, will reading be damned. All the years together with John are payment enough. When I was a boy, he gave me stability, sustenance, and care when I thought I'd be better off rolling up in a ditch to die."

"You're not the only fella to feel like that after the Civil War." Henry rubbed his chin thoughtfully.

John Brinkman's longtime lawyer was one of the smartest men Blake knew. He'd been representing the Five Sisters Ranch for years, knew the operation better than anyone besides him and John. Henry's desk was an orderly display of dedication. Blake doubted the man ever let anything get under his skin, let alone his business notes and ledgers. Before Blake had arrived that morning, the attorney had placed six straight-back chairs in a single line a few feet in front of his desk so everyone would have the same vantage point. Several large racks of antlers decorated the walls or were in use as coat- and hat racks, displaying the man's love of hunting. Even though Henry had a perfectly good clock on the wall, he withdrew his pocket watch from his snappy-looking black vest and flicked it open.

"It's eight ten," he said. "They'll be arriving anytime."

"And you won't give me any hint before they do? I've never been good with surprises."

A smile played at the corners of his lips. "As you've said about one hundred times this morning, and as I've replied one hundred times, you know I can't. That would be breaking the law . . . and my word."

"Thought as much. But even if you could, I don't think you would. You like watching me sweat."

The middle-aged bachelor walked over and grasped Blake's shoulder. His brown hair was combed, and his mustache, which rivaled any gambler's, was neatly trimmed. Henry might be working, but even John's lawyer wasn't immune to the idea of five young, unattached women. Eden had a limited supply of those.

Henry dropped his hand and patted down his vest. "Let me get you a cup of coffee."

"Only if you add a couple of shots of whiskey."

The outside stairs reverberated. John's daughters were on their way. After all these years, he was about to see them again . . .

Henry went to the door before they had a chance to knock. "Welcome!" he said in a sincere voice as the first black-frocked young woman moved over the threshold. Blake noticed that she wore gloves—of all things—and a shawl draped her shoulders. The gloves looked out of place in Eden, a town composed mostly of stockmen, miners, and farmers.

Mavis. Blake recognized her instantly—the oldest, and the one who'd liked to direct him, the orphan boy, around like he was a puppy. She'd grown tall and slim. Nothing like the pudgy girl who'd sought him out and tried to make him play dolls with her. One time, telling him she'd been sent out to the meadow to gather flowers and needed his help, they'd spent more than an hour exploring the hills and dales around the ranch. When they'd returned, Mrs. Brinkman had been frantic with worry. Blake suffered the scolding of a lifetime, as well as censorious looks for a week from Celeste, their mother, for endangering her daughter. Mavis never let on that the whole thing had been her idea in the first place.

"Blake?" Her mouth dropped open. "Is that you?"

Of course the scar answered for him. He nodded as her sisters followed her inside. The heavy silence in the room made Blake swallow.

"May I?" Henry asked, gathering their shawls.

To Blake's surprise, the sisters weren't alone. A man stepped into the room behind them. He quietly closed the door and took up position near one of the windows. He was tall and wore expensive clothing. Blake thought he caught a whiff of a spicy aftershave. The fellow tried to catch Blake's eye, but Blake wasn't in a mood to be friendly—even though he knew Henry would be sorely put out if he wasn't.

Which has married? Just another fact John didn't get to know about his daughters.

With no correspondence to speak of, the facts of their lives had been a mystery to Blake until that very moment.

"Thank you for coming," Henry said to the women. "I'm Henry Glass, your father's attorney." He held out his hand to them one by one. "I've represented your father's ranch for many years. Some of you might remember Blake Harding, your father's right-hand man and foreman."

When they glanced his way, Blake expected them to flinch at the sight of his scar, but they didn't. "Pleased to see you again," he mumbled.

They all nodded, their smiles tight.

Seems everyone's on edge.

Henry seemed to know what Blake was waiting for. "Could I ask you please to introduce yourselves, perhaps beginning with Mavis, who I know to be the eldest?"

Mavis smiled. "Of course. I'm Mavis Brinkman Applebee."

Ah, so she married the man standing by the window.

These women had almost broken John's spirit. And they broke his heart more than a time or two. Blake wasn't going to let them off the hook just because they finally decided to show up.

Dressing them down to their pantaloons with a sharp tongue-lashing would feel so good.

His gaze shifted to the next sister, standing at Mavis's elbow. She was as tall as Mavis but instead of brown hair, hers was a dark blonde, golden like a spring sunrise.

"I'm Belle Brinkman," she said in a clear, strong voice that matched her straight posture.

Something clicked in Blake's memory: *Belle. A chatterbox, to be sure.*

Her face, a tad too round to be considered oval, was striking, with high-set, distinct cheekbones and lovely eyes. Of the five, she resembled their mother the most. Blake watched her attention glide over to her sister's husband and linger. He didn't think too much about it until the fella's regard softened, bringing color to her cheeks. Blake looked away. He didn't want any part of her deceptions. She'd once hit him over the head with a candlestick, angry over something—he didn't remember the why.

The third oldest, and the only one with strawberry-colored hair, spoke up next, a shy smile on her face displaying a dimple on her right cheek. Henry's impressive bookshelf had caught her interest. He remembered Emma and the adoring toddler eyes she'd cast in his direction.

His gaze shifted to Lavinia, who shyly introduced herself. She had been learning to walk the last time he'd seen her, and drooling from a newly sprouted bottom tooth.

Has it really been that long?

She wore a hat that covered most of her dark hair, and the black netting on the top looked a bit ragged. The small strawberry birthmark on her neck that resembled an hourglass was still there. He imagined she'd be shocked to know he'd once helped change her diaper.

"Then you must be Katie," Henry said to the youngest, an eighteen-year-old version of Belle, with her lighter hair and blue eyes. They might be mistaken for twins if not for the beauty mark under the corner of Katie's bottom lip.

No one could deny John had sired a gaggle of beautiful girls who held themselves with dignity and poise. Blake felt mightily outnumbered.

Katie smiled. "That's correct, Mr. Glass. I was an infant when I left Eden. I must say, the town is much more rugged than I ever expected."

Henry chuckled. "Don't let that trouble you, Miss Brinkman. We have some charms the big city doesn't. Now," he said, clapping his hands together once, "first let me say thank you to everyone for making the long, difficult trip. I extend my condolences about your father. His death was a shock to us all." Henry's expression clouded over for a moment. "John was a healthy man. Even with the broken leg, if infection hadn't set in, he'd be alive today."

Blake dropped his attention to the floor. *And you all wouldn't be here. Only death moves your compassion. For shame, little ladies, for shame.*

"I'll bring another chair around for you, Mr. Applebee," Henry said. "Of course you're welcome to sit by your wife." He glanced at Mavis and smiled. "I didn't mean to leave you out, but I wasn't aware any of the girls had married."

The fellow pushed away from the windowsill, and Mavis straightened.

"I'm sorry for the confusion," she said. "Mr. Atkins is not my husband. Mr. Applebee passed away last month. This is Belle's gentleman friend, Mr. Lesley Atkins. He is our escort."

Explains the earlier look.

"Oh!" Henry said in surprise. "Well, we appreciate you taking the time out of your schedule to ensure the Brinkman sisters' safe arrival, sir. I know John would have been duly grateful, as am I."

"It was my pleasure," Mr. Atkins replied. "I can assure you, having five beautiful women to watch over is not an imposition." His gaze once again strayed to Belle.

Right. Blake shifted his weight from one leg to the other. Henry must have caught Blake's expression, because he arched a brow in warning.

"Unfortunately," Henry went on, "the reading of the will is a family-only affair. I'll have to ask you to leave."

Belle stiffened. "But we're practically promised," she said. "What could be the harm?"

Blake discreetly wiped the smile from his face, enjoying the show. *She reminds me of John fighting for water rights two years ago.*

Henry was firm. "I'm sorry."

She softened. "Mr. Glass, can't he please stay? When our business is finished and we've seen the ranch, we're headed right back to Philadelphia. His parents are throwing a large party." She smiled tenderly at Mr. Atkins. "Which in all likelihood might be an engagement party."

Poor fellow.

Henry blinked twice in quick succession, a sure sign his patience was wearing thin. "No. I'm sorry, Miss Brinkman," he said in a kind tone. "That's not possible. Your father was explicit in his directions. I'm here to carry out his last wishes."

"Then why does *Mr. Harding* get to stay? He's not family." She cast a disapproving gaze Blake's way.

Heat sprang to Blake's face. He knew his scar was shining.

Good question.

"According to your father, Mr. Harding *is* family. He's been invited to be here, just like the rest of you. He has no idea what is written in your father's will." Once Mr. Atkins had excused himself, Henry said, "Please, take your seats and get comfortable. The unknown is what's difficult. I can assure you that as soon as we have this taken care of, you'll all feel better." Henry smiled and waved his arm over the row of chairs, looking a little anxious himself.

Blake was the last to sit, taking the chair to Mavis's left.

Henry opened the folder resting on the center of his desk. He hooked his wire-rimmed glasses over each ear. "Let's get to the business at hand, shall we? I'm sure you're all curious to know what John had in mind for the ranch and all of his children."

He cleared his throat. "As you girls must know, your father was worth a great deal of money. It's not evident from the state of his ranch house, but the barn and stock are of the utmost quality. After your

21

mother left Colorado with you children, he threw his heart and soul into making the ranch profitable. An operation to be proud of that would support you and your mother. Something substantial. To say he succeeded is putting his accomplishments mildly."

The audible gasp from at least four of the five sisters made Blake blink. Turning, he glanced down the row. At the same time, Henry looked up from the paper in his hand. His eyes narrowed. "You *are* aware of your father's holdings, of course?"

The eldest three leaned close together, whispering frantically.

What's going on? Blake had no idea.

Belle cautiously raised a small hand, only chest high.

"What constitutes a great deal to you, Mr. Glass?" she asked, all coyness in her voice gone. "We had no knowledge that our father's estate had any particular worth."

Henry's brow crashed down. He shot Blake a questioning look, and then again cleared his throat. "The ranch alone is worth over two hundred thousand dollars. But all this has been spelled out in numerous letters he's sent over the years. Along with the monetary support he sent for your mother and you."

CHAPTER FOUR

M avis surged to her feet, but Belle pulled her back down. The three younger sisters just sat in stunned silence, their bewilderment almost comical. Blake dredged up a smidgen of pity.

Visibly shaken, Mavis could hardly get her next words out. "What? What are you saying? All these years, our father has been in contact with us? I can assure you, Mr. Glass, we have not received *any* letters from our father—or anything else. No contact at all."

Henry reached out two placating hands—his way, Blake assumed, of calming the girl's runaway emotions. The youngest, Katie, already had a handkerchief out and was dabbing her watery eyes.

"Please," Henry said. "Let's take a moment to figure out—in a calm and collected manner—what's going on. I posted many of the letters to your mother for John myself." He paused, frowning. "John received a good many responses over the years, all communicating that Celeste was not ready yet to return to Colorado, and that you girls were flourishing in Philadelphia. She implored him not to interfere with your lives." His color deepened as reality set in. "John did receive a note from Vernon Crowdaire, letting him know that your mother passed last year. My condolences."

A stunned silence filled the office. Mavis lifted a shaky hand to her mouth, and Belle just stared, her face a twisted mask of anger.

"Our mother passed away *long* ago," Belle said. "Fifteen years, to be exact."

In that second, it became apparent to Blake what had happened to the correspondence—and the money.

"What are you implying?" Katie whispered anxiously. "That Aunt Velma and Uncle Vernon purposely kept our family apart? They've been our guardians for *fifteen years*. They'd never do such a thing."

Emma was shaking her head.

Henry pulled out a handkerchief and wiped his forehead. "If that's what happened, it's atrocious, but I have to admit, after what you've just said, it sounds plausible."

Lavinia cleared her throat, looking frightened. "Vernon Crowdaire was the only person allowed to pick up our mail. I remember going into the post office and being turned away. Vernon said that was because he'd forbidden the postmaster to deliver to anyone but him. He said he didn't want any of his business correspondences to be lost, that his charges were too flighty to be trusted."

"Is that legal, Henry?" Blake asked, his interest sparked to the mystery. "If letters were addressed to Celeste?"

"Absolutely not. But that's not to say he didn't pay off the clerks and postmaster who were doing his bidding."

Blake suddenly felt like going to Philadelphia, finding their guardians, and taking matters into his own hands. His anger at the girls ebbed as he took in their confused expressions. The pain John had endured because of the Crowdaires was sickening. They'd ruined his life.

If, that is, the girls are telling the truth.

"After your mother's passing, or what John thought was her passing last year," Henry went on in a steadier voice, "he'd hoped at least one of his now-grown daughters would write to him. Take an interest in him or the ranch. Come get acquainted."

Blake stared at a spot on the wall behind Henry's head.

And the disappointment killed him. Just like that. Well, not exactly. Still, if he'd had hope of any kind, he'd have fought the infection with conviction. Is it possible the women are acting now, to cover their deceitfulness over the years? They could have planned this explanation, knowing how despicable they'd be perceived for ignoring so many requests from John. Are they trying to pull wool over the eyes of a country lawyer and a cowhand? Acting innocent and confused?

Blake decided he wasn't quite ready to believe them.

Mavis glanced at her sisters and then briefly at him. "I can promise you, Mr. Glass, Mr. Harding, we knew nothing of Father's letters—or support. If I'd known, I would have come at his first bidding. We were told he disowned us after our mother moved away. That he was bitter and vengeful, even a dangerous man. Uncle Vernon said our mother had kept that information from us to protect us from the truth, but he thought we should know." She sniffed and looked away for several long seconds. "A grave injustice has been done to our father, our mother, and to us. I'm sure I speak for my sisters when I say my heart is shattered. We were kept from him intentionally and unlawfully."

"This is a bit difficult to believe," Blake angrily bit out, unable to keep silent any longer. "John has sent support for years. Enough money so that every single one of you could be raised in style. He didn't ask for anything in return, just hoped for a little of your time one day. To get to know you. To love you in person."

They were staring at him as if he'd sprouted big, ugly warts all over his face—and with his scar surely turning red with anger, he essentially had. At this point, finding a whit of compassion for any of them was nigh on impossible. They might be pretty to look at, but they'd broken John's heart, his spirit. "Just one of you could have reached out to him, taken an interest. Even without the money. Just one . . ."

Henry pointed a finger. "Blake. Temper your anger. You don't know all the facts."

"I think I know enough," he said, trying to rein in his tone. "Would that have been so difficult, Mrs. Applebee, Miss Brinkman?" He waved his hand. "All you Miss Brinkmans? Amazing how you show up now, only when he's dead and there might be something of value to inherit. Why am I not surprised?"

"Blake!" Henry shouted. "Get ahold of yourself. That's more than enough."

Belle leaned past her sister so she could look him in the eye. "We have *never* received anything from our father. Not one word. Not one penny. When I was a little girl, I used to dream he might send me a doll for my birthday. Or a pretty dress for Christmas. All I heard was that he didn't want daughters, he wanted sons. That if he wanted us, perhaps he'd have come to Pennsylvania himself. I won't let you lay this debacle at *our* feet, Mr. Harding, no matter how much you think we're to blame. We are victims, just like our father."

Her voice was strong, but Blake didn't miss the tremble in her lips as she turned away.

"Ladies! Blake! Please," Henry blurted, reaching out in supplication once more. "Please. Settle down. Figuring out what happened will take time—more than we have today, or even this month. But I assure you, no one will get away with such an immoral deed, if indeed the Crowdaires are to blame." He took a deep breath. "For now, let me get on with the reading. Later we'll come back to this situation and try to determine what actually transpired with all those letters and bank notes."

Silence settled over the room. Where Belle looked angry, the rest of the girls looked confused and sick.

"Besides the cattle ranch and the silver mine farther south, your father owns five businesses in Eden. A mill and lumberyard, the café in the hotel, a tannery and leather shop, the livery where he has a partner named Maverick Daves, and an apparel store called the Toggery. He didn't start these businesses. Townsfolk came to him, needing to sell, because he had the cash to help them out. They each had an agreement that they could buy the businesses back if they ever wanted. Most just moved out of town."

"And he always gave them more than they were asking," Blake threw out. He stared straight ahead, refusing to look at the sisters.

Henry leafed to the next page, taking a moment to look it over. "The mine has never been worked under John's ownership and sits vacant at this point. It's to be split evenly between the five girls." Henry looked up. "If you haven't heard, this area is rich in silver. The other businesses are to be drawn from a hat, so that each sister receives one. After drawing, if you want to make trades, that's allowed. John's hope was that having actual stock in Eden would encourage you to stay. Get to know the people and the area. Perhaps make his town your home."

God forbid.

There was movement in the chairs beside him. Someone murmured. Someone else daintily blew a nose. Outside, the rattle of a wagon rolling by and the neigh of a horse could be heard clearly over the strained atmosphere in the office.

"He leaves a thousand dollars to the town of Eden for improvements." Henry looked up and smiled. "I don't know if you've heard of the Canyon of the Ancients. It's a rock formation thirty miles away with Pueblo and Anasazi ruins. John believed as the attraction gained in popularity more people would come to Colorado to see the beauty and greatness. They'll need a place to stay on their journeys."

The girls remained silent.

"The ranch will be split in half. Half to the Brinkman daughters and half to Blake Harding, who's worked the place for the last eighteen years."

Annoyance left Blake in a zap of surprise. He pushed against the back of his chair, wondering if he'd heard correctly.

Half of the ranch? Why did John cut me in, in such a big way?

Time seemed to slow down, and the floor under his boots tilted. Because of his good friend, Blake had just become a rich man.

"You'll all be wealthy beyond anything you could have imagined. But where the ranch is involved, there are a few stipulations. To be awarded the fifty percent of the ranch—which is the largest piece of John's estate at this time—all five sisters must remain in Eden for six months. That's a short enough time that if you have ties back in Philadelphia you don't want to break, your stay here won't disrupt them too much. It's also a long enough time for you to get to know Eden and perhaps desire to remain here, on the land John loved, and his father before him. If you decide to return to Philadelphia before the end of six months, you'll each be granted fifteen thousand dollars. Accepting it forfeits your claim on the ranch to Blake. You may do what you want with whichever business you each acquire. You may not sell the mine for five years."

Finally, Blake chanced a look down the row. The girls were glancing around in confusion.

Henry made a dismissive waving motion. "Please don't worry too much about all the particulars at the moment. It's a lot to digest in one sitting. Concerning the businesses, there are managers running them now who will continue until you take over the reins, whether that's right away or not at all, if you choose to sell. I'll go into greater details after I read the letter John left, and after you've had a little time to absorb such a shock.

"The ranch is the largest holding, and will be worth the most. If after the six months you decide you want to sell, you can do so, but all sisters have to be in agreement so it's the full fifty percent of the ranch that would be sold—not ten, twenty, or thirty. Most importantly, Blake gets the first chance at buying your fifty percent at a fair market price. If he doesn't want your fifty percent, you can sell to whomever you choose. If, after six months, you decide you all want to keep the ranch, the sisters who want to remain in Eden can do so, and anyone who wants to return to the city can, without giving up her share."

Everyone sat as still as marble. Blake doubted if they'd remember any of the details at all.

"And now, here's a personal letter from John."

Henry pushed his glasses higher on the bridge of his nose and began to read aloud.

Blake braced himself. He hadn't expected any of this.

I'd still give it all up to have John back.

"My dearest daughters, if you're hearing this now, I have passed from this world into eternity and am now reunited with your mother. I cannot tell you how happy that makes me. I have missed her deeply, and am now comforted that we are again together.

"Welcome to Eden. I hope after Henry explains everything, you will understand why I made the decisions I have. There is much I'd like to say to each of you, and so much I'd like to learn about you. But now, that is not possible. I want you to know that I do not blame your mother for taking you away. She did what she felt she must to keep you safe, away from Indian skirmishes and death. It is true; your lives were in peril every day. Back then, Eden was a much different place than you see now. Indian raids were common. The cemetery usually added one or two fresh graves each month. Our ranch was remote, rough, and mere survival required hard work. Harsh winters went on for months. Too few females were here with whom she could share her feelings. But her breaking point came when the couple at a ranch a few miles west was murdered and scalped. Katie had only been born three months before. At some point, everyone

has to make a choice as to what they will endure. Celeste made her choice and took you back east, despite the ongoing war. That is a day I never forgot."

Henry cleared his throat and continued.

"Blake, you have been like a son to me. After those days when my family left, you kept me sane. You made sure I ate, and the chores got done. You are the reason I survived. Since then, you have worked tirelessly at my side. Thank you for that. I hope you know I couldn't have loved a son more."

Hot moisture sprang to Blake's eyes, and he glanced toward the window.

"Daughters, Blake Harding is a good man. He's smart and capable, with a good, level head on his shoulders. If you decide to stay in Eden, you will need guidance to keep the ranch running smoothly. Knowing his character as I do, I expect him to watch out for you all and make sure you learn our ways, which may be different from the way you were raised. My most ardent wish is that the Five Sisters Ranch will always be owned by Blake and my daughters—and eventually your offspring."

Loud gasps ricocheted around the room.

"The Five Sisters Ranch?" Mavis repeated in a tear-filled voice.

Henry nodded. Blake sat, stunned. More than once he felt curious eyes turned his way, but he kept his gaze trained forward.

John never let on about his intent for the property—or, maybe there had been a hint or two, now that I think back.

He'd always assumed John meant to keep him on as foreman, but he'd never dreamed of ownership of Five Sisters. The reality made his head buzz.

John's monthlong battle with infection was still as fresh as a knife wound across Blake's heart. The last days of delirium, when John drifted in and out of consciousness, imagining his daughters and wife had returned, were agony. He cried their names and babbled promises, the emotion in his pleas enough to make a hardened killer weep with pity. Blake had done his best to ease John's strife, spending hours at his bedside, wiping his sweaty brow and drying his tears. Before the end, John had rallied, becoming once again the man who'd raised him, offering comforting platitudes about death not being the end, just a new direction. He had tried to ease Blake's own distress, knowing that he was dying.

Blake looked over. Now all five sisters were crying. Some wiped at wet cheeks with snowy-white hankies adorned with their initials. The teary faces finally softened his mood.

Henry continued reading.

> *"There's Brinkman blood flowing in your veins, even if you don't recognize it yet. You're fighters. Fortitude is each of your middle names. Now I smile, thinking of all the beauty your presence will bring to my beloved Eden. It's almost as if the whole town has been holding its breath, waiting for your return.*
>
> *"I must sign off, as I have other letters that need writing. I remain your loving father..."*

Henry stared at the back wall for several long moments, then stood. He moved to his sideboard and began pouring water from his blue-and-white porcelain pitcher into tumblers. He brought two to Mavis and Belle first.

"Please, have a little water. You've had a shock."

Mavis reached out and took the glass.

"Miss Brinkman?" he said to Belle, but she shook her head, her face clouded. The two eldest had scooted around the youngest three like protective hens.

Henry handed the water to Emma and went back for more. "I say we finish up later. You've had enough for one day. So much more than what you were expecting—any of us, actually."

"I think that's wise," Mavis said. She stood and straightened her black mourning dress, and the others followed her lead.

Henry nodded. "Good. But tonight, after you've rested, please join me for supper as my guests."

Blake breathed a sigh of relief. As soon as they were gone, he'd head to the saloon for a beer. *Or whiskey.*

"B-but, we couldn't eat, Mr.—" Belle began, wiping away a stream of tears.

"No buts. You have to eat. As difficult as this is, life goes on. It's what your father wanted. I've reserved a table at Mademoiselle de Sells for seven tonight. We can get better acquainted." He cut his gaze to Blake.

"Me too?" *I didn't hear anything in the will about having to socialize.*

"All of us. Does the time work for everyone?" He looked at the women.

"Seven will be fine," Belle said, and the others nodded.

Henry clapped his hands together. "Wonderful. Anything you need, just ask Mr. Simon at the hotel."

Blake went to the door and pulled it open to a gust of warm, dry air. He reconsidered the whiskey. The day would be hot. The ranch might have problems with the river sooner than they'd planned. As much as the Five Sisters had been his life before, it was all the more so now.

One by one, the women thanked Henry and Blake and left, youngest to oldest. Mr. Atkins was waiting at the bottom of the stairs.

Henry released a deep sigh after they were out of earshot. "That wasn't so bad."

But Blake hardly heard him. Below, Mr. Atkins offered one arm to Belle and another to Lavinia, the other three sisters latching together at various points.

Not so bad?

The surprise that accompanied the news that he was now half owner of the ranch had made him overlook the other half of the equation: that he was now a business partner with the women he'd been disparaging in his mind for years.

"Blake?"

"Yeah? I'm just thinkin', Henry."

"I bet you are. Congratulations. You've worked hard to get where you are today. I know John would be pleased. You and his girls finally getting together again after all these years."

After the Brinkman sisters had crossed the street and disappeared through the door of the hotel, Blake turned to face his old friend. He wished he could be as happy as Henry looked at that moment, but trouble was brewing. He felt it in his bones. One of those women was going to want to develop the land, every meeting would turn into a sparring match—or worse, one of them would marry some fellow who wanted to bring in sheep.

He thought of Ann, his wife, dead four years. Marcia, his infant daughter, living only half an hour after her birth. His brother. John. He'd lost so much—and now he'd gained a lot too.

Life in Eden had just taken a sharp turn. In which direction still remained to be seen.

CHAPTER FIVE

T he girls filed into the hotel room in stunned silence. Even though
they'd only been gone an hour, the bed had been nicely made, the
floor swept, and the windows opened to welcome the fresh, clean air.
The room was cheery, albeit simple. Everything about Eden was simple.
The complete opposite of what Belle was feeling inside.

When they'd left the lawyer's office, sights Belle hadn't seen before
jumped out before her eyes. Their father had adored Eden—a father
who had, in all reality, loved them as well. That revelation was still so
razor sharp she wanted to fall to her knees and weep. At the end of Main
Street, near the hotel, an enormous rock face jutted several hundred
feet to the sky. No fortress she'd ever seen in a book looked as strong, as
impenetrable. In the other direction was a line of businesses flanked in
the distance by lofty mountain peaks. Grassy plateaus of sunlit emerald
preceded the gorgeous snowcapped heights. Fatigued from the long trip
and anguished over finally confronting their father, even in his death,
she'd missed all this grandeur earlier. She turned back to the door, where
Lesley waited.

"Thank you for walking us back," Belle said, clasping his hands. So
much was running through her head, she'd barely been able to explain
to Lesley what the lawyer had said. She'd said nothing about Vernon

and Velma. That bit of gossip would send his straitlaced parents into hysteria, and they needed no more ammunition to think her beneath their beloved Lesley. Perhaps her inheritance would soften them. One could hope.

He rubbed his thumbs over the backs of her hands. "You know I'm always happy to help in any way." His green-flecked blue gaze held her spellbound. "Once we return, opening bank accounts may prove difficult for you and your sisters. Husbands usually do that. But I'd be honored to introduce you to my banker. My whole family has been with him for years. With our recommendation, he'll be open-minded, I'm sure."

"You're a godsend, Lesley. I'm so thankful you took the time off to accompany us." Her heart welled with sadness. She hadn't yet been able to express how the news about her father had affected her. That would take far more time to come to terms with.

"Are you sure there isn't anything more I can do?" His gaze searched hers. "Lawyers are notorious for their twelve-letter words. I'm sure Mr. Glass is no exception." His smile was warm. "If you'd like, I'd be happy to explain anything that seemed confusing."

Lesley. So steady. So reliable. He didn't mean to make her feel inferior. And if she were honest, the prospect of never being in Mavis's situation was so appealing as to outweigh such minor aggravations. Lesley had money he wasn't afraid to spend, and he often did so—on her. In a life with him, there'd be no scrimping, no mounting debts. Was that so wrong to want?

Am I the only one who sees the world for what it is? A place that requires struggle to stay alive.

Without warning, several of Velma's favorite sayings popped into her mind: "Being poor quickly gets old." "Marrying above her status is the only chance for a woman to improve her lot." "It's just as easy to fall in love with a man who has as with a man who hasn't." "Having an empty coffer when the debtor comes to call makes an old woman out of a maiden."

Belle vowed that if she could control her thoughts, she'd never think of that duplicitous woman again.

She forced a smile. "Just your being here means so much. All we need is some rest and time to talk things through. Thank you for understanding."

He pressed his cheek to hers and then proceeded to his room at the end of the hall. She was grateful he wouldn't be far. The trip from the lawyer's office to the sanctuary of the hotel's four walls had taken less than a minute, but that was long enough for her to notice the abundance of men watching them from all four directions. Even with Lesley at her side, the curious glances were unnerving.

She'd never be comfortable living in such a place—"rustic," as Lesley called it, and with so few women. She'd seen him notice the fine layer of dust on her shoes and the sandy grit on her fingers. No matter her father's wealth, this town was the antithesis of everything she'd done to improve her social station.

The sooner we're out of Eden, the better.

The five of them stood like mannequins in the center of the room. "Katie, Lavinia, come over here." Belle patted the tall, quilt-covered bed. Their faces looked wan and moist, the shock still apparent in their expressions. "Climb up. And you too, Emma. Come over to this side, where there's plenty more room." She circled the bed and put out a helping hand.

We'll get through this moment, this hour, and then decide the best course of action. How could Father have expected us to stay here now that he's gone?

If Belle had to decide this moment, she'd take the fifteen thousand dollars and return to Philadelphia as quickly as possible. Her insides trembled at the thought of so much money. Enough to last a lifetime. Enough to make her swoon right now.

And for each of us. How generous Father had been. Even after waiting for years to hear from us, to no avail.

Mavis sat in one of the chairs by the window, rubbing the end of her absent finger through the padded finger of her glove—a habit when she was troubled. Lavinia untied the ribbons under her chin and held her latest creation in her hands, staring. Unable to afford buying new, she'd refashioned the same headpiece over and over. Katie nibbled her lips. Whereas Emma's dimple usually looked so attractive, strain lines now marred her pretty face. Belle's heart ached to see her sisters so out of sorts.

"We mustn't worry," Belle said, sitting in the other chair. "I know you all hurt as deeply as I do thinking Father believed we had betrayed him. We didn't know the truth." Guilt pushed down on her shoulders. "If we'd known, we would have come right away. There's no question about that."

She glanced around the dead-quiet room. All gazes were lowered to hands or the floor, or eyes were simply closed.

"We must be pragmatic. Father wouldn't want us to fall apart now, thinking about his feelings. We're Brinkmans. As strong as he was. As strong as Mother had to be to protect us." In reality, she wanted to collapse in Lesley's arms and cry for a year. And still, she knew that would do little to fill the deep hole she felt in her soul.

"I don't understand," Emma whispered, reclined on the pillow, her arm thrown over her eyes. Strands of her hair had fallen free from her French twist; the color reminded Belle of strawberry frosting. Emma worked in a wool-and-fabric store in Philadelphia, and deeply loved the owners. They'd taken her on as a daughter when she'd needed the connection most. "What did Mr. Glass mean, Father sent us letters and money?" She lowered her arm and sat up. Her crinkled brow of worry was one Belle was used to seeing from her sensitive sister. "Could our aunt and uncle really be that despicable? I just can't, just can't . . ."

"Don't call them that," Belle replied curtly. "They aren't our relations. And now that we know how they've betrayed our whole family, the very idea of them sickens me."

Katie shook her head. "I don't believe any of it!"

Mavis finally raised her head. "That's because you've known no other mother and father besides them. And because their treachery hurts too much to consider."

"But . . . but Uncle loaned me the money to go to normal school. It was generous . . ."

"It was *our* money to begin with." Belle had to make her understand. "And he's drawn you out a schedule to pay *him* back."

"Maybe it's a cruel trick, and Father was really as crazy as the Crowdaires said," Lavinia whispered, trancelike, almost as if she'd missed the whole conversation.

It didn't go unnoticed by Belle that Lavinia had not called them by their names. Her analytical sister had dark good looks, so unlike their mother. *But maybe exactly like our father?* Besides loving the finer things in life, she also adored a room filled with chattering children. The proprietor at the tailor shop where she worked had eight little moppets and recruited Lavinia often to watch them when she had errands. It was a toss-up which part of her monthly income came from needlework compared to child rearing. Nothing made her happier than their smiling faces eager to see her.

"Maybe he paid Mr. Glass to *say* he sent letters and money as another way to hurt us," Lavinia went on. "Or Mr. Glass and Mr. Harding could be in cahoots to cheat us out of our inheritance."

Belle didn't believe that for a second. Henry Glass seemed to be a straight-up fellow. And Blake Harding? To her surprise, it wasn't his scar that popped into her head when she thought of him again, but his piercing blue eyes and the deep affection he clearly felt for their father. She hadn't liked him like she had Mr. Glass, but she didn't sense he was a crook. "No. Mr. Glass's loyalty to Father was apparent. He's on our side. And you saw the signed will yourself," she went on. "He could be disbarred if he's lying."

Agitated, Belle stood and looked out on the town. Several cowboys trotted down the street and halted at the sheriff's office, kitty-corner to the hotel. From the other direction, a stagecoach pulled to a stop below her window. The shotgun messenger climbed onto the top of the stage and began handing down luggage to the driver, who climbed to the street below.

"To me, it's obvious." Belle kept her gaze trained on the men below. "The crooks we know as the Crowdaires hid the letters for Mother from the beginning. They absconded with money intended for our upbringing. That's why they were able to move to a finer house, take trips, buy expensive clothing. As much as I hate to believe it, that's the truth of the matter. Don't you remember the tailored garments *she* loved?"

"Yes," Lavinia blurted. "Something new all the time. I hated when we had to wait on them like servants once they retired to the parlor. Little girls wearing white aprons, using a tray for sherry, and curtsying." She shook her head. "We were such fools."

Emma wiped at tears. "We were children."

"But we grew up," Belle whispered. "We should have suspected something."

A woman was being helped down from the stage. And then a small boy. She had a short conversation with the driver, pointed at a trunk, and then, son's hand in hers, turned and entered the hotel. *Another woman to join the ranks of the few.*

"I wonder why Mother kept us with them for so long," Lavinia said, and then paused to swallow down her grief. "I was young, but I think I remember her speaking now and then about moving on."

"She did," Mavis said, nodding. "But it didn't make sense at the time, with the fighting. The war was still going. I think she felt safer with the Crowdaires."

Belle glanced around the street and behind the buildings for as far as she could see through the window. She needed to get outside, forget about this for a few moments. "I wonder where the church is," she murmured. "That's where Father's grave would be." She felt drawn to searching for it, but leaving the hotel room would mean walking down that boardwalk again, to face the men's curious eyes.

Katie took out her hankie and blew her nose as tears spilled over and ran down her face.

"I wonder if Mother knew about *any* of Father's letters," Lavinia choked out, wiping at her own tears. "Would she have returned? Brought us with her? She probably thought Father didn't want her anymore after she abandoned him."

Belle glanced toward Mavis. Their leader was being very quiet. "What do you think?"

"There's no one besides the Crowdaires in the position to execute a deception of this magnitude. You're all too young to remember, but they weren't that well off when Mother brought us to their home, looking for a place to stay until she could decide what to do. I'm not judging Mother for taking us away from Eden, but I do remember she was a strong woman, nothing like the mother you all remember, who became sickly and remained in bed, weak and confused."

Katie's eyes grew large. "Do you think . . ."

Everyone gasped.

Belle went over and put her arm around Katie. "Thoughts like that won't do us any good. Mr. Glass said he would get to the bottom of how all this transpired. I suggest we concentrate on the problems at hand. Tonight, he may want our decision about the ranch and whether we're staying in Eden. I suggest that before we discuss further whether to upend our lives, we take time to reflect and relax. Our minds and hearts are full to overflowing." She glanced around. "At least mine is. Let's wash our faces and see if we can't find the church where Father is buried. At this moment, I feel the need to be close to him."

"Reflect?" Emma sputtered. "What do we have to think about, Belle? You're not actually considering *staying* in Eden, are you? We know absolutely nothing about cattle, horses, or ranching—let alone running any of the other businesses. My vote is to take the cash offer and go directly home."

"I disagree," Lavinia said. "Staying in Eden sounds like a challenge. At the very least, an adventure. I'm keeping an open mind." She turned toward Katie.

Katie looked despondent. "I don't know what to think. I've never pictured myself doing anything other than teaching. Does Eden even have a school?"

Mavis leaned forward in the chair, seeming drained. "Belle's right," she said. "We have much to learn. Not only about a father we don't remember, but the home he's built, the town he's lived in, and the friends he's made. We may never have this chance again."

"Home?" Katie asked, confused.

"Eden. As Mother said, he lived and breathed the country here. She said the land was his glory as well as his downfall. I wish I remembered more, but I was busy watching over my sisters." She winked, and then a bittersweet smile played at her lips. "And I loved every minute. Now come on, let's go find the cemetery. We'll feel better. We're not made of glass. We're John Brinkman's daughters. We better start acting like it."

Belle nodded her agreement.

Emma climbed from the bed. "Mr. Harding is rather frightening, with that scar running down his neck. I wonder what happened to him. Does anyone know?"

"I don't," Mavis said. "But I do have vague recollections about how painful it looked back then to a little girl."

Belle went to the washstand and splashed water on her face. With a washcloth, she blotted dry her cheeks, forehead, and chin. "As Mother used to say, character and strength are more important than looks."

Lavinia slipped off the bed, joined Belle at the basin, and began to freshen up as well. "That's funny coming from you. Lesley is *very* handsome."

Belle smiled. At least the girls were smiling again after this exchange, and Mavis didn't look quite so glum.

A loud blast rent the air, followed by a thunk in the siding beside their hotel window. Everyone screamed. Lavinia and Emma fell to the floor, and Mavis, who was still sitting by the window, flew across the room to crouch behind the bed next to Belle. Katie stood in front of the mirror, her eyes frozen wide in fear.

Was that a gunshot? Belle glanced around from her position. No other shots sounded. *Is it safe to get up? Was it just a random volley?* Painful knots twisted her belly. Slowly, she stood and inched toward the window.

"Get down," Lavinia breathed. "You'll be killed!"

After a few moments, Belle peered around the curtains. Everything down on the street looked normal. "No one seems upset out there. There's a couple people looking around, but that's it. I guess all is clear."

Emma hugged herself, her eyes as large as saucers. "Famous last words—until a bullet flies through that window and strikes me in the head. One more reason to get on a homebound stage as soon as possible."

"I agree," Belle breathed out, thankful no one had been hurt. They couldn't possibly stay in a town where gunshots were such an everyday occurrence that the residents barely reacted. Emma was agreeable to going back to Philadelphia, but Belle had better think of some ideas to sway Mavis. Her older sister had the most pull with Katie and Lavinia. If not, Belle would be stuck here, without Lesley. This was a sticky wicket just when Lesley was so close to proposing. If the vote were taken now, there'd be two for home, one to stay, and two undecided. Katie would want to please Mavis, Belle was sure. Action was needed.

CHAPTER SIX

B lake wandered down the street he knew like the back of his hand but barely saw a thing. As much as John had wanted his girls to return to Eden, Blake never once thought they actually would. Too many years had passed. Mixed feelings swirled inside, causing his gut to twist like a wet rope. Truth was, without John, Blake didn't fit anywhere anymore. Sure, he had the ranch, and the ranch hands were loyal, but John had been his *family*. Without him, Blake was alone, as if he were standing in the middle of the desert, without a direction to go.

He turned into an alleyway alongside Poor Fred's Saloon to escape all the curious stares from the townsfolk. Had word already gotten out that he'd been included in the reading of John's will?

Leaning on the cool board siding of the saloon, he lifted one boot and placed it against the wall as he pushed up his hat and ran his palm over his forehead, thinking of Ann. How he wished his wife were still alive. They'd met the night of the harvest social, and it had been her laugh that had first captured his heart. After her death, her father and sister moved on, looking for work down south. Ann had been a good listener who gave his concerns deep thought. His time with her had been too short. As well as loving her deeply, he'd valued her opinion like gold.

What would she advise me today? And Marcia? Thinking about his infant daughter was too painful to even try. Frustrated, Blake pushed those memories away . . .

What will the Brinkman sisters decide? Taking the payout would leave the ranch strapped. There wouldn't be money for any new heifers next year, or the purchase of the chunk of land John and I had been eyeballing, saving any extra cash like misers. That opportunity will disappear in the blink of any eye if the sisters return to Philadelphia.

His face heated. He had no real right to feel angry, but he did anyway.

Suppose if I work like a dog, I'll be able to hold the ranch steady and see it back to the present holdings in a few hundred years.

As much as he hated to forfeit such a huge chunk of money, the Brinkmans' staying in town might prove even more problematic. What if, after six months, they sold out to the Diamond J, the spread he and John had been fighting for years for trying to dam the river?

Be a partner with the snake who owned the Diamond J? Nope, won't do it. At least if the Brinkmans take the money now, I'll be holding the reins. I'd have to let a few men go. None of 'em would be happy.

John had been so proud when they'd had to enlarge the bunkhouse. It was a sign the ranch was profitable, really making money. But there was no help for what he'd have to do.

"Blake?"

Turning, he saw Clint Dawson leading his horse up the alley.

"You okay?"

Blake didn't miss the concern written in the sheriff's eyes. Everyone knew Clint had taken John's passing hard as well.

"How'd it go today?"

"Me and the Brinkmans are partners in the ranch, split fifty-fifty." He hadn't meant to blurt it out, but he was still astonished at the outcome.

Clint gave a long whistle. "Congratulations. That's a windfall. John always did think of you as a son."

A lump of regret pushed up Blake's throat. *Everyone will think the same thing, and why not? It's true.*

But the money wasn't why he'd stayed so long at the ranch. The land, the dilapidated house, even the five little girls, had felt like home since the day he'd set foot on the property. He nodded, unable to dispel the uncertainty hanging over his head.

"Too bad I don't have something substantial to hand on to my son, when my day arrives," Clint said. "I'm sure Cash would be mighty grateful if he didn't have to clean stalls for the rest of his life." He closed his mouth. "Sorry, pal, didn't mean to make you feel bad." Clint stepped close to clasp Blake's shoulder. "We all miss John. Nobody's going to be forgettin' him anytime soon."

Blake hefted a sigh. "To top things off, we're having supper together tonight at Mademoiselle de Sells to get to know one another." He glanced away, feeling mulish. "I'd rather not go."

The tall Coloradan chuckled. "Can't say as I'm not more than a bit jealous. Spending time with not one, but five, beautiful, *rich* women? What more could a man want?" He shook his head. "Imagine John leaving you all that."

"Truth be told, hearing I'm now a well-off landowner does have my brain in a fog. When Henry summoned me to the reading, I figured John had left me a token of his friendship. Like a watch or rifle. Maybe a few acres. Not half the ranch."

"And you're complaining about an evening of fine wine, steak, and conversation. You should be horsewhipped. How about I take your place? I doubt those women will even notice the switch. I remember those little tykes well enough," he said, with a thoughtful nod of his head. "The oldest one was bossy."

"You remember Mavis? She's now Mrs. Applebee."

45

Clint hooked a thumb in his belt, his lips curled up in amusement. "I sure do. Like it was yesterday. I was somewhere around sixteen or seventeen, I think. John hired me to do chores out at the ranch. Mrs. Brinkman was doing the washing, so John had the little ones with him in the barn. Let's see, I don't believe the youngest had been born, so there were just four of 'em, but that was enough little-girl madness to spin my head around. Couldn't get a thing done with watchin' 'em." He gave another hearty laugh. "Worse than a gaggle of geese—and Mavis dogged my heels all morning, telling me this and that. It'll be interesting to see how they turned out. Did Mavis's husband come as well? Is she still roundish?"

"She's widowed. And no, tall and slim. Pretty too. They all are."

Clint thoughtfully rubbed his chin. "What do you make of 'em?"

"They're nice enough," Blake hedged. *If you don't get too close.* "I'll find out more after supper."

"They staying on? Eden could use a few single women prettying up the town."

Blake couldn't blame the man for being excited. Most women there were either grandmothers or already married with a passel of kids hanging on their skirts. He thought how bravely Belle Brinkman had looked him in the eye, a silent challenge written on her face.

She's no shrinking violet. No way, not by a long shot. "Don't know yet."

"By the way, heads up to possible trouble," Clint said, gathering his reins. "I ran into Moses and a couple of your hands today. Having to report to a buncha petticoats isn't sitting very well with 'em. There's been talk around the bunkhouse of quitting."

"Moses?" Blake couldn't believe it. The ranch hand had saved Blake's life during the Civil War, when Blake was just a kid secretly tagging along with his older brother. His chest tightened. If Moses hadn't stitched up the wound that gave Blake the scar, Blake would have died. He was eight years older than Blake, and the two had always been close.

"No, not Moses. Mostly Praig."

Blake shook his head. "That doesn't surprise me in the least. Praig is happiest when he's picking a fight about something. I'm amazed Moses was even riding with him. The two don't usually mix. I've had to step between them more than once."

Clint shrugged, and Blake turned to walk with him toward the livery. He had hours before supper. He'd saddle up and head back to the ranch. Check on the men. With what Clint had told him, leaving the men alone longer than necessary didn't feel prudent. With the arrival of the Brinkmans' stagecoach, everyone seemed as spooky as yearlings. Him included.

CHAPTER SEVEN

avis looked at the calling card Mr. Glass had given her before they'd left his office that morning. "This is it," she said, glancing at the gold paint on the large window. "Mademoiselle de Sells." She returned the card to her reticule. "I'll bet the food is delicious."

Eden had turned out to be larger than Belle had anticipated. Instead of just one or two straight streets, the town contained a multitude of smaller, curvier roads and alleyways that connected to the large main street, as well as others that splintered from it. This charming area made Belle think the street planner had tossed a handful of noodles onto the wall and then said, "There, that will do. No newcomer will ever be able to find his way out." Here, the lane was narrow and there were buildings lining it. And surprisingly, even though Main Street, on which the hotel was located, was dirt, the smaller alleyways were paved in cobblestones. Darkness had yet to fall, but flickering lanterns hung along the route, making the area feel inviting. Many of the shops stood vacant, waiting to be leased. Although quite bare of detail, they reminded Belle of drawings she'd seen of Italy, Paris, and London. At least *this* area of town coaxed her in. She was surprised just how much she liked it.

A smile appeared on Katie's lips for the first time since the morning. "I *hope* it's delicious. I'm embarrassed to say I've worked up quite an appetite. I think I could eat one of those huge steaks we saw along the way in the train stations. I'm feeling quite unladylike."

"It's the mountain air," Belle replied, realizing she was hungry as well. "Or maybe it's all the searching we did in the cemetery. There were so many gravestones. Even with five of us, investigating the churchyard was a task." She looked down at her feet. "And my toe still aches from stubbing it. I wonder if Mr. Glass has arrived? Or Mr. Harding?"

"Look." Emma discreetly pointed to a figure coming their way. "There's Mr. Harding now. Our partner." He was looking the other way and hadn't yet seen them.

Mavis palmed her gloved hands nervously. "Should we wait, or go inside? I feel like a fish out of water. I doubt my every move. What's proper here in Colorado?"

"Let's go in," Lavinia whispered, reaching for the door. "Hurry. Mr. Harding makes me nervous. Hopefully Mr. Glass is already inside, at the table."

"Too late," Belle said under her breath. "Smile, girls. He's seen us. Entering now would be impolite."

Blake's step faltered, but only for a moment. Then he came on, a strained, uncertain smile on his face.

Does he find this as difficult as we do? Jealousy stirred when Belle realized he'd shared every day with their father for the past eighteen years, but his own daughters hadn't had a single moment.

He stopped and touched the brim of his hat. "Good evening, ladies."

Belle smiled, then remembered how rudely he'd grinned when Lesley had been tossed from the room. He was taller than she'd noticed, and certainly strong, but he wore the same black string tie he'd had on that morning, and somehow it didn't suit his sun-darkened skin and wind-mussed hair. She pictured him on horseback, shouting orders and laughing at a ribald joke. So unlike Lesley, who rarely changed from his business attire.

Not trusting herself to say anything genuinely polite, she waited for Mavis to respond.

"Good evening, Mr. Harding," Mavis said. "It's nice to see you again. The weather couldn't be any prettier."

"You're right about that. This is the best time of year in Colorado. Temperate."

His gaze shifted Belle's way, but lingered for less than the beat of a butterfly's wing. She could see why the man frightened Emma. She was sure his eyes could see into her soul. And at the moment, the jagged line that ran down his neck looked more noticeable than ever. Emma edged closer to her.

"Were you able to find the restaurant without a problem?" he asked. "Sometimes newcomers find our streets a bit confusing—especially in this part of town." He looked around, seeming ill at ease.

"We were, thank you," Mavis replied, glancing at the door.

He sprang forward as if just now realizing they were waiting for him to oblige. "Please, allow me," he said, opening the door.

A wave of delicious aromas cascaded from the tiny restaurant, enveloping Belle. Her mouth watered. "Thank you, Mr. Harding." She stopped behind the others crowded into the tiny reception area, well aware Mr. Harding was only a step behind. She realized she *did* remember him.

Perhaps it's his voice. I remember something about him being angry with me. Could that be?

The establishment seemed so different from the few she'd glanced inside in the main part of town. The entry was lit with lanterns, and a very pretty young woman stood at a desk by a closed door. She was dressed in a frilly white frock, and her face lit up like the sun when she smiled.

"Welcome to Mademoiselle de Sells," she said with a French accent. Her gaze touched on each of the sisters' faces, then landed on Mr. Harding. "Your table is ready if you'd like to be seated."

"Thank you, Amorette," Mr. Harding said, the hard edges of his personality seeming to melt away. "Is Henry here?"

When she shook her head, the abundance of corn-silk–colored curls around her face and shoulders bounced and bobbed. Belle had a hard time looking away.

"No, monsieur. He is not." She glanced at a rectangular metal clock resembling a carriage that sat on a shelf behind her. "You are a few minutes early. Knowing Henry, he'll be along soon."

A look of panic briefly crossed Blake's face. "I'm sure you're right. If you'll show us to our table, we'll wait for him there."

Her bright smile reappeared. "Very well. Please follow me."

The dining room was beautiful. The bricked-in room only had five tables—four small and one larger that sat in front of a window. A courtyard outside provided the view. The large table was set for seven but could have easily held more. They were the only diners so far. A candle burned in the center of each snowy-white tablecloth, with long fingers of wax cascading over the brass candlesticks toward the tables. Baskets of flowers were attached to the walls. The shiny wooden floor was spotless. All in all, Mademoiselle de Sells was enchanting.

"This is lovely," Lavinia whispered, her gaze moving around the room.

Blake pulled out a chair for each of them, Belle last, and then took his seat across the table from her. She unfolded her napkin and placed the cloth on her lap. No menus were offered.

"Thank you, Amorette," he said, making the name sound like a caress.

Are the two of them sweethearts? Why doesn't Lesley say my name like that? As agreeable as her beau was, he'd never invoked shivers down her spine like Mr. Harding's voice did. Belle was surprised to feel a pang of jealousy.

Blake gifted the waitress with one of his rare smiles. "Can you please ask Jean-Luc to send out something to drink?"

Mavis looked at Belle, her expression unreadable, and Belle remembered the reason they were there. *Are we just supposed to sit silently through dinner, mutely agreeing to whatever Mr. Harding and Mr. Glass, friends of Father's, want us to do? No.* Belle knew what she wanted. Take the payout, and as soon as a respectable time had passed, head straight home, where she'd accept Lesley's proposal at his parents' party. Down the table, Katie touched the rim of the pretty china teacup in front of her, and Lavinia chewed on her bottom lip, a horrible habit she'd picked up on the train ride west. *Where has our gumption gone?*

"So today we went in search of our father's grave," Belle stated, not liking the picture of incompetence they were creating for Mr. Harding, the man their father had given fifty percent of his ranch. She looked across the table.

We aren't a group of wallflowers, so we'd better stop acting like we are.

Mr. Harding's brows shot up. "You did? I'm sorry. I should have anticipated you might want to see John's grave. It's not in the cemetery, but out at the ranch."

"Yes. A man driving a wagonload of wood enlightened us on that point. Said Father used to hire him every year to supply the orphanage."

"That would be Nels Carson. I'll be happy to show you around the ranch tomorrow, if you'd like. Henry and I thought you'd be tired from your trip and would need a day or two in town to rest. But that can be remedied first thing in the morning, if you're up to it."

Belle looked around at her sisters, who said nothing. "We're up to it, Mr. Harding. We didn't come all this way to stay in our rooms and sleep, I can assure you."

"Fine, then."

There was a note of irritation in his tone. Maybe he didn't like being corrected. It was wrong of her to provoke him, but remembering his rude grin earlier, she added, "I assume Lesley will be welcome."

"I don't see why not."

Mr. Glass entered the room, Amorette leading the way—as if anyone could get lost in the postage-stamp–size establishment. He stopped to hang his hat next to Mr. Harding's on the way.

"I apologize for keeping you waiting. I got caught up in paperwork, and I lost track of the time." He looked around the table at all the expectant faces. "I assume everyone had a pleasant day? And time to rest? Coming all the way from Pennsylvania is no small feat. Again, I apologize for my tardiness."

A man emerged from what Belle thought must be the kitchen door with a round tray and glasses. He placed them on the table, left, and returned quickly with a bottle of red wine. He opened and poured.

"Compliments of your father," Mr. Glass said. "He wished he could be here when you arrived, but I know he'd still be glad that his daughters are finally in Eden."

Everyone lifted a glass, sadness in their eyes. Belle watched Mr. Harding over the rim of her glass as she sipped her wine. On the rare occasions he did smile, it was more with his eyes than his lips. His nature seemed serious, and he left most of the talking to Mr. Glass.

But Father trusted him wholly, and that says a lot.

After a few minutes of chitchat, Mr. Glass got serious. "I've been contemplating what you said earlier. About not receiving any letters or support from your father. I took the time this afternoon to put together a few documents listing the funds he sent throughout the years. You're welcome to come to my office and review them."

"Thank you, Mr. Glass," Belle said. "I, for one, would like to see that."

"I'm at your disposal at any time."

Jean-Luc was back with the first course. At this restaurant there were no choices, only what the chef had prepared. That was fine with Belle. The cold mushroom bisque was superb. She promised herself that before she left town she'd sneak back for another serving. The thought made her smile. When she looked up, she found Mr. Harding gazing at her.

A loud pop sounded outside, followed by several more.

Belle flinched. *Gunshots. Again?*

The others startled and gasped. Katie, who had lifted her water glass, dropped the tumbler to the tabletop.

"What the devil?" Blake barked, pushing back his chair.

More gunshots. A lantern in the courtyard exploded into a shower of glass that hit the window with a clatter. The echo of galloping hoofbeats quickly faded away.

Deep-voiced French words, sounding like obscenities, could be heard coming from the kitchen, and Amorette stuck her head into the dining area and looked around, wide-eyed.

Blake excused himself and went outside. With her napkin, Emma helped Katie mop up the mess. Lavinia's face had lost all color.

At ease, Mr. Glass lifted his wine and took a sip. "I'm sure that was nothing to be worried over."

Belle placed a hand on her galloping heart. "Are random gunshots a regular event here? A bullet almost came through our hotel window earlier today."

Emma's eyes were as large as saucers. "It could have killed any one of us."

Mr. Harding returned just in time to hear these comments as he settled back in his chair. "All's quiet now," he said. "Probably a cardsharp caught cheating at one of the saloons."

"If he's cheating, is he an outlaw?" Katie asked, shock giving way to curiosity. "Maybe he killed his opponent with those shots."

"If that's the case, Clint Dawson, the sheriff, will deal with him," Mr. Glass assured them. "Our sheriff keeps a steady hand on the happenings in Eden. You won't hear many guns. They're few and far between."

Emma spoke up. "We won't if we don't stay." With a tipped eyebrow, she challenged her sisters. Her face was deathly white, and her hands shook as if she'd been out in a snowstorm.

The heart of the conversation had yet to be discussed. Emma's comment wiped the smile from both men's lips.

Having his daughters in partnership at the ranch was John's dream, but not Blake's. Things would be so much simpler for him if they decided to take the payout and go home, despite the financial hardship it would entail. He felt like a turncoat, but the words had come from Emma, not him. He couldn't stay his curiosity any longer. "Is that your decision, then? To take the lump sum and return to Philadelphia? Six months *is* a long time."

Henry shot him a dirty look.

"Our father's wish is not our own," Belle supplied, echoing Blake's thoughts. "We have lives to live back in the city. We won't give those up easily."

Mavis arched her brow in Belle's direction. "Not all of us, Belle. I look forward to the challenge of staying in Eden, and the change of pace. It's almost as if my dream has been placed in my lap. I'll not run away in fear."

"No one is running," Belle replied forcefully but kindly. "We're being practical instead of romantic." She reached out and touched Lavinia's hand. "Isn't that right?"

Lavinia hesitated. "I love our home, of course, but I also truly enjoyed our walk around Eden this morning. The view of those far-off mountains is breathtaking. Something I could get used to. And back in Philadelphia, we'll have to find somewhere new to live."

Belle almost looked like she was going to be sick. Blake glanced at Katie, his hope growing. "And you, Katie? How do you feel about the decision at hand?"

She shrugged. "I'm confused. Much like Lavinia, I want a little of both."

Henry, the sly ol' fox, smiled like he had an ace up his sleeve. "In that case, now's the time to share a little surprise. This morning you all suffered a major shock, so we're in no condition to hear any more."

Mavis tipped her head. "And what surprise would that be, Mr. Glass?"

"About ten years ago"—he smiled at Mavis, the one already in his corner—"you would have been thirteen. John began thinking about the ranch house, which remains almost exactly as it was when your mother gave birth to you five. Investing in a larger house for just him and Blake felt foolish. Instead, he had plans drawn up for a structure befitting a prosperous ranch such as the Five Sisters, and his beautiful five daughters, in case you returned. And also a smaller structure attached, with a covered porch—for Blake. He wanted to be prepared, but not wasteful. The plans are ready, a building site with a view of the mountains chosen, and the ground prepared. The lumber list is at the mill. After the passage of five or six years, his hope began to fade, but he gave me the authority to begin the project as soon as you arrived and proclaimed you were staying, even for just the six months. He wanted you to be comfortable."

"You mean after he died," Katie choked out. "Isn't that right? He knew we were never coming back." Large tears rolled down her face, and Emma took her hand in comfort.

Mr. Glass nodded. "As soon as your decision is made and the verdict is to stay, I'll give the go-ahead, and Blake will hire carpenters. With agreeable weather the new home would be finished within a month or two, if not sooner. The decorating will be up to you five."

All the girls sat with stars in their eyes, thinking about a grand new house. Decorating. Parties. The same look Blake remembered Mavis and Belle, as small girls, wore the day their pa surprised them with a freshly constructed dollhouse made from wood off the ranch. Emma, who had been around three, scurried back and forth grabbing the small furniture and messing things up as Belle and Mavis tried to kindly intercede. After Celeste took the girls away, John stored the dollhouse in the barn loft for many years. One season, Blake discovered it was gone. He assumed John had finally given it away to some family or the orphanage.

Belle set her wine goblet on the table. "Are you trying to bribe us, Mr. Glass?" she asked, frowning.

Yes, Blake thought, but in solidarity with his friend, he said, "Henry wouldn't bribe anyone, Miss Brinkman. Especially not John's daughters. You're free to go anytime you want."

"Blake . . . ," Mr. Glass said, low, shooting him a look of warning.

The chastising gaze Mavis sent to Belle almost made him smile. Clearly, more was going on at this supper than the players wanted the opposition to see.

"I'm not trying to sweeten the pot," Henry said to Belle. "Your father's done that for me. But I won't beat around the bush. He wanted you to stay. Make Eden your home. That has been his ardent wish from the moment your mother left with all of you in tow. I wasn't around back then, but Blake was. He's attested to that fact many times." He cut a look at Blake, a smile pulling the corners of his lips as if a fond memory had taken hold. "We've heard about you all for many, many years. It's really nice to finally meet."

Put in her place, if kindly, Belle's face turned a pretty shade of pink. If it wouldn't have been bad manners, he'd have happily pointed it out.

"Please, accept my sincerest apologies," she said. "My comment was uncalled for. Whatever reasons I had, they were not enough to be rude to either of you. You're just trying to do our father's bidding."

Henry chuckled. "John always said you were spirited, Belle. And I can see that he was right. Eden needs a woman like you." He smiled around the table, nodding. "Like *all* of you. You would make a difference here. Just this last day, I've felt a hum in the streets. It's because of your arrival. People are curious. They're sitting back to see what you do. I honestly can say I hope you'll stay. Don't disappoint them." He looked at Mr. Harding. "Or us."

In a move that even surprised Blake, Henry glanced at the ceiling of the restaurant as if he were looking up to heaven. "Or him. Your father, John Brinkman."

CHAPTER EIGHT

B elle sat up in bed, her quick breaths shallow in the dark room.
Mindful of Mavis sleeping soundly next to her, she wrapped her
arms around herself and glanced at the window, opened just an inch.
The curtains stirred, and cool air caressed her heated skin. The night
was quiet. No more gunshots.

Mavis fumbled with the sheets. "Belle? What's wrong?"

"Nothing."

"Did you have a nightmare?" Mavis reached out and touched her arm.
"Things will work out. No need for you to bring your worries to bed."

Belle shook her head. "No, not a bad dream. Just thoughts of
Father, and how he longed for our return. It's a stone on my chest. All
those years of waiting . . ."

Mavis placed her pillow against the delicately carved wooden head-
board and sat up, drawing the bedding up with her. "I know. When I
begin to feel overwhelmed, I try to think of something else."

"Like what?"

"Darvid. About happier times, when we first met."

Belle didn't have memories like that, though. Even thoughts of
Lesley wouldn't chase away the deep sorrow wedged inside like a sharp
knife. This trip had not turned out the way she'd envisioned.

"I wonder if they have the makings for molasses cookies downstairs? A few dozen hot from the oven sounds good."

Belle smiled. Sometimes the five of them got up in the middle of the night to bake some delicious creation. Lavinia would always eat a little too much and feel sick. Katie usually fell asleep on a chair nearby but never wanted to be left out. Thank God they had one another. Belle knew she wouldn't be able to get through this without her sisters. A smidgeon of her distress evaporated. "I appreciate your effort to cheer me up. Do you know the time?" Belle lit the candle on her nightstand.

"My watch is across the room, on the dresser. Do you want me to get it? I can, if you want. Or get you some water?"

Mavis looked rested even though the moon was still bright in the window. Her lacy, high-necked nightgown ruffled under her chin, and her rumpled tresses framed her face in softness. No one would ever guess she was a twenty-three-year-old widow.

"No water, thank you. Having a drink will only make me need to use the chamber pot—and I'd rather not. Remember that yellow chamber pot we had as girls?" She gave a quiet laugh, feeling better with each moment that passed. "I was always fearful of falling in."

"Yes, I do. And it was so large and always so cold. Velma would get so angry if we forgot to empty it."

Belle shivered. "I'm just coming to grips with what they did to our family. If not for them, who knows what would have happened? Mother and Father may have reunited." Hot tears suddenly threatened in the back of her throat, but she pushed them away. "We'll *never* know. The Crowdaires need to be brought to justice. We can't let them get away with what they stole from our family—and I don't mean the money. For years, I've ached for a father's love but hardened my heart thinking he was a monster. Vernon never let a day pass without besmirching his name, setting our minds against him. If only it were possible to do things over. If only . . ."

She felt more than saw Mavis nod. "I know. I worry about Emma, Lavinia, and Katie. They were too young to have any recollection of Father at all. At least you and I can remember a few things."

Is that true? If Belle concentrated, she thought she could recall being picked up and held in their father's arms. His scent. The deep, rumbling sensation of his laughter. She thought he might have liked to cup her cheek with a work-roughened palm, but she couldn't be sure.

And Blake? Do I remember him? Or did I imagine the mysterious boy who liked to stay in the shadows unless dragged out by us girls?

"You're lost in thought again," Mavis said softly. "I think being here will spark more memories from our past, and of Father in particular. At least I hope so. I know on the trip here, everyone was in agreement that we'd come, listen to what our father's lawyer had to say, visit his grave and the old homestead, and then return to Philadelphia and resume our lives. But Belle, think about all Eden has to offer."

"Six months is too much to ask!"

"Not really. Not in the scheme of our whole lives. Why do you want to run home to your catering job? You dislike it, from all you've said. Have you changed your mind?"

"That's not the reason, and you know it. I loathe restaurant work. It was just a way to supplement my stipend and pay some of the expenses that Vernon, the cheat, was always complaining about. I'll not go back to spilling hot soup and scalding coffee everywhere. And I won't have to—not with the money from Father. Mavis, you *must* reconsider." Belle felt like she was being strangled. "Don't forget my plans with Lesley."

Mavis was gazing at her, questions in her eyes. "What plans, Belle? I don't want to be cruel, but could your *plans* be hopeful thinking? He hasn't asked you to marry him yet, and you've known him now for a year."

"He's been dropping hints. I wouldn't exaggerate over something so important."

"But do you love Lesley? Can you spend the rest of your life with him?"

"I-I *think* I do. I can't see myself with anyone else." Having to defend her feelings to Mavis stirred resentment. She knew Mavis had settled by marrying Darvid. He was a friend, but their marriage had turned out well, in spite of that. "What is love exactly, anyway?"

"I think the answer to that is different for each person," Mavis answered thoughtfully. "The security and friendship Darvid provided is one kind of love, but I'm sure that might sound boring to you."

Mavis was right about that. Belle would never settle for merely security and friendship. She'd rather remain a spinster. Love stirred the soul, making thoughts of anyone else impossible. Love flew you up to the stars on magical wings. Love made even the dreariest day look sunny and bright. At least that's what Belle believed.

Lesley and I are almost there. We just need a little more time.

Mavis smiled kindly at her silence. "The party you keep speaking of . . . ," she went on. "You believe it's to be the announcement of your engagement?"

"I do," she said with confidence. "Lesley's parents have been planning it for weeks. I know they'd be very unhappy if I decided to delay my return." *Especially Mrs. Atkins.* Belle pictured the woman's cranky frown, an expression Belle had already seen more times than she could count.

"We'll never have a chance like this again."

Feeling obstinate, Belle frowned. "What chance is that?"

"To do something really extraordinary with our lives. If we take Father's money now and turn the ranch—the thing he loved the most in the world—over to Mr. Harding, we'll never know what we might have accomplished. To me, it feels like Father is here, alive, asking us one last time to come back to Eden. Making a hasty decision before we know all the facts doesn't feel right."

A warm gust of wind through the gap in the window made the candle flame dance and the shadows move across the wallpaper. Mavis pleaded with her eyes, a tactic she knew worked all too well on Belle. "It's what Father wanted," Mavis said. "A father who loved us dearly. It's also the best option, monetarily speaking."

Disgruntled, Belle sighed. "So Mr. Glass says."

"No one can know the future, Belle. Not even you."

"Maybe the ranch can't withstand a payout of seventy-five thousand dollars, so they're tricking us to stay."

Mavis pushed back into her pillow. "You're being cynical. We're all still young. Handing the operation over feels like giving away a treasure that was meant for us. What if we really could be a benefit to the ranch? Or the town? Isn't that a captivating thought?"

Belle scoffed. "Our father and Mr. Harding have been running the ranch for years. Do you believe you know better than them?"

"Not better than them, but we could contribute something different. We're Brinkmans. This is our destiny."

Belle rolled to her elbow, suddenly warmed inside. *Is that true? Does each person on earth have a predestined purpose? Something significant she's given a chance to fulfill if she chooses to accept the challenge?* For years, all she'd worried about was making a good match and being a wife. Back East, that was what women did—unless they wanted to go into service of some kind. But here, in Colorado, all kinds of possibilities existed. Her future was a blank slate. What she chose to write on it was up to her.

"Belle?"

"I'm thinking."

Mavis softly laughed. "Good."

"You're making this very difficult, you know. It's ironic that the tables have turned. You were the one who didn't want to come, and I had to talk *you* into the trip. I just don't know how Lesley will take the news."

"You don't think he'll wait six months?"

Lesley was her best chance at a good marriage, a respectable life. A social standing in Philadelphia that no amount of money could buy. "I don't know." Her gaze strayed over to the darkness of the night outside the fluttering curtains.

"He will if he loves you. Better to find out now . . ."

"The others might not agree. Emma is set on returning. Tonight, she may have convinced them of her reasons. Katie was shaken by the gunshots. I may not be your only obstacle."

Mavis laughed. "I can't believe you said that. With both of us working together, the others don't stand a chance. Remember the time we had fifty cents saved between us? You and I wanted to go for ice-cream sundaes, and they wanted to go to the zoo. You know how that turned out." She winked. "Or all the decisions about what to see on our yearly theater excursion? When we stick together, we're unstoppable. I'm confident that if we desire it, Father's wish will come true."

Mavis threw back the covers and stood. "Let's go wake the others and take a vote."

Belle started. "Now? Are you afraid I'll change my mind?" *What if Lesley doesn't understand? I'll be tossing away my whole life. Mavis can't grasp that. This is a new beginning for her. A way to run away from the hurtful memories of a dead husband, a broken-down apartment building, a tedious job. She has ample reason to want to begin anew. But I may be making the most catastrophic mistake of my life.*

"Maybe." Mavis pulled on her robe. "I won't be able to sleep until I know the outcome."

Belle's stomach pinched as she watched Mavis fasten her sash. In the blink of an eye, their lives had changed. She just hoped they'd all be smiling when the six months had passed.

CHAPTER NINE

"Take it outside," Clint Dawson growled through a clenched jaw as he held Praig Horn, one of the Five Sisters ranch hands, facedown on the bar, his arm bent around his back. "You're drunk. Get out of town and back to the ranch or I'll toss you in jail."

The big man jerked and struggled, but was unable to free himself from Clint's iron grip. The snootful of whiskey was working against him. Bedsides the bartender, it was just Clint and Praig.

"Let me go, tin star. Or I'll—"

Clint grabbed a handful of hair and shoved Praig's face onto the bar, knocking over his shot glass. Whiskey went everywhere. The man just wasn't listening. "Or you'll what, Praig? I've had enough of your foul mood. Go home and sleep it off."

"I ain't workin' for no woman, no matter *who* she is. Not right for a man ta be told anything from a she-cat!"

"Yeah, yeah, you said that before." Summoning his strength, Clint leaned back and hefted the thick-bodied weasel off the bar, walked him to the door, and shoved him through. He didn't believe he'd get the hell out without help.

Praig landed in a heap on the porch. "Harding thinks he's high and mighty now that John's dead," he slurred. "Running the ranch. Well, he's not. He's still just one of us."

"Go home." Clint slammed the door and ambled back to the bar. The sleepy bartender sank back down onto his chair. Clint stared at his whiskey, his usual good humor gone.

Blake's gonna have trouble with Praig. He'll sleep off his bender, but not his animosity and hate.

Clint took a sip from his glass. He'd wanted to be alone tonight so he could do some thinking. Instead of going to Poor Fred's, his usual drinking establishment just a few buildings down from his office, he'd opted to walk a quarter mile to the outskirts of town and the Spanish Trail Cantina, a rundown adobe building along the Old Spanish Trail.

A Mexican owned the place, and since Clint was the sheriff, his first drink was always on the house—if he so chose, which he didn't. Miguel Angel Alvarado and his grown son, Santiago, were having a difficult time making ends meet as more white settlers came to Eden and the Spanish community died off or left. Miguel's other son, Demetrio, two years Santiago's senior, was locked up in Sugar House Penitentiary up Salt Lake City way. He'd gotten into trouble in Santa Fe, and, as harsh as the conditions were at the prison during a fifteen-year sentence, the alternative was worse. The other two outlaws who'd been convicted at the same time, with a long list of priors, had swung by the neck until dead.

Clint shook his head and took a drink, feeling a mite bit insignificant. His birthday was coming, and he didn't like the thought of adding another year to the thirty-six he'd already lived. Loneliness edged in on him. He had Nicole, his sixteen-year-old half sister, whom he'd taken in when their mother passed. And his fourteen-year-old son, Cash, who was more of a man already than most grown fellas in town. Clint's life was full, so to speak, but still, something was missing.

Sighing, he got back to gathering wool. The Old Spanish Trail cut through town, the route going north from Santa Fe then veering west toward California. But the traffic on it was nothing like twenty years ago, when he'd come to town as a sixteen-year-old kid.

The good old days. The memory made him smile. Lifting his shot glass, he tossed back what was left. He remembered twenty mule-pack trains appearing on the horizon as they made their way toward Eden, one vaquero in the lead, one at the rear, maybe three more in between, their tall sombreros keeping off the sun as the mules trudged along. With three trains or more a week passing through, Miguel's cantina had been booming with traders. Money and whiskey flowed like water. Miguel had had three or four girls working the room and a mariachi band pounding out music. Souvenirs from Mexico, South America, the states and territories were abundant.

Clint lifted a boot to the brass kick rail, thinking how his bones felt old and stiff. Back then, in his teens, he would drop whatever he was doing to meet the traders on the edge of town. The Mexicans would smile and toss him jerky, candy, or another treat they'd bartered for along the way in trade for his help in unrigging the animals. They didn't go to the livery, where they'd have to pay per head to put them up for the night, but to an old abandoned barn on the edge of town that had a large corral. They'd unpack while telling all kinds of stories—wild, rowdy, and at times salacious, just the kind a kid his age wanted to hear. When they were done, they'd leave one of their men behind with their goods, several large guns, bags of bullets, and an easy trigger finger—or at least that's what they always told the boys.

Clint chuckled and shook his head. He'd bought the line easy enough and stayed far away from the tempting stash. He was as wild as the next young lad, but he knew better than to tangle with traders whose lifeblood depended on what was in those packs. They'd just as soon sell him as be his friend.

After the animals were taken care of and their supplies and belongings were locked in the barn, those not on guard duty would head straight for this cantina, first stopping at, in a roundabout way, the sheriff's office. They'd drop a dollar coin into a lockbox dedicated exclusively for overnight use of the barn and corral. The town had made a fair amount of money off the old corral over the years. Not so now. Eden was lucky to see one train a month anymore.

"Amigo," Miguel's son Santiago called to Clint as he came down the creaky stairs in the back of the cantina. He was dressed in his typical black shirt embroidered with colorful thread on the shoulders, seams, and pockets. His tight-fitting black pants were like a second skin. Even though it was one o'clock in the morning with the day well spent, *and* he was still too far away to tell, Clint knew there wouldn't be a speck of dust on him. He was just that way. Clint long ago expected the twenty-four-year-old to have returned from Santa Fe with a pretty senorita on his arm.

Maybe some men are destined to remain single. Like me.

Behind the bar, Santiago flashed a wide smile. "It's good to see you, my friend. But I am surprised. It's late. You have trouble in town? I rarely see you at this end of Eden, where the ghosts live." He chuckled softly, then went over and nudged the sleepy bartender, a paunchy, middle-aged man who got up, yawned, and slowly made his way from behind the bar and out the back door.

"Turned in at midnight. Found I couldn't sleep so decided to take one more walk around town. Ended up here." He looked around at the empty cantina. "You want to close up? I'm on my way out the door."

Santiago opened the cash box under the bar and began transferring the money into a brown leather bag.

"No, no, we'll stay open as long as you like. You want another whiskey? A night 'sombrero,' perhaps?"

Clint laughed, scraping his boot off the kick rail and straightening up. He stretched his aching back, realizing that, besides the small interruption from Praig, he'd been standing in the same position for more than an hour. "Gracias, but no. I'm gonna be cussing myself tomorrow for staying up this late. I'm too old for nights like this."

He smiled at his friend's raised brows.

"Old?"

Clint nodded. "I advise you not to do it, my friend. It's no fun, getting old. And I don't need any more coffin varnish to help me get there."

Santiago feigned a wounded expression. "You hurt me. We serve only the best—for you, that is." He reached under the bar and lifted a half-full bottle of whiskey. The white label read "Pure Kentucky Bourbon Whiskey, Aged 10 Years." That was a bald-faced lie, which everyone knew. First of all, the distillery that made it was located in Santa Fe. But the label made the whiskey somehow more respectable than homemade. Several bottles of Santiago's home brew lined a shelf under the mirror on the back bar, accompanied by six bottles of tequila, a brain-numbing elixir brought up from Central America. Two bottles of mescal, with large worms at the bottom, gathered dust at one end.

Mexicans are a hardy bunch.

Clint laid down several coins, considered the deserted cantina one last time, and started for the door. "Everyone else has more sense than me, I suppose. Adios."

"I hear the Brinkman sisters have come to hear John's will."

Stopping with one hand on the door, Clint glanced back. "That's right. All five of 'em. It's a pity they didn't show up before he died."

Santiago slowly nodded. "I liked Senor Brinkman. Good men are hard to find. I can't help but wonder what kind of girls they are." The unsaid implication hung in the air.

Clint wasn't touching that topic with a ten-foot pole. He shook his head and shrugged.

Santiago slapped his hand down on the bar, the sound reverberating around the quiet room. "The past is the past, as they say. Go home and get a good night's sleep. All is well in Eden tonight." He flashed a winsome smile as Clint walked out the door.

The night sky was clear and sparkling, with an abundance of bright stars. A cool breeze chilled Clint's skin. To the south, the dark silhouette of the faraway San Juan Mountains reached high into the sky, bringing a sense of longing into his throat. He loved this place as much as any man could. John Brinkman didn't have the corner on that. Eden was home. And he'd told himself during the Civil War that if he made it out alive, he'd head back to Eden and never leave again. He'd kept that promise for the last fifteen years.

The thud of hooves echoed up the road. Not that odd for someone to be traveling by night, but by the sound, Clint judged that there was more than one animal, perhaps a handful. Just to be safe, he crossed the road and stepped behind the outcropping of tall moss-covered rocks they called Castlewood. As he waited, he lifted his Colt several times, making sure his weapon was nice and loose.

The sounds came closer. Due to the darkness, it was still too soon to see who approached. A rider appeared in the center of the road. A mule came next on a lead, then another and another after that. Before the rider was alongside the cantina, Clint stepped out.

"Howdy," he said. "Who goes there?"

The rider reined up, and his mules stumbled to a halt. From what Clint could see, he was leading a fair number of pack animals.

"Captain White," the mule skinner called back in a soft Southern accent. He wore a light-colored shirt and a buckskin coat that picked up the gleam of the two lanterns still burning outside the Spanish Trail Cantina. His long, rawhide whip was coiled and tied to the front of his saddle. "Just making my way up from the mining camp along the Animas River, and before that, Santa Fe. Who goes there?"

Knowing full well it was too dark for Captain White to see him in his dark clothing, he came close and stuck out his hand. "Sheriff of Eden. Clint Dawson." Hanging back in the shadows was another man on horseback. Perhaps there was yet another at the end of the train. "What're you packing?"

The man didn't have to answer, but Clint hoped he would. He tried to keep an eye on strangers.

"The usual. Spices, foodstuffs, kitchenware, tools, clothing."

Although his words were friendly, his tone said he could have gone without being questioned.

"Stopping for the night?"

"Planned to, but we can move on if that's your preference."

Eden made money from travelers as well as freighters. They usually spent plenty on food, whiskey, and women. "I have no problem. I don't recognize you, though. Have you been through this way before?"

"No."

"There's an old barn on the north end of town. Follow the trail past Wild Turkey, Falcon Haven, and Deer Ridge, then turn right on Main Street and left on White Hawk. Road signs are well marked and easy to find. There's a large corral and barn. Also a stream behind and hay to feed. Costs a dollar a night. Payment made to me or in the sheriff's office before you pull out."

"Much obliged. I heard about that back in Durango."

Clint straightened. "Durango?"

"The mining settlement I mentioned on the Animas River. They just put a name to the camp. Should be official by next month."

Here was news he hadn't yet heard. That was the other function freighters and traveling salesmen served. They passed on information and usually knew things before anyone else.

When his horse fidgeted, Captain White said, "We best be getting on. Any establishments still open?" He looked over to the dark cantina and then back at Clint. When he smiled, Clint noticed he was missing a front tooth.

"Poor Fred's Saloon might be, or the Hole in the Floor; then again, maybe not. Either place serves a limited amount of foodstuffs, but you won't go to sleep hungry. That's the best I can offer."

Captain White gave a casual salute. "Good enough. Obliged again. We're headed to the barn right now. My monies are packed away. I'll stop by tomorrow."

I'll be keepin' an eye on you to make sure you do just that. "Welcome to Eden."

He stepped back, a signal that he was done talking and they were allowed to move on.

The captain gathered his reins and clucked to the tall gray beneath him. The animal walked forward tugging a tired-looking mule. It trudged forward, the pack on its back weighing between one hundred fifty and two hundred pounds, if Clint had to guess. A crate strapped to the mule's side looked suspiciously like it might contain dynamite.

Clint waited until the whole train had passed. He'd seen two more mule skinners and seventeen pack animals. He'd never heard of Captain White before, or seen the other two dour-faced men. They were strangers to these parts. Perhaps the lateness of the evening had them crankier than normal.

Or maybe they have something to hide.

They disappeared around the far corner, the brays of the weary animals dissipating into the night.

May as well follow along, make sure they do exactly as they said. I'm sure Captain White expects nothing less.

For a brief moment, a twinge of loneliness made Clint suck in a breath of cool air. He'd been dreaming about excitement, and now five new women had arrived in town, although he had no idea how long they'd actually stay. And an unknown freighter had shown up, dragging along seventeen mules. Things were looking up.

CHAPTER TEN

E arly the next morning, Belle took special care with her toilette in preparation for breakfast with Lesley. He wasn't going to like what she had to say. If there was any other way to settle the two opposing matters at hand, she wished an idea would present itself.

Belle arrived in the hotel café ten minutes early. She asked for the small table in the front corner, a nook, the last of a long row along the wall. The booths were elevated a foot off the floor by a wide step that ran the length of the room. She lifted her skirt and stepped up. The sky-blue curtains on either side of the alcove gave the tables a cozy feel. She was surprised by the quaintness and uniqueness of the establishment.

Another diamond in the rough for Eden.

She settled herself and smoothed her skirt, wishing she could do the same with the butterflies in her tummy. She glanced around, wondering if she'd get a chance to meet the woman she'd seen getting off the stagecoach, but she didn't see her in the few diners about. Although the Eden Hotel and Café was rustic, the building held a charm of its own. When she'd left her room, Mavis was reading. The room across the hall, where her three younger sisters were, was still quiet—as was the rest of the hotel.

A middle-aged woman came forward. Belle recognized her as the same waitress who'd been working the night before, when she and her sisters had returned from dinner with Mr. Glass and Mr. Harding, *and* the day before, when they'd arrived.

Did she ever take a day off?

She was average height, with brown hair drawn up at the back of her neck and twisted into a bun. Her pretty yellow dress looked freshly pressed. She was a spot of spring.

"Good morning, Miss Brinkman," she said pleasantly. "May I get you something to eat?"

"Yes, please," Belle replied. "For now, I'll have a cup of tea while I wait for my friend Mr. Atkins. He'll be joining me any moment," she added, feeling shy about being out alone so early in the morning. "Oh, and I wonder, would you have any honey to sweeten my tea?"

"Yes, we do. Collected from Eden's own beekeeper and made from high-mountain clover," she said with pride. "I'll get that for you right now."

As she moved away, Belle noticed that even the waitress's apron bow was neatly tied at the back of her skirt, presenting a nicely put-together picture. Belle wondered about her history.

Is she married, and if not, why? Had she been friends with Father?

If they were to remain in Eden, it would behoove her and her sisters to make some female friends.

Lesley appeared in the foyer, pulling his shirt cuffs out from his coat sleeves as if he'd just dressed. Spotting her, he hurried over, causing a new round of butterflies to hatch. Not because the sight of him set her pulse racing, but because of the difficult conversation ahead. She wished there was an alternative way to settle the situation—like cutting herself in half. One half could stay in Eden for six months with her sisters, the other half could go back to Philadelphia with Lesley.

He scooted through the tied-back curtains. As usual, not a strand of his nicely combed hair was out of place, and his face appeared as soft as a baby's derriere. His aftershave floated over and made her nose twitch. He took pride in his appearance, and this morning was no exception. As soon as he was settled, he picked up her hand. "How did you sleep?"

His overt expressions of affection always caused her a bit of discomfort.

"As well as I could after what we learned yesterday."

"Such a shock. I wish I could protect you from the turmoil. But at least your father didn't leave you penniless. That is a nice surprise."

She swallowed. *How on earth will I find the courage to say the things I must?*

"Coming from Philadelphia, everything in this tiny town must almost feel like a nightmare to you, Belle. I'm sure you're as eager to return as I am."

She gently pulled her hand away and set it in her lap. "Actually, I was born in Eden. This is where I'm from."

"Yes, well . . ." His nose wrinkled. "I'm keen for you to conclude your business so we can depart. I long to shower you with the love you deserve."

Why do his words feel so cumbersome today? "I'm impatient to have this sorted out as well, Lesley. I can promise you that."

Nerves skittered up her spine. His gaze was so direct, she felt as if he could read her mind. But he only smiled and said, "Will you girls get your bank drafts today? If yes, I can make arrangements for our journey back to Philadelphia on the Saturday stage. Or if you'd like to spend a few more days, actually see the ranch before you go, that might be the prudent thing to do. I doubt any of you will make this trip again."

Why is he writing off Eden so quickly? It's not so bad. Out of loyalty to her father, she felt compelled to defend the town. "Actually, Lesley . . . Mavis and I were discussing things last night. After we talked, we went and woke the others. We're not going to take the bank drafts Mr. Glass offered. We're going to stay in Eden for six months, as our father wished. After that, we can decide whether to sell the ranch or not. Of the two options, this is the better investment. Mr. Glass stressed that point many times."

Lesley's already pale skin turned chalk white. A moment of pity washed over her.

"Surely you're joking, Belle." He chuckled and shook his head. "Your sense of humor is a bit off."

"I wasn't . . ."

The look of amusement left his face. "You're not staying in this countrified place. It has absolutely nothing to offer a woman like you."

"We are. We'll make a lot more money this way," she hurried to state. Businessmen were always concerned with the bottom line, period, and Lesley's family was no different. They had made plenty of money in construction. Surely he'd understand that reasoning. "There's no better investment than land. I've heard your father say so many times. Six months is nothing compared to the money we'll make by selling to another buyer. The time will go by in the blink of an eye."

His face had lost all traces of pleasantness. "I hardly think so."

The waitress was back with a tray. She set out a small white porcelain pot along with a white teacup and saucer, both painted with purple pansies. She added a small crock of honey and a miniature pitcher of cream to the table. "I didn't ask if you took cream, miss, so I brought some anyway. Fresh this morning." She looked at Lesley. "What can I get you, sir? Coffee or tea?"

He just sat there.

"He'll have the same as me, please," Belle said quickly. She forced a smile, trying not to let the tension get the best of her.

The waitress nodded and walked away.

"Lesley, please. Say something," she whispered. "You're making me nervous."

The muscle in his jaw clenched several times, and he looked away, probably counting to ten. When his gaze came back to her, she could tell he was more than angry. If she had to guess, she'd say he was furious.

"What do you want me to say, Belle? What am I supposed to tell my parents when I return without you? Do you have any idea how awkward this is going to be? They'll never understand."

She didn't have the answers. "I can't. But you must know, must understand. I never expected this to happen. Not in a million years. None of us did. This was just as much of a shock to us as our wanting to stay is to you. It's not like I had this planned to hurt you."

She felt the hairs on her neck tingle in a funny way, and she looked up. Mr. Harding stood in the doorway, watching them. She forced herself not to look away for three seconds longer than was comfortable, then squeezed Lesley's hands. "I'm sorry." When she looked up again, Mr. Harding was gone.

"That's easy to say. They're just words."

He was right. Distress and culpability washed through her. Then she thought of her father and all he'd tried to do for his children. Maybe she wasn't being as self-centered as she'd thought. Her scattered emotions went to her sisters, and then finally to Mr. Harding and the way his gaze had just negatively assessed her actions.

Darn him. I should be focused on Lesley, not Mr. Harding.

The waitress appeared again with Lesley's tea. As if feeling the tension at the table, she set it down quickly. When she was finished, she looked at Belle. "Can I get you anything else, Miss Brinkman?" Her gaze shifted to a moody-looking Lesley and then back to Belle, her brow arched slightly in solidarity.

Belle shook her head, but when the woman turned to walk away, she felt compelled to say something more—if only to delay responding to Lesley. "Excuse me. May I ask your name?"

The waitress turned back. "Of course. I'm Karen Forester. Been working here at the hotel for seven years, and I know all about you and your sisters. The whole town is delighted you've finally come home." She hugged the round tray to her chest. "I always knew you would. You're all more beautiful than I ever imagined. John was a lucky man. Every New Year's, he'd tell me this was the year you'd return. He'd say, 'When they arrive, Karen, we're going to throw a party the likes this town has never seen. Mark my words.'" Her kind smile faded away, and she gave a small dip of her head. "You let me know if I can be of assistance in any way, Miss Brinkman."

Heat rushed to Belle's face. She hadn't expected to hear that she and her sisters were celebrities. It magnified the whole tragic mess. Her father sounded like the finest man ever born.

"I'm sorry," Karen said. "I didn't mean to embarrass you. Or remind you of how much you've lost." She dipped her chin once more and hurried back to the kitchen.

After she'd disappeared, Lesley reached across the table and touched her arm, his anger gone. His mollifying expression maddening. "There you have it. The crux of the matter. Here you're all prominent figures in a small pond. Imagine that. The Five Sisters is said to be the most prosperous ranch in West Colorado."

"*One* of the most," she corrected, not enjoying his tone.

He went on as if he'd not heard. "Who knows? Perhaps I'd want to stay on too, if I were in your shoes. I don't understand Mavis, though. How she condones this action. And Emma, Lavinia, and Katie? I'm sure you're the one to lead the charge, as usual. You're rather impulsive, you know."

"I told you it was Mavis. Not me."

He shrugged. "It's clear you're determined to have your way. Today I'll book passage for tomorrow's stage."

"Would you like to accompany us to see the ranch today?"

He shook his head. "I've no need to, like the five of you. And I'm anxious to get home. Barring any complications, I'll be home by next week."

Relief coursed through her. Then a thought struck her. "Does that mean . . . ?"

Lesley smiled a benevolent smile just as Belle saw her sisters entering the lobby. "Yes, I'll wait. Then, when you're home, we'll remedy the fact that I haven't yet asked you to become Mrs. Lesley Atkins. You'll be pleased, I promise. And we'll have a beautiful wedding."

Reaching over the table, he lifted her hand and kissed her fingers.

CHAPTER ELEVEN

B lake paced Henry's office, waiting for John's daughters to show up. They'd agreed last night to meet there again in the morning. Blake had just assumed that meant the same time as yesterday. He glanced at the clock on the wall. He'd arrived at eight, and that was more than an hour ago. He was used to rising early; too much work needed doing to sleep in, even if he wanted to.

A few minutes ago, Henry had discovered he was out of coffee beans and had gone downstairs for more.

Finally. Footsteps on the stairs. *Henry must be on his way back.*

The door opened. Belle Brinkman, finished with her rendezvous in the café with Mr. Atkins, swished in. She was clearly ready to get on with her day, as if she hadn't just broken that man's heart. She seemed light and her face was flushed—with guilt? Or happiness? Blake remembered how pretty she had looked last night, how her eyes opened a bit wider when she contributed to the conversation, how the soft scent of her perfume distracted him. Disgusted with himself, he shoved the thoughts away.

Her gaze landed on his scar.

"Miss Brinkman," he said, feeling a recurrence of his earlier anger.

They aren't to blame, he reasoned with himself. *They never received any of the letters. They were victims, just as John had been.* The memory of John in his final hours, reminiscing about his precious girls as he struggled for life, was still too vivid for him to completely let the resentment go.

She glanced around, obviously looking for Henry.

"He went to buy coffee beans downstairs. Ran out yesterday. There's none left in the pot . . ."

Turning away, he rolled his eyes at his own stupid babbling. He sounded like a blathering fool. A long crack in the ceiling caught his attention. This room—and the whole town—must look shabby to John's daughter. Henry kept his office and adjoining living quarters neat as a pin, but its bones were getting old. Looked a little ragged and tired—just like the rest of Eden.

The heck with the Brinkman girls. They can just get back on that stage and return to Philadelphia, for all I care.

"Where're the others? On their way?"

She clasped her hands tightly in front of her skirt, looking ill at ease, the brightness of her expression gone. "After breakfast, they decided to take a short walk. See some of the town. They should be along anytime."

He went to the window, wondering which way they'd gone. He didn't see one female belonging to their family—or to any other.

"What's wrong, Mr. Harding? Are they in danger?"

"That might depend on which way they went. Some parts of the town can be rough. Did they mention what they wanted to see?"

She hurried to his side, put her hands on the sill, and leaned out, looking both ways. "No. Just things."

"I'm sure they'll be fine, but I'd prefer you waited for me next time you plan to go sightseeing. When you want to walk, or see John's grave, I'll be happy to show you around to your heart's content."

Not actually happy, but I will because I told John I would.

"*Are* they in danger, Mr. Harding?" she asked again, an edge to her tone. "I want them to be more than fine. Will more men be shooting off their guns?"

When the door opened again, he was expecting to see Henry. Instead, in walked Trevor.

His ranch hand jerked to a stop when he saw Miss Brinkman and whipped the hat from his head.

"What is it, Trevor?" Blake asked. "If you're looking for Henry, he's downstairs in the mercantile."

"I just came from there. I'm looking for you."

"Miss Brinkman," Blake said, remembering his manners, "meet Trevor Hill. He works for the ranch—and now you, I guess."

"I'm pleased to make your acquaintance, miss," Trevor gritted out. "And I'm sorry about your pa. That was real bad, the way he died. I'd not wish that on—"

Blake loudly cleared his throat, and Trevor snapped his mouth closed.

Belle's brow wrinkled and she briefly searched Blake's gaze. "The pleasure is mine, Mr. Hill," she finally said.

"Just Trevor, ma'am."

She smiled. "One more face to recognize at the ranch will be nice. I know I have a lot to learn, but I hope you'll be patient."

Trevor's gaze shot to Blake.

Blake shrugged. *She didn't mean anything by that, did she? She's just making polite conversation.* He tried to signal as much to Trevor, who still looked worried. Blake would bet his last nickel that none of these women were up for such a challenge. *Why would they be? When they went back to the city, they'd be as rich as could be.*

No need to panic just yet—that was what he'd told the men yesterday.

"Uh, we need to talk, Blake," Trevor finally said.

"I'm listening."

"Maybe we should speak in private. I don't want to alarm anyone in the room, if you get my drift."

Belle's back went straight.

"This is John's daughter. If she's anything like him, she's tough." He smiled to himself. *Anything but.* "I'm sure whatever you have to report won't shock her too much." He looked her way. "You won't faint, will you?"

She shook her head.

Trevor shrugged. "Praig up and left. Took two of the men with him."

What the hell! Blake, who'd been admiring Belle's profile as Trevor talked, jerked his attention back to the ranch hand. "What do you mean, he left? Why would he do such a thing? Right before roundup, no less?"

Trevor scuffed his boot at nothing on the wooden floor. "Some of the men have been grumbling about working for five lady bosses. That's five more than they signed on for. Guess they finally made their decision."

Belle blinked and looked between them.

"How'd they decide that? We haven't heard their official decision yet." He chanced a quick look at Belle, wary of what he might see. The girl was more stoic than an Indian when she wanted to be. "My bet is they head back to Philadelphia by next week. Miss Brinkman, what do you have to say?"

She smiled, and Blake felt the full force of all those straight, white teeth.

"We spoke about our options late last night. We have come to a decision, but decided not to say anything until you *and* Mr. Glass were present."

So that's how she's playing it . . .

Trevor shook his head. "The men had a spy planted in the hotel café this morning. Heard 'em talking about staying in Eden. And maybe even bringin' in sheep."

"A spy? Who?" Blake demanded.

"Praig."

"Once sheep were mentioned," Trevor went on, "he beat it back to the ranch with the news as fast as he could ride. Didn't take much to convince the men to leave. Sheep and cattlemen don't mix."

Belle gasped. "A spy? Are we the *enemy*? Were the men not loyal to my father?"

"Yes on all counts, miss," Trevor said.

Blake couldn't believe his ears. The ride to the ranch was forty-five minutes by wagon, or fifteen on a galloping horse. "You sure he's gone for good? Maybe you got the story wrong. I can't spare a single man."

Again, the nod. "Sure I'm sure. He cleared out his belongings. Told Tank he's heading where men are respected and they don't have to work for no woman." He glanced at Belle. "No disrespect meant to you. I'm just repeating his words."

"None taken."

Blake felt like pounding his fist into Praig's face. He'd told the men to be patient. Not to jump to conclusions. "I should have fired Praig the first time he talked back. Wherever he's going, he won't last long. He's too lazy."

Belle gave him a long stare. "Why did you keep on a slacker?"

"I need to get back to the ranch before Praig can recruit any more hands," he answered, avoiding her question. "Who'd he take?"

"Riley and Bush."

Blake felt like cursing. "That leaves Garrett, Tank, KT, Moses, you, and me. We can get the roundup done with six men, but the job won't be easy. Long hours and hard work. We've never been this shorthanded before."

"Praig's been stewing for a fight since John's death," Trevor explained to Belle. "Almost like he was challenging Blake. And maybe he was." He glanced at Blake and then Belle. "Maybe hearing what John left you was the last straw. Even though he quit, I don't think he's gonna let this go. It's personal to him."

Trevor has a point.

"You best watch your back, Blake."

Blake rubbed the back of his neck, thinking how the last conversation he'd had with Praig hadn't been civil. "I'm thinking the same thing."

Steps echoed up the staircase. Either Henry was back, or the rest of the Brinkman sisters were finally on their way.

"What's this about a roundup?" Belle asked as Henry stepped through the door. The lawyer held a brown bag and a stack of mail in his hands. "Are you speaking about the cattle?"

"Nothing to be worried over. We'll get the roundup done and the cattle ready for the stockmen that're coming to drive 'em to the stockyards in Santa Fe, just like every year before. Our fall roundup is much smaller than spring's."

Even though they'd be shorthanded for the upcoming work, Blake could live with it. What he couldn't live with was a man who was always stewing for a fight. That was Praig. If it was a beautiful, sunny day, he'd find something to grumble about.

"Sounds the opposite," she said. "You sure you know what you're doing without my father?"

The apprehension in her voice turned his anger to annoyance. *Is this what I have to look forward to? My decisions questioned on things they know nothing about?* In that case, he was doubly glad they probably wouldn't be sticking around. "Yes, Miss Brinkman, I do, I assure you."

Henry, who'd been listening intently, set his mail and the bag on his desk. "What'd I miss? Sounds important."

Before Blake could answer, Belle turned to the attorney. "Some men at the ranch quit because they don't want to work for me and my sisters. One, named Praig, sounds like he'd like nothing better than to cause trouble. Seems he has a history with Mr. Harding. Mr. Hill thinks Mr. Harding needs to watch his back." She looked between them. "Does that mean he'd actually try to *kill* Mr. Harding?"

There was no guile in her eyes, only open, honest concern—and a genuine interest in the operation of the ranch. Begrudgingly, he had to admit that she reminded him of John at that moment.

She turned back to Henry. "What should we do? Inform the sheriff?"

Blake shot Trevor a look that said, *See what you've done? If you would have waited ten minutes, all this could have been avoided.*

"We were expecting disquiet sooner or later." Henry stepped closer. "We shouldn't be surprised."

Blake nodded. "Yeah, we were. You see, Miss Brinkman, the men—"

"If we're going to be working together for six months, perhaps you should call me Belle. And I'll call you Blake, if that's all right with you?"

Blake's heart thwacked in his chest. He couldn't believe what was happening. "We are? Going to be working together, that is? Have you and your sisters come to a decision?"

She nodded.

"You're staying in Eden?" He hadn't meant to sound so shocked—but in reality, he was.

Her gaze went to each of the three men, and then she laughed. "Blake, you look as if you've been dealt a death sentence." When he didn't answer, because of his shock, she looked to Henry. "May I call you Henry?"

A wide smile split Henry's face. "That's fantastic news, Belle." He rushed forward and gave her a fatherly hug. "Of course you should call me Henry. You won't regret staying, I promise." Henry's face fairly beamed with happiness.

Blake hoped his friend knew what he was doing.

"And as I said before, I'm Trevor," Trevor added quickly. "You or your sisters can come to me with any problem you might have. I'll be happy to help."

"Thank you, Trevor. I'll be honest. I was overruled." Her eyebrow tented. "I was against staying in Eden. The decision still has my insides in a knot. I'm keeping in mind what Henry said about the ranch as the better investment six months from now. And as of this morning, it sounds like we'll actually be able to help as well."

Blake rubbed a hand across his whiskers, remembering he hadn't taken the time that morning to shave. "Help? In what way?"

"You're short men for the roundup. Three, if I've counted correctly." A flash of heat rushed to Blake's face.

"Do you ride, Belle?" Henry asked, his silly grin irritating Blake further.

"I do. But my experience has been with a sidesaddle in the park, on a mount that was not much larger than a pony. I've never ridden astraddle, and I don't have the right clothes. Is there a clothing store in town?"

"Absolutely," Henry chortled. "A small place called the Toggery— one of your new businesses. They should have whatever you need in the young men's department. By now, they're open. Your father had an account at every establishment in Eden. You'll have no need for cash. Don't worry about getting lost—Blake will show you the way."

Blake gawked. *Henry must be loco. Belle could get seriously hurt.*

"Henry, you don't intend to let her ride."

She lifted a brow. "*Let* me?"

"The only way to learn is to ride," Henry replied. "After a day or two, she'll be comfortable." He smiled at her, and she smiled back, puffing out her chest.

Of all things, thought Blake.

Blake was reminded of her excited smile when she'd entered the office. "We best get movin'. Who knows what's going on out at the ranch. Trevor, go get a buggy from the livery and bring the other Brinkmans out when they show up. I'm shanghaiing Gunner for Belle." He looked at Henry. "You coming with us?"

"You betcha. Let me do a few things here while she gets her duds. I'll be ready when you are. I wouldn't miss this for the world."

CHAPTER TWELVE

C lint waited as long as his impatient instincts would allow for the mule skinners to come into his office on their own to pay the overnight fee. Early morning was long past. The clock on the wall chimed quarter past ten. A few hours ago, on his way to the café for breakfast, he'd taken a roundabout route to make sure Captain White hadn't skedaddled without paying. The mules stood peacefully under the large trees in the corral, head to tail, swatting off flies.

Stepping outside, he was brought up short. Four of the Brinkman girls stood by the hotel entry, gazing around with interest. He wondered if they were frightened to leave the hotel without an escort.

Time for a proper sheriff's welcome, he said to himself as he strode forward and touched the brim of his hat with a forefinger. "Good morning, ladies. You must be John Brinkman's daughters."

In a flurry of nods and smiles, one replied, "Yes."

"Sheriff Dawson, at your service. Welcome to Eden. This day has been a long time coming."

All wore black dresses that were a bit too fancy for their new town. "I can't remember Eden ever having so many new women at once." *Pretty too.* "You're creating quite the stir. Let me know if anyone bothers you, and I'll take care of them right away."

All four straightened.

Maybe not the smartest thing to say. He hooked a thumb over his shoulder. "My office is over there." They'd have to be blind to miss the large sign, but pointing it out couldn't hurt. "I've heard a lot about you."

"And we you."

Mavis, if he were to guess, gave a slight tip of her head. The strawberry-haired one would be Emma. Lavinia was giving him the stink eye for being so bold as to introduce himself, and the blue-eyed baby with the honeycomb-colored hair must be Katie. Blake had described them perfectly. He took a quick glance around for Belle. He wondered at the wrist-length gloves Mavis wore even though the weather was nice. *Is she too uppity for Eden?*

"You must be Mrs. Mavis Applebee. And these are Emma, Lavinia, and Katie Brinkman. But, ladies, aren't we missing someone?" He smiled mischievously as they glanced between themselves, visibly astonished by how much he knew about them. "Surely you can understand how news of your arrival would spread quickly."

All three blushed at his compliment.

"Belle preceded us to Mr. Glass's office," Mavis replied. "That's where we're headed now."

An unpleasant smell wafted by on the breeze. Mavis waved one gloved hand in front of her face, and the others wrinkled their noses.

"That's the tannery," Clint said quickly, wanting to make it known he wasn't to blame. "Ol' man Little must be soaking his hides today. I'd be honored to escort you to Henry's," he said, to change the subject. The office was just across the quiet street.

"Thank you, but that won't be necessary," Lavinia said, the earlier narrow-eyed expression having given way to a smile. Her dark hair looked velvety in the early light as the upswept curls glimmered and her brown eyes snapped a challenge. "We can cross on our own, Sheriff Dawson."

"You sure? Now that you're in Eden, I'd hate for anything to happen." He wasn't ready yet to let them go.

Right then, the first of seventeen mules rounded the corner, heading toward them, with Captain White leading the way. The mule brayed loudly, his pack swaying with each step.

The captain's timing couldn't have been better. Clint gave Lavinia a satisfied smile, and she looked away. Her spirited response made him chuckle.

Captain White pulled to a halt in the road before them. "Sheriff, we're on our way out of town, but first I intended to stop by your office and pay what I owe. The security of having our merchandise locked in the barn last night was a boon. I wish all our stops provided such accommodations." His gaze moved slowly over John's daughters. One of his men rode closer when he saw the pretty display of femininity.

"You can pay me now, if you'd like. Or stop by the office. Either way. The pay box is just inside the front door. You can't miss it."

The girls stood quietly, listening.

"I'll leave payment in your office, if you don't mind."

"Not at all." He wouldn't share the fact he'd been on his way to their camp, suspicious they might try to leave without doing just that. "What's your end point?" he tossed out, friendly-like.

The third man's eyes narrowed, presumably not liking Clint's meddling. Clint didn't blame him. He'd feel the same if the tables were turned. Captain White, an expert in diplomacy, masked his reaction with a smile and scratched under his hat. "Agua Mansa."

"Ah, California. A long trip. I'm surprised you're not stopping over for a rest and trading." *Or have you already?* "These Easterners just showed up. Perhaps you're carrying some souvenirs these ladies might like to buy."

Why am I trying to get them to stay on? That strange pull inside was back.

White gave a fake laugh. "Can't. I have a schedule to keep. Bartering for a herd of horses and mules we'll be bringing back this way. If we don't show up on time, they may sell to another with cash in hand."

As they pulled out, Clint did his best to memorize their faces. Sugar House, Utah's territorial prison, was located just outside of Salt Lake City, a few days' ride from where the Old Spanish Trail meandered through Utah on their route. Clint knew several marshals who worked at the penitentiary, and they had been grumbling about the conditions. There'd only been two prison breaks since Clint had become sheriff, and all the escapees had been killed in the recapture. By his way of thinking, the fact that the mule skinners didn't want to barter at all or stay around town for any length of time was unusual. On the other hand, Captain White could be telling the truth. Maybe they'd lingered too long in another town and now had time to make up. Who could say?

Mavis, Clint saw, was studying the long train as the animals trudged by. Her profile was one of intelligence and beauty. She resembled John around her eyes and nose—but softer, sweet. She caught him watching and dropped her gaze.

"You know, Mrs. Applebee," Clint said low, for her ears only, "I've met you before a time or two. I'm sure you don't remember, but I do. When you were a child."

A crimson line crept up her face. "I'm sorry. I don't. You must have been just a boy."

"No, ma'am. I was about eighteen."

The middle rider passed, and then the final man behind the last mule.

"That was exciting," Katie gushed when the road was again clear. "Those men were like nomads, going from one town to the next. I can't imagine a life like that. And caring for so many animals." She shook her head in astonishment.

"Ready to go?" Traffic was booming today. After a peddler's wagon driven by an old Chinese man rolled by, Clint put out both elbows and waited for someone to take hold. "By now, Henry will be wonderin' where you are." He felt a brief moment of disappointment when Emma took one arm and Lavinia the other. Surprised, he realized he'd been hoping for Mavis. The women lifted their skirts as they stepped across the multiple droppings the pack animals had left behind. He enjoyed having one sister on each arm, but it was the nonchalance of the oldest that had piqued his curiosity the most.

CHAPTER THIRTEEN

Belle sat on Trevor's gelding, the noontime sun shining warm on her back. Blake and Henry had brought her on a roundabout way out to Five Sisters so they would end up on a rise that afforded the best view of the ranch. They forked their horses, three across, taking in the Colorado scenery.

Cradled between two forested highlands was a large valley. Along the distant stand of trees she could make out a river, but couldn't tell from here whether the flow was swift or slow. She was able to pick out a grove of cottonwood trees and tall, magical aspens. Several windmills in the midst of the ranch yard turned slowly in welcome, and vines that she thought might be honeysuckle twined up their legs.

"To the right," Blake said, pointing, "is the old homestead. She might look rickety, but she's stood off many a bad snow year as well as torrential rains—and the big winds we can get in the spring. She's kept us just fine all through the years." He pointed again. "That's where the new place will go up."

His voice was low and calm. By his tone, there was no doubt how much he loved the land, the ranch, and everything in between. Although the hint of resentment told her he liked that old house just fine and didn't see a need for a new one. Belle didn't dare look over to see the expression on his face.

"No argument she needs a little loving care," he said. "But as Henry said, there'll be a new one going up soon enough. Until then, I'm sure you and your sisters will want to stay in Eden at the hotel, where the accommodations are comfortable and there's the eatery downstairs."

Since she wasn't sure yet what she and her sisters would decide on that subject, she ignored his comment. A smattering of aspens grew on the slopes between them and the ranch. In her mind, she imagined the clacking of the rigid, almost heart-shaped leaves and rolling soft strips of white bark between her fingers. *Is that a childhood memory? That plus the feel of velvety-soft grass beneath my bare feet?* They had no aspens in Philadelphia. She'd never gone barefoot outside before. *And what of the unfamiliar, deep voice calling to Mavis and me?*

Henry touched her arm. "Belle?"

"Beautiful," she murmured, shaking off the gentle squeeze of her heart. "Every bit as lovely as you said. I can see why Father loved the ranch so. Back in Philadelphia, we're used to breathing coal dust and smelling grease on the streets." She took a deep breath and held it for several seconds. "This air smells so sweet."

She took in the barn as well as the corrals and a rambling bunk-house with a high-pitched roof. Leaning forward in her saddle, she felt an unsettling pull toward the land. *This was Father's dream, not mine. The place is a means to an end, right? This is not where my heart belongs. In six months, I'll be back home with Lesley.* Disconcerted, she pushed the questions away, glancing at Henry and then at Blake. The men seemed lost in their own thoughts.

"Henry, concerning the new house . . ." She felt awkward voicing her opinion on such an important matter, one that would usually be reserved for men. She had to realize she was now a partner—at least for the time being. Her views mattered. She wasn't dealing with Vernon and Velma anymore. "I know your heart is in the right place, but I'm not sure taking on a huge debt would be prudent. Such an undertaking must be substantial. Spending all that money just so we can live comfortably seems almost sinful."

Henry was looking at her in wonder. Blake still gazed out at the valley.

What must they think? They don't realize we sisters have worked since the day we finished school. We've saved prudently all our lives. She knew the meaning of a dollar and didn't like wasting a cent.

"A frivolous, unneeded expenditure," she went on, trying to make a point. "Until we know more about the accounting books and income, I think we should wait. I feel moderately certain my sisters will agree. If Mother could live all those years in that little house, I'm sure we'll be able to as well. We never asked to be pampered. Or for a fuss to be made."

Henry chuckled. "Sorry, Belle, but that decision isn't up to you and the girls. Or Blake, for that matter. John felt strongly about building. If you're to stay on, even for only the six months, the new homestead will go up as planned, along with the smaller one for Blake. Knowing I'd follow through on his wishes made John able to die in peace. If you do decide to sell after the allotted time, which you have every right to do, the additions will make the ranch's worth go straight up. Those rich Easterners are taken in by our big and bold ways. You needn't worry about the cost. Long ago, your father opened a separate account to pay for it. The money is just sitting there, waiting to be spent. The Five Sisters can afford it."

She chanced a glance at Blake. He was a difficult man to figure out, but she thought she knew what his carved-in-stone, unreadable expression meant. Driving up the price would make his ability to buy them out that much more problematic.

Blake doesn't appear flush with cash, not like Lesley and his family, who throw money around like water.

"Indeed. The money is there," Blake agreed, although he'd not taken his attention off the ranch stretched out before them. "John spoke often of the new place for his *daughters*."

The way he'd said "daughters" made her sit straighter. She could tell he didn't like them one bit, no matter how he tried to act nice. He thought them spoiled and arrogant. He was inconvenienced by them, but worse, he feared they'd hurt the ranch. The urge to strike squeezed her heart.

"So much land," she said with phony excitement. "I can only guess at how much it's worth. A true fortune. You must have speculators sniffing around all the time."

His mouth actually opened in surprise. "Is that how your sisters feel as well? Ready to sell off the first time you lay eyes on the place?"

"I've seen it before." She glanced over her shoulder at Henry to find he hadn't heard their comments—or was ignoring them. Either way, the hot stare Blake was sending her was meant, she was sure, to intimidate her. "Eighteen-plus years ago. So quickly you forget." She smiled.

His jaw clenched and released several times. "John scrimped and saved to add each and every acre to this place, for the likes of you. He talked of seeing your face when he showed you the land the first time, and how you'd love the vastness just like he did. I'm glad he's not here to hear you talking about the money selling it could put in your pocket."

A man stepped out the door of the bunkhouse, drawing Blake's stunned expression away.

Her smile faded. Even though he deserved a moment of unease for his lack of faith in her, she felt childish for baiting him needlessly. The fella on the bunkhouse porch glanced around as if he had a feeling he was being watched.

With a hard-set mouth, Blake drew his gun. Before Belle could even think to gather her reins, he shot a round into the air. Surprisingly, Gunner didn't even flinch.

Thank goodness he's not a flighty Philadelphia park mount.

The man on the bunkhouse porch shaded his eyes and searched the area in their direction. When he saw them, he waved his arm several times and then disappeared back inside.

"That'd be KT, one of the hands," Blake said sourly. "He's a wealth of information in case you find yourself in need of any answers . . ."

"If you're not around?" She filled in the blank and smiled. "Good to know. Thank you."

Blake nodded and took up where he'd left off. "The new barn was built five years ago. There are a few cattle here and there, but most of the corrals are almost empty." He shifted in the saddle. "A few head came wandering in, feeling the roundup drawing near."

That's so interesting. "They know the time of year? That's remarkable."

Blake glanced her way, his scar a deep scarlet. "Sure."

Belle noted his tone. *If he was ten when we left the ranch, then he's twenty-eight now.* Six years older than herself, since she was about to turn twenty-two in ten days. *Has he gotten any education, living here in Eden and working on the ranch since he was a boy?*

Blake stretched his legs, making his saddle creak. "Soon every one of those corrals will be full, and the ranch will look—and sound—quite different."

"This is only a small part," Henry stated, nudging his horse closer. "Your father, and now you and your sisters, as well as Blake, own tens of thousands of acres. The Five Sisters is huge. There's a reason she dominates in Colorado."

Henry was looking at her, gauging her reaction. Suddenly, she wanted him to be proud of her. She didn't want to fall short in his eyes. "I can't wait for my sisters to arrive," she said, the weight of his scrutiny making her fidget. "I don't remember the house, but I'm drawn to it. I'd like to go inside."

"This may sound strange," Henry went on, "but I'm feeling rather fatherly at the moment. I think I know how John would've felt today." He withdrew his handkerchief and actually blotted his eyes.

Hot pinpricks jabbed at the backs of hers. As hard as Belle tried to keep the moisture at bay, a tear slipped out, which she quickly brushed away. "I have the impression he's somehow near. Do you think that's possible?"

Henry nodded. "I do."

Blake kept quiet.

"Mother said the only thing he ever talked about was Eden," she breathed, mesmerized by the sight before her.

Henry shifted his weight. "And you girls."

Guilt pushed at her lungs.

Henry took off his hat and pointed toward the mountains. "Your land runs all the way to the base. And you'll find a lot of highland open pastures. That's where your cattle feed in the summer and fall, before the snows hit. After the roundup, Blake will take you and your sisters on a pack trip so you can see the whole ranch."

She glanced at Blake. "You will?"

His eyebrow twitched.

"We'll camp?"

"There aren't any inns or hotels out there. Just soft grass and fresh air."

"What about Indians?"

Blake leaned his forearms on his saddle horn. By the gauge of his smile, he was about to exact his revenge.

"What about 'em? Most live on the reservations to the south and east, but not all. Renegades cause dustups from time to time, but we've learned to live with 'em best we can. We've a mutual respect for one another."

She mulled that around, thinking of her mother. Then she caught sight of movement. "Look." Belle pointed to a buggy approaching at a quick pace. The spinning wheels kicked up a plume of dust on the dirt road.

"That would be your sisters," Henry said. "We best get down there so you don't miss all the fun. I expect they're excited to be back after eighteen years."

Following the men's lead, she nudged her horse into a jog. Right now, she wasn't sure whether Blake was their partner or an enemy. Belle wasn't sure about much, except the beauty of the land, the invigorating way it made her feel, and the fact that, with the amount of acreage Henry had mentioned they had to explore, six months suddenly felt like it would go by awfully fast.

CHAPTER FOURTEEN

*L*ook at this place," Belle called to her sisters as her horse jogged toward the parked buggy, the large saddle feeling slippery under her denim. The pants were incredibly comfortable, and the baggy shirt over her loosened corset felt daring. Mr. Buns, the friendly fellow at the clothing store, had assured her all the women loosened their stays while riding so as not to faint. Blake had insisted she buy a hat as well, to protect her face from the sun. Even though the temperatures were mild now, she was glad he'd pressed the point. "Isn't the place a sight? And the journey was exhilarating. I can't wait for the ride back to Eden."

Her sister's astonished faces almost made her laugh. A warm Colorado breeze played with the bright-blue scarf she'd tied around her neck at the last minute, thinking of the cowboys she'd seen walking around town. She'd never thought of herself as a tomboy before, but perhaps she was.

"I'm amazed at the vastness," Emma gushed. Her strawberry hair was a mess from the buggy, but she didn't seem to mind. "I envy you the ride, Belle. You left without giving us a chance to tag along." She glanced about. "Are there more horses like the one you're on?"

"Plenty. You'll all have a horse of your own, if that's what you want." Blake kept his gaze far away from Belle and the biting tongue she'd shown. His anger didn't dissipate quickly. "We have several horses that would suit. Dusty comes to mind. As well as Sugar. And Gem. We don't have any sidesaddles. You'll have to ride Western and purchase clothing like your sister's. Our horses are used to guns and lassoes but not flapping material or silly hats. We don't want anyone to get hurt."

Lavinia reached up and readjusted the droopy brim she'd added to her hat that very morning with a few well-placed stitches.

Trevor set the brake and stepped down.

Henry chuckled, looking as comfortable in the saddle as he had behind his large desk. He wouldn't let anything go wrong with the transition in ownership of the ranch, Belle was sure.

"These comfy garments take no time at all to get used to."

Intent on showing off, she threw her leg over the back of the large saddle and began to dismount. Gunner was much taller than the Hackneys she was used to riding. Her foot kept descending farther and farther, until one of her hands slipped from the cantle. Gasping, she grasped for the long leather ties on the back of the saddle, catching herself just in time before she hit the ground.

Suddenly Blake was at her side. "You'll get the hang of it," he said curtly.

When did he dismount?

"Go more slowly next time, until you're used to his size."

Embarrassed, she ran her hand up and down Gunner's sleek neck. "I've fallen hard for this smart cow horse. He took care of me as if he knew I was inexperienced. Is that possible?"

"Sure." Trevor spoke up just as Blake opened his mouth to answer. The cowboy was handing down her sisters one by one from the black-upholstered buggy seat. "He ain't no dummy."

Belle kissed the horse's soft muzzle. "I believe it, Trevor. He was so calm and collected. I never felt frightened at all. Not once."

Blake glanced at Henry and then at Belle. "All we did was walk and jog."

"Still. Feels like I've been riding him all my life. You were worried, Blake—I noticed it in your eyes. Then you saw how well the two of us were getting along." She gave him a genuine smile, and he actually smiled back. She reminded herself that Blake had meant a lot to her father and had asked her to be patient. She'd try harder.

Trevor hooked a thumb over his back, pointing to the bunkhouse. Several men politely waited to be introduced. "Looks like we've attracted attention."

Blake glanced over. Tank and KT stood expectantly on the bunkhouse porch. *At least those men are loyal. The fall roundup will be no picnic without the deserters.* Just as he was about to wave the men over, Belle grasped his arm.

"Wait. Let me tell my sisters what's happened. Especially since we're the reason."

Mavis's brow fell, as did Emma's at Belle's serious tone.

"What?" Katie whispered. "It's rude if we don't acknowledge the men now that we've seen them." Her gaze slid surreptitiously back toward the bunkhouse, but she kept her head cocked just so, and her lashes lowered.

Blake was sure the other men had no idea they were being watched. He almost chuckled and wondered how she did that.

"You're right, Katie," Belle replied. "But you should know before meeting the men that three ranch hands walked out this morning, and may even be a menace to the ranch, to Blake, or even to us. They refuse to work for a woman, and especially not more than one. It's important we don't scare the rest away. Every hand is needed for the roundup this week."

Their eyes widened. Lavinia glanced at Mavis and then Emma. "What's a roundup?" Emma whispered. Blake shook his head and caught Henry's amused expression. Belle had established herself as the leader, having been privy to inside information.

"Are we ready?" He looked Belle in the eyes for the first time since her comment about the speculators. He wasn't sure of her intentions— yet—but he wondered if she'd only been trying to get his goat. "Can I call them over?"

"You have *my* permission."

Ignoring the innuendo, he waved his arm. The two men stepped off the porch and strode over to the group.

"Boys," Blake said loudly, "I'd like you to meet John's daughters." He nodded to Mavis and noticed the girls had arranged themselves in a line from oldest to youngest.

Do they remember their father used to have them do the same thing before supper each night to see if they'd washed their hands—or at least the three oldest? He hid his smile as a warm, homey feeling squeezed his chest.

"The girls," Blake said with a swish of his arm. "The boys." Another swish.

Belle rolled her eyes.

Chuckling, he dipped his chin. "This is Mrs. Mavis Applebee. Miss Belle Brinkman. Miss Emma Brinkman. Miss Lavinia Brinkman, and Miss Katie Brinkman. They'll be staying in Eden for six months— maybe longer—and are equal partners in the Five Sisters. I expect you to treat them accordingly."

Blake pointed to Tank first. "This is Tank Bellus. He's been at the ranch approximately a year. Signed on this time last year for the roundup when one of our men got hurt. He's not our cook but rustles up most of the meals around here."

Tank smiled and nodded his head.

"And that's KT Brackston. He's been here longer." He looked questioningly at KT.

"Over three years now," the hand mumbled, more shyly than Blake had ever seen him act. KT nodded at Trevor, who stood behind him, and then at Henry.

"Pleased to make your acquaintance," KT added, and Tank nodded his agreement. "You can count on us. We were loyal to your father and will be just as loyal to you . . ." He looked at each of them. "Five. Don't be afraid to ask."

"Are there more men?" Mavis asked, glancing about with her gaze landing on the barn.

Blake nodded. "Yes. Two others. Moses and Garrett. They're out mending fence. You'll know Garrett by the black-and-white paint he rides."

A shout brought them all around.

At the far gate behind the homestead, Garrett came at a gallop, a limp body slumped across the front of his saddle. Moses's horse followed behind, running free.

Blake bolted in their direction.

When Garrett reined up, Blake eased down the body of his friend. Moses's face had been badly beaten. With Moses cradled in his arms, Blake started for the house. Behind, he could hear the others following, and Trevor telling the girls who he was. They arrived at the house just as Trevor had begun the story about Moses finding a wounded Blake on the battlefield when he'd gone searching for his brother. Blake owed Moses his life—and John his future.

Henry hurried up the porch stairs and opened the front door.

Blake went straight to John's room, turning Moses's large body to angle him through the narrow bedroom doorway. He laid him down, and the others filed quietly inside. Blake positioned the pillow and began unbuttoning Moses's shirt.

"What happened?" he asked as he worked.

"Ambushed by Praig. That snake never gave Moses a chance to fight back. Being a ways down the fence line, I saw some of what happened, but not all."

Blake glanced up at the girls. They were lined up at the foot of the bed, their faces drawn down in concern. *Should I ask them to leave? Besides Mavis, have any of them even seen a man unclothed? It's none of my business. They'll leave if they want or stay if they want. What's important now is seeing to Moses.*

"Praig and Moses have been at each other's throats since you gave Moses more authority around the ranch," Trevor said softly in the quiet of the room.

Blake's hands stilled. "He's been here the longest and is oldest, even countin' me. Makes sense."

"Not to Praig. You know how he feels about . . ."

When Trevor's words faded away, Blake glanced over his shoulder. The cowhand was gazing at Moses's still body lying on the bed. "Moses didn't like him speaking against you and John either," he went on. "None of us do, but Praig liked to rile him most because he's colored. Needled him night and day."

Blake looked up. "I didn't know it had gotten that bad."

"Just since John's death," Trevor said. "Moses didn't want nothin' mentioned. You had plenty on your plate already."

Blake kept working. When he finished with the buttons, Henry leaned over and lifted Moses so Blake could slip off the shirt and undershirt, revealing his bruised and bloodied chest. He chanced a quick glance to the foot of the bed and caught Belle's gaze.

"How can I help?" she asked, her voice unsteady. He was relieved not to see any of the distaste some women might show toward a colored man. He didn't know what he'd do if she had demanded they remove Moses from her father's bed.

"Heat water and fetch towels from the closet," he replied. "We need to wash off the blood to determine the extent of his injuries. I think I feel at least one broken rib."

She turned, and her sisters followed.

"I'll get the medicine box from the bunkhouse," KT said. "Anything else you can think of?"

Blake shook his head. His blinding anger was making it difficult to think.

"Tank," Henry said, "ride into Eden and get Doc Dodge. Also tell Clint to be on the lookout for Praig."

With Tank and Trevor gone, the room felt larger. Belle returned carrying a pot and towels draped over one arm. She went to the other side of the bed, next to Henry. "It's not that hot yet," she said, placing it on the nightstand. "But we have more heating." She looked at Moses, her eyes blinking in rapid succession. "He looks quite weak." Across the bed, her solemn gaze found Blake's eyes. "Will he live?"

"Depends on what's happening inside. Won't know until the doctor looks him over."

The other sisters stood just inside the door.

"His eyes fluttered," Belle said as she dipped a cloth into the pot, wrung out the excess water, and began gently washing his face. "I think he's coming around."

Blake picked up one of Moses's hands. "Moses, can you hear me?" he asked softly, fear and anger warring inside. He couldn't lose Moses after losing John. It may be a selfish thought, but still, he just couldn't.

"Blake?"

The ranch hand struggled to open his cut and bloodstained eyes, already swollen twice their usual size. Blake placed his palm on Moses's forehead, and his friend calmed down immediately.

"I'm a stupid fool to let Praig get the jump on me."

"Shh," Blake said. "Don't try to talk. Just rest." He watched Belle as she carefully cleansed away the blood and dirt. "You're gonna be all right. Tank's gettin' the doctor."

"Don't need no doc. Just help me up and I'll get back to work."

"Nothin' doin'."

Moses struggled to look around, his puffed-up eyes obviously painful. When he realized he was in John's bedroom, he fought harder, but let loose a moan and cringe of pain. Finally, Blake convinced him to settle.

"Clint better lock Praig up for his own protection," Blake murmured. He was talking to himself, but in the quiet room, everyone heard his words. This beating hadn't just been on a lark. Based on the severity of Moses's injuries, Praig had been aiming to kill.

Belle, finished washing, began drying Moses with a soft towel, going slow and gentle. Blake stood, glanced at her four watching sisters. Mavis's blue eyes held concern. Emma's emerald, fear. Lavinia's cocoa, anger. And in Katie's cobalt, an innocence he hoped wouldn't be squashed flat her first week in Eden.

But when Belle stood, her sky-blue eyes, more unsettled than any storm front, held him transfixed. They were deep, filled with stories, memories, regret, and . . . guilt? He felt powerless to look away and instinctually knew she felt exactly the way he did inside.

Praig was out there somewhere, carrying a festering chip of hate on his shoulder. He was unhinged enough to do this to Moses just because he didn't like the color of his skin. Blake wouldn't let him touch any one of John's daughters. If Praig Horn could do this, he could do anything.

CHAPTER FIFTEEN

A s soon as he arrived back in town, Henry went straight to the
sheriff's office to see if Clint had found Praig and to inquire if the
sheriff's younger half sister, Nicole Day, wanted to make easy money by
staying out at the ranch with Belle.

John's second oldest had insisted on remaining to help with
Moses—who had three broken ribs but would heal—and to see how
the roundup worked. Henry had tied his horse to the back of the buggy
and driven the other four sisters back to Eden in abject silence, an indi-
cation they were shaken by what they'd witnessed.

Nicole packed a bag while Mavis gathered a few essentials for delivery to Belle. Nicole was usually game for just about anything; she did
odd jobs around town and on the ranches. Henry thought she could be
a friend for Belle. She'd stay in the house and help show her the ropes.

He was too diplomatic to say this to anyone, but he hoped Nicole
could also ride interference between Belle and Blake. Those two were
circling each other like wolves from rival packs. After witnessing their
argument earlier, he knew Belle could skillfully get Blake's goat. But
Blake didn't realize just how sensitive Belle really was. She covered her
hurt with bravado. He hoped Blake would figure that out sooner than
later.

Now, back in his office, Henry went about straightening his desk. He was exhausted. He wasn't one to hang out in a saloon every afternoon or evening, but tonight he needed a beer. Something to take the edge off his ragged nerves. He'd head over to Poor Fred's, listen to the chinwag as he drank a mug, and see if anyone knew Praig's whereabouts. Or that of Riley and Bush. He also wanted to see what people were saying now that John's daughters had arrived. The best place to find out much of anything was bellied up to the bar.

But first, he tackled the task of writing several ads to run in the *Santa Fe New Mexican*, *Cheyenne Daily Leader*, and Denver's *Rocky Mountain News*. The girls would need permanent help once the new home was built. A cook and a housekeeper. He wondered if there were other employees a flock of young women living miles out of town might need.

A warm goodness slid through him as he remembered their faces as they'd climbed out of the buggy today, before Garrett had come galloping in with Moses. Yes, someone who might help them decide to stay after the six months were up. He'd have to give that idea more thought.

Feeling older than his forty-five years, he stood and stretched. If he didn't get moving, he just might fall asleep stretched out over his desk. He went to the door, turned the sign, pulled down the shade, and locked the door.

He entered his living quarters from a door in the back wall of his office. Well, they were less living quarters than bachelor's cave. Small and easy to keep. A tiny sitting room held two chairs, a small table, and a stool opposite. His bedroom was about the same size as the sitting room, with just enough space for his bed, a dresser, and a wooden wardrobe constructed from intricately carved birch wood, the satiny texture shiny.

He paused at the framed photo of his mother and father, melancholy tightening his chest. He'd been in love once, long, long ago, with the daughter of his mother's best friend. But she didn't feel the same. After her rejection, he threw himself into law school and his profession.

Shrugging off the mood, he splashed several handfuls of water on his face, scrubbed briskly, then washed again. He toweled dry. After checking his reflection, he lifted a light jacket from the haphazardly tossed covers of his unmade bed. He was about to go out through the back door, but felt movement on the front steps.

Everyone local knew he closed up shop around five thirty. Maybe one of John's girls had a question. With a fleeting thought for the beer he should have already had in his hands by then, he tossed his coat back on the bed and entered his office. He opened the door to a stranger.

A woman stood before him, her hand firmly grasping a small boy's. She was pretty, perhaps midthirties, with soft-looking caramel-colored hair and striking blue eyes.

"Hello," he said, surprised. "May I help you?"

"Yes, I hope you can. I'm sorry to show up so late in the day. Earlier, Johnny wasn't well. I've been waiting for him to feel well enough to come along. I didn't have anyone to leave him with."

Ah, a newcomer.

The boy looked about three, four, or five—Henry wasn't much good with children's ages. His sandy-blond hair was in need of a trim, and his flushed color and faraway look said he truly was ill. Henry put out his arm in invitation.

So much for that beer.

"That's fine. Please, come in. I'll do what I can to help." His curiosity more than roused, Henry walked with her to the chairs in front of his desk. "Would your boy like to lie down? I have a bed in my rooms behind the office. Perhaps he'd be more comfortable there."

She brushed back the hair that had fallen over her son's brow. "Thank you, but no. I think he'd be frightened."

"Fine, then." Henry waited until she and her boy were both seated, after which he went around his desk and took his own seat. "What's this about?"

She glanced at her son, around the room, and then back at him. "I heard about John Brinkman dying." A shadow of grief crossed her face. Again, her gaze skittered from his. "A Denver newspaper with a halftone image showed up at my place of employment."

"Yes, it's been hard for all of us. We'll miss him greatly."

She nodded. "I was shocked, seeing his image. It was also the first time I knew his full name."

"You're a friend of his?" He couldn't help but lead her; she seemed so befuddled, and a bit weak. He wondered when she'd eaten last.

"Yes, I was. A *good* friend."

His attention went on high alert. *What does that mean?* The beer he'd been dreaming about flew from his mind. "Why don't you begin with your name and where you're from. Whatever you tell me is completely confidential." He glanced at her boy and smiled, but that didn't produce any response.

"First, I must say that I have no money to pay you."

All right. He'd done charity work many times. The Mother of Mercy Orphanage was one of his steady customers. "That's not a problem."

"Thank you. My name's Elizabeth Smith. My son and I are originally from Virginia, but have been living in Denver since just before his birth."

"About four hundred miles from here."

She nodded. "It took almost all my savings just to get here." When she put a protective arm around the boy, a slim band of gold on her fourth finger glimmered in the lantern light.

Could this all be an act? Why do I feel suspicious? He didn't know.

"I'm sorry to be so evasive, Mr. Glass," she said. "I understand you were John's attorney, and are still the attorney for his ranch and businesses. I would have gone to someone else if there'd been another in town."

This is getting more interesting by the moment.

"That's all right. I can handle more than one client at a time. Like I said, what you tell me remains within these walls. Don't be frightened."

The small smile his comment induced seemed to break the ice. She let out a large breath and rubbed Johnny's back. The child was being unobtrusive, fiddling with a small toy he'd pulled from his pocket. His flushed cheeks weren't a good sign, or his glazed eyes.

"Johnny is John's son."

Henry snapped his gaze up to hers.

"It's true."

Could that be? Had John known of a son? Surely not. He would have included him in his will. And he would have brought him and his mother here to Eden long ago. Sent support, as he'd done for his girls all their lives.

An instant dislike pushed up within him. His first thought was that Elizabeth wanted to cash in on John's dying. Just because the boy was named Johnny didn't mean a thing. *She'd seen the announcement about his death, knew he was worth a fortune, and came sniffing around to see what she could find. Who could refute her story? Or maybe the boy's real pa put her up to the charade. They might be working together. Or . . . she might be telling the truth.*

Unable to control himself, his gaze dropped once again to the child, looking for any resemblance to his friend. If this was John's son, Henry felt sure he hadn't known of his birth. He'd have been overjoyed.

So many questions . . .

Elizabeth's hands began to shake. He'd taken so long to reply, she was probably frightened to death. "Have you eaten today?"

She sat looking at him.

"Mrs. Smith?"

She shook her head. "I just had enough for Johnny to have a little soup."

"Before we go any further, you need to eat." Henry couldn't turn a blind eye to her distress, even if she was lying. She didn't have any extra weight to lose. Most likely she'd had little to eat on the trip there. He stood, circled the desk, and helped her to stand. "I'm taking you back to the hotel. Johnny will be more comfortable, and I'll have supper brought to your room."

Tears sprang to her eyes, and she looked away.

"Come on," he said gently. Throwing caution to the wind, he hefted the small boy into his arms. "I assume you're rooming across the street since you said the hotel, but I have to ask because there is a boardinghouse in town too, though no one ever seems to find it when they're new."

Her face turned up to his. "I didn't know. I'm sure the cost is much more affordable than the hotel. Can you direct me?"

"Later. If need be. Tonight you're staying in the Eden Hotel, where there's a kitchen right downstairs."

"Thank you, Mr. Glass."

He held back the offer for her to call him Henry. She could be playing him for a fool. He had to keep a professional distance as he researched her story—once he got one from her. Heat from Johnny radiated through the child's clothing. *The boy in my arms might be John's son!*

"As soon as you're settled, I'll fetch the doctor."

With the boy in his embrace, they descended the stairs in Eden's evening light.

John, do you have something to tell me? Is this boy your son? Did you know Elizabeth on one of your trips? I'd greatly appreciate any clues you can send my way . . .

CHAPTER SIXTEEN

B elle paced the front room of the old ranch house, dying to get outside and walk the premises. The doctor, who was exceptionally friendly, had seen to Moses and bandaged his broken ribs. They were to watch for signs of internal bleeding, such as severe pain in the abdomen, coughing or vomiting blood, and something else he'd whispered to Blake after darting several wary looks at her. She'd caught the word *urine*. At almost twenty-two years old, she wished the men would stop treating her like a child. Moses, awake now—and pumped full of morphine for the pain—had demanded to be taken to the bunkhouse and his own cot.

Strange how suddenly this place feels like home. Alone and in the quiet, it was as if she'd never left. She wrapped her arms around herself and willed memories to resurface. The sink along the far wall. The cooking stove in the corner. Two bedrooms, one of which had been her parents', and the other, hers and her sisters', later to be taken over by Blake. She had learned that, after her father passed, Blake had gathered his things and moved into the bunkhouse. He was there now with Moses and the men.

She went to the window, noticing a fine layer of dust on the windowsill. Her parents must have been very unhappy. *Why else would Mother leave? Father's letter had blamed the Indian raids, and yet that didn't seem like enough. Life is a paradox. Will we ever know the truth?*

She sucked in a deep breath. She was supposed to be waiting for a woman that Henry was sending out to stay with her. *To act as chaperone. Why?* This was now her ranch, and her sisters'. *Do I need a chaperone in my own home? That's ridiculous.* Feeling trapped, she stepped out onto the porch, the early-evening coolness calming her. Mavis, Emma, Lavinia, and Katie would be back out tomorrow, after they'd rounded up riding and work clothes.

The lonely call of a mourning dove drew Belle off the porch. She meandered down a path toward the corrals and stuck her hand through the wooden boards. The few cattle inside watched her with cautious eyes, hanging back against the far fence. Skirting the other two corrals, she headed for the barn. The door was heavy, and she had to put her shoulder into the wood to slide the beast open. Several cats darted away. With ease, they bounded up the tall posts and disappeared into the loft. In the second stall, Gunner had his head buried in a mound of hay. He lifted it for a moment when she looked in, then went back to eating.

Leaving the barn, she did her best to pull the heavy door closed. She started up toward where she was told the new place would be built. The sun had set. A brisk chill raised gooseflesh. She realized she should have found a jacket in the closet before venturing out.

Reaching the flat top of the hill, she turned a full circle. *Beautiful view. Perfect place for the new house.* There was an abundance of trees to the left. Beneath them, she spotted a small cemetery. *Father's grave?* As she got closer, she noticed not one, but four, graves, one of fresh-looking dirt, the other three, old grass-covered mounds, beaten down by the weather. *Who could they be?*

A sorrow deeper than the depths of the ocean filled her. This was the closest she'd been to her father in eighteen years. Her father, who'd loved her, rested right here.

She inched to a stop in front of the new grave. A towering ponderosa pine stood guard only a few feet away. A handful of smaller, whimsical blue-green evergreens with upturned tips bobbed in the breeze. *A nice place to rest,* she thought. *A nice place for eternity.*

JOHN COLUMBUS BRINKMAN
BORN MARCH 11, 1830. DIED AUGUST 15, 1880.
HUSBAND TO CELESTE MAY FIELD BRINKMAN.
PROUD FATHER OF MAVIS, BELLE,
EMMA, LAVINIA, KATIE, AND BLAKE.

And the epitaph: NOTHING SOOTHES A MAN'S SOUL LIKE A WIDE-OPEN VISTA.

That made Belle smile. The view here was gorgeous. Father would never tire of the sight.

Thank goodness you had Blake with you for all these years, Father. I'm so happy he was here to be your son. I'm sorry so many years had to pass before we came home. I hope you know we would have come sooner, if we'd known. Please forgive me for not doing more to find out about you.

A twig snapped. Frightened, Belle spun around. Blake had warned her extensively about the ranch hand named Praig, and here she was, out walking around alone at dusk.

It was Blake. He stood back, giving her time. She was sure he wouldn't come up unless invited. She smiled and motioned him forward.

"I see you found your father's grave," he said, his voice bringing a surprising peace to her jittery heart.

So much has happened so fast. Learning about Father's death, then the trip here. The inheritance. The stunning discovery Father wasn't the scoundrel we'd all believed.

And now this all-encompassing feeling she got whenever she took in the sight of these mountains, the ranch, the old house. Even the man beside her. All parts of her father. She wished with her whole heart she could have him back. Even for one minute.

"I did. I hope you don't mind?"

"You need to be careful, at least until we find Praig." He held her gaze. "This isn't a game. You understand?"

She nodded. "How's Moses?"

"Still feeling the effects of the morphine. He fell asleep a few minutes ago."

He shifted his weight from one leg to the other, gazing at her father's grave. He seemed to be wrestling with a problem in his mind. The mourning dove that had been breaking her heart suddenly fluttered down onto the grass a few feet away.

"Will you tell me about him?"

"Your pa?"

She nodded. "Your father as well, by the words on his headstone."

"I didn't have anything to do with that. Henry took care of all his last wishes."

"I see."

He was hurting too. The long grass around the perimeter of the small, quaint burial ground waved gently, and she had the urge to step closer to him, but she didn't. The peace here was intoxicating.

"John was a darned good man. Best I've ever known. He fed the Andersons through a hard winter, making sure they had plenty to eat after Mr. Anderson hurt his back. He did the same for Widow Lang and her granddaughter. Sent the Greens' twins to a hospital in Denver when Doc Dodge couldn't diagnose the problem at hand." He shook his head thoughtfully. "Made sure the orphanage had firewood and food. He never turned anyone away, no matter their problem. There're too many instances to list."

"Did he ever talk about us?"

A sentimental smile crossed his lips. "All the time. He'd worry I'd get sick of listening and said so, but I didn't. I liked how reminiscing made him feel. He wondered about you. What you looked like. What your characters and behaviors turned out to be. What you liked, or disliked. If any of you had married. He had his opinions from when you were babes." He turned his head and winked at her. "'Now Belle,' he used to say, 'she's my firecracker. I pity the man who she decides to marry. He better be strong, because I've never seen a spirit on any of my girls like I do in her.' Then he'd chuckle and shake his head, recounting a story I'd heard about a thousand times about you wanting a toy Mavis was holding, a little doll your mother had sewn out of cloth. You were only about one, too young to know about temptation, but somehow you did. You hounded Mavis until you got it—keep in mind you could barely crawl at that time." He shook his head. "Once you had the toy, you plopped down on your diaper and held it out in offering until Mavis came close, eyeing the toy. When she was within reach and put out her hand to take it, you jerked it away, making her cry."

Belle tried to hold it in, but a strangled sob slipped out between his words. She'd thought she could handle learning more, but out here under the blue sky that her father had loved so much, she realized just how much she'd lost, how much they'd all lost. Standing in front of a grave instead of him—alive, vibrant, and happy—caused an unendurable agony. Heartbroken, she dashed at the moisture on her cheeks.

He cut his gaze to her.

"I'm sorry," she whispered. "I really do want to hear."

"You sure?"

She nodded. "My tears, though. I'm embarrassed . . ."

"Don't be. Just shows you have a heart." He went back to staring at the graves. "For all these years, I didn't think you did. Now I know different."

She looked at another grave, the one with the oldest, most faded headstone, beaten and shabby from the weather. Several of the chiseled-out letters had crumbled away, making reading it a challenge— except that it bore the same name as her father's. Her grandfather, John Brinkman. This land had been in her father's blood for years, and his father's before him. No wonder he couldn't leave it when her mother had decided to go to Philadelphia. That would have been a sentence worse than death.

"Whose grave is that?" She pointed to a smaller, simpler marker. "Cranston Field. Do you know?"

Blake nodded. "I do. Your mother's father."

Another grandfather. How special. She studied the dates, her mind filling with a thousand questions. She was about to ask when she noticed Blake's gaze anchored on a plain wooden cross set off under a copse of aspen all by itself. *Could it be a grandmother, or a sister or brother I didn't know about? Why is that person set away from the rest?*

"The wooden cross. Whose is that?"

He stood so still he reminded her of the pictures she'd seen of Michelangelo's *David*, only clothed in Western attire. His pants encased powerful thighs, and a blue chambray shirt that looked as soft as the clotted cream they served at her favorite teahouse in Philadelphia covered his potent chest and arms. She was on his right side, so she couldn't see the scar. *How painful that injury must have been. And it had something to do with Moses.* But when she raised her eyes farther, it was the devastated look in his thundery blue gaze that captured her completely.

"My wife. Ann. Only eighteen. And my daughter, Marcia. They both died in childbirth."

He glanced her way for only a second.

The mourning dove called out again, and Belle thought she'd never heard anything so sad. *Blake. A widower? Lost a wife and daughter on the same day. How could he stand it?* Her heartbreak was complete. She should say a soothing word, but what? There was nothing to cure a pain like that. Nothing that could ever make his world right again.

"How long ago?"

He kicked at a mound of grass. "Four years."

What to say? Or do? She felt rooted to the ground.

"Blake, I'm so, so sorry—"

He put up a hand to silence her. Surely, his visits here were usually alone, to be with his wife and daughter. And now her father too. The briskness of the wind made her shiver.

Or was that caused by the souls lingering in the dancing trees?

Blake cleared his throat and turned away. He was over the pain long ago. Over everything, as a matter of fact. He just needed to get through each day, and then one day, to his surprise, a certain hour would be his last. That's what John used to say. "One day at a time, one breath at a time." Blake understood that completely. He looked off at the mountains. "You have any recollections of making mud pies?" he asked, embarrassed when his voice came out thick with emotion. He waited for her answer.

She shook her head. He began a slow walk in the grass. She followed.

"You should. One day, when your ma was large with Katie, she kept Lavinia with her and sent John and me out from underfoot with you, Mavis, and Emma. John had the bright idea to take his girls fishing. Well, that lasted all of two seconds. Mavis found a shallow spot in the sand, safe with boulders that cut it off from the river. There, the three of you ended up covered in mud, freezing cold from splashing each other—and us—even though it was the dead of summer. And boy, could you chatter like a magpie. You'd *Blake* me this and *Blake* me that." He chuckled. "Your ma was none too pleased with us on our return."

The story brought a smile back to Belle's lips.

"You don't remember?"

Again, she shook her head, a tender look in her eyes.

Spotting a group of riders coming up the long and winding road that led to the ranch, he pointed, thankful for a diversion. He recognized the fellas. One was the town's mayor, a man who sometimes stood in for Clint when the sheriff had more important things to attend to—like hunting Praig, Riley, and Bush. Moses hadn't said anything about the other two men being there, but they still had to be questioned. The other rider was a hireling from one of the saloons. Out in front was the woman they were escorting: Nicole Day. She rode as well as any man. Belle was in for a treat.

"That would be your companion." His chuckle sounded strange, even to his own ears. "I don't think the ranch has ever seen so much activity in one day." He slid his gaze to hers, and her lips tipped up. "You have a way of disrupting things."

"I hope in a good way. And I hope it calms down soon. A person can only take so much."

"You're telling *me* that?"

"Yes, I am. Let's go see who they sent to hold my hand," she said with a note of cynicism. "I can hardly wait."

"Don't be turning up your nose at help. You haven't been here but a few hours. I promise you, you'll be glad Nicole's here. And then tomorrow we can expect more Brinkmans. Things around the Five Sisters are really looking up."

CHAPTER SEVENTEEN

B elle liked *this* Blake. Easygoing, with a smile now and then and a joke thrown in for good measure. The other Blake was too intense. She didn't know how to handle *him* at all. "I won't turn my nose up. I'll be nice and welcoming to Nicole."

The men in the group split off and headed for the corrals in front of the bunkhouse while a woman, dressed in pants and a shirt just like Belle, headed in the direction of the house and then rode right up to where she and Blake walked.

"Hey there, Blake Harding. Haven't seen *you* around for a while. What've you been doing? Hiding out in the hills from all these Brinkman women?" She laughed and dismounted with ease as if she'd been doing it all her life.

Blake gave a hearty laugh that went right up Belle's spine.

"Belle," he said, loud enough for the newcomer to hear him, "meet Nicole Day, Sheriff Clint Dawson's sister. She's as good a protector as any man. Six bears and a wolf couldn't intimidate her."

Belle bristled at his amused brow. He ran an affectionate hand down Nicole's horse's blaze. "How was the ride out? See anything peculiar?"

"You're the only *peculiar* thing out here, Harding," she joked, then looked straight at Belle.

Are they flirting? Nicole is pretty enough. For that matter, so was Amorette at Mademoiselle de Sells. Blake's wife has been gone for four years, after all—that's a long time. A sharp twinge of jealousy pricked her. *Where did that come from? Blake is practically my stepbrother. Surely seeing him settled with a wife again would have made Father happy. I need to remember that. Besides, Lesley will be waiting at home for me. He's going to propose. He said so just this morning.*

She'd gotten everything she wanted.

And—she smiled—now she had the chance to make her first proper girlfriend in Eden.

"Let's not get carried away, Nic. This is Belle Brinkman. It's good of you to come out for a few days, show her the ropes. We'll be able to use a hand during the roundup too, if you're staying that long."

"I can't stay but a couple of days. Still, I was happy Henry thought of me to babysit your new partner. I can use the money."

Belle's smile vanished.

Oh boy. Blake jerked straight and cut a warning look at Nicole. "Stop teasing, Nic. You're just trying to get a rise out of Miss Brinkman. She may look all soft and citified, but she's smart and tough too. Just like you." That wasn't the exact truth, but he didn't want to inflame Belle any more.

Nicole laughed and stuck out her hand. "I'm just teasing, Belle. Hope there aren't any hard feelings on your end. I can promise we're going to be good friends before long." She shrugged. "And by all that's reasonable, I *am* sort of babysitting. Aren't I? Why so prickly?"

Nicole stood quietly with an outstretched hand. Blake knew that wouldn't last long if Belle didn't respond. Turning, he took Belle by the arm and extended it until the girls were forced to grasp hands. With his large hand covering theirs, he pushed them up and down, smiling as wide as he could. Nicole seemed to have already forgotten the whole scene, but Belle's nostrils flared, and he didn't think he'd ever seen eyes so narrow.

122

"Nicole didn't mean any harm. She just doesn't seem to have a filter. You'll get used to her kidding."

"I doubt that." Belle dropped her hand as if she'd been touching cow dung.

This wasn't going well. The men came from the bunkhouse, mounted, and rode up to join them.

"I appreciate you escorting Nicole out." Blake pointed with his hat. "This is Mick, a good fellow. And this is Donald Dodge—he's mayor of Eden. You met his brother, Ray, earlier."

"Oh, the doctor?" Belle asked.

"That's correct, Miss Brinkman," Donald said, a much thinner man than his sibling, who was large and fit for a man of her father's age. Smile lines cradled the mayor's lips, and his eyes were kind. "I'd like to officially welcome you to Eden. I would have done it the day you arrived, but I just returned myself. We've wondered for years if you'd return. Your father would be a proud man today." He glanced around in the waning light. "It'll be good to have more Brinkmans in town now that John's gone."

He touched the brim of his hat. Blake watched as the men turned their horses and began the trip back to town. He needed to check on Moses. Now that Nicole was here, she could take over where Belle was concerned. At least until tomorrow. But there wouldn't be much sleep. He and the men would watch the house and ranch in case Praig came prowling in the night.

The distant cry of an early coyote made Belle's head whip around. Nicole gave a soft snicker. "Blake, where do you want me to put my horse?"

"I'll stable him for you."

Nicole reached up, untied the overstuffed carpetbag secured to the back of her saddle, and held it out to Belle. "Your sisters sent you your things."

Instead, Blake took the heavy satchel from Nicole's hands. "Come on, let's get you two settled. Can either of you cook?"

"I can . . . in Philadelphia," Belle said softly. The immensity of her situation seemed to be finally sinking in. "I don't know about that old stove I saw in the house, though."

"What are the men cooking in the bunkhouse?" Nicole asked.

"That isn't a half-bad idea. You two want to join us since there isn't much food in the house? Might be easier than doing everything yourself."

Nicole nodded. "That'd be my vote. Everything tastes better if someone else does the cooking. What about you, Belle? Want to wait a day before tackling the stove?"

In the darkness, Blake couldn't see her reaction. Cooking on an outdated stove probably sounded as appealing to her as ringworm. He came to the realization that she and her sisters were going to need a whole lot of coddling. Not that he held a grudge against them. He'd had a lifetime with John, who'd taught him everything he needed to be a rancher and a man. Passing on the information to his own daughters seemed like the least Blake could do. And he would. With a good attitude, to boot.

"That's exactly what you'll do. If you don't mind the men."

At the house, Blake went in first and began lighting the lanterns. "Why don't you take a half hour and get refreshed? Then I'll send someone to escort you down."

"Surely we don't need a bodyguard on the ranch," Belle said, surprised.

As golden light filled the room, Blake was astonished once again that he was actually looking at Belle Brinkman. He had a vision of himself at ten, looking at her through the crack of the pantry door. Now that she was here, he'd not let Praig or anything else hurt her.

"Until Clint finds Praig and locks him up, you do." Clint's baby sister squished up her face in protest but didn't buck his orders. "You just be ready in half an hour to experience the meal of a lifetime."

"Supper in the bunkhouse." Belle actually smiled, and a glow came back into her dark-blue eyes, transforming them to jewels. "That sounds like an adventure."

Blake stepped out into the quiet night thinking the exact same thing.

CHAPTER EIGHTEEN

It was ten minutes after eight o'clock by the time Henry finally located Dr. Dodge, as he was leaving the Hole in the Floor Saloon. Elizabeth and her son, Johnny, had been tucked away in the hotel for more than an hour. He'd had a steak supper sent to her room along with a bowl of chicken soup for the child. As he and the doctor hurried through the streets on their way back, Henry couldn't get Elizabeth's story out of his mind. The timing was actually right. He'd never have remembered otherwise, except that John had taken an extended trip to Denver because Blake and Ann had wed and he wanted to give them a few weeks of privacy. Ann hadn't wanted to leave town because her sister was just getting over being sick. Since it had been years since John had any time away from the ranch, he'd volunteered to go instead, leaving them the house. Henry had made the arrangements for him. A week in Denver, and another in Santa Fe.

Matching the doctor's long strides, Henry hurried after him through town. John had seemed different upon his return. Happier. Relaxed. That could have been the result of Blake finally marrying, but then, perhaps a different reason was responsible. It was the most content he'd *ever* seen his friend.

How sad that John hadn't brought Elizabeth back here. Or knew that he'd sired a son.

"You're mighty quiet, Henry," Ray Dodge said, a concerned tilt to his brow. "What's on your mind? Other than this young boy you've just met?"

"Just been a helluva long day, I guess." *And it's not over yet. Not by any means, whether I like that fact or not. Look at me. Here I am, believing Elizabeth's story without an ounce of proof.* He thought of the depth of concern in her blue eyes.

She could easily be a schemer, just after John's money. When John died, Henry had wired the sad news to his friend, Judge Harrison Wesley, a circuit judge that resided in Denver. When a person of such substantial wealth passed, news traveled fast. Elizabeth could be from anywhere. And Johnny could be anyone's son.

I may be her attorney, but I'm also John's and the ranch's. I can't turn a blind eye to their needs just because she walked in with a sad story. No, I can't and I won't. Proper steps will be followed. I'll do my due diligence. I won't leave one stone unturned. But what does she actually want?

They hadn't gotten that far in the conversation before he'd insisted she return to the hotel and eat.

The men strode into the Eden Hotel. Only two tables in the café were taken. Karen Forester glanced up from filling salt and pepper shakers on the counter. She set them aside and hurried forward. "Hello."

Henry nodded. "Did they eat the supper I had sent up?"

"Every last morsel."

"Good." He headed for the stairs. "Thank you. Be sure to put that on my account. And anything else they might need while they're here. I think she'll be too shy to ask, so please check with her in the morning by knocking on her door, if you don't mind."

"Not at all. I'll write myself a note so I don't forget."

At room six, he quietly knocked on the door. It wasn't a few seconds before the door opened.

"I've brought Dr. Dodge."

Relief crossed Elizabeth's face. Her hair was down, brushed, and a long braid now fell down her back. She still wore the same skirt she'd had on earlier, but she'd changed into a soft-blue blouse that brought out the color of her eyes. Weary lines fanned out from their corners and cradled her missing smile.

"Thank you, Mr. Glass. I don't know how I'll ever repay you. But I will, I promise."

He waved the comment away.

"I can't pay you either, Doctor. I want you to know that up front."

"No need to worry about that right now," Dr. Dodge replied as he strode for the bed where the small boy lay between sheets only, his face flushed with fever. He placed his palm on Johnny's forehead and immediately pulled off the top sheet. The child was too sick to react, but his eyes followed the doctor's moves. "We'll need ice, Henry," he said over his shoulder. "More than they'll have downstairs. You'll need to go to the icehouse."

Turning, Henry started for the door, but Elizabeth caught his arm before he stepped out.

"Your kindness means so much to me," she said. "I never expected this to happen. And having—" Her voice broke, and she looked away.

"Please, Mrs. Smith," he said, "you don't need to keep thanking me. Any decent man would do the same. Let's concentrate on getting your son better, then we'll worry about the other issues. And you needn't worry about the money. Each year, Eden sets aside a sum for truly needy widows." She *was* a widow, so to speak, if what she said was true. There was no evidence yet that she was lying. He shouldn't just label her a deceiver because what she'd told him was difficult to believe.

Actually, what she told me is easy to believe. And at face value, the boy's age matches up with the trip John took. I'm not much of an attorney if I can't see the picture that's emerging right before my eyes.

"I'll put in your request for it, if you'd like."

And cover the cost myself of anything that goes over the amount. John would do the same for my son and his mother.

"Right now, though, I need to get that ice." He went to her ceramic water pitcher, which sat in a large matching bowl. He took up the bowl. "You best let me go."

She stepped back, an amount of relief softening her expression. "Yes. Thank you." She gave a small smile when she realized she'd just thanked him again.

Henry found himself bounding down the stairs. At the bottom, he spotted Mavis and Emma at a center table in the dining room. The sight stopped him in his tracks.

John's daughters are here. Is his son upstairs?

Mavis saw him and waved him over. "Henry, would you like to join us?"

The trust in their eyes almost did him in. Here he was, daydreaming about the beautiful woman in room six who claimed her son was their half brother. *Does she believe he's entitled to part of John's fortune? How would I ever explain that?* He'd pledged to John that he'd always look out for his girls. *Wouldn't John also want me to look after a son he never knew he had?*

"Thank you, but no. I'm on, er, I have to . . ."

Mavis sat forward, concern in her eyes. "Karen told us about the poor little boy upstairs. How you fetched the doctor for him. How is he? If there's anything we can do . . ."

"They're newcomers," Emma added. "Came in on yesterday's stage, just a day after us." Her smile resembled John's.

Karen appeared with a small plate of cookies and set them on the table between the two young women. "You off again, Henry?"

"Yes. To the icehouse."

Emma covered her mouth. "For the child?" She looked at her sister and then at Karen. "He's quite sick, then?"

"The doctor is with him as we speak. He has a high fever."

Karen's brow creased. "Where's she from?" she asked.

Blast. He needed to shut his mouth and get moving. "I'm really not at liberty to say. You'll have to ask her."

"You must be representing her," Karen said. "Interesting." The waitress had a habit of ferreting out information about anything or anyone in Eden.

Mavis cocked her head, her concerned sympathy deepening. "Do you know her, Henry? Is she family? Maybe a sister or a cousin?"

His intimate involvement *would* look that way. "No, no, nothing like that. Good evening, ladies," he said and gave a polite nod. "I really must be on my way. Doctor needs that ice now."

And I really don't want to give out any more information or be backed into a corner where I'll have to hedge on the truth. That's not the kind of man I am. But until I know more, I can hardly make a fair call to all concerned.

Pivoting on his heel, he made for the door like a frightened boy. He welcomed the coolness of the night on his face. He cut between the buildings on the shortest route to the icehouse, located down by the river and behind the rocks opposite the Spanish Trail Cantina. Walking briskly, he crossed the road and weaved beside the Hole in the Floor saloon. Its name boasted of a urinal at the foot of the bar. It wasn't exactly a hole, but more like a slanted trough to accommodate anyone who didn't want to make the trip to the outhouse. Henry avoided the establishment like a sore tooth.

The moon gave off enough light that he didn't have any trouble seeing Saint Rose along the route. The half-French, half-Spanish priest stood in front of the adobe church, looking at the stars.

"Padre?"

The priest searched out Henry from the direction of his voice. "Ah, hello," he said. "The beautiful evening made it impossible to stay inside."

"Yes. I noticed you're stargazing. Are you looking for anything in particular?"

"Everything in particular," he said evasively. "But in reality, from my bedroom desk where I was reading, I noticed two shooting stars, and thought to take a walk. Since then, there've been two more." He gave a small laugh. "Where're you off to in such haste?" He looked down the road toward the Spanish Trail Cantina, the only business left in that direction.

"Not the cantina. The icehouse. We have a sick child. The doctor sent me."

"I see. I will keep him in my prayers. What's his name?"

Henry swallowed. "Johnny."

There was a moment of pause. "We wouldn't want to lose another John, now, would we? Please send word tomorrow on his condition."

"Will do," Henry called over his shoulder as he rushed away. *That's strange. Two Johns?* It was a coincidence, to be sure. Henry didn't believe in signs. As a lawyer, he dealt in hard fact. Period.

Sure you do. If that's the case, why did the hair on the back of your neck prickle? Is Johnny really John's son?

If yes, they'd all been given a great gift. *But how will the girls feel? And Blake? How would he handle this amazing discovery, if indeed Mrs. Smith's story proved true?* Henry had to be sure before anything could be said. He'd make Elizabeth understand. *And what if she won't agree? What if she insists on making her claim right away? Mavis and the rest are just coming to grips with losing their father and finding out he wasn't the monster they'd been led to believe. They need time. And that's exactly why I need to search out the truth. I'll do my best to be as sure of the boy's parentage as I can be before anything is said. Will I be able to talk Elizabeth into waiting?*

That was what he'd find out soon enough.

CHAPTER NINETEEN

The velvety black sky glittered with stars as Belle and Nicole made their way from the house toward the bunkhouse, a savory, warm aroma wafting about on the air. When Belle had picked up a lantern to bring along, Nicole made a face but kept her comments to herself. The girl might be used to walking around in the dark mountains of Colorado, but Belle wasn't. Who knew what could be lying in wait on the path? Compared to Philadelphia, this was true wilderness.

It is difficult imagining Mother living here for any length of time.

Freshening up had taken some doing. The water pump, which had been agreeable when she'd needed water to clean Moses's battered face, had been cranky and pushed her God-given patience to the limit. She'd almost worked her arm out of the socket until Nicole stepped forward. With finesse born of experience, she had water splashing forth in seconds.

Finished with her bird bath, Belle discovered Mavis had forgotten to send her shoes. She'd be forced to wear the heavy boots like the ranch hands wore beneath her dress. *This is dinner in a bunkhouse. With a handful of rough-hewn men. Surely my footwear doesn't matter.*

As they walked toward the bunkhouse, she held the light with one hand and her shawl with her other, being careful not to twist her ankle on a rock. Out in the corrals a horse nickered, followed by the howl of a coyote. Nicole hadn't done a thing to prepare for supper except coil her thick brown hair into a French twist, which, in its messy way, looked very stylish. The girl had slipped on a leather coat with fringe along the arms and bottom. Westerny, but also soft and feminine.

At the windmill, Nicole paused, plucked a blossom from a climbing vine, and stabbed it behind one ear.

"That's sweet," Belle said, trying to fill the awkward silence. "And your jacket is attractive. I've not seen one like it before."

Nicole's lips pursed in amusement. "Thank you. It was a Christmas present from my brother. Mr. Little, the old man who tans the leather, is a friend of mine. Sometimes I work at the tannery. He must have told Clint I'd been eyeing the coat."

They were making progress. Belle nodded, then directed her gaze back to the stars. Maybe if she got to know Nicole a little better, they could be friends. Belle was older; she'd make the first move.

"Blake told me your brother is the sheriff of Eden?"

Nicole glanced over. "Yep."

"But you're so young. I'd think a sheriff would need to be a bit older, what with all the danger involved."

"He's my half brother, so he's a lot older. In his thirties."

Darn. Belle remembered that fact now that Nicole had pointed it out.

"We had the same ma. When she died, I moved in with Clint. It's not all that mysterious."

Her defensive tone made Belle reach out and touch her shoulder. The last thing she wanted was to make matters worse.

Nicole stopped in her tracks. "Save your pity."

"I'm not pitying you. I'm just trying to get to know you better. So we can be friends."

Crossing the porch, Nicole took hold of the door handle and was about to step inside when Belle caught her shoulder again. "Shouldn't you knock? What if someone isn't dressed?"

Nicole gave an incredulous laugh. "Women expected in the bunkhouse for supper?" She snorted out another chortle. "And you don't think they're ready for us? Oh boy. You do have a lot to learn." She turned back to the door and stepped inside.

Feeling shy, Belle followed. She softly clicked the knotty pine closed as she kept her gaze riveted on the latch. *What will I say to these men?* She heartily wished she'd declined Blake's invitation and eaten the loaf of bread Mavis had sent out. She'd also found a small crock of butter and preserves as well. That could have kept her until morning. Uncomfortable nerves skittered down her spine, and she knew she'd have to turn around sooner or later.

She turned.

The messy room she'd expected was nicely arranged, neat, inviting. And larger than she'd anticipated. The area wrapped around in the shape of an *L*. One candle burned in the center of a rectangular table, another on the fireplace mantel, and several lanterns burned around the room. At the turn that she figured led to the beds, a large colorfully woven curtain hung—perhaps an Aztec design—sectioning off the area.

Tank stood at the stove with a large wooden spoon in hand. KT appeared as if he'd just stood from the chair behind him, and Trevor stepped out from behind the drawn curtain, a welcoming smile on his face as he worked the bright-red bandanna around his neck.

Blake, hunkered down in front of the hearth, promptly stood and dusted his hands. It was apparent all the men had donned clean clothes, washed up, and combed their hair. There wasn't a hat in sight.

"Welcome, ladies," Blake said, his gaze going directly to her shawl and then to Nicole. "May I take your wrap, Belle?" He strode forward, took the lantern from her hands, blew out the flame, and set it on the mantel. "And your coat, Nicole?"

Belle drew the light shawl off her shoulders and handed him the garment. "Thank you," she replied, keenly aware of the other men in the room.

"My pleasure. But I do recall asking you two to wait for one of us to come fetch you. I was about to step out the door."

"We got impatient," Nicole said, lifting one shoulder. "Are you mad?"

He shook his head, a smile teasing his lips.

My, he's in a good mood tonight. She hadn't known Blake long, yet she felt like she had; she was getting used to reading the slight changes in expression that signaled his mood. She glanced around.

"How's Moses?" She presumed his bed was behind the curtain with the rest of the men's.

"Sleeping again." Trevor moved to stand beside Blake and her. "He's pretty banged up. Tomorrow he'll feel even worse. But keeping him in his bed when he's awake has been difficult."

Nicole pranced over to the stove in the corner of the room that was clearly used as the kitchen, took up a folded towel, and lifted the lid off a large, cast-iron pot.

"Hey, who gave you permission to peek?" Tank said, taking the hot lid and almost dropping it as he hurriedly slapped it back in place. "You're gonna let out the heat. I've been working on this all afternoon."

"It's not a soufflé," she retorted in a razor-sharp tone. "It won't fall and be ruined."

Blake put out his hand to them both. "No need to squabble. Belle, why don't you have a seat over here? You too, Nicole. Trevor was just about to set the table."

"I was?"

Blake sent him a glance.

"I was." The ranch hand laughed and went over to Tank. "You have a tablecloth somewhere? Blake wants the table to look nice."

Tank scratched his head.

Belle took the seat Blake had intended and glanced around the room. The pie safe had several drawers below the two main doors. "Perhaps in there?" she said, pointing. "May I help? I'd like to."

"No," all four men said at once.

Disregarding their outburst, Belle stood. She'd never make it through tonight if she had to stay in that chair until dinnertime. She was too nervous. She crossed the room and opened the drawer in the pie safe. *Asserting myself feels much better.* There were several tablecloths. She chose a yellow one with tiny blue flowers and carried it to the table.

"Well, I'll be," Trevor exhaled, looking astonished. "I've never opened that drawer before. I don't ever recall us having a tablecloth either."

It's not so different from corralling my sisters. As she shook out the cloth, Nicole lifted the candle. Belle applied the covering and smoothed out the wrinkles. Nicole replaced the brass candleholder and then shoved her hand into her pockets.

She winked at Nicole. "Teamwork."

"What's your fella think of you staying out here at the ranch tonight?" Trevor asked. "Seen him wanderin' around town like a lost puppy. He staying in Eden? Or going back to Philadelphia?"

With the stack of plates Tank had set out, Belle went back to the table and began to place them around. "Lesley is going home tomorrow." Guilt at staying out here and not seeing him off on the stage edged in. "He has work there and nothing to do here. I plan to stay for six months and then return to Philadelphia as well."

There, I've said it. That's the decision we reached, but why is it so difficult to voice? Once the six months had passed, she was free to do as she wished. *Father wants us to be happy. His letter said he understood we might already have commitments of the heart. If Darvid hadn't passed on, Mavis would have a difficult decision to make as well.* As it was, Belle was the only one who seemed torn by the decisions at hand.

Trevor looked surprised, Tank's hands went directly to his hips, KT swiveled from feeding the small fire, and Blake's eyes narrowed. None of them said a word.

"He's certainly understanding, this fella of yours." Nicole lifted an innocent shoulder. "And you're not even in town on his last night?" She made a small, disapproving sound in her throat and then circled around behind Tank.

So much for friendship.

"He understands," she said a bit too forcefully. *Who am I trying to convince? Them or me?* "I never knew anything about the ranch until yesterday. Or about my father, until a few weeks ago. Lesley realizes I need time to come to accept all the changes in my life." *Does he really?* "It's not something one does in a day or two."

Her face heated, recalling their breakfast that morning. *Shouldn't I be more distressed at our parting? It feels like I should. After all we've been through and his being so considerate to make the trip with us.* She could have gone back into town with her sisters, at least for the day, to say goodbye, but her mind had been set on staying at the ranch. Their ranch. *Her* ranch. Here she was, being heartless again. She could change that if she wanted. She knew she should, but would she?

When her gaze locked with Nicole, one of the girl's eyebrows reached for the wooden beams overhead. *Even she knows how thoughtless I've been.* If Belle had been more considerate, Nicole wouldn't have had to make the trip and Tank wouldn't have had to cook a fancy supper—all to feed her when she was too incompetent to use the old stove. She'd put them out because the view of those tall, distant mountains had woven a spell around her heart.

"You don't owe any explanations," Blake said, looking uncomfortable. The whole room looked uncomfortable.

Trevor brought over the salt and pepper shakers. "He's right. You're the boss now, along with Blake. We don't mean any disrespect. Just making conversation. Wondering what to expect. If you marry Mr. Atkins, he'll be one of our bosses along with Blake. No one here would like to see that happen, him being an outsider."

"Trevor!" Blake scolded. "Keep your thoughts to yourself. What Miss Brinkman decides to do with her life does not revolve around what anyone on this ranch thinks, and that includes *you*."

Tank ducked his head, and KT looked away.

"Course not," Trevor said. "All I meant was—"

"Drop it." Blake's tone pinned Trevor to the wall, and Belle actually quivered. "This is her first night on the ranch. Let's let her enjoy the charm in peace." He smiled at her as she set out the silverware. "We've already put her to work."

It was a moment before she realized the work comment was meant to be teasing. Everyone seemed to let out a sigh of relief. Nicole actually went over and patted Trevor's back. The poor guy looked as if he'd just lost his best friend.

"Dinner's served," Tank called, his face shining with pride.

"Should I make a plate for Moses?" Belle asked, fearing her appetite had fled with the subject they'd just discussed. She should put herself to good use.

"I just checked on him, and he's still asleep." Trevor stepped over the long bench at the table. "That morphine does a fine job. If I ever get banged up, I want some of that."

"Sleep's the best thing for him." She glanced at the table, wondering where to sit. "He'll mend faster that way. Do you have assigned seats, or should I sit anywhere?"

Blake motioned to the head of the table, next to where he stood.

"I couldn't."

There was that charming smile again. "You can and you will."

She inched toward him, a warm glow heating her insides. She chanced a look into his eyes. "Don't you sit there?"

"Not tonight."

Aware of the men's gazes, as well as Nicole's, Belle seated herself at the head while the rest used the benches along each side. There was plenty of room. The thought gave her pause—it was only because of the deserters, who were still out there.

So much was happening so fast, Belle felt as if she'd lost her footing. Still, one glance around the friendly faces brought a smile to her lips. She'd figure it out. It would just take time, and she had six months.

CHAPTER TWENTY

"W haddaya mean you're goin' out of town?" Blake asked in surprise from the buckboard seat as he stared down into Henry's
face. He and Belle had just arrived in Eden, having gone into town for
supplies. Exhausted, she sat next to him in silence after exchanging
pleasantries with Henry. Three busy days at the ranch had passed in the
blink of an eye, and the roundup was scheduled to begin the following
morning. As much as Belle had taken to Gunner, and to riding in a
Western saddle, Blake wondered if her interest in the ranch would wane
as soon as the novelty wore off.

Henry lifted a hand and shaded his eyes against the morning sun. A
wagon rattled by in the street behind him. Shouting and laughter came
from Poor Fred's Saloon even though it wasn't yet seven in the morning.
"Exactly what I said. I have business I need to straighten out in Denver.
Tomorrow morning, I'm starting for Santa Fe to catch the train."

"Can't it wait?" Blake tipped his head toward Belle, who was a bit
rumpled in her three-day-old clothes. She'd given him a mean eye earlier
when he told her the cattle didn't care if she looked presentable, so not
to fuss. She'd been unusually quiet on the wagon ride in. *Is she missing
the amenities of the hotel—or Mr. Atkins? Does she regret her decision to
stay?*

Nicole had ridden her horse alongside the wagon, but as soon as they were within a mile of town, she'd taken off to who knew where. The rest of the sisters had yet to make a showing out at the ranch, each day sending a note explaining why their arrival had been delayed. One day, Lavinia had had a headache and didn't want to suffer through the ride out, and another day, they were catching up on their correspondence and writing letters home to friends. *That sounded suspect. Were Mavis and the other three put off after one glimpse of the ranch? Had the house been too rustic? The men too rough? The whole idea of the cattle ranch operation too daunting?* He didn't know what to expect when he saw them.

Henry frowned. "Unfortunately, it can't wait."

"What is it?"

"Just business. I'm not at liberty to say."

Strange. Blake knew of nothing that would take precedence over John's daughters in the attorney's thoughts and business. Whatever put that frown on his face meant trouble. But Henry wasn't going to spill his guts here in front of Belle, or he would have already. Blake would corner him later, when they were alone. Maybe it had to do with the search for the girls' guardians, Vernon and Velma Crowdaire. Perhaps he didn't want to say anything and upset Belle.

"Have you forgotten we're starting the foundation next week?" Blake asked. "Fall is just around the corner, Henry. If we want to be finished before the onset of winter, we need to get moving. That doesn't leave much time."

"You'll have to deal with it."

"Fine, then. I'll watch over construction as well as bring in a thousand head of beef shorthanded. That's not asking much. You run off to Timbuktu or wherever it is you have to go," he said with a short tone of his own.

I can't handle all the sisters. Belle has been taxing enough with all her questions and suggestions—and almost getting kicked by a steer, smashed in the head by the beam Tank was carrying on his shoulder, and scalded by trying to pick up a hot coffeepot. And yet, she hasn't complained about a single thing. Actually, if I admit it, I'm a bit impressed.

He sighed. "Any news on Praig? Clint bring him in?"

Henry shook his head. "Nothing. It's like he disappeared into thin air. Perhaps he realizes what will happen when you get hold of him. Maybe he's gone for good."

"I don't think so." Pushed by agitation inside, Blake rested his foot on the brake.

"Look, Blake, in the midst of the events of the last three days, I actually forgot about breaking ground on the house. Perhaps I can put the trip off one week, if you think that might help."

"A week would help a great deal. I'd appreciate that."

"I'm not making any promises just yet," Henry went on. "But it might be doable."

Belle flicked a piece of dust from her shirttail. "In Mavis's last note, she mentioned a small boy at the hotel who's sick. How is he, Henry? Are they staying in town long? I saw them, if indeed it's them, from the window as they got off the stagecoach."

Henry's face seemed to tighten even more.

What is going on? Belle wouldn't have picked up on the change in Henry's usual mannerisms, but Blake sure did.

"One question at a time, Belle," Henry said, annoyance back in his tone. "That would be Johnny Smith. He's doing better. He and his mother, Elizabeth, are from—out of town. I don't know if they're planning on staying in Eden, since I just met her myself. The doctor isn't sure what made the boy sick, but today he's doing much better."

By the hurt look on Belle's face, Henry's tone had cut her to the quick.

Henry's face softened. "They had been staying at the hotel, but his mother took a room at the boardinghouse. I imagine they'll be there for a time."

Belle perked up. "That's good news. From what I've seen, Eden needs all the women it can get."

A voice called out, "Belle!"

Giddy happiness slammed Belle when she saw Mavis and Lavinia rushing toward the buckboard. She stood up and put out her hand, which Henry took to assist her down. After three days on the ranch—and her pride in tatters—she'd learned there was no shame in asking for help. She was drained and dirty. She was going straight to the hotel for a hot bath and planned to soak until the water turned to ice.

She and Mavis fell into each other's arms. Her sisters were such a welcome sight—especially after all the hours with snippy Nicole. None of them had been away from one another overnight until Mavis had married and Katie had gone to the normal school. *Could I really leave them here and return to Philadelphia in six months?*

That sentiment was pushed away when Mavis looked her up and down with a critical eye.

"Belle. You look awful."

Belle couldn't stop herself; she glanced back at Blake. It was the same thing she'd been telling him all morning. He shrugged and looked away.

"I *know* I do! I can't wait to sink into a tub of bubbles up to my chin. And wash my hair. I love a nice white-vinegar-and-chamomile tea rinse. It's going to feel so nice after days of sun and wind." She reached up and felt the tangled mess. "The weather has punished it horribly. After I'm finished, I'll have a steaming cup of tea and a double order of toast and jam." She rubbed her backside, not caring if the men saw her. "My bottom and legs ache horribly from riding astride. You just wait. It's nothing like sidesaddle. I'm actually looking forward to tightening my corset and donning a dress."

Lavinia hooked her arm through Belle's, and Mavis did the same on the other side. They started toward the hotel, but Belle stopped, pulling them to a halt. She turned back to the wagon.

"Blake, how long does loading supplies take? I don't want to hold you up." From beneath the brim of his Stetson, his intense gaze made her senses spring to life. Her sore muscles and mussed hair weren't the only things that had taken a beating out at the ranch. So had her sanity. "Or . . . or do you need my help?" she asked tentatively. *Please say no.* "I did come into town in place of KT and told you I'd do anything you needed."

"You riding back with me?"

"You know I am."

"Thought you may have changed your mind when you got back to Eden."

She threw back her shoulders.

He chuckled. "I can handle the supplies on my own. Take some time off. Get your bath. As a matter of fact, stay in town and rest up."

The thought was tempting, but she forced herself to reply, "Nope. I said I'm going back to the ranch with you, and I am. But as long as I'm here, I'd like to take advantage of a few . . . things, if you don't mind. Will you possibly be busy for two hours?"

His mouth twitched. "Stay two days. I don't mind."

Henry shrugged. "I wouldn't turn that down, Belle."

"I can't. The roundup is set to begin in the morning. I intend to be there. Just tell me how long you'll be loading and whatnot, and I'll find the wagon wherever you are. I won't be late."

She didn't miss the amused look on Henry's face. He seemed to have gotten over whatever had caused his mood swing. She'd never seen him like that before, but then, she'd only known him four days.

"Fine, then," Blake said in that voice that had a hint of lazy attraction. "How's eleven sound? That give you enough time to—"

"Plenty." An overwhelming sense of happiness welled up inside Belle. There'd been challenges the last few days, that was for sure. *Dodging puddles on the streets of Philadelphia was nothing compared to the constant dangers of life on the ranch. Or the dispiriting realization that Nicole is ten times better at every chore than I could ever dream of being.* Still, as she'd watched how tirelessly Blake worked at everything from rehanging a gate to caring for Moses, she'd developed an admiration for the life and business he'd built with her father. She didn't really have the words to describe their partnership or what they were to each other. *Family* didn't quite seem right yet. And neither, she realized during their talk at the gravesites, did *brother*. Whether Blake was giving her instructions, haranguing her about being careful around the horses, or praising her for a simple deed any child could do, she felt something she wasn't yet sure about. But she was eager to see where it led.

CHAPTER TWENTY-ONE

L aughter wafted out of the open door of Poor Fred's Saloon. Santiago Alvarado stopped on the boardwalk in front of the establishment and watched John's daughters gather in the street as Henry helped the one dressed in denims down from Blake's wagon. He'd heard the news about their arrival more than once, but this was his first sighting. Standing in the shadows, he was sure they wouldn't catch him staring.

No one could claim John hadn't done a fine job siring such a herd. Dios! There isn't an ugly one among them. Two more black-clad young women exited the hotel, only to pull up when they saw their three sisters in the street. As they dashed forward, their cheerful voices caused a stir inside Santiago. This was what family was supposed to be. Unable to stop a smile, he leaned a shoulder against a corner post. Not often did Eden see such beauty all in one place. *God has blessed me this day.*

"Santiago," a voice called from inside the saloon. Homer, a town local, stumbled out. "Want a drink? Something better than that Mexican whiskey you serve at your place? First one's on me." The man's breath, now that he was close, was enough to drop a horse to his knees. Santiago discreetly took a step back.

"Gracias, but no. I have business to attend to." He bent his head in the direction of the wagon. "Stopped for a moment to enjoy the show."

The drunk leaned forward, catching his balance with a palm to the porch rail. "Would ya looky at them girls," Homer slurred. He laughed loudly. "I hope it ain't a hallucination."

One young woman in particular caught Santiago's eye. From her silliness, jumping around and hugging her sisters, he'd guess her to be the youngest. Her light hair sparkled in the sun, and her smile was infectious. Something caught her eye, and she stilled. Santiago followed her gaze to a broken-down Chinese peddler.

Homer laughed again, and she glanced their way. The vividness of her blue eyes sent a shock through Santiago's person. Most likely she couldn't see him under the overhang of the building, but he smiled anyway, just in case. He'd been told by more than one pretty senorita that his smile was deadly and his face would charm an angel. He'd never really cared all that much about his looks, but now, here, right before his eyes, was a prize to be won. *Gringos be damned.*

From the turn in the road, the stranger he'd been waiting for came riding up the street, a black bandanna tied to his saddle horn as a sign of identification. Santiago watched him smile and politely doff his hat to Brinkman's daughters. As the rider drew closer, Santiago stepped onto the dirt road nonchalantly, as if crossing was his only intention.

"Buried behind the old barn on White Hawk Road," he whispered as the rider passed closely. He took one quick glance up to see if the man had understood. The man dipped his chin and kept going. The whole exchange took no more than a couple of seconds. On the other side of the street, Santiago stopped, turned back, and returned his attention to the young women who had by then moved to the entrance of the hotel.

Blake Harding was pulling the buckboard into the side street between the mercantile and Poor Fred's. Henry, at the top of the stairs, disappeared into his office. The rest of the town was quiet.

Anxiety slithered down Santiago's spine. He'd been careful; nobody suspected a thing. Still, he turned and scanned the street, more thoroughly this time. Padre Francisco stood by the sheriff's office. He carried his tall walking stick that resembled a shepherd's staff, and his long brown robe fell to the ground, stopping just above the man's boots. The wide-brimmed straw hat he wore didn't cover his eyes. When their gazes met, the priest smiled and dipped his chin in acknowledgment.

He saw! And is making a point that I know he saw. No. That's not possible. My back was to him when I gave the message. He couldn't see my mouth. It's all speculation.

Santiago looked away. *Who cares if the padre knew anyway? He wouldn't say anything.* Santiago was certain of that from the many years they'd known each other, and the many scrapes he and Demetrio had gotten into as boys. Padre Francisco had an inventive way of looking at things.

A hot pain sliced through Santiago's heart. Any thought of his older brother brought such anguish that Santiago found functioning difficult. Demetrio shouldn't be locked up like an animal. The small cells at Sugar House Penitentiary were dug into the ground, the access at the top the only available light. At night the guards lowered down a tub for the men to do their business.

It was true that Demetrio had thrown in with an unscrupulous group of men, but when they went to rob a Santa Fe business, he'd had no knowledge they intended to kill the owner in retribution for something else. One witness testified that Demetrio, who'd never been convicted of any other crimes, had been waiting with the horses when the shopkeeper was murdered, and so he'd gotten a lighter sentence. But fifteen years in prison was still more than he deserved. Today, Santiago had set a plan in motion. To make up for the guilt he felt at not telling their father when Demetrio first began disobeying small laws. For now, Santiago could breathe easier. And that's what he intended to do.

He drifted toward the hotel. *"Hola."* He looked at the young woman who had caught his eye. He wasn't wearing a hat, or he'd have swept it from his head.

Her face deepened in color. "Hello," she replied softly. The other girls quieted and turned to gaze at him, all pretty, but different from one another. The oldest one stepped forward. "Hello, sir. I'm Mavis Applebee, and these are my sisters."

Again, he made a small bow with his head. "Yes, I know." He warmly smiled and let his gaze stray back to the youngest, the one with the sky-blue eyes and honey-colored hair.

Mrs. Applebee pointed to the sister dressed like a nice-looking young man. She might be wearing the clothes of a vaquero, but there was no disguising what was underneath. "This is Belle."

He smiled and dipped his chin. *"Hola."*

They all seemed to like his Spanish, because they smiled and tittered every time a Spanish word rolled off his tongue.

"This is Emma, Lavinia, and Katie."

Ahh, Katie. I will know you better. You will be mine . . .

Katie blushed as if she could hear his thoughts. "We're pleased to make your acquaintance, Mr. . . . ."

"Alvarado. Santiago Alvarado. Our fathers knew each other well. John made a point to open his doors to us. He hired me and my older brother many times. He was a good man. My condolences." Daringly, he picked up Katie's soft hand and, bending forward, kissed the back of it, lingering much longer than was proper. He didn't even need to look up to hear the stir he'd created.

"Mr. Alvarado." The panic in Mrs. Applebee's voice almost made him chuckle.

"Perdóname," he said, and quickly followed with the English: "Forgive me. I was overcome with the sunshine in your sister's eyes."

Across the street, Blake came out of the mercantile with a large sack resting on his shoulder. He stopped and stared. Santiago knew that look all too well. After a moment, Blake moved on around the corner to where his wagon was parked.

"Mr. Harding would like me to walk on, but I'm of a mind to invite you all to tea." He looked to the door of the hotel and the café inside. "My treat."

"That's a kind offer, but I need to rest," Belle replied, her eyelids drooping.

"Ahh, the vaquero is weary." Again, he let Katie see his gaze lingering on her face, but kept it far from her lips. "But I will hold you to another time. My father and I own a business in town. The Spanish Trail Cantina, on the southeast end of Eden. Come see us, if you are brave enough." He winked and they all smiled—even Mrs. Applebee, who acted like a mother hen.

"We will, Mr. Alvarado," Katie said, her voice not as timid as it had been just a moment ago.

"Good. I will watch for you." He gave one more small bow and walked off, feeling ten feet tall. *How many men have been brave enough to approach John's daughters?* Not one that he'd seen today. *And not only that, but invite them to tea?* Santiago Alvarado, or Lion Heart, as Demetrio liked to call him, had staked his claim.

CHAPTER TWENTY-TWO

"B elle, are you ready for more hot water?" Lavinia called from the
other side of the cloth screen. "The delivery boy just brought some."

Belle lolled in the oblong silver tub the hotel had sent up a half
hour ago. With her washed hair wrapped in a towel, she scrunched
down into the bubbles as far as she could go, letting the lavender-
scented water soothe away her aches and pains.

"Please. There's just enough room for one more bucket. Then I
must get out and dress. I feel guilty for not helping Blake, at least a
little. Knowing him, he'll finish up early and leave me behind without
a second thought. I have no illusions about that man."

Lavinia inched her way in, the weighty bucket swaying between her
legs. Both hands gripped the wooden handle, and water came precari-
ously close to slopping over. As careful as she was, water splashed on her
dress and the floor. She made a face. "This is difficult."

Belle dunked deeper into the bubbles. "Be careful not to hurt yourself. That looks heavy."

"I am. Scoot to the side so I won't burn you when I pour this in."

Belle promptly obeyed. The sound of the door opening was almost
concealed by the splashing of water.

"They had everything you wanted at the Toggery," Emma called while the crinkle of paper being unwrapped and crumpled filled the room. "Two more pairs of pants like you bought before, and two more shirts. That was all of the smaller sizes they had. Mr. Buns, the clerk, will put in an order for the rest of us. It'll be at least a week before the garments arrive, but he's promised to send them to the hotel the moment they do."

Belle smiled at the silly name. She'd met the man on her visit to the shop with Blake. He'd seemed nervous; Henry had told them the shop managers were all aware that one of the girls would be its new owner. Just wrapping their heads around the ranch was so overwhelming, she had no idea when they'd feel ready to divvy up the other businesses.

She'd made an effort to put Mr. Buns at ease; still, he had dropped several items, stuttered twice, and had to search for more than five minutes for the account book. "Thank you," Belle called to the ceiling. "Wearing those same grubby clothes for another day would have sent me to my grave."

"Don't say such a thing," Emma replied. "What you're doing out at the ranch is no small feat." She cleared her throat. "I do have to voice my concern about the Toggery without sounding overly prideful about myself. Whichever sister ends up with that establishment will have a task on her hands. I was horrified to see what they consider a dress-and-hat section. It's like Mr. Buns doesn't realize there's more than one sex. *One* dress, *one* hat—that looks as if it's been there for ten years—*no* gloves, scarves, or unmentionables. I'd have to guess most women in town sew their own things."

Belle felt a smile. "I'm sure one of us will bring the place up to snuff in no time. The clerk is nice enough. He was very helpful—when he wasn't fainting with fear."

Lavinia and Emma both laughed.

"Yes, I'll give you that," Emma said in agreement.

"I'm sorry about taking the last of the riding clothes." Belle swished the warm water around, enjoying it immensely.

"Don't think a thing of it," Emma replied. "I'm planning to stay in town for the time being. I'm not ready to start ranching yet, but I do intend to in the future. We all must make a concerted effort to learn everything we can. Six months will pass quickly."

Belle lathered her washcloth with the lavender soap and began scrubbing her arms and legs a second time. "Have either of you met Nicole Day?" she asked, keeping her voice casual.

"No. Who's she?" Lavinia asked.

"The sheriff's younger sister."

"Really?" Lavinia said. "How old?"

"Sixteen."

"We met the handsome Sheriff Dawson yesterday morning," Emma said. "Are you sure they're brother and sister?"

"Yes. His half sister. I can find out more about her on the way back to the ranch."

Lavinia knocked once on the screen and looked around. Belle plunged down into the sudsy water.

"Don't do that, Belle," Lavinia said. "Blake will think we're nosy."

"He already thinks I'm nosy, and every other bad thing that a person can be. Anyway, I don't care. We need *something* to talk about on that long wagon ride back. By the way, where did Mavis and Katie make off to?"

"I'm not sure," Emma said. "You almost finished? If you get dressed, we can go find out. I like exploring the town. There're actually quite a few shops and restaurants. I hear with the mining that's exploded the last few years, Eden has grown quite a bit."

"Blake says you should be careful where you go. Speak with Henry before wandering off. And if you do go out, go in pairs—not alone."

"You're getting to know Blake quite well." Lavinia's tone held a mountain of meaning.

"What do you expect? We've been working together for three days." Belle reluctantly stood and reached for the towel folded on the chair. Being careful not to slip, she stepped out of the tub and dried herself. Securing the towel around her body, she crossed the room to the bed, looking over her new clothes.

Emma smiled as Belle picked up her new shirt and looked over the garment. "Whoever thought I'd be so excited over a man's shirt?"

"I'll drop off the dirty clothes at the laundry house for you," Emma said. "I spotted it one street over."

"You're learning the town." Belle couldn't hide her envy.

"And you're getting to know Blake and the ranch. The ranch hands and all the rest. We all must do what we can and then share our knowledge."

Belle brightened. She was beginning to feel a little down about leaving soon. "That's a wonderful idea. Today's Monday. Let's plan a meeting as soon as most of the work with the roundup is done. We'll each give a short talk on what we've learned. How does that sound?"

"How does what sound?" Mavis asked, stepping through the door.

"That after a few days, we get—"

Mavis stepped quickly to the bath screen and looked behind it. "Where's Katie?"

Belle gaped at Lavinia and then Emma. "We thought she was with you. She must be in the other room."

"No. I stopped there first," Mavis said, shaking her head. "I've been across the street at the mercantile."

The walls closed in on Belle as she dropped the towel and quickly pulled on her unmentionables, not caring who saw her nakedness. "She's probably downstairs in the café. Did you look there?" All that mattered was Katie, and that she was safe.

Blake made it quite clear we weren't to go off on our own.

Mavis had assumed a general's posture. "I glanced in on my way to the stairs, looking to see if any of you were there. Did she say anything about going anywhere?"

"No," the three said at once.

"The last time I saw her, I was going to my room." Belle fumbled twice with the stiffness of her corset. "And she went into hers. You left with her to fetch Emma's book. That's why I thought the two of you were still together."

Mavis's mouth was a hard, straight line. "She was still there when I departed for the mercantile."

Finished lacing, Belle slipped her arms into the shirt and quickly fastened the buttons. Next she pulled on trousers. The girls were already headed for the door. "Wait until I pull on my boots," Belle barked. "And we need a plan. We can't just fly out the door." She buttoned up the fly and, with her fingers, quickly racked her wet hair back and tied it with a ribbon.

"Belle's right." Lavinia stood with hands on hips. "Mavis and I will find Blake and tell him. Then we'll search up and down Main Street, as well as that small touristy area where we went to supper. Check all the stores and alleys. Someone may have—"

Lavinia's voice broke, and Belle gently put her hand on her sister's shoulder.

"Nothing bad has happened to Katie." Belle prayed her words were true. "Emma and I will go alert Henry and then search up and down Falcon Haven and the Old Spanish Trail that runs through town. She's just wandered off. Distracted by . . ."

"That handsome Santiago Alvarado?" Emma whispered. "She wouldn't, would she?"

"No, she wouldn't." Belle headed to the door. "She has more sense than taking up with a man she doesn't know." She let the others precede her through and then locked the door with a shaky hand, shoving the key deep into her pocket.

Nothing would be worth losing Katie. Not all the money in the world, or even learning about Father and our history. We have to find her, and quickly. A deep dread began to burn inside. As she followed the girls through the hall and then down the stairs, she wondered if this had anything to do with Praig Horn. Moses's beaten face and broken ribs flashed through her mind. *That man better not have touched my little sister or I'll kill him with my bare hands.*

Plunging out the front door of the hotel, Belle grasped Emma's arm and followed Mavis and Lavinia, already on their way to the mercantile to look for Blake. When she and Emma reached the building, they bounded up the outside steps to Henry's office, but the room was empty. Belle crossed the office and pounded on the door that led to his private rooms. No answer.

How could he be gone when we need him most?

CHAPTER TWENTY-THREE

W hat now?" Emma gasped, looking around Henry's vacant office, the fear and panic in her voice all too evident.

"We head one street over," Belle stated firmly. "We'll enlist the sheriff as we pass his office. He's supposed to keep citizens safe."

They raced out the door and took the stairs at a run. Belle caught her toe but righted herself before falling face-first into Emma's back. When their feet hit the street, they took off, Emma struggling to keep up in her dress.

Who can we trust? Is the handsome Santiago to blame? She'd noticed the way his eyes feasted on Katie. *Did Emma remember Praig, and the trouble with him?* She'd not bring that subject up now and worry her, since doing so wouldn't help their situation.

Breathing hard, they clamored into the sheriff's office only to find it empty as well.

"Where *is* everybody?" Belle blurted in frustration. Each moment without Katie was another moment something atrocious could be happening. She stepped outside and cupped her hands around her mouth. "Sheriff!" she shouted. She called out a few more times before a tall man she assumed was Sheriff Dawson came running up the street.

He pulled up. "What's wrong?"

"My baby sister is missing! We fear for her life."

His gaze cut in several directions and then back at them. "How long has she been gone? What makes you think she's in trouble?"

"We're wasting time." She glanced at Emma questioningly.

"Over an hour, Sheriff," Emma said. "Not much more than that."

He gave a noticeable sigh, relaxing his stiff shoulders. "That's not long. Maybe she's visiting and forgot to tell anyone."

Belle narrowed her gaze. The last thing she wanted to do was stand here and argue. "Who does she have to visit? She doesn't know anyone!"

He put out his hands as if they were hysterical women who needed to be calmed. They weren't hysterical—*yet*. They needed to know that Katie was safe.

"It's plenty of time for any number of things too despicable to name to happen," Belle said. "As well as being kidnapped or killed. Have you forgotten so quickly about Moses? I assume his attacker is still running free since I was just in your jail and all the cells are empty."

His mouth twisted at that. "I just got in an hour ago—after searching all night for Praig. And I've sent more than a dozen telegrams to outlying towns. Finding someone who's on the run is more difficult than you might think."

His voice grew louder with each word, but she didn't care. Perhaps he didn't like being questioned by a woman many years his junior. *That's just too bad! I'll question President Hayes if I have to.* Nobody was as important to her as her sisters.

She stomped her foot. "Blake's told me there're places in town respectable women shouldn't go alone. What if Katie accidentally wandered there? Are you refuting that claim?"

"No, I'm not."

"Are you going to help?"

His jaw clenched. "Of course. Where's the rest of your band?"

"Band?"

"Now *you're* the one wasting time."

"We split up," she answered quickly. "They're searching the north part of town, and we're taking the south part and the Old Spanish Trail. We need your help."

The sheriff spotted a young boy walking their way. "Dan, go ring the bell at the Protestant church. When people begin to congregate, tell them we're looking for the youngest Brinkman girl. Her name is Katie. Been missing for about an hour."

"Sure, Sheriff." Dust kicked up as the kid bolted away.

"All right. I'll go down to the end of town and come up the Old Spanish Trail. You two look into the shops on Falcon Haven. When we're finished, we'll meet back here. Same if you find her."

As the sheriff jogged away, Belle's heart trembled. She glanced at Emma to see her sister's teeth worrying her lower lip as they hurried along. They couldn't handle any more tragedy. They'd been through enough these past two months—and that wasn't even taking into consideration all the years their guardians had been lying to them about their father. Katie's joyful laughter wafted through Belle's mind.

Not Katie, Lord. Please don't take her too.

CHAPTER TWENTY-FOUR

B lake was at the livery, a wooden box of horseshoes hefted in his arms, when the tolling of the church bell brought him up short. Shoving the container over the open tailgate of the buckboard, he looked across the vacant field and picnic grounds to the church. A small boy was hauling up and down on the bell rope.

Maverick Daves, the smithy, stepped to his side. He wiped his smudged hands on a towel looped through his thick leather belt. His bare arms were moist from his work over the forge. Rings of sweat stained his shirt. "I wonder what that's about."

Several townspeople had already gathered around.

Blake pondered the same thing. *The Brinkman girls? Naw, couldn't be. But I won't get a lick of work done until I know.*

"I'll go see," he called over his shoulder, already on his way.

"What's this about?" Blake called out as soon as he was close enough.

The boy stopped ringing. "Sheriff had me sound the alarm. Seems a girl's gone missing. John Brinkman's youngest. Her sisters think she's in trouble."

Blake cut his gaze up the road. "Where are they?"

"Don't know."

Confound it! He should have left one of the hands with them at all times, just until they were familiar with the town and with what they could and couldn't do alone. If they weren't so shorthanded, he'd have escorted them himself.

He ran back to the livery, informed Maverick what was going on, then veered behind the building, cutting through the paddocks. *May as well begin with the older, rougher part of town,* he thought, taking the footpath to the Old Spanish Trail.

Scents wafted over from Mrs. Gonzales's food stand. The old woman was hard at work over her *comal.* The flat cast-iron pan appeared plenty hot as she fried a large white tortilla over an open fire.

"*Buenos días,* senor Harding," she said as she watched him approach, sweeping her leathery arm over her offerings of tortillas, black beans, and rice. She hadn't yet started her beef strips, but when she did, the aroma would pervade the whole town. The small shed with a long, colorful Mexican blanket hanging over the door was her office, and gave her a bit of shade to work in. In less than an hour there would be a line ten men long, waiting patiently for a midmorning meal. "Why the bell? Trouble?"

"I'm looking for a young woman." He put out his hands and mimed a pretty shape.

Her creased bow crinkled.

"A *niña.* Gringo. Pretty. You see this day?"

She took a moment to flip the tortilla, which was browning nicely around the edges. "No."

"No?"

She shook her head.

"All right. Have you seen anyone leaving town?"

"*Vendedor ambulante,*" she said, pointing to the trail leading past the Spanish Trail Cantina toward Santa Fe.

"A peddler's wagon?" he mumbled to himself. On its way out of town. Surely Katie would know better than to engage with a stranger. "How long?"

Her brow wrinkled again, and then she held up her hands, placing one finger over the other.

Half hour. He needed a horse. He'd come to Eden in the wagon, but there was no time for that now. "Gracias!" he called over his shoulder as he sprinted toward the cantina. The town seemed unusually quiet. Horses were usually tied everywhere, and now he didn't see a one. He took the cantina steps two at a time and crashed through the front door. The old man the Alvarados had tending bar looked up, as did the few men at the bar. Santiago appeared on the landing at the top of the stairs.

"You have a horse saddled?" Blake called up.

"Yes, my gelding out back. What's—"

"I'm taking him!"

"No problem, amigo."

A few seconds later, Blake galloped down the trail, the sun glaring under the left side of his Stetson. Today would be unseasonably warm. But that didn't matter. All he could think about was Katie in the back of that peddler's wagon.

The narrow road was no more than five or six feet wide. Ironwood, scrub trees, and taller pines spotted the surrounding hummocks, making visibility difficult. The road swung around a slight hill to the right. Blake knew this territory well. Too bad he'd shed his weapon when he'd gotten hot, stashing the Colt under the wagon seat. He felt naked without a gun.

Instead of following the road, he reined the gelding to the left to climb the gently sloping ground. He slowed as the terrain became steeper, letting the animal catch his breath. Women were bought and sold around these parts all the time—a crime, of course, but a crime difficult to stop with so many men and so few women. Heading straight up, the horse dug in, pushing off with strength on every step. Nearing the top and wanting to stay out of sight, Blake dismounted, tied the reins to a tree, and proceeded the rest of the way on foot.

There it was, just moving out of sight: a small peddler's wagon and a rider alongside. The red-and-white paint made the wagon easy to spot in the distance. He knew a few of the dealers that came through Eden, and some even stopped out at the ranch now and then, but this wasn't one of them. He backtracked to the horse, mounted, and galloped off.

As he got closer, he slowed to a walk, dried his face with his bandanna, and then stuffed it back into his pocket. A group of five or six buzzards circling slowly in the sky sent a warning down his spine. A young woman was worth a good sum of money. If indeed these men had Katie, they wouldn't just hand her over without a fight. He needed to slow down, be careful. Bungling this could get Katie Brinkman killed, as well as himself.

CHAPTER TWENTY-FIVE

B elle almost collided with Mavis as they each rounded the corner in front of the Toggery at a full run. Mavis pulled up, breathing as hard as she and Emma were. "Where's Lavinia?" Belle blurted, not wanting to lose another sister. She was heartsick. The last twenty minutes hadn't turned up a clue.

"She headed for the sheriff's office to see if Sheriff Dawson is back yet." People she didn't know—all wearing worried expressions—hurried by, helping in the search.

"Did you find Blake?" Belle asked. "Does he know what's happened?" That was the only thought keeping her sane.

A smudge of dirt marred Mavis's forehead. "No. He wasn't in the mercantile, and I was told he may have gone over to the livery."

Belle looked to the end of the street. She'd already been to the livery. *Was going back a waste of time? Mr. Daves, the smithy, hadn't said a thing about Blake—but I never thought to ask about him either.*

"What are we going to do?" Emma's voice was as soft as a baby bird's. "I can't believe Katie left the room by herself. It's so unlike her."

"She *has* to be here somewhere," Mavis stated in a no-nonsense tone that always alerted Belle that her older sister was close to tears. "Did you tell Henry? What does he think?"

Frustrated, Belle clenched her fists. "He wasn't in his office. If he knows, it's not because of us telling him. At least we've rallied the sheriff—and the whole town. She'll turn up. She has to."

Then why didn't she hear the bell already and come running? What if she's not able to respond? Or even to hear it?

"I'm sure you're right," Emma said, unable to hide the fear in her eyes. "Did anyone check that small business area on Hidden Creek where we had supper? Mademoiselle de Sells? All those small shops there need to be searched. Maybe she fell sick and is lying in an alley all alone, fighting for her life."

Belle nodded. "Yes, all those small, empty shops. She could be in any one of them." *Hurt or dying.* "Good thinking, Emma. You and I will go there next."

Lavinia hurried up the road, her face shiny red to match her eyes. The hem of her black dress was caked with mud.

"Anything?" Lavinia gasped out as soon as she was close enough.

Belle shook her head. "No. Not a thing. And we still don't know if Blake and Henry even know what's transpired. I'd feel so much better if they were here."

All three turned when Sheriff Clint Dawson came jogging up to the group. A sheen of moisture on his face was proof he'd taken their request seriously.

"Has Katie turned up?"

"No," Belle answered, feeling angry at the man. *He's supposed to keep people safe!* Katie's disappearance seemed like it was his fault. "Where else can we look?"

"I have men checking the buildings around town, but I've yet to hear back."

Emma let out a low moan, and Belle slipped an arm around her back.

"It's time I get a posse mounted and extend the search," he said. "Did anyone thoroughly search the hotel? Could she have gone into the sitting room and fallen asleep in a chair in a dark corner?"

"We thought of that a little while ago," Mavis said, her back stiff with worry. "The woman who works in the café helped us search. She unlocked every room."

"What about the deserted restaurant across from the hotel?" he asked. "The boards would have to be pulled off the door."

"Yes, that's been done."

The sheriff let go a deep sigh. "All right. As soon as I hear back from the man searching the outskirts and vacated buildings, we'll mount up and begin a sweep of the outlying land. You girls best go back to your room so nothing else happens to the rest of you."

Mavis looked him in the eye. "You've got to be kidding."

"Exactly," Belle added, a hint of exasperation in her voice. "I think you forget we're Brinkmans, Sheriff. Our father and our grandfather helped to build this town! We won't quit until we have our sister back—and not a moment before."

CHAPTER TWENTY-SIX

Fifty feet from the peddler, Blake called out. "Hello, wagon!" A picture of Katie bound and gagged in the back kept rolling around in his head. He remembered the night Mrs. Brinkman, after supper was finished and the dishes were dried and put away, had let each older girl, with her help, hold two-week-old Katie for a few minutes. Blake, still feeling like an outsider, hadn't expected a turn. When Mrs. Brinkman had asked, he'd shyly nodded, carefully balancing a pink-faced Katie in his arms. The tiny blanket-wrapped bundle hardly weighed anything. And Blake had been astonished at how awake the infant was. He'd also been moved by the warmth he'd seen in Mrs. Brinkman's eyes when she regarded him. *Had she wanted a son?* In the candlelight, Belle sidled up, tipping her face as the infant gazed up at them with all the trust in the world. The memory was one of his favorites.

Blake's heart tripped. *Katie has to be alive. She just has to be.*

The rider looked back. Blake watched him lean over and say something to the driver. The wagon rolled on, but the rider pulled up and waited for him.

Blake plastered a wide smile on his face as he watched the man's gaze take in the sweat under his armpits—and then fall to his thigh, where his Colt should be strapped. To his relief, Santiago's horse did have a canteen looped around the saddle horn, plausible for a man setting off, but no saddlebags or bedroll. Selling himself might prove difficult.

The man was white. Middle-aged. Had seen his fair share of fights, judging by the scar at the side of his eye, another on his chin, and a disfigured nose.

"Howdy," the man said, low, out of the corner of his mouth. "Only a fool ventures the Old Spanish Trail without his weapon." He narrowed his eyes. "Or a desperate man. Which're you?"

Blake took a deep breath and slowly let the air escape through his mouth. He reached up, lifted his hat, dragged his shirtsleeve across his moist brow. "I've been called worse, I guess," he replied after a half-hearted chuckle. "Fool or buffoon. But it can't be helped. I never did take to guns; the loud blast gets my ears every time, as well as spooks my horse. Gave up on 'em long ago." He looked around. "Hot for this time of year, ain't it? Seen any banditos?"

The fella blinked back his surprise and then slowly smiled, revealing a row of stained and broken teeth. All Blake could think about was the retreating wagon.

A sly smile appeared. "Banditos? Not today."

Blake slouched in his saddle. "That's a relief." He started forward, and the man followed. "I'm on my way to the mining camp on the Animas River. Are you with the wagon ahead?"

"You talk a lot—for a stranger."

Blake shrugged noncommittally, but squeezed his mount. The horse extended his stride, forcing the other fellow to jog to keep up. Hoping not to get shot in the back, Blake pushed the horse into a slow lope. Soon, he was only a couple of lengths away from the wagon. He slowed to a walk. The other fellow reined up beside him, clearly perturbed.

Blake strained to hear anything. A woman's cries or struggles. But there were only the buzz of katydids, his horse's footfalls, and the crunch of wagon wheels on the dry earth. *Is Katie in there, bound and gagged?*

Has the worst already happened? He finally rode up alongside—to find an ancient Chinese peddler holding the reins.

"Well, howdy," Blake said, hoping that if Katie was inside, she didn't make a fuss if she recognized his voice. "I've been wondering who was driving." He felt a little more optimistic now that he'd seen the rider's companion. He couldn't be more than five feet tall. "I'm sure glad to meet up with y'all. Don't like riding by myself since I'm unarmed. There's safety in numbers, my pa used to say." He grinned like a fool and hoped he wasn't about to get the back of his head blown off. He didn't see any weapons on the driver, but that didn't mean the man didn't have a revolver hidden beneath the robe he was wearing or under the seat. His guard had plenty of firepower, though. Enough to make Blake a bit twitchy.

There! A sound. Maybe a boot heel along the floorboards. This deep sensation I have can't be wrong. Hold on, Katie. I'm coming, but this can't be rushed.

Blake pretended he hadn't heard a thing and began plotting how he'd take the rider first and then the driver. Beating up an elderly man didn't sit well with his conscience. Maybe after he had the tough-looking guard subdued, the driver would give up and hand Katie over. *What are the chances of that happening?*

A metal pot, a lantern, and other odds and ends hung from hooks on the side of the wagon. "You have any food for sale?" he asked. "It's a far piece to my destination. I set out rather off the cuff. This burning in my belly won't keep me for seventy-eight miles, give or take a few."

The peddler looked his way and studied him for several seconds. "Off cuff? Why dat?"

"I'm a messenger delivering a communication to the foreman of the Rio Grande Railroad Company. After getting my orders, I got to talkin' in the saloon, like men do. Being stupid, I rode out without any supplies. Now it's too late to go back. I should have packed a few edibles for the trip, but I didn't. I have money if you have any eats to sell." He waggled his eyebrows at the wagon and licked his lips. "Maybe you'd like to make a dollar on your ride down the trail? Whaddaya say?"

The rider was even with him again, and Blake gauged the distance between them.

"Message?" the peddler said. "Let us see."

Blake tapped his temple under the brim of his hat and smiled. "All up here. Every last word."

"You share with us, I give *eats*," the Chinese peddler said softly. "Not charge friend. Eats for free."

"I couldn't do that. Don't take charity. Never have. I'll pay my share. Besides, the message is private. Only to be given to the foreman. You fellas don't want me to lose my job, do ya?" He'd begun pleading about halfway through his little speech—and ignored the way the rider's gaze kept searching out the driver's. They wouldn't kill him just to kill him, but he had no doubt they would if they suspected he was really hunting for Katie.

The driver shrugged. "When we stop."

"I hate to beg, but I can't wait that long." He rode close to the wagon now. The guard moved to within arm's length. "My stomach is near on—"

A low, garbled "Help!" sounded from inside.

If he heard the cry, Katie's captors had as well.

Blake lunged across with his right arm and grasped the handle of the pot dangling on the side of the wagon. Swinging wide, he smacked the rider square in the face. The man fell from his horse like a sack of potatoes.

Before the guard hit the dirt, Blake swung back. The peddler halted the wagon and scrambled up in the seat. Several small silver daggers glittered in his hands. Blake had seen throwing knives like these before. They were fast and deadly.

With a speed of a rattlesnake, the Chinese peddler flung the first blade.

Blake spurred his horse, and it bolted forward. The blade sank deep in the leather skirt of his saddle. From the corner of his eye, Blake saw the peddler again raise his arm. Without thinking, he hauled back on the reins, then turned the horse on his haunches as a blade sizzled past his ear—and another his forehead. How many did the old man have?

Arm up again! This time, as if cutting a steer, Blake spurred with his left heel, making the horse jump to the side. The dagger impaled the canteen, and water spurted everywhere.

Blake charged the wagon. The frightened horses danced in their harnesses.

The driver must be out of knives because he'd turned to clamber inside.

Blake galloped forward, leaned from the saddle, and pulled the Colt from the holster belonging to the unconscious man on the ground. He vaulted onto the side of the wagon. Instead of entering from the front like the peddler had, he yanked open the back door.

Blake stared down the barrel of a shotgun.

A cry of pain pierced the air. The small man rocked to the side, and the shotgun fell to the floor with a clatter. Blake jumped forward and struck him in the head with the butt of the Colt.

Katie! Bound and gagged. Her eyes swollen red. Beaded sweat rolled down the side of her face, mixing with her tears. But there was no mistake. If she hadn't kicked the peddler's knee out from beneath him, Blake would be dead right now.

Relief coursed through him.

"I'll be right back, Katie. Give me one minute to make sure the other fella doesn't wake up and give us trouble." He cast a confident look at the knife thrower. "He's out good. I'll have you out of here quickly."

Blake jumped out into the sandy loam and strode over to the unconscious outlaw. The man's bloody face was smashed into the dirt.

The anger Blake felt at the sight of John's youngest bound and gagged smoldered in his gut.

Without any hesitation, he struck the man full force over the head again with his gun to be sure he remained unconscious until things with Katie were squared away.

He turned to the sound of a fast-approaching horse arriving in a plume of dust.

CHAPTER TWENTY-SEVEN

A cry of joy sprang from Belle's lips when she spotted Blake riding up the street with Katie behind him, her arms wrapped around his middle. Her face, covered with dirt and grime, showed the tracks of her tears, but it was still the prettiest sight Belle had ever seen. Blake's hat was pushed back, and there was no mistaking the grin on his face.

"It's Katie!" she called out. "She's alive!"

Along with Lavinia, Mavis, and Emma, Belle ran from the boardwalk after their tenth circuit around the town, searching every building from top to bottom as if for the first time. A congregation of people followed behind Blake, and Santiago rode proudly at Blake's side, his gaze straying often to her sister.

"What happened?" Lavinia called when they were within hearing distance. "Katie, where've you been?"

"Shame on you, Lavinia," Mavis chastised. "That can wait. How are you, Katie?" she asked instead. "Are you hurt?"

All Belle could think was, *Thank God!*

The two groups met in the middle of the street in front of Poor Fred's Saloon, and everyone pushed in tight. Santiago, looking more dashing than ever, dismounted first. He reached up and plucked Katie off the back of Blake's mount, setting her feet on the ground beside him.

Once her feet hit the dirt, Belle and the rest rushed forward, circling, petting, kissing.

"I'm all right," Katie said softly. She kept her gaze fastened on the ground between them. Her hands trembled, and when her face clouded over, Belle thought she was going to cry. "I'm just so thankful Blake found me." She turned into his arms and wrapped her own around him, causing a murmur in the crowd. She placed her head on his chest and closed her eyes.

Belle, thinking how much Katie hated confined areas, pushed back at the crowd. "Give her some breathing room. She looks white. You're not going to faint, are you, Katie?"

Katie shook her head.

"So what happened?" a man standing behind them called out. "Where've you been? The whole town's been searching for almost two hours. The sheriff and his posse are still out looking."

Santiago turned and glowered at him, causing a hush to fall over the crowd.

Katie opened her eyes and stepped away from Blake. "I was kidnapped."

Everyone gasped.

"The Chinese peddler and his hired man left with more than they arrived with," Santiago said with a sneer. "It was Blake who found her. I secured the scoundrels in the back of the wagon and drove them back. They're parked in front of the cantina."

Hot shivers coursed down Belle's spine. *And what did they intend for Katie? A life worse than hell.*

Blake still hadn't said anything. She turned to him.

"Thank you," she said softly. "You saved our little sister. You're our hero. We can never thank you enough."

Blake smiled shyly. "Without Katie's fast thinking, I'd be a dead man now, and she'd be on her way to Santa Fe or Mexico. She was pretty heroic herself."

Emma reached out and stroked Katie's shoulder. "Really? You saved Blake? Tell us what happened, Katie. Why did you leave the hotel room?"

Shame crossed Katie's face. "I was so stupid. Please forgive me. I—"

"Shh," Belle said softly. "Nobody's blaming you. Accidents happen, and that goes for a slip in judgment as well. We're all"—she looked around at the townspeople she was finally beginning to recognize—"just thankful you're here, safe and alive. Nothing else matters."

"We just want to know what transpired," another person called.

Katie took a deep breath, her lips wobbling.

Belle thought her little sister must be the strongest of them all.

"I was sitting by the window in my room when the peddler's wagon I'd seen before parked behind the hotel. At my teachers' school in Philadelphia, I'd read about Chinese medicine. Their remedies are so old. So fascinating."

The crowd pressed tighter, trying to hear. Katie's breathing became labored, and sweat slicked her forehead.

"Back up, everyone," Belle said. "Please give her some space. She doesn't like confined spaces." Blake offered Katie his arm as support.

"Mavis had gone to the mercantile," Katie said, "so I thought it couldn't hurt if I hurried out before the peddler passed through and asked a few questions."

She looked around apologetically, and Belle wanted to pull her into a hug, but she knew the townspeople, who had helped immensely in the search, did deserve to know. And the only way to make them stop asking would be to tell them the tale.

"The peddler was agreeable and only too happy to bring out a sample of a cow's gallstone, dried and sealed in a jar. Then a hornet's nest and snake bile. Then he began speaking about"—she snapped her mouth closed and leaned close to whisper into Belle's ear—"a male dog's long part, if you know what I mean. But he said the word that begins with a *P* to me." She looked around. "I became frightened. I thanked him and went to leave, but he grasped my arm. I pulled away, but someone grabbed me from behind and pressed his hand over my mouth. He wrestled me into the back of the wagon and locked the door."

Katie's face had turned pasty white.

"You don't have to talk about it, Katie. You've said enough already." She shook her head. "I want to, Belle. I must!"

"Let her speak," Blake said, low. "Better to talk now than have nightmares later."

That made sense to Belle. She noticed Blake's scar for the first time in a while, the one that had been so frightening when they'd first met. Now it seemed a part of him—a good part.

Tears leaked from the corners of Katie's eyes, and Santiago handed her a white handkerchief to wipe them away.

"I thought I would die. The walls pressed close. I couldn't breathe. The man was so large. I had no way to fend him off. He bound my hands and feet and then gagged me. I was sure I'd never see any of my sisters ever again." Katie gulped for air. "The wagon became hot. I cried and prayed. I prayed so hard I thought my heart would explode." She looked at them all for several long seconds. "The worst part was that you'd never know *what* had happened to me. You'd worry and search, and the whole thing would be awful, because I know how I'd feel if any one of you went missing." She reached out and touched Belle's arm, then Mavis, Emma, and Lavinia. "I don't think I could live through that. The wagon wheels turned and turned. Anger replaced my fear. I was furious at the men, but I was also livid at our father for living here! For demanding our return to this wretched place! Mother was *right* to take us away. Danger lurks on every corner. I had a lot of time to consider each and every moment. I wished I was back in Philadelphia. I thought if only I could get back there, where it's safe, I'd never leave again."

With trembling lips, she swallowed and then wiped more tears, which had again filled her eyes.

"And then I thought I heard your voice." She looked into Blake's face. "But I wasn't sure. I worried my mind was playing tricks. The gag was extremely tight. I'd only have one chance to alert you to my presence. I tried to calm myself, waiting for the right time. What if they killed you? I couldn't bear that thought."

Blake squeezed her shoulders.

"When I heard you speak like a country bumpkin, my heart rejoiced. That meant you knew I was there, and were trying to trick them." She smiled at Blake and looked around.

Belle encouraged her with a nod.

"But still I doubted. What if I was wrong? What if it wasn't Blake? What if whoever was out there rode off without helping? Fear almost overtook my resolve. I called out as loud as I could. Suddenly, they were fighting. Soon the old peddler appeared in the back, and I thought he was going to kill me because he hefted a shotgun." Her voice grew quiet. Blake tightened his hold. "But he didn't shoot me. He pointed the barrel at the back door and stood there. A moment later, Blake opened the door. That's when I lifted my bound legs and kicked the peddler from behind as hard as I could. He fell and dropped the gun."

Blake smiled. "Katie saved my life. I wasn't fibbing about that. The shotgun was aimed point-blank at my face. There wouldn't have been much left if he'd pulled the trigger. I'm in her debt."

Belle stood back as Blake started for the hotel with Katie under his arm and Santiago on her other side.

We were blessed to have found her before it was too late.

But one thing still worried her.

Is Katie right about Mother? Is Eden too dangerous for us all?

CHAPTER TWENTY-EIGHT

U nsettled by the day's events, Blake decided to remain in town for the evening to make sure Katie and her sisters were doing all right. After leaving them in the hotel room, he'd gone out and walked the streets, unable to get the picture of John's youngest in the back of the peddler's wagon out of his mind. If he didn't have the roundup tomorrow, he'd have booked a room himself. As it was, shorthanded, he couldn't spare an extra day. Finally, he'd ended up in the hotel café for supper. Blake folded his napkin and set the cloth on his now-empty plate.

"Is there anything else I can get you, Blake?" Karen asked. Perhaps he was being too conspicuous, dining in the hotel, but he wondered what was going on in the girls' rooms. He was sure as the sun would rise tomorrow that they were all together. *Will they decide to return to their city lives and not even last a month?* To his surprise, the thought disappointed him. He'd enjoyed the last three days. Belle asked intelligent questions. She'd ridden next to him and endured being saddle sore. He'd bet she'd shape up into a competent hand if she gave herself the chance.

Henry came through the hotel door just then.

Where has he been all day?

"Henry!"

Seeing him, Henry started for his table.

"Pull up a chair."

"I heard what transpired with Katie. How terrifying. And how fortunate to have your fast thinking. In a few hours, who knows what could have befallen her? I'm indebted."

"Nobody's indebted to anybody," Blake replied. "I'm just glad it's over and Katie is in one piece. Dr. Dodge just left her room. He's been checking in every few hours." He took a sip of his coffee and noticed the dark circles under Henry's eyes. "Where were you all day? After our talk in the street, you all but disappeared."

"I had business in Dove Creek. Got back an hour or two ago, and have been in my office."

Dove Creek? It was a small town north of Eden. *What could Henry have to do there?*

The whole thing sounded suspicious to Blake, but he'd not question his friend. He seemed to have a problem he was wrestling with.

Is going to Denver part of it?

Karen approached the table. "Henry?"

"Just a cup of coffee, if you have it brewed."

"Sure do. Coming right up." The waitress hurried away.

The two men looked at each other.

"What do you think the girls are contemplating after today?" Henry asked.

"Their applecart's been upended," Blake said thoughtfully. "And I really can't blame 'em in the least. When Belle told me she was staying in Eden tonight with Katie, the look in her eyes was unclear. None of the sisters would meet my gaze."

Henry shook his head.

"The thought of what could have befallen Katie freezes my insides, Henry. As cold and brittle as any blizzard." He looked out into the darkness on the other side of the window. "Before you came in, I was considering going up to their room to see if Belle had a moment to talk before I start back to the ranch." He switched his attention to the coffee at the bottom of his cup and then glanced at his friend. "I feel anxious inside. I'd like to speak with her, but I don't even know what I'd say."

"We can't make up their minds for them. And we can't make them stay."

"No, we can't. But in less than a week, I've become pretty used to having 'em in Eden. I can't say I won't be sorry to see them go."

"Yeah, I know what you mean."

Henry smiled at Karen as she set a cup and saucer in front of him as well as the sugar bowl. She knew him well—and the rest of the town too.

She stopped and tipped her head. "What's got you two fellas so down in the mouth? I'd think you'd be celebrating tonight."

"Nothin'," Blake said, knowing that wasn't the truth at all.

Henry slurped the hot coffee. "You go see if Belle wants to talk while I drink my coffee. Now I'm as interested as you are to see what they're thinking. Can't hurt to ask. You are their partner . . ."

Blake stood. Henry's nudge was the push he'd needed. "I think I'll do just that. I'd like to know what the future holds."

CHAPTER TWENTY-NINE

Blake found himself in front of room number three listening to undecipherable murmurs coming from within. Without giving himself time to decide what to say, he lifted his hand and rapped his knuckles on the wood. The low hum of conversation stopped.

Mavis opened the door, still dressed as she'd been earlier.

"Evenin', Mavis," he said, a little unsure of what to do with his hands since his hat still hung on the hat rack downstairs. "How's Katie tonight?"

Mavis opened the door wider so he could see Katie, Emma, and Lavinia sitting on the bed. Belle was in one of the chairs by the window. Belle watched him intently.

Suddenly feeling shy, he dipped his chin and smiled. "Ladies."

Still in her riding clothes, Belle stood and came over to the door. "Would you like to come in, Blake? I can get a chair from the other room. You're welcome to join us."

"I was actually wondering if you might have a moment to speak with me in private, outside. You know, with the roundup tomorrow, I just wanted to get a few things organized." *Well, that was a stupid thing to say. What on earth would she need to help with?* "You're a partner in the Five Sisters." He jerked his gaze up to look at the rest of the girls. "You all are."

Belle lowered one shoulder and looked back at her sisters. "Katie, you'll be okay if I go out for a minute or two?"

Katie sniffed. "Of course. I'm not a child."

Her smile looked like a scared little girl's. Blake didn't miss her red, puffy eyes. The direness of the situation had probably hit her after she was alone with her sisters. He didn't blame her in the least.

Belle looked up at him. "All right, let me grab my shawl."

At the dresser, she draped a feminine garment over her shoulders. "This is going to look silly with my pants and boots, but it's the best I can do at the moment."

"We'll get you a real jacket tomorrow," Blake said.

If you decide to stay.

Feeling like a square peg in a round hole, he followed Belle down the hall to the stairway, then descended into the hotel lobby. The café was quiet, most of the diners gone. Henry sat alone, a small smile on his face. Belle saw him and hesitated, but Blake directed her toward the door. He plucked his hat from the hat rack and donned it as they proceeded out into the night.

She gazed up at him, bringing a strange rush into his head. "Would you rather sit inside?" she asked. "The place looks pretty empty, so we'd have our privacy."

"I've been sitting in there for the last two hours. I need some fresh air."

She glanced up. "I thought you would be gone by now, on your way back to the ranch. Can the horses see in the dark?"

"They do fine, especially when they're familiar with the way. I'll head back to the ranch as soon as we talk."

She stopped. "This sounds serious."

"It is. We're worried about Katie. And the rest of you."

"We?"

"Me and Henry."

"He sent you to find out?"

Blake shook his head. "Nope, not at all. I've been pondering the situation for hours and couldn't stay away any longer. Are the five of you headed back to Philadelphia?" he asked straight-out. Beating around the bush never was his style. He was a straight shooter and always would be. He motioned to the bench in front of the hotel wall. They'd have a little privacy there. "Would you like to sit?"

Belle nodded and sat on the hard pine seat. She pulled her shawl more firmly around her shoulders.

Leaning forward, he rested his forearms on his thighs, knitting his fingers together in an attempt to calm his nerves. His sun-weathered hands looked dry, lined. He wouldn't win any beauty contests. The glow from two lanterns hanging on a nail nestled into the corner posts gave off plenty of light for him to see Belle.

He turned his head and looked at her. "Well, don't keep me in suspense."

"I don't deny that Katie wants to go home. The sooner the better."

"What about the rest of you?"

"I'm surprised to say Lavinia wants to stay, at least for the six months. While she was searching the town for Katie, she discovered the orphanage. She hasn't stopped talking about it since. I can tell she's anxious to get involved, which would be wonderful for the orphans—and also for her. She's always loved children and dreams of one day having a houseful of her own. If we do end up staying in Eden, I doubt we'll see much of her out at the ranch."

He nodded. *One to go, and one to stay.*

"To each his own. What about Emma? How's she feel?"

"She waffles back and forth, agreeing with whoever's talking, but leans more on the side of returning. She has a job in a knitting shop."

She glanced at his face, and he noticed her chapped lips. *She needs to wear her hat while she's ranching.*

"Don't laugh. I know that sounds silly, but she's worked there since she got out of school and loves the owners. They've been very caring and are more like parents to her than our detestable guardians ever were. The woman never had a daughter of her own, so she's taken Emma under her wing and taught her all she knows about wool, and the business. I think she fancies Emma marrying one of her sons. Emma's rather an expert on sheep and the different types of wool they produce. You should speak with her about her favorite subject sometime. I'm not surprised Praig heard her talking about sheep. She's written the owners faithfully every day, so if a vote were cast tonight, I believe she'd choose to return."

Woolies! Not my favorite subject at all!

"When and if we go back, we'd need to find a new place to live since we've learned the truth about the Crowdaires."

Belle shivered, and Blake wondered if she even realized she had.

She went on. "But that shouldn't be too difficult with the funds we'd have from Father's will." She gave a small laugh. "Since I know your next question will be about Mavis, I'll save you the effort. She's sympathetic to Katie's fear and Emma's homesickness, but she has hurtful memories of Philadelphia. Darvid's death, for one. I think she's willing to begin afresh. Take on a new life—here in Eden."

Two to go, one to stay, one undecided. What about you, Belle? How do you feel about Eden? About me?

"I know Katie wants to be a teacher," Blake said. "She'd have a chance if she stayed on because Eden's schoolmaster is about a hundred years old. Maybe that's not enough to sway her. I've never heard what *you* do in Philadelphia. I'm assuming you had a job too. You've never said what that is."

"That's because I'm shockingly bad at it. It's just a means to an end."

"I hardly believe that."

She sent him an incredulous stare. "I work for a caterer. Four nights a week."

Belle? A waitress? He couldn't picture that in the least after seeing her ride and ranch. "And your vote?"

"You already know how I feel. I'm promised to Lesley. You've met him yourself." The smile on her lips didn't reach her eyes. "He's waiting for me. And he wasn't all that pleased I'd committed to stay for the six months. So, until then, unless we go home early, I'm just biding my time."

Home? This is your home, Belle. You just don't remember that yet.

He pushed his spine to the wall, feeling it bite into his back and ground his wandering thoughts. "Yeah, that's what I figured." Rolling his shoulders, he sucked in a breath of fresh air. "So we begin the roundup tomorrow. That's what I really wanted to discuss," he said, changing the subject. "If all goes well, we'll be finished bringing them in, in about a week or two."

"Is that usual? Sounds like a long time."

"Pretty much. I'm factoring in our shortage of help. But we'll get the job done, the calves branded, the six-month-old bulls castrated, and the heifers checked for disease. It'll be a lot different without John. I still can't believe he's gone."

He blinked out into the darkness of the street. *After the girls leave, the town will feel so much lonelier than before they arrived. At least back then, everyone was hoping they'd return. Now that they're here, everyone would be sorry to see 'em go. Me included.*

CHAPTER THIRTY

Belle reminded herself that Blake was still grieving her father as well. He'd lived with him for eighteen years. *They must have had an incredible bond.* Blake hadn't said much, but at the strangest times, his eyes would fill with pain, and she'd know he was remembering. *He isn't made of steel, like he'd have me believe. And he doesn't have the support of four sisters to lean on.*

He'd looked so sad earlier, his head bowed as he listened to their plans about whether they'd leave Eden and return to Philadelphia. She needed to be support for him. Maybe talking would help.

She laid her hand atop his warm, entwined fingers to make a point. "We had a father who *loved* us, Blake, who *wanted* us, who was waiting for our return." She dropped her gaze to the boardwalk and shook her head. "Month after month, year after year. If that isn't the saddest thing I've ever heard, I don't know what is." She closed her eyes for a moment, letting a puff of cool air calm her mood. If she didn't get her emotions in check, she'd cry. "If only we could go back, do things over. I'd not trust Vernon and Velma for one second. I can see so clearly now how they manipulated all five of us. It's criminal."

"You're right. About the criminal part. But you're not to worry over them. Henry is doing his best. He'll find 'em. Until then, you let that go. If not, it'll eat you alive."

"It's difficult."

He nodded, looking at her hand still on top of his own. Slowly, she drew it away and folded it with her other. "Will you tell me more about my father? All we have are Mavis's memories. And mine, which are few and vague. We were so young when we left Eden. When I think back, I don't know if what I'm remembering is real or fantasy. We're desperate to know more about him. The man he was, the husband, the father. Please, Blake. You knew him so well."

Blake stared off into the darkness—the street was quiet, and the businesses closed. "On long winter nights, John shared a lot with me. It was his way to relive the memories. Keep them alive. I was only ten when I came to the ranch, and you all left a few months after I arrived, but I have all kinds of stories I think you'll enjoy. I'll be happy to pass on anything you'd like to know. John would want me to."

Excitement swirled within. She stayed the impulse to jump to her feet and run for her sisters. For now, she'd let Blake tell what he wanted. She'd pass on the information later. A warm feeling of home wrapped around her, and she didn't want to break the spell.

He glanced at her and then away as if deciding how much he should say.

"Please, don't spare my feelings."

"At times John would look so unhappy. And as a kid I didn't know any better than to ask him why. As far as I knew, he had a roof over his head and beef on the table. In my boy's mind, I couldn't conceive what he had to be sad about."

"What did he say?"

"'On occasion sadness, seriousness, or melancholy are better than carrying on and making jokes. It's when a person's deep in sadness that his heart's growing wiser.' I don't know if he read that somewhere or what. After he'd said it, he smiled and ruffled my hair, but I could tell his heart wasn't there. He was smiling to make me feel better." Blake's gaze softened. "Don't get me wrong, he was a happy man too. He wasn't always remembering back."

Belle wiped tears from her face.

A dog barked and then ran into the street on the heels of a scraggly cat. That was enough to lift the blanket of sorrow that had draped itself over her soul. "Do you know how he met my mother? Did he ever tell you?"

"You sure you want to know? It's sort of a sad story as well."

"I do—we all do. We've speculated many times."

"All right. I'll tell the story just like he told me. We were out minding the herd on a cattle drive. The coldest August I remember—a night so dark, with hardly a star to find, the campfire a bed of coals. I was grown by then, 'bout eighteen. He got talkin', more to himself than to me, and let the whole story roll off his tongue, loosened by a tin cup of whiskey. He'd been down all day, and I later learned that day was his anniversary. Sorry, I don't remember the date, but Henry might know."

Belle closed her eyes as she listened to Blake's velvety, deep voice. She could imagine her father opening his heart to the prairie sky in mourning for his lost family.

"Your grandfather Brinkman started the ranch but died when John was almost twenty. Eden was little more than a dot in the sand. About six or seven years later, I think, one day in late fall, a few settlers came along in a handful of wagons on their way to Oregon. They'd gotten lost and were hundreds of miles south of the usual trail that crossed the Wyoming Territory. Fearful of being caught in a snowstorm, they trudged on even though they said they had a wagon lagging behind. They were right. An early storm hit that week, bringing two or three feet of snow. Out checking the cattle one day, John found the stray wagon. Its driver, your other grandfather, Cranston Field, was deathly ill, and his daughter, your mother, frightened. John drove the wagon back to the ranch and tended Mr. Field for several days, doing his best to keep him alive. He fetched the doctor, but nothing could be done. Before the man died, he begged John to care for his daughter. Said they didn't have any other relatives that he knew of, or anyplace to send her. Well, your mama was a pretty young woman. John said she was tall and carried herself with dignity. She had an oval face with large blue eyes, hair the same color as yours, and a smile that would melt the snow. John was lonely, already liked her, and was on his way to falling in love. So they married."

Belle sat up. *Just like that? Mother had hardly known Father a few days, and she'd had no other option but to become his bride?* This was the first she'd heard of any of this, and the hasty union didn't sound romantic at all. It sounded scary. "How old was she?"

"I'm not real sure. Henry might know. Young, though."

"How young is young?"

"If I were to guess from the stories I've heard, I'd say sixteen or seventeen." He shook his head. "That's just a guess."

"And Father? How old was he?"

Blake chuckled. "I knew that was coming."

"And?"

"Twenty-six? Twenty-seven? But like I said, check with Henry. He has more of the facts written down, whereas I have more of the memories in my head."

Well, their meeting wasn't the romantic story Belle had imagined, but it did, in a way, explain how her mother could go off and leave their father, taking her daughters away. From what she'd just learned, her mother had never chosen to live in rustic Eden in the first place. Maybe didn't even want to marry John Brinkman—or anyone. She'd said her vows out of necessity, with nowhere else to turn. Still, she'd borne five daughters with their father. *Didn't that mean anything? Hadn't they fallen in love after six years?*

"You're awfully quiet," Blake said, breaking the silence.

She played with the tassel of her shawl. "Their marriage sounds like a business deal. We'd heard from Vernon how deplorable Father was, and so we all just thought . . ." She glanced up at him, feeling like a child who believed everything was meant to be a fairy tale, when she knew, especially after this month, there wasn't such a thing.

This time it was Blake who reached over and placed his hand on hers. "We can't know everything about the past, so best not to speculate. It's fine to have your musings. Nothin' wrong with that. But you're pretty fast to write love off."

What does he mean? She studied his face, trying to find the answer.

"Who says they weren't in love?" His coffee-scented breath brushed her face. "How does having to wed out of necessity change anything? Maybe in the beginning . . ." He looked off into the street. "That sweet union between two people, when it's done right—and what I mean by that is it's wanted by both parties, given and taken in gentleness and openness—is mightier than any sword of the strongest steel, and possesses the power to accomplish anything in the world. If that love is nurtured, there's no stopping . . ." He swallowed and glanced down at the boardwalk.

Of course he's remembering his wife, Ann. How much he must have suffered.

"According to your father, he and your mother had a bond of love that would last forever. I believed him—and you should too. I don't even remember my mother."

"Tell me, Blake. I've been wondering about your family. Please."

He withdrew his hand and stood. "That's a story for another night. I need to get back to the ranch, so I best get movin'."

She surged to her feet, missing the warmth. "But I have so many more questions!"

"There's plenty of time. You're not leaving tomorrow, are you?"

She shook her head.

His little-boy grin said he'd known all along she wasn't going anywhere, but she didn't care. She smiled back. He'd already given her, *them*, so much.

"Take good care of Katie." His eyes searched hers. "I'm sorry she had to go through such a frightening ordeal. The thought of what could have happened still raises the hair on the back of my neck. Watch her close so she doesn't become fearful of everything, like—"

He snapped his mouth closed and looked away, breaking their gaze.

"Like? Like who? My mother?"

"I didn't mean anything. I'm just rambling. I need to get to the livery, hitch up my team, and get movin'. I'm my own worst enemy, relaxing all evening."

She gave a soft laugh. "I'm sorry I backed out on helping at the roundup. I know how shorthanded you are, but I don't want to leave Katie. Not just yet. We're all so close that when one hurts, we all do as well. I think tomorrow we'll spend a quiet day in the hotel not doing much of anything."

"That sounds like a worthwhile plan. Don't worry about the ranch. We'll get through fine. I have the men . . ."

"But not Moses."

Blake shook his head. "Nope, not him. Not riding yet, anyway. Takes a little longer than that for ribs to heal. But he'll help with the cooking. He's a hard man to keep down."

There was a history between Blake and Moses, but she didn't quite know what. Later, when she and Blake had another chance to talk, she'd ask him. And about his life with her father, and before. And what wound could have caused such a scar.

The scar. It's practically invisible to me now. Tonight had been all one-sided.

The hotel door opened and Henry stepped out, his gaze tracking back and forth between them. "Belle." He dipped his chin. "Blake. You have a nice talk?"

"I'm just heading out," Blake said, stepping around the question nicely. "I've things to get done before the rooster crows tomorrow."

She reached out and touched Blake's sleeve. "*Thank you* for sharing your memories. It felt like Christmas tonight, the best Christmas I've ever had. I look forward to hearing more when you have the time. I'll pass on everything you said. You're going to be an extremely popular man around the Brinkman girls."

He dropped his gaze to the boards under Henry's feet.

She didn't want him to leave. *Is the reason because he'd known Father so well? Shared quiet talks, worked over problems, shared the secrets of their souls? Or is it more than that?* Her heart felt full and warm and overflowing with wonder. She liked the sensation and wanted to keep it forever. Still, she knew that was silly and impossible. "Have a safe trip back to the ranch." She turned to Henry. "It *is* safe for him to drive the wagon at night, like he's going to do? He wouldn't tell me the truth if I asked, I'm sure."

Henry laughed, a warm expression moving over his face. "Sure it's safe, Belle. Should I head out to the ranch with the contractors tomorrow, or after today, are we putting the construction on hold?"

Both men stared a hole through her forehead.

"Considering the circumstances, Henry, it's best we wait."

Henry nodded and started across the street toward the mercantile and his upstairs office. "Thought as much. Good night, you two."

"Good night," she called to the attorney's retreating back.

She thought she and her sisters had already made the tough decision, but now it had to be discussed some more. If she had anything to say about it, nothing bad would ever befall them again.

CHAPTER THIRTY-ONE

H enry looked at the clock on his bedroom highboy. Seven o'clock. Was that too late to call on Elizabeth? He needed to speak with her. He'd been circling the situation for hours, even during his ride back from Dove Creek. Any chance at sleep tonight depended on whether he was able to put a few of his ducks in a row.

He grabbed his hat and went out the back door. The boardinghouse, simply named The Boarding House, was two streets over, between the livery and the Hole in the Floor Saloon. Not the best side of town, to say the least, but that was why the rates were affordable. Unlike the smaller shops and businesses, which sat on one side of the street or the other with an alley behind that backed up to another business, the boardinghouse was a large, freestanding building, three stories tall, and took up two lots. It was squarely set in the middle of the parcel of land, and accessible from either Falcon Haven or the Old Spanish Trail.

Henry had offered to pay so that Elizabeth could stay in the hotel until the matter had been resolved, but she'd flatly refused. *What matter? Even if Johnny were John's son, nothing in the will provided for him.* He couldn't change that. The Brinkman sisters and Blake weren't obligated to do a darn thing if they chose not to, but knowing them all, he felt pretty certain they would. She'd said the boardinghouse suited her fine and that she'd pay him back just as soon as she was able. She wasn't looking for charity.

No, just an inheritance. Which could rightly be her son's, his mind countered. *Could be, but might not be. John had never mentioned his liaison with Elizabeth once in the last four years, which a lonely man might do at one point or another, one would presume. There are so many ifs, ands, or buts with this predicament.*

Arriving at the boardinghouse, Henry's resolve began to melt. He'd never been shy before, so why now? Striding up the dirt path to the wraparound porch, he mounted the steps. Not needing to knock, he quietly stepped inside and went directly to the parlor, but found it empty.

I should've known.

Henry pushed through the kitchen door. Sebastian, the widower who owned the place, came in through the back door at the same time. The man was tall and thin; the only hair left on his head was a line above his ears. "Henry, hello. What can I do for you?"

Now he was stuck. He'd wanted to get in and get out unnoticed, but that game was up. "I was hoping to speak with Mrs. Smith, but I see she's already retired. I'll come back in the morning, which I should have done in the first place."

"She just turned in not three minutes ago. Would you like me to knock on her door?"

"No. Her son may be asleep. I wouldn't want to wake him."

"Actually, I'm here."

He turned. Elizabeth stood in the doorway, clutching the curved handle of a blue-and-white porcelain pitcher. The pottery appeared heavy as she rested the bottom on her other palm. He swept his hat from his head.

"I've come for fresh water. I spotted several ants floating in this," she said in explanation. "Did you need to see me, Mr. Glass?"

"I did. I mean, I do. If you can spare a moment."

Her light-brown hair was swept up in a messy bun on the back of her head, and she looked tired. He wondered what she'd done all day.

"I have time. Let me dump this and take some fresh water back to the room."

He nodded, still holding his hat. "Of course. I'll wait for you on the porch."

The two men stood in silence as she worked the pump, refilled her pitcher, and then disappeared in the hall as quietly as she'd come.

Sebastian leaned back onto the counter. "Business?"

"Isn't it always?" Henry replied a bit defensively. Everyone knew he was married to his work, obtaining a good amount of his clientele from the railroads, as well as the several mines and ranch owners around the area. He never socialized or had female companions, so Sebastian's comment struck a nerve.

"Fine, then," Sebastian replied curtly. He'd received the message loud and clear. He started for the doorway between the parlor and the kitchen. "I'll just be off myself. I presume you'll make sure Mrs. Smith is safely inside once you're finished with your jawing?"

"I will."

"And put out all the lanterns except the one by the front steps?"

"Yes."

Sebastian left the room. Henry started for the front door, wanting to be outside, in the cool air, before Elizabeth reappeared. He walked around one side of the porch and then settled on the north side of the building, which faced the Toggery across the street.

Henry stood when Elizabeth came out the front door. She'd added a shawl across her shoulders, and he couldn't discern the look in her eyes. He didn't know her well. She approached rather slowly, and he realized the last few days must have been strenuous for her.

"Thank you for agreeing to speak with me." He waited as she took a seat. "I understand it's late, but I've been gone all day. I have several matters I'd like to clear up, but first, how's Johnny? Is his fever gone?"

Her face softened. "Much better, thank you. He sat up most of the day. Seeing him so sick gave me a fright. I don't know what I'd do if I lost him too." She gave a wobbly smile.

Henry didn't miss how she'd tacked on the word *too*. She'd lost John and now didn't want to lose his son as well. That was understandable—if she were telling the truth. He hated feeling so hard-hearted, but he had an obligation to John. To Blake and the girls. He had to have the truth.

A wagon rolled by, moving toward the edge of town and the cantina. The driver glanced over, nodded to Henry, and then looked back at the two donkeys pulling his wagon.

Henry adjusted his posture. "I don't mean to rush you, Mrs. Smith, but I need a few questions answered. I sent a telegram today to a friend of mine in Denver. He's a judge who knows many people. I went to our neighboring town of Dove Creek to do it so nobody here would be alerted. I want proof of who you say you are before I tackle your case. I hope you can understand my reasoning. John Brinkman was a good friend of mine. I've been his attorney for years. What you claim is quite difficult to prove, especially since he's passed on. What I'm leading up to is this: I'm going to need answers from you tonight to a handful of personal questions. In all honesty, I don't know you from Adam. It's time to dig deeper into your claim. And too, even if what you say is true and Johnny *is* John's son, I'm not sure that will result in any type of monetary compensation for him. What is it you hope to accomplish here? I can't bring John back from the dead."

For one instant, her nostrils flared the tiniest bit. *Did I strike a chord? If yes, what had it been?*

CHAPTER THIRTY-TWO

Henry gave Elizabeth time to gather her thoughts. She looked rattled, and he didn't blame her. He didn't want to know the details of John's and her private affairs, but he had a responsibility to get to the bottom of Johnny Smith's paternity. Elizabeth was the one who had opened the can of worms, but he was the one who would have to sort through the facts.

She dropped her gaze to the boards beneath his feet. The evening was cool. A host of night sounds broke the silence around them. The hoot of an owl. A coyote serenading the moon. He fought not to look at her. Now, in order to help her son, she'd have to tell a stranger about meeting John and the few days they'd spent together. Pity grew in his belly. *Raising her child on her own couldn't have been easy.* Why he should care so much had him a bit mystified, except that she might have meant something to John. What kind of a woman was Elizabeth Smith—a name he was sure she'd made up to cover her true identity in case things didn't go as she hoped?

"Mrs. Smith?"

"Yes, I heard you. I knew that I'd eventually have to explain everything if I came to Eden. I don't blame you, Mr. Glass; it's just a bit private, if you can understand. Please don't feel bad about having asked.

You want to know when and where I met John, and how Johnny came to be."

"That's right. Since John never mentioned you, I have to be skeptical. My position demands it."

They both took a breath and sat for a moment looking at each other.

"What you say will be kept in the strictest confidence. You can trust me."

She nodded. "It was five years ago April. I came to Denver with my longtime employers as the nanny to their three children. Each day, for several hours, I'd take the children and tour the parks, the museums, or for a carriage ride around the city. My employers were very wealthy. Any expense was not too much for the children."

"You're a nanny?"

In the dim lantern light, he watched as her cheeks grew rosy. He hadn't meant to cause her embarrassment. Her direct gaze and the way she held her chin made it difficult for him to believe she was lying.

"I *was* a nanny. And I loved my job. Since leaving, I've taken in sewing to survive. I've never before said this much to anyone, Mr. Glass."

He nodded.

"Mrs. Masters, my employer, knows a small portion of the truth. I had to tell her something when my condition began to show. She insisted Mr. Masters needn't know the details of my leaving their employ, which I'd been in for ten years. First in service and then as a nanny. After I moved and got set up as a widow in Denver, she wanted to help. Insisted on sending a small stipend. I want you to know, Mr. Glass, I've kept track of every cent, intending to pay her back. Without her help, I don't know what we would have done."

He rubbed a palm across his mouth, admiring her bravery. Not everyone would admit to such a past and risk ridicule and expulsion. He reminded himself to stay introspective. She hadn't yet proved her story.

"How did you and John meet?"

"Five years has softened the pain, but speaking about John is still difficult. We didn't know each other long—two ships passing in the night, you might say—but those few days were wonderful. A time I'll never forget." She took a breath. "We first met at the Denver Park. I had my little ones, ages three to eight, gathered around, and we were watching two small white bunnies hiding under a hedge. Every few minutes one would gather the courage needed to dash out, hop around on the lush green grass for a few moments, and then race back to his spot of safety in the blackthorn hedgerow, causing the children to laugh uncontrollably. John had been walking on a trail and heard us. He came to see what was going on."

Henry kept any expression off his face.

"He wore a pair of tan slacks, a midlength coat that was much too warm for the day, and a brown cowboy hat. The children were only too happy to answer his questions, and he seemed in no hurry to move on. As a matter of fact, he stayed with us for the rest of the day, walking and talking. He said he was a rancher, but didn't say where—or if he did, I didn't hear him. I had to keep a close eye on Leanne, the youngest of my charges, who was enthralled with a pair of mallards. I didn't want her to slip into the pond."

She looked off into the darkness and then back into his face. "What can I say? John and I liked each other. He was funny and kind. After hours spent caring for the children, speaking with an adult who was interested in my thoughts and opinions was nice. We held similar views on many topics."

Henry could understand that well enough.

"The next day, John was there again, waiting for us to arrive, with a large basket of food and a blanket. He'd brought a kite, a ball, and numerous other toys. He had such a wonderful way with the children. I found myself hanging on his every word, but I was still cautious, not knowing any of his history or where he was from. I didn't want to appear forward, so I didn't question him. The week passed with each day the same. We grew closer. That scared me. I'm an orphan. I'd been single all my life. It wasn't as if he was holding back about himself; we just found other things to talk about. Then one day, after hours spent sightseeing, he invited me to have supper with him after the children were put to bed and I had time to myself. I didn't know what to do. I struggled with whether I should encourage the budding relationship because of how we'd feel when we parted. Because parting *was* inevitable. I lived in Virginia with my employer's family. John hadn't even hinted at anything more."

If she was making this up, she'd done a good job with the details. She described John true to form. He enjoyed the small things in life, like fried chicken on a blanket, laughter, the feel of rain on his skin. She'd perfectly described his clothing and mannerisms. Was Johnny Smith really Johnny Brinkman? The thought brought Henry great excitement.

"That evening, after dinner, he invited me to his hotel." She looked Henry straight in the eye in challenge. "I'm not a loose woman, Mr. Glass, and I was thirty years old. Hardly a girl. I went because I wanted to, asking nothing from John in return."

He gave a slight nod but didn't say anything.

"Late that night, back in my hotel, I was awakened by Mrs. Masters. Practically in hysterics, she told me to pack the children's things. She'd ordered a carriage that would arrive any moment to take us to the train station. Because of the sensitivity of the subject, I won't share why she ran off without her husband's knowledge except to say he had broken her heart. I wanted to leave a note for John but didn't have time. I believed I'd be able to send a telegram to him later, to his hotel, after we arrived wherever we were going, but he'd checked out as well. I didn't know where to find him."

Poor John. Two women lost to him. One intentionally, the other by mistake. Henry wondered if that was really the case. "You said earlier that you'd seen an announcement about John in a paper?"

She nodded.

"Which one?" He'd supplied the obituary along with a photograph for halftones to several publications. John was an important figure in Colorado.

"The *Rocky Mountain News.*"

Correct. "What did you say you do for a living now?"

"Alterations in a tailor shop. That's where I saw the paper. A customer left the copy behind after a fitting. I was stunned to see John's face after all those years."

Henry studied the sentiment that had just thundered across her face. *Either she's a darned good actress or she's truly moved.*

The timeline worked.

A few feet over, Sebastian stepped out the front door. He looked at them a few moments before saying, "Your boy's woke up. He's calling for ya."

Elizabeth surged to her feet. "Thank you."

Sebastian nodded and disappeared inside.

She turned back to Henry.

"Are you all right staying here while I look into your statements?" he asked.

"Yes, thank you."

"Don't worry about the board. I'll take care of that. Can you give me a few weeks? I know that sounds like a long time, but I can't see it happening any sooner."

She nodded and hurried away.

Henry remained on the porch alone, thinking of his life since coming to Eden to do work for the railroads. That felt like a lifetime ago. Caught up in his work, he hadn't been lonely. Not so now. His chest pushed in with thoughts of going home to his quiet rooms above the mercantile instead of to a wife and family. He glanced at the door Elizabeth had gone through not two minutes before.

How will all this turn out? He was staring his most challenging case to date in the face—the face of a small boy.

CHAPTER THIRTY-THREE

In the quiet darkness of the morning, a wagon pulled up to the bunkhouse. Blake blinked several times to make sure he wasn't seeing things. Maverick Daves, the livery owner, held the lines of his team. Belle was at his side, Emma and Lavinia squished in next to her. They wore men's clothes, much as Belle had been in for her few days on the ranch.

"Well, what'a we have here?" he said, unable to hide his delight at seeing Belle back on the ranch so soon. He'd pretty much thought about her the whole ride from town and then most of the night, robbing himself of much-needed rest for the day ahead. John's dream of having his girls on the ranch meant a lot to him. But that didn't matter right now. He had the cattle to worry about.

Rubbing a hand over his unshaven face, he wrestled with inner conflict. *It is John's quest I'm concerned about, isn't it?* Just because seeing Belle now had his heart feeling light didn't mean a thing, and he wouldn't waver. *Losing Ann and Marcia darn near killed me.* Giving your heart could be deadly, a risk he never intended to take again. That pain had cut him at his knees. He'd never forget the day Ann went into labor—only to die hours later, along with his tiny daughter.

What about the conversation with Belle outside the Eden Hotel? So many feelings I'd thought dead.

KT stepped from the bunkhouse porch, followed by Tank. Both men helped the sisters to the ground. Blake had dwelled on their conversation last night for hours as he went about dressing, tacking up, and handing out orders. *So what if Belle had hung on every word? She was starving for knowledge of her father, nothing more.* Still, he couldn't deny he'd been moved by the wonder in her eyes and the way the sentiment made him feel.

Maverick stayed on the wagon seat. "I'm headin' back straightaway. As soon as I drop this gear at the house." A trunk and two carpetbags sat in the back of the wagon. "You have anything to go to town?"

The liveryman had an extra smile in his voice, and Blake knew why. He'd just spent a nice forty-five-minute drive talking with Belle and her sisters. "Naw. Thanks, though," Blake called as the smithy turned the jangling rig around. "Thanks for bringin' 'em out." The three young women were lined up and ready for orders, the ever-changing hat Lavinia wore so often nowhere to be seen. He narrowed his eyes. "I think."

Belle stepped forward. The wounded side of her he'd seen last night had been replaced with tenacity. She'd done some soul-searching—and maybe a little healing too. She had plans to show him what she was made of. "You have any complaints, Harding?" she asked playfully.

"Not a one."

She nodded. "Good. You and your men will be sufficiently pleased we decided to help. Don't you forget—we're Brinkmans." She puffed out her chest and looked around at the waning darkness. A few crickets still chirped in the dew-wet grass.

"So you've come to help with the roundup? All of you?"

She gave him a snappy look. "That's pretty obvious, isn't it?"

"Now that you mention it, I guess you're right." He liked pulling her leg. "Does this mean you're staying the six months?" Blake dared to ask, serious now, and totally uncertain of what her answer might be.

Caroline Fyffe

She shook her head. "No. Just that we didn't feel right leaving you high and dry. From what you've implied, there's a lot of work to be done. We've put off everything, like drawing our businesses, until the roundup is over. We may be inexperienced women, but there're things we can do to lighten your load. I'll help with the cattle, and Emma and Lavinia will assist with meal preparations. Just point them in the right direction . . ."

"Whaaa?" Trevor stepped out the bunkhouse door, pulling his suspenders up over his shoulders. He looked between the three with delight. "I thought I heard girlie voices out here. Did you change your mind about helping, Belle? You were getting pretty good in that Western saddle a few days ago."

"Maybe. Can I ride Gunner?"

Trevor's face fell. Like a child, he cut his gaze to Blake and then back to Belle. "He's my best horse. I have a couple others you might like. A smaller mount might suit you better."

Belle flounced over to the sound of a few chuckles and put her arm through Trevor's. "But I like Gunner. He and I are friends."

He actually lowered his head. "Sure, go on ahead. I don't mind."

"Mind *much*," Tank said with a laugh. "He thinks more of that gelding than he does his ma. If he says you can ride him, you're pretty high in his book."

Trevor pointed to the row of saddled horses on the far end of the bunkhouse. "He's over there, all ready to go. You're welcome to him."

She followed Trevor's gaze. When she spotted the horse, a small smile pulled her lips.

"How shall we proceed?" Emma asked.

"Tank put on a side of beef early this morning," Blake replied.

Lavinia gasped. "Earlier than this?"

Tank's lopsided grin made Blake laugh. "Just after midnight. Moses is inside packing the saddlebags. He's moving slow with his bandaged ribs, but he's getting around."

204

Emma, looking a little unsure, stayed close to Lavinia. *Perhaps she's been talked into this against her will.* Blake couldn't imagine what growing up with four sisters must be like. A moment of sadness pulled at his thoughts as he remembered his brother. *Long gone, but not forgotten.*

The sun had yet to rise. The fact that Belle and her sisters had gotten out here so early said a lot, the generous gesture not lost on him. Maybe they *did* have ranching in their blood, like John always said. Blake had thought those words were just wishful thinking, but now he realized perhaps ancestry did play a role in the way people behaved.

Lavinia's eyes went wide. "Then we should go in and help." The high, bright-red shoes she'd worn for the last few days had been replaced with ratty work boots.

"He'll welcome the help," Blake said. "He may be shy at first, but don't let that stop you. With the long days, we'll be especially hungry. By the way, where'd you get the duds?" He glanced at Belle. "I thought you bought up the last. Did the store get a new supply?"

"After our meeting late last night, we sought out Karen Forester." Lavinia placed her hands on her hips, looking self-assured. "She's a world of knowledge. She rounded up garments and boots from the townspeople. As soon as we replace them with our own, we'll give these back."

Blake nodded. "Fine, then. If your mind's set. You've arrived just in time for our departure. The horses are saddled, and we're setting out to different pastures as soon as we have our saddlebags packed with grub." He hitched his head. "I'm sure there's breakfast left inside if anyone's hungry."

Garrett came out of the barn leading his mount and joined the circle, unable to hide his pleasure at seeing the girls.

"That's right, Garrett," Blake said, not blaming the ranch hand in the least for the sudden spring in his step. "We've got us more help than we figured. Belle'll ride with me and KT to the south pasture. Garrett, Tank, and Trevor, go north."

Moses appeared, a cup of coffee in his hands. Blue strips of fabric wrapped his middle and all but covered the shirt of his long johns. A greenish-brown bruise still marred the right side of his face. He hadn't said anything about Praig, but Blake could tell he was stewing. He was a free man now but had grown up in slavery—and bore the scars to prove it.

"Moses!" Blake chuckled at his friend's surprise. "Your help has arrived. Lavinia and Emma are at your service. You won't have to peel that mound of potatoes alone."

Shocked, Moses took a stumbling step back and sloshed coffee down his front. "Oh no." His eyes were large at the prospect. "Nothin' doin'. I'll saddle up and help with the doggies."

Belle, having gotten to know Moses from their supper in the bunkhouse and later on the ranch, dashed up beside him and gave him a fierce hug. Moses's face screwed up in pain.

Blake coughed into his hand. "Not so hard, Belle. Ease up a little."

"Oh," she gasped and pulled back. "I'm sorry. I hope I didn't hurt you."

"Not *too* much. I came out to get help luggin' the saddlebags out. I'll just go right back in and pack another, being Miss Belle is joining ya."

Blake stepped onto the porch to follow. "I'll fetch the others."

Inside, he stilled his friend's arm as Moses moved to lift one of the loaded leather bags. "You're still sore. Let the girls work. This is their ranch. They need to feel connected—unless we want them running back to the city."

Moses studied him for a good five seconds.

Blake couldn't take the scrutiny any longer. "What?"

"It's good to see that look back in your eyes, Blake." He placed his large, warm palm on Blake's shoulder. "Been too long. Wasn't sure if it'd ever return."

Heat rushed to Blake's face. "I don't know what you're talking about. Just thinkin' about all the work there is to do. Cattle to brand, cut, doctor, and no one else to do it but us. I better get my backside in that saddle."

Moses winked, and then a smile stretched across his sore-looking face. "Just keep tellin' yourself that. You know I'm right."

Blake hefted two heavily loaded saddlebags over one shoulder and another two across his arm. He made for the door before Moses had a chance to say anything else.

"Get your bags, boys!" he called, anticipating the day with new fervor. "We've work to do."

Moses had struck close to home. When Belle laughed and joked as she was now, out in front of the bunkhouse, she reminded him so much of John. As pleasing as it was, it was painful too.

And what about the other feelings she conjured up inside him? The longing for intimacy he hadn't felt for four long years.

That scared him more than he'd like to admit.

CHAPTER THIRTY-FOUR

After an hour of riding, Blake reined to a halt. KT and Belle followed suit. They had crossed several large, flat, prairielike pastures as they approached the sloping terrain that led to the mountains. KT told her they'd look for the main herd as well as strays. When the cattle began to miss the others, they'd get restless and start a slow migration back toward the ranch, where they were rounded up a few times a year, and their feed supplemented in the winter. This way, they didn't have to ride quite so far.

"Thoughts?" KT said, turning in his saddle to look at Blake.

Belle was already hungry, but she wouldn't dare say anything to Blake. If the men could hold out until lunch without dipping into the saddlebags, so could she. To arrive at the ranch before the men left, she and her sisters had had to rise at an absurd hour. Karen's early wake-up knock had hardly left them time to eat. She'd gobbled down two hard-boiled eggs and a cup of coffee and thankfully accepted a stack of French toast wrapped in paper for the bumpy wagon ride out to the ranch. The clomping of Gunner's feet covered the frequent and embarrassing growls of her empty stomach.

Blake pointed to a hill covered in large rock outcroppings. "KT, you go up and over. Belle and I'll go around. I don't think she's firm enough in the saddle just yet to be pushing beeves through brush and over rocky ground."

"I can do—"

"I'm in charge," Blake interrupted. "At least *this* year. Next spring may be a different story. Until then, you'll follow my orders."

KT loped away without a word.

"He follows orders."

She harrumphed.

"We'll go this way." He pointed with his chin to a path.

"A cattle trail?"

He nodded. "What else? We're looking for cattle. A cattle trail seems like a smart place to start."

Again, she realized he was right.

The trail was only a foot wide. Tender green sprouts of new grass interspersed with the long, dry stalks from last year. The land challenged her heart. *What would Father say if he were riding beside me now? Would he be as happy as I feel?* They followed the path around the perimeter of the hill. Blake rode along, content with his thoughts as he scanned the underbrush and shrubberies.

She resisted admiring his form. By the way he sat in his saddle, it was obvious he was exceedingly strong, but his fluid movements also reminded her of a ballet dancer. She smiled to herself, thinking how he'd hate that comparison. Wide shoulders turned this way and that like a ship's boom, strong and straight. He glanced back to check on her often.

Those intense eyes, the way they light up when he laughs.

She'd like to know what he was thinking.

"You ever been to the ballet, Blake?"

He didn't even turn her way. "You're supposed to be looking for cattle."

"I am. I can think and look at the same time."

He twisted and regarded her, assessing her every fault, she was sure. "Why do you want to know?"

She lifted a shoulder. "Just wondered. You don't look like a man who would enjoy the arts." That was a lie. She wanted to see what he would say. He looked like *the* art himself. She made a valiant effort to appear to be searching the scrub oaks on her side of the trail. "But I could be wrong."

He chuckled. "You are. I've been twice. Once in Denver, and once at a small theater in Santa Fe. I enjoyed the performance greatly."

They rode on in companionable silence as she pictured him dressed in a suit, comfortable in a balcony seat upholstered in burgundy velvet, absorbing a romantic pas de deux between a striking prima ballerina and her handsome counterpart.

"You're pretty quiet over there," Blake said, breaking the silence.

"Just doing my job." She smiled when he glanced over. "How come we're riding so slowly? This would go much faster if we loped, or even jogged. You're not walking because of me, I hope."

"Nope. The last thing we want to do is startle the cattle and have them scatter. We want to sneak up on 'em and kinda suggest nicely they begin moving north, toward the ranch. If they scatter, it'll triple our time. That's why it's important to have more hands to do this job. Normally, we would have had two more sets of riders going east and west."

She thought about that a few moments. "How do you figure that?"

"Counting myself, we usually have eight wranglers. Sent out in pairs of two, we can cover all four directions. We lost three and gained one."

"If that's the case, shouldn't you have sent out three teams of two?"

He shrugged and looked away.

"Blake?"

"Just watching out for your reputation. Us riding alone wouldn't look right. At least, I didn't think so. Besides, you're just learning the ropes."

Her mouth dropped open. *Did he allude to us as a possible couple?* She was practically promised to Lesley, but, actually, she recognized he was right. *Thank heavens one of us thought this through. But does that mean he considers me a romantic interest?* She cut her gaze to the top of the horizon as heat rushed to her face.

His plan made sense, and Belle couldn't complain. If left to her own devices, and her preconceived notions, she'd have galloped up to any cattle she'd have spotted, making the chore all the more difficult. *Blake's right. I do have a lot to learn.*

The warmth on her shoulders felt like a heartfelt hug from her father. All her life she'd been a meticulously clean lady, proper in all ways. The sheen of sweat on her skin now actually felt good. Earthy. She glanced over. Blake didn't look hot at all. He was used to being out in the elements. He was as cool and collected as a cucumber-cream finger sandwich.

When she laughed, he glanced over, his face void of expression. "Something funny?"

"Just enjoying the ride."

Belle couldn't help but recall everything Blake had told her last night. Such a windfall of family history. She'd gathered Mavis and the rest around in the hotel room and shared how their parents had met and then married when their grandfather died. As she'd been with Blake, her sisters had sat spellbound, listening. They knew so little about their past. Their mother was alone and destitute, and their father the hero who married her to calm her dying father. The story could be in a novel, but with a teary ending instead of a happily ever after.

Affection surged into her throat as she thought of the graves back on the ranch. *So much love and heartache. What would giving myself to a man I hardly knew be like? Had Mother been terrified?* She glanced at Blake. *Father must have been much like him,* she thought. *Strong. Bronzed by hours in the sun. Was he as quiet and introspective as Blake?*

Or loud and humorous? Belle chanced another secretive peek. She was sure Blake still had so much to tell.

"You used to like to walk down to the corral and give apples to the horses."

She glanced over. He still looked all business, and yet he was about to give her another polished gem from her past. His memories were a part of her, locked away and out of reach. He was the connection. Somehow, out here in the wide-open sunshine, he'd picked up that she'd gotten sentimental and was remembering back.

"You and Mavis," he went on, his deep voice mixing with the sound of insects in the background, the call of a hawk, and the footfalls of their mounts. "Your ma would watch you from the porch of the house. You two would walk down to the corral hand in hand and wait for the friendlier broomtails to come to your side of the fence. John had taught you how to hold the apple slice on your flat-open palm. I kept an eye on you from the other side of the corral. Your eyes would grow as round as walnuts until the horses' probing lips took the treat, and then you'd burst into laughter." He glanced over, a self-satisfied grin on his lips.

Feeding apples to horses? Do I remember that? Frustrated, she searched her mind, trying to find a trace of what Blake had said. *Nothing. But there is the fact I never went to the park in Philadelphia without a sackful of sliced apples for the park ponies . . .*

"Belle? You've gotten quiet again. That makes me nervous."

Warmth pushed through her. "Just thinking. Trying to remember. Thank you for sharing. We're not seeing many cattle, Blake." Despite the clouds that had begun to gather in the sky, the sun was especially warm. "Where's KT? Is he coming over the hill?"

"No way to tell about KT. And there may not be any cattle in this spot. That's why it's called a roundup. You have to be patient. They could be anywhere."

She nodded, enjoying the ride. She thought back to when they'd first arrived in Eden, sparking a question she'd had from the start.

"Are you and Amorette sweethearts?"

The trail had narrowed, and he'd taken the lead.

Blake's head bobbed as if in shock, and he turned to look at her, a silly grin on his face. "Who? What did you just say?"

"Don't act like you don't remember the beautiful woman at Mademoiselle de Sells. The two of you were friendly, so I just wondered. There's no shame in admitting . . ."

He barked out a laugh. "No, Amorette and I are not sweethearts. She was a good friend of my wife's, that's all. I don't get to see her much these days."

The trail widened out. He pulled up and waited until she was again at his side. "So, what's Lesley like?" His gaze challenged her. He was getting her back for asking a personal question. "You two know each other a long time?"

Except for a few moments ago, she'd not given Lesley much thought over the last several days. There had been the excitement of being on the ranch for the first time in eighteen years, and then Katie's abduction. He'd popped fleetingly into her mind when she'd been telling her sisters how their parents met and married, but for the majority of time, *Blake* had commandeered her thoughts. The deep timbre of his voice had made her all but forget the sound of Lesley's. Shamefaced, she glanced away.

"Belle? You hear my question?"

"Sure."

Velma had introduced her to Lesley and had been in favor of the match. Belle blinked several times, having never thought of that angle before. Velma had also been very interested in the progress of their friendship. *Did that mean anything?* She'd never asked Velma how she knew Lesley, or what she knew about Lesley's family business. *The Atkinses and the Crowdaires didn't travel in the same social circles . . .*

"You're taking so long to reply I thought you didn't hear me."

"I've known him about a year, and we've been stepping out for several months. He's tremendously smart. He's twenty-seven and works for the family business. They're draftsmen, architects, and investors in real estate." She glanced his way. He had his hat tipped up and was screwing the top back onto his canteen. "Which means they draw intricate plans for large homes, office buildings, and a few warehouses."

"I know what an architect does. You see all those books in the ranch house? I've read 'em all. Your pa insisted I spend my evenings wisely. I'm well read, if nothing else."

"*That's* why you don't sound like the other townsfolk I've met. I haven't been able to put my finger on why, but that makes perfect sense." She smiled, thinking of her father and Blake settled in comfortable chairs, blankets over their laps as they read by the light of a lantern.

"Oh, really?" His voice was thick with cynicism. "You've been evaluating me and comparing me to everyone else?"

"Well, yes . . ."

"And is Eden so different from your home?"

His tone reminded her of the day they'd first met in Henry's office. When he'd hated them all for being so heartless. That felt like a year ago. "Yes, again. I'm sorry if you think I'm being uppity, but the differences are vast. Eden is nothing like Philadelphia. Nor are its people, climate, or opportunities. But that doesn't mean I like Eden less." She gave a small shrug. "I'm coming to like it more."

"You've skillfully changed the subject from Mr. Atkins. Are the two of you getting married? I just need to know how many hands I'll have to let go once you and your sisters take the payout and leave."

Irritation sizzled inside Belle. "Who says we're going to give up our shares of the ranch? We can still be owners even if we don't live here, can't we? After we stay the six months? That's what Henry said."

He looked away and rubbed his chin. They rode along, side by side, thinking about everything except cattle.

"Sure," he drawled, cowboylike.

He's never sounded that way before. He's angry.

"But to get to that point, you'd have to winter in Eden. I don't think you're tough enough for that. This part of Colorado gets real cold, and there're times when we're snowed in for days. I can't see you enjoying it that much."

Angrier than before, she turned in the saddle and glared at him. "Don't be selling us short, Harding. How on earth do you presume to know what's to my liking and what's not to my liking? And whether I'm a hothouse flower or a spiky cactus? We've just met. I barely know you from any of those other men I've seen walking down the street of that hick town you call Eden. And you certainly don't know *me!*"

He nodded. "True enough."

That's it? That's all he's going to say? What nerve.

"Maybe that architect might want to move to Colorado, do a little ranching," Blake finally said. "Did you ever consider that?"

"No, I haven't. And I hardly think that's a possibility. Lesley enjoys spending a day in a museum or art gallery. He doesn't like a speck of dust on his shoes. I hardly think he's going to walk around Eden, where manure is plentiful. Or where the only art to see is a view of the faraway mountains."

"Doesn't he ever work?"

The innocent tone made her want to snap. *He's baiting me. How could I be so stupid, to fall for his shenanigans?*

"Of course he works! But he enjoys leisure as well." *Why am I even responding?* Unsettled by Blake's questions, she kept her face turned away so he couldn't see her agitation. She'd enjoyed today so far, riding the lonely countryside with Blake—until he began asking all these unanswerable questions. *Darn the man.* She opened her mouth to tell him what she thought, but he snapped his fingers and pointed.

Twenty feet off, grazing peacefully, were about thirty steers.

"Keep quiet. I don't want to chase 'em down if we don't have to."

They looked edgy, ready to bolt.

"What do you want me to do?"

Again, he rubbed his chin for several long moments. "One thing I *don't* want is to get you hurt."

"I'm not going to get hurt. Tell me what to do."

"Fine, then. Just know if you face Gunner at a steer and the critter tries to dart away, he'll cut the steer—I mean, cut him off. Be ready or you'll end up on the ground. And keep your weight in your heels. There's no shame in grabbing the horn if need be."

He sure doesn't think much of me. "I can ride." She looked down at the rope tied to her saddle. "Should I get this out?"

He shook his head. "I want you to quietly ride over to that clearing and just stand there while they settle. Once they see you coming, they're gonna get edgier than they already are. I'm gonna circle around that way, pretty far away, and then come on them from that side." He pointed. "Then we'll both push 'em back the way we've come. Slowly. Don't be frightened of the cattle. They're afraid of you—or I should say, your horse."

"Blake, you're beginning to make me really mad. I told you—I can ride!"

"On a park pony and a sidesaddle. I've a good memory."

So he did. She'd been hoping he'd forgotten that statement, but she'd been wrong. She felt totally comfortable in the Western saddle. The creaky-soft seat was much too large for her, but she could manage. The saddle horn, bound with supple leather wrap, was comforting. She could grab it in case she lost her balance—which she'd only done a few times. Nothing was going to make her fall.

"That was then," she replied, buoyed by the wonderful feeling the elements around her had created. The gorgeous cerulean sky dotted with puffy white clouds reminded her of dollops of fresh-whipped cream. The sunshine mixed with the crisp, sweet-smelling air. The fact that Blake sat on his horse twenty feet away, watching her every move, didn't hurt either.

Excitement pushed at her insides. "As I was saying . . . that was then, and this is now. Let me show you how it's done." She sank into the heavy stirrups as she'd seen him do many times. "Watch and learn."

CHAPTER THIRTY-FIVE

S louched over a stack of official forms, Clint silently cursed the paperwork that went along with being sheriff. He'd put the task off for months, and now he was paying the price. The pencil wobbled in his hand. *Damn it.* He'd always been a clumsy writer because he had difficulty holding his pencil. Mr. Edwards, his teacher, had taken delight in rapping his knuckles with a ruler more times than Clint liked to remember. *Give me a pitchfork any day.* Cleaning ten stalls sounded like a vacation over writing one lousy report.

Movement outside caught his eye. He glanced up.

At the sight of Mrs. Applebee headed his way, his arm jerked forward, knocking over the stack of documents. They flew out and scattered on the floor, settling just as the oldest Brinkman daughter walked through the door. In her hands was a large tray from the hotel's café.

He bolted to his feet, hoping she didn't notice the mess strewn everywhere.

She stared, and then her gaze flew up to his, a comical twist lifting her mouth.

"Good day, Mrs. Applebee." He totally ignored the littered floor.

"Good day, Sheriff Dawson," she replied, still holding the tray.

"What do we have here?" He came forward and lifted the red-and-white checkered napkin protecting the food. "Fried chicken! My favorite."

"Food for the prisoners—not that they deserve any."

Okay, so the meal wasn't for him. He could live with that.

"If it were up to me, I'd let them starve."

He had to give her credit. Not once since she'd come through the door had she looked over to the cells that held the two men who'd absconded with Katie Brinkman, each wearing a wicked stare.

She has guts, to say the least.

Reaching forward, he took the tray and placed it on his desk between the reports. Just like the first time they'd met, she still wore the gloves that looked so out of place. Her sisters didn't, and he wondered why she was different. *Does she have a strange sense of style?*

"Kind of you. I was about to head to the café myself. To pick it up."

She hedged a small smile. "Not kind at all, Sheriff." Her nostrils flared just the tiniest bit. "I went to the café to pick up lunch for Katie and myself, and Karen was just finishing up with this. I mentioned that I was planning on speaking with you, so she asked if I'd please bring this over. They're shorthanded today."

All right, she did the nice deed for Karen, not for me, and wasn't too timid to say so. He liked a woman who was up front. Left little room for confusion. Still, his bubble did burst, at least a little.

"Well, I thank you anyway, for saving me the steps."

She eyed the mess on the floor. "Do you need help?"

"No, ma'am. Thank you all the same. You said you had a question for me?" He did his best to look agreeable. "How can I help?"

"I'd like to speak outside."

He nodded and let her lead the way out. On the boardwalk, she took a deep breath as if she needed to clean her lungs.

"Sheriff, I can't be away from my sister for long, so I must make this fast. Because of what happened yesterday, Katie is terribly frightened.

Every time she hears footsteps in the hotel hallway, she about jumps out of her skin thinking those disgraceful men are back. It's unsettling with them so close. How long will they be here?"

"Until they're tried and sentenced for their crime."

"And how long will that be? I have no idea how things work around here. Everything is so small and close together. In Philadelphia, the police station is blocks and blocks away from everything. Knowing they're right across the street is discomforting. Isn't there anything else you can do with them?"

"Do, Mrs. Applebee? What can I do? We have to wait for a judge to come through on his monthly rotation. And that too can be hit-and-miss. I've put out a telegram, but now we just have to wait."

Her toe began a steady tap on the wooden boardwalk as she considered his words.

"Your office is kitty-corner to the hotel. We can easily see it from my room, where we spend much of our time. Is there really nothing you can do, or are you just saying that?"

Affronted by her question, Clint straightened. "I don't lie, Mrs. Applebee. I assure you there are no other buildings secure enough to hold those men. If they were to escape, they'd be a real threat to Katie, or anyone else, for that matter—have you thought of that? What's worse? Having to see the place where they're locked up, or having them kidnap another unsuspecting woman?" As irritated as he was by her accusation, he couldn't help but admire her concern for her sister. "There is something you could do, though."

"Me?"

"Yes. Close your curtains. Don't look out. Or move to another room. That would solve everything."

She folded her arms. "I can't see the wind, but I know it's there. Every time we take a walk, Katie will be reminded."

"Sheriff!" one prisoner yelled. "We're hungry! That fried chicken smells good."

He ignored the men. "I'm sorry. There's no other place to keep prisoners. After what's happened, I assume you and your sisters will be returning east. None of you bargained for such a wild and unlawful place, I'm sure."

"We're taking one day at a time. Do you know the men? Do they have a reputation in Colorado?"

"I've never seen 'em or heard of 'em before yesterday. I'll let you know if I find out anything substantial."

"I appreciate that."

"Perhaps Katie would feel more comfortable out at the ranch? I can arrange for transportation. I heard your other sisters went out early this morning . . ."

Her mouth pursed. "My, news gets around."

Warmth crept up his neck. "Yes, ma'am. It does."

She looked over her shoulder and through the doorway at his paperwork scattered haphazardly over the floor. "You're sure I can't be of help, Sheriff Dawson? Your paperwork is taking over your office."

"No, I was just . . ." He gave a hearty chuckle. She smiled for the first time since her arrival. "I do appreciate your concern. I can straighten out my own mess, which I plan to do just as soon as you leave. I'd just rather be chasing after an outlaw then filling out a mountain of forms."

She departed, and he walked back inside, wondering if he should have taken her up on her offer to help. He wouldn't mind spending a few hours in the same room, even with her spiky attitude. He hoped maybe next time she stopped by, the fried chicken she brought would be for him.

CHAPTER THIRTY-SIX

B lake was thankful it was finally time to quit for the noon meal. Belle looked like a well-worn cleaning rag that needed to be tossed in the wash bucket. Tangles of hair dangled in her dirt-streaked and sun-burned face. She'd placed her hat firmly on her head, but at the first sign of action, the Stetson had tumbled to the ground and landed in the dirt. Then it had been dislodged by a gust of wind that had come up from the clouds gathering in the sky. Startled by a calf, Belle had knocked the hat off again herself when her arm jerked up in surprise. After dismounting to retrieve the headpiece and then remounting Gunner several times, which wasn't easy on the tall gelding, she'd cursed quietly and stuffed the nuisance into her saddlebag, against his strong protests.

"Belle!" he called loudly as she pushed five unruly steers out from behind a grouping of trees and toward the herd KT tended half a mile away. Once the steers caught sight of the others, they'd trot along by themselves to join the herd. "As soon as you get those on their way, come over and let's eat. It's time for a siesta. I don't know about you, but I'm more than ready."

You certainly are, judging by your slouching shoulders and sunburned face.

He'd risen at three thirty and eaten at four. The thought of closing his eyes, even for five minutes, was all-consuming.

Raising her arm, Belle waved back and forth to signal that she'd heard him. He admired her gumption. She'd not complained one iota. He smiled, remembering the first time she'd faced a steer that had a mind to go the other way. Gunner had dropped down and cut the bovine, sending her sharply to one side. Surprised, she screeched, grabbed the horn, and pulled herself back aboard as Gunner continued to do his job. She'd hung on like a badger to a raw steak. Her gaze had sought his, which pleased him. Once she'd regained her balance and hunkered down into her seat and stirrups, the cow horse gave Belle her first real lesson. Soon the steer had been turned back, and a beautiful smile had blossomed on her face.

Blake unbuckled the saddlebags attached to Banjo's saddle, watching Belle from the corner of his eye. The shade felt good. *What was I thinking? Today will be much too long and demanding for her to keep up. I should have known better than to allow her to come. She could have stayed back with her sisters and helped Moses with the cooking.*

Setting the leather bags on the ground, he loosened Banjo's cinch, hobbled his front feet, and then slipped off his bridle, having already watered the horses at a nearby stream. He plopped down on a grassy spot and began unloading the food. Belle, on a sweat-stained Gunner, started toward him, slumped in her saddle.

He stood to go help, but she waved him away.

"Go on and eat. I can do this myself." She passed him at a slow walk toward the trees where Banjo grazed.

Ignoring her, he followed behind. She reminded him of John in so many ways. *His stubbornness, for one. And that serious tilt to her brows, another. Amazing how that happens.*

"At least let me help you down. You're going to be sore, I can tell you that."

"It won't be anything new."

"I think you're wrong."

She halted. Her face twisted into a grimace when she moved to swing her leg over Gunner's back.

"Swing it forward, over his neck."

When she realized what he meant, she obeyed, lifting her far leg over the front of the saddle. She wasn't too proud to reach out with both arms. She might say she didn't want help, but she'd complied without much coaxing.

He lowered her to the ground. She groaned when her boots touched earth. Once her feet were squarely under her, she stood in his arms a few moments, leaning into his embrace and letting him take most of her weight.

She gave a strangled laugh. "I don't think I can walk. Every muscle in my body is on fire."

"This is my fault. I should have realized the light riding you've done over the last few days wouldn't prepare you for all-day gathering. I'm sorry."

"If you're really sorry, carry me over to the food."

He laughed. "I can do that." Without another word, except her gasp of pain, Blake swung her into his arms and strode forward. Her eyes closed, and her chin dipped to her chest. After a few more steps, he hunkered down.

Belle shook her head. "I don't know how you can stand my smell."

He gently rolled her onto the grass, stifling a laugh. "Who says I can?"

"I'd hit you, but my arms feel like limp rags." She flopped onto her back and smiled up into the branches of the tall pines and oaks. "Ahh. Shade never felt so good, or the earth beneath my back. I think I'll stay here the rest of the day—and through the night. You can come fetch me in the morning."

Instead, he went to fetch her saddlebags and turn Gunner out. She didn't stop him when he left. Soon, he was back with her saddlebag and began digging through them. "Let's see what treasures you have. Several pieces of fried chicken, biscuits, jerky. What's this?" He held up a small jar of honey, which hadn't been in his fare. "Moses is already playing favorites, I see. And a baked potato cut into manageable slices."

She wasn't responding, just lying there, looking up at the trees.

"How long do we have?" she mumbled.

She was in so much pain, they really should quit for the day. Head back to the ranch with the cattle they had, even if that would extend their work tomorrow. There was no good solution.

"As long as you need. We're in no rush."

"How much work is left for today?"

"A good four to five hours of gathering, and then the ride back to the ranch with the cattle. We'll have another break to eat before that, though. We'll arrive long after dark."

"I'm sorry for not keeping up."

"You're keeping up just fine."

"After I eat and rest, I'll feel better. How long do you *usually* take?"

He unwrapped one of his chicken legs and took a generous bite. "I like to rest the horses at least a half hour or so." He chewed and swallowed. "But like I said, we can take longer today. That's fine with me."

"Nope. My father wouldn't have, and I won't either."

"Your father was never out of the saddle. He felt the most comfortable on his horse."

She turned her head and looked up at him. "*His* horse? Who has his horse now?"

The chicken leg polished off, he tossed the bone over his shoulder. "Strider? He's been turned out with the broodmares since he fell on your father."

"Can I have him?"

Blake thought that over.

"Blake?"

"We'll see. He hasn't been worked at all. Might be a handful."

She crossed her arms over her chest and closed her eyes.

225

"Aren't you going to eat? You need food to keep up your energy."

"First, I need rest. We got up before sunrise, and this soft grass is heavenly. My eyes feel like they're full of sand. I can't wait to bathe and be clean again. It's amazing how much dust those critters kick up."

She yawned noisily, not even trying to be a lady.

He unwrapped his biscuits and dug in, grabbing another chicken leg with his other hand. She might not feel like eating just yet, but he was starved. He couldn't wait, even to be polite.

He wiped his sleeve across his mouth. "Seriously, Belle, we're in no rush. After our noonin', we can take the cattle we have and head back. There're no hard-set rules stating how long we have to stay out. I'm pretty sore myself."

"You're a liar," she said softly. He almost missed her statement with the swaying of the tree branches.

He shrugged and looked out to the horizon, enjoying the food more than he could say. "Storm's brewin'."

Her eyes opened. She lifted her head and looked around. "You think? Is that a bad thing? What happens if it rains?" Jerkily, she sat up and looked around.

"Eat your food." He handed over her saddlebag. He'd been riding and ranching since he was a kid, so being that exhausted was difficult to imagine. He smiled to himself, remembering the first ride where he'd gone out with John. He liked that memory—and realized Belle might too. He unwrapped a plump breast from her stash of food and handed the chicken over. He raised his brows in a silent command that she eat.

"I remember the first time John took me out hunting strays," he said, listening to her eat as he stared off at the horizon. Tree branches swayed in a gust of wind. She stopped eating, waiting for him to go on.

"Keep taking bites or I'll stop talking." He pointed at the half-eaten chicken breast. "I had little experience riding because me and my brother hired ourselves out to farmers, for the most part. By the time I came to Eden, I'd spent more time behind a plow than wrangling cattle. Anyway, back then John had maybe a few hundred head. This was before the railroads and silver discoveries in the mines, so population around here was much sparser. My first day in the saddle felt like the longest day of my life. We finished after dark, and much to my disgrace, John had to lift me down, like I did for you today. My legs buckled and I fell to my knees. From that day on, though, I've been in the saddle every day—unless I was off the ranch. It's been a good life."

When she didn't respond, Blake glanced down, expecting to see the chicken bone picked clean. Instead, her cheeks were wet with tears. He hadn't meant to make her sad. She'd been so eager for information the night before, and today too, he'd thought she'd like the story.

"Belle, I'm sorry. I didn't think—"

She rolled over in the grass and buried her face in her elbow. "It's all right." Her voice was wavery with emotion. She took a loud sniff. "I do like to hear. But it's painful too. We could have been a family again after Mother died—or maybe even before that." She turned her head and glanced up at him, her face contorted in pain. "I'm so thankful he had you! Thank you for staying here, keeping him from being a lonely man." She rolled to a sitting position, sucking in several large breaths. "I wish I'd had a chance to speak with him, know him, live in his house. We were led to believe he despised us. Why would we want to know a father who didn't want us?"

Her face crumbled as a dark cloud passed over the sun, closing out the light. She angrily dashed at tears. She looked so miserable. He threw caution to the wind and carefully, so as not to hurt her, pulled her into his arms and cradled her against his chest.

"Shh." He gently stroked her back. She moved in close, letting him cuddle her, not pulling away or telling him to stop.

"What I don't understand is why he never came after us. Why he didn't search us out to see for himself if we were really well and happy." She looked up into his face through a pool of tears. "Do you know, Blake? Why didn't my father come find us in person?"

"Of course I don't know for sure; I can only speculate," he replied softly, feeling her pain. He pulled her closer, thinking of the hurtful times, the lonely nights. "Your mother rebuffed in a stringent way his many offers to come and fetch you back. He wanted to come for you right after she left. He did. But her letters—the ones we believe now were written by your uncle—told him not to. That she wasn't ready to return. That he'd disrupt all your lives. When I was young, I remember he used to tell me that Celeste was coming back, just as soon as she was stronger. Just as soon as the girls were a little older, so she wouldn't worry so much. But a couple times a year he'd receive a letter saying she wasn't up to the journey quite yet, or the weather was bad, or that she'd wait after the holidays. He'd tell me, 'Soon, Blake. I'm expecting them soon.'" Blake glanced off, the feel of Belle in his arms grounding him. "But time goes by faster than you think. A workday may go on and on, but a year? That's gone in a breath, or a shout. Soon one year is three, then eight, then eighteen."

She sniffed and rubbed her face into his chest. The four years since Ann's death felt like a day. The eighteen since his brother was killed, a heartbeat. "I can understand John's reluctance," he said. "When your life is full, you keep moving, keep hoping, keep working. The only thing that keeps you sane is your dream, and your desire kindles that. You can't bear to be proven wrong. So you stay busy, making your life happen, doing good where you can. That was your father. John kept writing, waiting. Then, after a handful of years, a letter came saying she was happy with her life and liked where she was living. The girls were well and grounded. None of them could face the harshness of living in Colorado. They'd keep the lives they had in Philadelphia."

She gasped. "But, he could have come anyway! He should have made sure!"

"I agree. We know that now. But back then, if he'd gone in search and found you as your mother said, not wanting him, his dream would be dead." She shivered, and he stroked her back, fingering the silky texture of her long ponytail. "I'm sorry for you, Belle. And I'm sorry for John as well. All of you."

A strong gust of wind slapped him in the face, and along with it, a smattering of rain. Belle sucked in a surprised breath, and he hunkered over, protecting her.

"I feel like a sparrow tossed in the wind," she whispered into his ear. "I'm pitched this way and that, not knowing what I should feel anymore. Sometimes I want to fly up into the sky, then up to the mountaintops where I won't have to worry about anything."

"I know you do, sweetheart. You've been through so much." He stroked her back. "I wish I knew what to say to make things better. All I know is, life's hard. One day to the next you never know what to expect. I just take things one day at a time. You should too."

When the cloud above let loose, she pulled away. They scrambled to gather up the food, stuffing chicken, apples, and the two slices of huckleberry cake they'd yet to eat back into the saddlebags. With that done, he stood and pulled her to her feet.

"Let's make for that overhang." He pointed to the hillside, where he knew they'd have protection. "We can stay out of the worst until these clouds pass."

"What about the horses?"

"I'll go back for them once I have you out of the weather."

She put her hand to his chest, stopping his steps. "I'm fine, Blake. A little water won't hurt me. I feel better now that I've cried. Seems it's all I do lately." She looked up into his eyes. "Thank you for listening. And for wanting to help."

He had to look away before he embarrassed himself. The depth of her soul was right there for all the world to see. Thing was, he wanted that look for himself. The realization took him by surprise.

"You're welcome," he said, primarily to send his mind in a different direction. "I'm here for you, Belle. I want you to know that."

Her smile wobbled, and she turned away, walking awkwardly toward the horses, her stubbornness her badge of honor. She'd help him and not be coddled.

He stood in the downpour marveling over the new feelings that had worked their way to the surface.

CHAPTER THIRTY-SEVEN

After five days of ranching, Blake had insisted Moses take the girls back to the hotel so they could bathe and rest in comfortable beds, as well as check on Mavis and Katie. Belle was relieved. She felt like the sole of a worn-out shoe that had walked a thousand miles. Just the day before, she'd lost the soreness from the saddle, but her arms still felt like limp rags from lugging the hot branding iron to the wranglers waiting to push the red-hot metal into a poor animal's hide. The chore was difficult to watch. Most times she looked away. After several seconds of the sizzling brand with hide and hair burning, the calves would jump up, bawling so loudly it broke her heart. Their tails quivered with pain as they raced away to find their mamas. The practice seemed cruel, but Blake assured her marking them was the only way to keep the cattle from being rustled.

All the while, Katie was never far from Belle's thoughts. Mavis had sent word out to the ranch that her little sister was feeling better and was now comfortable going downstairs to the café to eat instead of taking all her meals with Mavis in the room. They'd shared a few walks around town and visited Henry. Karen Forester, the motherly waitress, was always there to help. And friendly Dr. Dodge checked on her every day. That was all fine to hear, but Belle still needed to see her sister's progress with her own eyes.

"I'm exhausted," Lavinia mumbled.

"That's because you've been a mighty help to me, missy. You too, Miss Emma *and* Miss Belle." Moses held the reins in his large hands and worked the brake with his foot as they rattled down a steep grade in the road. "I couldn't have done all that cookin' without y'all, my ribs being as sore as they are." Turning, he gave them a wide smile.

"We were glad to help." Emma gripped the side of the wagon as they descended the hill. "I've never peeled so many potatoes in my life—my hands have been in water so long I don't think they'll ever lose all the wrinkles. Or plucked so many chickens. That's a chore I can honestly say is not close to my heart!"

Lavinia laughed. "That actually wasn't as bad as I was expecting. I'm just glad Moses didn't ask either of us to do the killing. I would have drawn the line."

Emma nodded, then grimaced when they bumped over a rough patch. "That bloody hatchet stuck in the post still gives me the shivers. Who would've done such a thing? I'm glad Blake didn't see any humor in it either."

Praig. Or possibly Nicole? The girl had taken an instant dislike to her, but would she think such a stunt funny? The action was most certainly aimed at her and her sisters since the hatchet had been stuck in the homestead's porch post, not the bunkhouse's. Poor Emma and Lavinia had been traumatized. And Blake had been fuming mad to think Praig might have sneaked onto the property when the men were gone.

Belle was too exhausted to even participate in the conversation. She wouldn't feel normal for some time.

"So you got to know our boy pretty good." Moses gazed over at Belle with a strange look in his eyes. From the affection in his voice, he was referring to Blake. The two shared a special bond.

"I did. As we all did."

"Was he patient with ya? Learning to ranch, I mean?" He cast another sideways glimpse, his brow arching at her bedraggled condition.

A bath in the hotel couldn't come fast enough.

"Yes. He was, Moses. But why on earth are you asking? He was a perfect gentleman the whole time." *Well, mostly.*

She thought of how tenderly he'd held her in his arms as she'd cried out her heart concerning her father. She still felt like she had an ocean of tears welling at the surface, ready to gush forth at any given moment. They'd never be completely gone. She'd been the most steadfast against their father for many years, and because of that, she had the most regret.

"Just wonderin', is all." He slapped the lines over the horses' backs as the buckboard leveled out. "Get up there, you two lazybones! These gals have things to do!"

"How long before we reach town?" Emma asked, her eyelids at half-mast.

"Approximately a mile. You'll be there before you can count to a thousand."

Belle sneaked a look back, all three too drowsy to count to ten. "We'll take your word for it, Moses." She wondered if he would tell them what had happened to Blake's family. Each time she'd asked Blake, he'd skillfully avoided the topic.

"Moses, we're curious about Blake," Belle said. "He's half owner of the ranch, so it's natural we'd want to know a little about him. I've inquired a couple of times, but we've been interrupted or he changes the subject."

Moses glanced over, the dark skin of his forehead crunched in consternation. "I don't like talkin' about nobody, Miss Belle. Especially not Blake."

She glanced at Lavinia and Emma for help.

"Please, Moses," Emma said quickly. "It's kinder to learn from you if he's reluctant to speak of his past. We're going to be working so closely together."

"Are you staying, then?" he asked, also cunningly changing the subject. "You and your sisters will be part of Eden? Your pa'd be so proud if he was alive."

Moses wasn't stupid. He'd turned that around on them in a heartbeat.

"We can't say for sure," Emma replied. "Depends a lot on how Katie feels."

He shook his head. "I sure don't like what you told me about that. Her being stole away."

"Neither do we."

Slapping the reins over the horses' backs again, he sent the team into a trot. "What would you like to know?" He had to raise his voice to be heard over the racket of the wagon and horses.

Belle straightened. "Where's Blake from? And how did he get the scar?"

They rounded the final corner before town. Moses would drop them off at the hotel and then pick up more supplies.

"Well, since we're here now, I don't have time. Sorry." In front of the hotel, he worked the brake.

Belle was just getting ready to climb down and hurry inside before anyone noticed her peeling nose and windblown hair when the tall sheriff came striding over. He held out his hand. "May I?"

Mortified at her appearance, she forced a smile. "Thank you, Sheriff. I appreciate the help." To his credit, he didn't mention her state. He helped Emma and Lavinia out as well.

"I was wondering if you might pass along a message to your sister? Mrs. Applebee. She asked a favor of me a few days ago, and I've taken care of the matter."

The three of them were intrigued.

"Just tell her that the men in the jail are gone. I've transported them to Dove Creek, a small town north of here. They'll stay there until a judge arrives. After that, I can't promise where they'll go." He looked from one to the other. "Katie won't be bothered anymore, worrying about seeing her abductors so close. If I can work it out to only use Blake as a witness, she may not even have to testify."

"That's thoughtful, Sheriff. Thank you so much."

He dipped his chin and strode away.

Katie's kidnappers. That was such a horror, still. Mavis and Katie must have been living in that shadow all week.

She rushed upstairs, eager to see her sisters.

CHAPTER THIRTY-EIGHT

Excited to see Katie, but nervous too, Belle stopped in front of her sister's door and gave a light rap rap rap. Karen had been in the hotel entrance when they'd arrived and told them Mavis was with Katie in her room. Lavinia and Emma stayed back, waiting for some slices of the chocolate cake Karen had just iced to bring up to the room in celebration of their return.

"Katie? Mavis? It's Belle."

The door flew open. "Belle!" Katie vaulted into her arms. "Is the work finished?"

Mavis stood behind, looking relieved to see her. For most issues, they worked best together in a group, but Mavis had had to deal with Katie's frightened state by herself for the last five days. They exchanged glances as she and Katie embraced.

Belle moved into the room but stayed off the inviting bed. She didn't want to mar the pretty yellow quilt with her dusty clothes. "Not yet, but Blake—the kind soul that he is—sent us back to town to rest. I didn't argue. I can't believe Mother lasted there for as long as she did. Just warming water to wash with is a task. I didn't know how easy I had it in Philadelphia with our cast-iron pipes. Such an indulgence." She held up her arm and flexed her bicep. "I've developed muscles, albeit I'm sore. I think Lesley will be surprised when we meet again."

"I don't think he would recognize you at the moment." Mavis winked and squeezed in for her own hug. "It's good to see you, sister. Where's Lavinia and Emma? They returned as well, didn't they?"

"Yes. Down in the café, waiting to bring up a dessert to share in celebration of our returning alive. They should be here any moment."

Katie's eyes sparkled. "I can't wait to see them. Mavis and I have done some exploring and have much to share. And we've become friends with the new woman, Elizabeth Smith, and her darling little boy. They came into the café, and we invited her to join us. We talked for so long, Johnny actually fell asleep in my lap." Katie turned and smiled at Mavis, as if not wanting to leave her out of the conversation. "She's remarkable, Belle. She does needlework like Lavinia. We have a lot in common. And Johnny is just the cutest little boy . . ."

Mavis's expression said they hadn't been out of the room as much as Katie would like for her to believe. Her little sister still suffered from the effects of those outlaws. That reminded her of the sheriff's message.

"That sounds wonderful, Katie. And I'll be all ears after I soak in the tub. But I better get back to my room now, because Karen is sending the boys up with the water. Before I forget, Sheriff Dawson sent a message."

Mavis perked up. Belle wondered about mentioning it in front of Katie, but her sister needed to face her demons to vanquish them. A wound not cleaned out often festered and became worse. She'd not let Katie become a victim of her own fear.

Katie tipped her head. "Oh?"

"Yes. He met our wagon as we came into town just now. He wanted both of you to know he procured a place for his prisoners in the small town of Dove Creek. They're no longer in Eden. You can rest assured you will not be seeing them until the trial—and maybe not even then."

Katie stepped back as if she'd just noticed Belle's condition. "Look at you. Your poor face. Your nose is peeling. Peeling!" she said again, emphasizing the words. "Velma would be scandalized."

Did she really just notice, or is she changing the subject so she won't have to acknowledge what transpired?

Katie cocked a chastising brow. "You know how Velma hated the sun. Never allowed us to get any at all, and was horrified if we came home with the slightest color on our faces. And if our freckles appeared . . ." She shook her head. "She'd be shocked to see you now."

"Yes, I remember well the many lectures from *that woman*. I don't give a whit about her." Katie's eyes widened. She must have forgotten or put aside their guardians' traitorous sins.

Katie's gaze dropped to the rug. "I'm sorry," she whispered. "I didn't mean to mention Velma. Believing what they did is difficult for me."

Reaching forward, Belle ran her hand down Katie's arm. Katie was the youngest, so she had no recollections of the ranch, their father, or their mother. It was no wonder she'd bonded with their caretakers. "I shouldn't have reacted the way I did. But I do think you should try to reconcile the facts in your mind. The sooner you do, the better you'll feel. We all have a lot to work through." She went over to the gold-leaf oval mirror above the washstand. "Oh! I *do* look a fright. The light here is much brighter than in the dark kitchen at the ranch house." She fingered the bridge of her nose, dismayed. "Lots of freckles. Who would have thought they could appear so quickly? I'll need to send for a milk plaster too." She touched her chapped lips. "I hardly recognize myself so bronzed. I must go." Kissing them both on the cheeks, she headed for the door. "I feel like going out tonight. Maybe let's ask Henry and go to Mademoiselle de Sells again."

Mavis's eyes brightened.

"But we don't have any money yet—at least not much," Katie responded. "Besides, I like staying here in the hotel. I like this restaurant best."

Why? Because you're afraid to go anywhere else?

"You forget, little sister, we have accounts all around town. Henry said we're welcome to use them. I've put in five days of hard labor. I'd like a night out." *And to get you out and show you danger isn't everywhere just waiting to pounce.* Belle grasped the doorknob. "Has the doctor been by lately?"

Mavis nodded. "A couple times a day. He's been particularly attentive." She picked up a bottle from the nightstand. "He gave Katie this to help her sleep."

"I've only used it twice."

Fondness welled up. "Good. I'm glad he's been a help." She winked. "As soon as I'm behind the soaking screen, come in and visit. I've missed you both, and we have lots to catch up on." Katie didn't meet her gaze. As a matter of fact, she'd backed away and was facing the window. *Is she locking herself into a prison of her own making? Had that happened to Mother? Like Blake alluded to?* Belle wouldn't let that happen—not his day, week, or year. She was back now, and could help Mavis strengthen Katie. They'd figure out a way. They had to.

CHAPTER THIRTY-NINE

T he room was a welcome joy. *How good it feels to be back.* What she once thought plain and simple was now luxurious. Belle had only stayed in this room three nights since first arriving in Eden. The cheerful colors were inviting. Mavis, perfect housekeeper that she was, had the place immaculate. Running her hand over the soft quilt, Belle imagined how good the mattress would feel tonight after she had bathed, was filled with a wonderful concoction from Mademoiselle de Sells—and sated from a glass of wine, or maybe even two. Giddy with excitement for the evening to come, she wanted to send a message to Henry right away.

At the window, she glanced across the street to his office. The attorney had been scarce the last week, and she wondered why. Of course, she'd been out at the ranch, but even before that, she'd noticed his demeanor had changed since their first meetings. He seemed preoccupied or worried.

Taking a deep breath, she slowly let it out. The last few days had been exhausting, but other feelings had taken her by surprise. And every single one concerned Blake in one shape or another. He was about the only thing she thought about from dawn until dusk. She could hear his voice right now, as clear as if he were whispering in her ear. Her insides fluttered, and her heart felt light.

What is love?

She still didn't know for sure, or how it felt. Her conversation with Mavis drifted through her mind. She compared the last few days to what she experienced when she was with Lesley. Confused, she wrapped herself in her arms.

What have I gone and done out at the ranch? A lot more than work.

Going to the tall wardrobe, she opened the door to see what dress would be suitable for tonight. Taking the skirt of her lilac gown, she fluffed out the lengths, having not worn the garment since she'd arrived. She loved the slightly scooped neckline with the delicate ecru frill lace. It was dark, and could pass for mourning if she added her black shawl. The dress fit her figure to a *T* and made her feel pretty.

Yes, this will be the one—

A horrific buzzing erupted from the bottom of the wooden structure. Gasping, she barely had time to look down before she stumbled back and fell. But not before she'd seen a large rattlesnake, coiled and ready to strike.

Belle screamed, scrambling backward, but her britches caught on something, holding her firm. Inside the wardrobe, the snake had the advantage of being a foot off the ground. Its head moved slowly back and forth, as if gauging where to strike.

With another scream, she pushed back with all her force. Her pants ripped. She clambered backward like a crab escaping a seagull. She had to get away before the serpent sank his fangs deep into her throat.

The door flew open, and Mavis rushed in.

"Stay back!" Belle shouted. Her face, drenched in sweat, felt hot and prickly. Her gaze darted around. A snake of that size had to be quick as lightning. "Get out! Get out! There's a rattler in the wardrobe!"

Sherriff Dawson appeared in the doorway, flanked by Santiago. Both men had their weapons drawn, and their hard eyes said they were ready to kill anyone trying to hurt a Brinkman.

She pointed. "Rattlesnake!"

That was apparent by the racket. She was shaking so hard her teeth clattered almost as loudly as the serpent's tail. Santiago came to her side at the same time Clint leveled his gun.

Bam! Bam!

Acrid smoke burned and soured the back of Belle's throat.

Silence.

She collapsed into Santiago's arms, violently shaking. Mavis rushed forward to take her from Santiago. Katie, along with Lavinia and Emma, watched white-faced from the hallway, the tray of sweets in their hands forgotten.

Sheriff Dawson holstered his gun and closed the distance to Mavis and her. His gaze cut to Santiago, then back at them.

"H-how did that th-thing get in here?" Belle whispered, amazed that she was even able to speak at all. If not for Mavis's support, she would crumple to the floor.

"That's a good question, Sheriff." Karen came through the door. "We've never had a snake in any of our rooms before, let alone in a wardrobe." She glanced to the window, which was open a few inches. "Can they climb up the side of a building?"

The boy delivering the bathing screen glanced inside the wardrobe. Clint nudged his shoulder. "Get that snake out of here."

Belle blinked and wanted to look away but was mesmerized. At least four feet long, the menacing creature hung limp in the boy's hands.

"Can they, Sheriff? Can a snake climb a wall?" Belle squeaked out. "Can it slither up siding and come in our window?"

"No," he replied flatly. "I've never heard of that. A tree, yes, the side of a building, no."

Mavis's eyes narrowed. "Then how? How did a rattlesnake get into our room?"

Sheriff Dawson rubbed his chin. "When was the last time you were in your room?" He looked between the two sisters.

"Belle's been out at the ranch, so I've been the only occupant. I left at eight o'clock this morning and have been in Katie's room since."

A shocking thought reverberated through Belle. "The doors of the wardrobe were closed, Sheriff! I expressly remember pulling them open. Could this have been deliberate? But who would want to hurt us?"

CHAPTER FORTY

U nable to concentrate on his work, Blake left the remainder of the branding and castration to the men while he made a quick ride into Eden. He should have driven the women himself. They'd been on his mind since they'd left with Moses an hour before, and because of it, he'd burned his hand on the branding iron—not once, but twice. A fumble only a novice would make. Praig Horn was still unaccounted for. He'd been stupid to take such a chance. John's daughters were his most pressing responsibility.

Rounding the corner into town, he slowed Banjo. The normal fifteen-minute ride on a galloping horse had taken him ten. His horse was breathing hard. A crowd was gathered outside the hotel doors, mulling around. *Why?* Henry dashed across the street, followed by one of the boys who worked in the hotel. Fear ricocheted up Blake's back. Just as he reined up and was about to swing his leg over the saddle, a long object flew out of Belle's second-floor window and landed square on Banjo's rump. His gelding snorted and bucked, and the object fell to the ground. Blake looked down.

Rattlesnake! What the hell? And not just any rattlesnake, but a large, black mountain diamondback—the kind that would give anyone nightmares. Its head was blown off, but the impressive row of buttons was still there for anyone's taking.

Dismounting, he tossed his reins over the hitching rail and pushed his way through the curious onlookers.

"Did you hear that scream?" one woman whispered to another.

"We'd know by now if she was bitten."

"I heard the rattler got all five."

Hell!

Alarmed, Blake took the stairs three at a time. The hall was packed with people. He shouldered his way into the room to see the sisters huddled together. Clint, Santiago, and Henry stood close by.

Belle's eyes widened when she caught sight of him, but she remained silent. Her face—the same one that had been suntanned and healthy-looking an hour ago—appeared as white as a sheet.

He stayed his impulse to rush to her side and instead went to Clint's group, glancing at Henry and Santiago. "What happened?"

Henry was shaking his head in disbelief.

"Well?" Blake barked impatiently. "Fill me in. A moment ago, a dead diamondback landed on my horse."

"The snake was in with Belle's clothes," Clint said, pointing to the tall wardrobe.

Again, Blake glanced at Belle. She could have been dying right now. The slow, painful death wasn't pretty. Ten years ago a ranch hand had succumbed to a deadly bite. Blake hadn't forgotten the ugly purple-black of the man's swollen arm. "The hell you say!" He swallowed down his fear. She was standing right there, but still he felt compelled to add, "She all right?"

"*Sí*, amigo." Santiago's squinty gaze moved slowly around the room.

Henry shook his head. "She's shaken up pretty bad. All of them are. And I don't blame them." His gaze caught Blake's and then Clint's. "We need to talk. Right now, in my office."

Henry was right. "And the girls?"

"Them too."

Santiago took a large step back. His gaze lingered on Henry, Clint, and finally got to Blake. "I will keep watch around town and let you know if I see anything suspicious." With a half turn, he came face-to-face with Katie and the rest of the girls. Blake didn't quite know what to make of the tender understanding that darkened his eyes.

"Katie?" The one word was a question and an answer.

She dropped her eyes and blushed.

He put out his hand to Belle. "You had a close call, senorita, but it will take more than one little rattlesnake to frighten John Brinkman's daughter." Without waiting for a reply, he turned on his heel and disappeared into the crowd of curious townsfolk still lingering inside.

Upstairs in his office, Henry held the door for the others. Blake came through the threshold first, followed by the girls. Clint brought up the rear. They stood around in silence.

Henry cleared his throat. "I'm worried. That snake had to be planted." Henry took in the girl's reactions. A little color had come back to Belle's face. For the past five days, they'd been worried about Katie. And now someone had decided to scare Belle. Who would be next?

"You think we're a target?" Belle asked. "With a snake? That doesn't make sense. I thought people were *waiting* on our return to Eden."

Henry paced the room, feeling as if a giant had his foot planted on his chest. "That rattlesnake didn't get into your wardrobe by accident, Belle. I should have anticipated this problem. Advised John differently. If the worst happens, the blame rests wholly at my feet. Most people *are* happy you've returned, I promise you that. But I think there's someone out there who, for some reason, is plotting against you."

Blake stepped forward. "You've been distracted of late, Henry. Is this what's been troubling you? Worry over the will?"

"No, not this." *Or could this be related? Are Elizabeth and Johnny involved?* He didn't like to think it.

"You think someone wants the ranch," Blake said, low, deadly. "For their gain."

Belle's eyes brightened, and she sucked in a breath. "Yes! That's it. If they frighten us enough, they think we'll take the payout and go home." She frowned. "That would leave Blake the sole owner."

Henry's jaw clenched and released several times. "The will contained a stipulation for that situation. If Blake were to die without an heir, the ranch would be auctioned off—and the proceeds would go to the town."

Blake and Belle stared across the room as if they were seeing each other for the first time. Since they'd returned from the ranch, Henry didn't miss the way Blake's gaze kept tracking back to her. Feelings had grown. Belle was the exact opposite of Ann, Blake's first wife, who'd been shy, solicitous. The two women couldn't have been more different if they'd tried, and yet it was plain Blake had fallen in love with Belle. Henry wondered if his friend even realized it yet.

"Any outfit would be tempted by the Five Sisters," Clint said, rubbing his chin. "Create a misfortune where Blake is accidentally killed and you'd have a shot at it."

It was all coming to light, Henry thought. John would never have assumed this could happen. "Five heirs would be too difficult to plot untimely deaths for, but without you girls here, there'd only be one target. Somebody either wants a crack at owning the Five Sisters, or they're interested in the payout Eden would receive after the ranch was sold."

"What about the gunshots when we first arrived?" Belle glanced at Katie and then the others. "Two different times they came too close for comfort. Could they have been intentional too? To frighten us away? And the kidnapping?" She gasped and went to Katie's side. "Maybe they'd have been content taking any of us, not just Katie."

Henry couldn't believe this was happening. "Makes sense to me."

He'd never seen Blake's face so set, so angry.

Clint nodded, his expression dark. "I'll ride up to Dove Creek tomorrow. Get answers from the prisoners one way or the other. If they were paid by someone, I'll find out."

"And the bloody hatchet that was left sunk deep in the porch post out at the homestead?" Emma's hands were shaking. "Do you think that's connected?"

"No doubt." Blake fisted and relaxed his hands. "And now the rattlesnake. Somebody wants you out of town. My fear is, he may be getting frustrated."

The Brinkmans' expressions made Henry think they wouldn't be sticking around Eden too much longer. They had their lives to worry about. *But where does that leave Blake? A prime target?*

Belle went to the window, glanced out, then turned to face them. "Nobody is scaring me out of Eden. Not today, not ever. I make my own decisions for when I stay and when I go." The firm set to her mouth reminded Henry of John. "Katie, I think you're the one with the most difficult decision. You know we love you and will stand with you." Her gaze went to Blake's as if to say she stood behind him as well. "What do you say? Are we going to cower in fear? Run away?"

"Whoever's behind this may become more aggressive," Blake responded, his gaze riveted on Belle. "Things could get worse. There's no telling how far he'll take things."

Henry was glad Blake was warning them of the growing danger. Until they knew what they were dealing with, everyone had to be careful. "We don't know that the culprit is a man. Could be anyone."

Even a mother with a small son?

"I wonder how they discovered the terms of the will," Clint said.

Blake nodded at Henry. "Where's the document been besides here in your safe?"

"Only out at the ranch." Henry didn't like what that implied.

Blake's expression darkened. "Could someone have read it?"

Henry shrugged. "Anything's possible."

"Praig Horn?" Belle asked.

Clint and Blake exchanged a long look.

"Could be," Blake said. "He was around the month John was dying. Most of the men stuck close to the ranch. But we have to keep an open mind. As much as I hate the idea, could be any of the men."

"Maybe Trevor?" Clint said quietly. "Even if you don't like to think it. Or it could be a person totally unrelated."

Blake nodded. "Or an individual from a ranch we've had trouble with. The Diamond J?"

Henry sat in his chair, drilling his fingers on the desktop. As much as he'd like to tell them about Elizabeth, he couldn't. They'd spoken in confidence. But if anything happened to one of John's daughters or Blake and they later found out Elizabeth was working with an accomplice, he'd never forgive himself. He vowed to press her harder the next time they talked. He had no other options.

"Trouble with a ranch?" Emma breathed. "What kind of trouble?"

Blake rolled his shoulders. "Where to begin? Over the years we've had run-ins a time or two. A couple years back, a disagreement over water rights. And last year, we had rustlers. Turned out to be a rancher losing his place to the bank and looking for any way to hang on. Being the largest puts a target on our back."

Lavinia went over to Katie, who was staring at her hands in her lap. She touched her sister's shoulder. "Our decision really depends on how you feel about staying, Katie."

Katie finally looked up. "Blake saved my life. We can't abandon him now." She looked at the people in the room. "We're Brinkmans," she said in a strong voice—the first time she had used it since her nightmare ordeal. "We need to show our backbone, stay, discover what's going on. For Father, if for nothing else." She tipped her head thoughtfully. "But if we just make our intentions of staying known, won't the person give up? We'll beat him."

Clint shook his head. "If only it were that simple. Any man depraved enough to go to all this trouble is determined. We need to find him—or her—before they succeed in another plot and one of you is killed."

Henry watched Belle and Mavis close in around their younger sisters. Katie had been through the most trying experience, and if she was still willing to stay in Eden, the rest would follow. Henry prayed John's will hadn't condemned one of his daughters to die. Or Blake. A day ago, the sisters' staying would have been the best news in the world. Now, he wasn't sure at all.

CHAPTER FORTY-ONE

The next day, after a stern lecture from Mavis that they'd all be fine in town without her, Belle sat atop a bluff at the ranch looking out over an empty prairie. Katie was doing surprisingly well, proving to be a stalwart example for Emma and Lavinia. Mavis was holding the three together.

We'll get through this one day at a time.

No cattle. All were in corrals at the ranch. She'd grown used to seeing the muscular steers grazing in large herds. The valley before her felt lonely, and the air seemed to stand still. She'd needed a break from the sorting, dust, and flies, so she'd ridden out a short way to see if she could spot any strays. Today was her birthday. She missed her father with a heavy heart.

How much different this day could have been if he'd survived.

She turned at the sound of a long whistle.

Blake.

Loping to her side, he reined in with ease, his movements again reminding her of a dancer. The hair around his collar was tousled from his gallop out. Wide shoulders leaned her way as he searched her face. His handsome good looks made her feel worse.

"You doin' okay?" He pushed up the brim of his hat. "Saw you ride out on your own. You know that makes me uneasy."

She was surprised at his tone—neither scolding nor annoyed.

"Just needed a little open space," she said without taking her gaze away from the view in front of her.

"A phrase your father said often. I'd find him out here in this exact spot just memorizing the horizon. I'm not surprised to find you here now."

Cutting her gaze to him, she was unable to stop two fat tears from spilling from her eyes. She could talk herself blue in the face, but that wouldn't change the way Blake's voice melted any of her resolve.

He leaned forward and gently brushed them away with his thumb.

"Father was so right; this ranch *is* in my blood. What am I going to do when the six months is over and I'm supposed to return to Philadelphia? I'm so confused."

He didn't respond, just sat at her side giving her the support she needed.

"Blake?"

"You'll have to decide that on your own."

Several moments passed. It was as if he were deliberately giving her time to think.

He reached over and touched her hand resting on her saddle horn. "Why so sad today?"

She gave a small shrug. "Don't know. Well, maybe I know. It's my birthday, and I'm feeling a little sorry for myself."

His brow arched. "Is that so?" He went for his inside pocket, making enough noise to make her smile. He pulled out an envelope. "Happy birthday."

She studied what looked to be a letter in his hand. "You knew?"

He nodded. "Henry gave it to me. It's from your father. He wrote one out for each of you while he still had the strength."

She couldn't speak for the knot lodged in her throat. Finally, she took the white envelope from his hand. "I-I don't know if I can."

A small smile played at the corner of his lips. "You can. I'll ride over there a ways and give you some privacy. Go on, Belle. He's waiting to speak with you."

Belle took great care opening the precious gift. Her pounding heart made her head feel dizzy. Taking the sheets from the envelope, she was careful not to let any get away in the breeze that had begun to stir the grass. She wiped her eyes with the back of her hand, noting the stains on the paper.

> *My Dearest Belle,*
> *Happy birthday! I can just imagine what a beautiful young lady you've become. If you look anything like your mother, rivers will still in your presence, and the sun will stop its track across the sky. I've loved you dearly through the years, and now have a story I'd like to share.*
> *I remember twenty-two years ago today as if it were yesterday. You came earlier than expected, surprising us both. Your mother awoke me with a hand to my arm. Fumbling my way into my clothes, I hurried to send for the midwife. The labor was long and difficult, and I was scared. For a while it looked as if you'd not come at all.*

Belle had to stop reading and search for her handkerchief in her pocket. She wiped her eyes and blew her nose. Glancing over, she saw Blake watching her. He gave a small smile, then looked away. Strengthened, she read on.

> *I paced the front room with Mavis in my arms, rocking and singing to her when she cried for her mama. Finally, the midwife came out with you in her arms. I took you, and she took Mavis, and we went in to see your mother. The room was so quiet after what had just*

transpired. You looked up at me with your large blue eyes in that perfect sweet face, wondering who your father was.

We thought all was well. The midwife left. After a few hours, we learned you wouldn't eat. No matter how hard Celeste worked, you refused her breast. You weren't a large baby to begin with, so in my mind, you wouldn't last long. Your cries sliced through me like a knife. We tried everything. By the second day, you were growing alarmingly weak. Rejected the sugar water we offered.

Time was running out. Against your mother's wishes, I bundled you up, mounted my horse, and rode off into the wilderness looking for the Indians. Not all the Indians were friendly. I had to be careful. Finally finding a small band, I approached slowly. They heard the crying infant. I offered the only thing of real value I had: my hunting rifle. They took you, Belle. The gamble was risky. That band of Cheyenne could have disappeared with you into the night since I had to go home to care for Celeste and Mavis. You stayed until I was sure you were eating as you should. Two days later, when I brought you back to Celeste, your cheeks were full and rosy. You had the sweetest smile I'd ever seen. And you'd learned to nurse. Don't know if your mother forgave me for that. She never said, but we were both thankful to have you home.

Now you know why I'll never forget your birth.

My special girl.

May this birthday be as special as you are . . .

All my love,

Father

A painful joy sprouted inside Belle. What a tale! And what a wonderful gift to hear the telling from her father's own hand. He'd saved her life. He was so brave and smart.

How will I ever get over losing him?

As she looked up and met Blake's eyes again, she knew how. She'd stay here, in Eden, working her father's land next to the man he'd loved as much as he did his daughters.

CHAPTER FORTY-TWO

U nable to stay away a moment longer, Blake rode slowly toward Belle, her face dipped toward the paper trembling in her hands as Gunner stood quietly on the knoll. Her demeanor as she'd read John's letter had moved him deeply.

How difficult to lose a father she'd just found.

She glanced up.

"Finished?"

A smile blossomed on her lips as she nodded. "I wish the letter was ten pages long. I could read forever."

"He was weak. Wanted to leave a letter for each daughter before . . ."

She sniffed loudly and then dried more tears with a handkerchief that looked soaked through. He pulled out his own and handed it over. *God in heaven, she's lovely.* She had no idea the vision she made in her saddle, the world at her feet and the sun's light muted by the clouds more golden than gold.

"Why would Mother leave? I know what Father's letter said . . ."

"Don't know. Possible her anxiety grew larger with each child she feared she'd lose. That's all I can figure. Until she had no other choice."

She shuffled one page behind the other. Her smile was back. She glanced over to him. "Did you know I was nursed by an Indian woman for two days right after I was born? I might have died if not for Father's fast thinking."

He shook his head, enjoying the closeness he felt. "I had no idea. John never shared that fact. Perhaps he was saving that admission for you alone."

She sighed deeply and looked off at the mountains, a light shining from within.

"Aren't you going to ask what *I* have for you? It is your birthday, you know."

Her gaze jerked back. "A present?"

He lifted one shoulder. "Sort of. Look in the first stall when you get back."

Again her face lit up. "Strider?"

He nodded. "I brought him in from pasture a few days ago. Been riding him. Gave him a stern talking-to as well. Go slow, get to know him, and you should be fine."

"Blake! I'm so . . . I can't . . . when did . . ."

Her happiness was easy to see. In her excitement, she was sputtering like a chipmunk.

"If I weren't on this horse, I'd give you a hug and kiss . . . I . . ." Her words trailed off, and she glanced away, her cheeks as rosy as any spring flower.

Without saying a word, he stepped off Banjo and dropped his reins, wondering if she'd dare to take the next step. It wasn't just the danger of the last few days. They'd worked together side by side. Like partners. Like more. It was the life he'd envisioned for himself and Ann, and he wasn't honoring her memory by refusing to live his destiny now that he had another chance at something good. He'd lain awake all night, thinking about life. He hadn't come up with many answers except one. He didn't want to lose Belle. Not now that he'd just found her.

Belle swung her eyes to his. Their gazes locked. She hesitated only a moment, then dismounted, took the two steps to reach him, and slipped softly into his embrace, wrapping him in her arms as well. Her cheek rested on his chest, both their faces turned toward the far-reaching mountains. They stood in silence for an uninterrupted minute, experiencing how their bodies felt together. No rush, no embarrassment.

He was determined *not* to think this through—he'd done all that last night. For once in his life, he'd follow his feelings. He pulled her closer.

"Belle," he whispered low. "Look at me."

When she looked up, he cradled her face with his palms, admiring her beauty. He traced his thumbs over her cheeks, marveling at the wonder of her. He didn't want to rush, but to enjoy every moment.

Finally, he lowered his lips to hers. She didn't pull away, only leaned in closer. A cool breeze brushed past, mixing with the warm sunshine. He hadn't realized until the moment their lips touched how much he'd desired her, thought of her, wanted her on a level unmatched by anything else.

What am I doing? Where can this go?

He had no answers, just the feel of Belle, the softness of her lips, the thunder of his runaway heart. And yet . . .

He was the first to pull away. As the impulse of the moment lessened, guilt filled him.

She's John's daughter!

"Blake?" She searched his face as he looked at the mountains.

She's practically engaged.

There were a thousand reasons why this was a bad idea. He'd gone and ruined her birthday. When she'd had happy stars in her eyes from her father's letter, he had to go and throw her into his confused fire.

What kind of a man am I?

"Blake, I'm sorry. I don't know what came over me."

She's apologizing to me?

He felt like a cad. Forcing a smile before looking into her face, he stepped away and chuckled, trying to bluff his way through his feelings.

"I do. John was never one to back down on a dare. You Brinkmans are all the same." He shook his head and smiled. "I know that didn't mean a thing, so you best just forget all about it. I already have."

Her face clouded over, and she stepped away as well.

He repositioned his hat and then forced another smile, needing to change the subject. "Did I mention what happened right before I came out here? Riley and Bush are back. Came begging for forgiveness. Said they let Praig confuse 'em in the beginning with all his fancy words. They claim they've got no problem working for any of you."

The frown on her face said she understood there would be no more kisses or talk about what happened. That almost hurt the most.

"Said they had no idea Praig was planning to fight Moses, get his revenge for always bucking him when Praig was riling up the bunkhouse against me. When Praig returned to their camp with a bloodied lip and cuts on his face, they packed up and rode out. They don't know where he is."

"Did you take them back?"

Her tone was no longer wistful, but angry. He couldn't blame her in the least.

"Told 'em I needed to talk with you first. See what you thought before I made any decisions. Moses hasn't any beef with taking 'em back on."

She cocked a brow. "Before *we* made any decisions."

"Yes. Exactly that," he replied, trying to make his tone light. The sadness in her eyes was difficult to bear.

She moved to Gunner's head to give the gelding a rub down his face. They were over the awkwardness of the kiss as much as they could be at this point, and for that, Blake was thankful. He tried another small chuckle, but she didn't look his way.

"What do you think about Bush and Riley?" he asked.

"I don't know. Do you think they have anything to do with what's been happening?"

He scuffed a boot. "I can't imagine either of them responsible. They've been harmless in the past. I think they just got caught up in Praig's nastiness and followed his lead. At least at the ranch we can keep an eye on 'em. They're under suspicion, just like everyone else."

At her expression of vulnerability, he wanted to kick himself. *What have I done?* One moment of weakness may have cost him her friendship.

She gave a deep sigh. "I have no objection. Having them back will make finishing the roundup easier."

"Yes."

"And I'll be able to spend more time in town with Katie and the rest of my sisters." She went to Gunner's side and mounted up with no help.

Blake rubbed a hand across his face and followed suit, knowing a marker had been passed between them. He'd miss her questions and presence by his side, but this was best. A little distance was exactly what they needed.

CHAPTER FORTY-THREE

That evening, after the small birthday celebration in Belle and Mavis's hotel room, Belle had a difficult time keeping her thoughts on track. Blake's kiss had changed her life—or at least mixed her up completely. If nothing else, it had shown her how little she felt for Lesley. She hadn't known a kiss could move the ground under her feet. Or whisk her to the highest mountain peak. The two worlds the men represented couldn't be more diverse. Her emotions had been running high yesterday after she'd read her father's letter, but still. There was much to consider.

"Belle, pay attention!" Emma scolded, holding the bowl filled with scrap papers that were inscribed with their father's five businesses. "This is important! You look as if you're five thousand miles away."

"Sorry. I *am* paying attention. After drawing straws, it seems Lavinia will choose first, followed by Katie, Mavis, you, and then I'll get what's left over. Lavinia, are you ready?"

Lavinia, in her pretty blue dress and with her dark-brown hair brushed to a high sheen, stepped forward as if in a Broadway play, eagerness moving across her face. Everyone was excited this moment had finally arrived. Since the reading of the will, one calamity after the other and then the roundup had made them delay. Henry had relayed that the townspeople were anxious to get to know their new bosses. They were beginning to fret, so the girls knew they should not put off choosing any longer.

All Belle had been able to do since she'd arrived in town two hours ago was think about Blake back on the ranch. *Why did he kiss me? It didn't make any sense at all.* But she had to admit the kiss had sent an eruption of delicious sensations flashing through her body. His warm lips, strong arms, and the feel of his chest were seared into her mind. The caress, which must have only lasted seconds, felt like a lifetime. She'd been able to think of nothing else since. They'd ridden back to the ranch in silence, and she'd been there when he'd given Riley and Bush the good news. The men were younger than she'd expected—younger probably than Katie.

Lavinia stuck her hand in the bowl and made a show of fingering all the scraps of paper before choosing. One more piece of the puzzle of their lives was about to fall into place. She withdrew her hand and carefully opened the fold. "I'm the proud new owner of the hotel café! I'll be working alongside Karen!" She clutched the scrap to her chest as if her fortune had just been revealed.

Belle was thankful the eatery hadn't gone to her.

Everyone smiled and cheered. The happy sentiments felt good after what they'd learned yesterday about being the targets of someone's scheme. Emma moved to Katie, whose face glowed with excitement. Katie enthusiastically put her hand in the bowl.

Opening the paper, she sucked in a breath. "I've got the mill and lumberyard. I know *nothing* about milling boards." Her gaze touched each of her sisters'.

"You'll learn," Mavis said. "Whoever runs the place now will help. Just think, you'll have your finger on the pulse of Eden as it grows. That's exciting."

She put her gloved hand in the bowl next and chortled after she pulled out a paper and read her lot. "The livery! I'm partner with

Maverick Daves. Oh my!" Her face flamed red, making Belle, and everyone else, take note.

"And you'll also be working with Cash Dalton, the sheriff's fourteen-year-old son," Emma said with a saucy laugh. "He may be practically a boy, but he's incredibly handsome." She nudged a flustered, scarlet-faced Mavis with her elbow. "Don't you think, sister? I became tongue-tied when I met him in the café a few days ago. Maverick isn't bad himself. Perhaps he'll ask for your hand. I wouldn't be surprised in the least."

Belle averted her gaze when Mavis subconsciously clasped one hand over the other, covering her missing finger. She knew Emma hadn't meant to hurt with her comment, but Mavis was overly sensitive about her plight. Belle snorted to herself. She finally realized more of the blame for that accident resided with Velma, instead of her. With their father's money, rightfully given to them when it should have been, she and Mavis wouldn't have been outside cleaning up refuse like a couple of garbage men. *Perhaps . . .*

"It's my turn!" Emma called, quick to draw a scrap of paper.

Belle didn't care what business she ended up owning. All she really wanted to do was be out at the ranch riding herd. Amazing how much the duty had grown on her in the little time they'd been in Eden. *Is that the real reason? Or am I missing Blake with my whole heart and soul?*

"What did you get, Emma?" she asked, trying to silence her annoying inner voice.

Emma beamed. "The Toggery! It's exactly what I wanted. I'm going to tear that place apart, enlarge the building, and import all sorts of pretty clothes for women made of the finest wool. You watch and see if I don't. You won't recognize the place when I get through with it."

"That will take some doing," Lavinia replied with an exasperated sigh. "Their inventory is shocking. Or should I say lack of inventory . . ."

Belle made a face. "That leaves me with the run-down leather shop on the Old Spanish Trail that backs up to Dr. Dodge's medical office. How exciting. Anyone except Lavinia want to swap? Please? Please?"

They all shook their heads.

"I didn't think so."

"Sorry, Belle." Emma was fairly glowing. "Looks like you're stuck with what you have. Everyone seems to like their challenge at hand."

"I've never even been out to the mill," Katie said. "Or seen it. Where is it?"

With the excitement over, Mavis lowered herself into a chair. "On the other side of the river. Clint told me there's a bridge just past the icehouse, across from the cantina. You won't be able to go down there by yourself, Katie. None of us will. At least not yet."

All color had drained from Katie's face. "No, I wouldn't want to. Did Henry say if the mill has an office in town?"

"He didn't. But that's an idea you might want to implement if they don't."

A knock sounded on the door. Belle's heart leaped, thinking Blake may have followed her into town like he had yesterday. Lavinia opened the door to reveal Henry.

"Good evening," he said. "How's the choosing coming along? Did I miss the fun?"

"Come in," Lavinia gushed. "I'm the new owner of the café downstairs. Would you like something delightful to eat? It's on me."

Everyone laughed, feeling Lavinia's lightheartedness. In Belle's mind, she and Emma had gotten the types of businesses that would be pleasing to a woman. She was glad.

"As a matter of fact," he said, coming in and closing the door behind him, "I've just finished a tasty bowl of stew from downstairs, thank you very much." He glanced around. "But I have other news. It's not as fun as what you've been discussing."

Belle moved closer. "Oh?" The news could be any number of things. She steeled her nerves.

He stood straight, legs slightly apart, looking every bit a protector. "I've had a reply to my telegrams regarding your guardians."

A hush fell over the room.

"The last known sighting of Vernon and Velma Crowdaire was at the shipyard. They were seen at the ticket office, but no one there has a recollection of where they went. I'm under the belief they paid off whoever sold them their passage. There were several ships leaving that day. One to France and two to South America."

The excitement Belle had been experiencing at the thought of those two getting their comeuppance vanished. *They'll escape. Walk free after all they'd done to hurt my family.*

"What can we do? Is there any way to find them?"

Henry dropped his gaze. "I won't lead you on. Searching for them in another country will be like finding a needle in a haystack. Difficult and expensive, but not impossible. Our end result may take some time. I do have several connections in both of those destinations. I'll send correspondence right away. Perhaps my letters will beat their crossing, but there is no telling. If that doesn't happen, our chances lessen more."

Emma leaned into Mavis's arms, her face a mask of hurt. Belle knew exactly how she felt.

Henry set a comforting hand on Lavinia's shoulder. "But I'll keep trying. The least we can do is keep them in hiding. Keep them from living the high life on the plunder they've stolen from this family. If they've planned for a time like this, and have a strategy laid out . . ."

"Finding them may be impossible," Belle finished for him.

He nodded.

"Well, at least we'll keep them on their toes," she said.

He smiled. "Now for a bit of good news. Everything is lined up. Construction on the house might begin as early as tomorrow. I suggest you start conspiring on colors and furniture. I know how much women like such things."

Belle gave him a look. "You're sure about the ranch house? We've talked about it at length, and we'd never want anyone to think that's why we're staying. We've lived in one bedroom our whole lives. Since we've arrived, sharing these two in the hotel has felt like a luxury. We don't need—"

"Belle! We've been over this many times. The ranch will be more valuable with a new home. Would you deny your father his dying wish?" He smiled kindly. "You need to come to grips with just how well-off you all are. We're not talking peanuts, I can assure you."

Someone else knocked on the door, and Emma answered.

"Good evening, ladies." Clint stood in the hallway, holding his hat. His brows shot up when he saw Henry.

"Please come in," Emma said, holding the door open.

"Only for a moment. I'm just back from Dove Creek."

Henry's expression grew dark and all business.

By the look on the sheriff's face, this was more bad news. "What did the prisoners say when you questioned them?"

"I didn't get a chance. They'd been released."

A gasp went around the room.

"What do you mean?" Henry barked. "Who would do such a thing?"

Clint held out a telegram. "Apparently, I did."

They all crowded in. The telegram said it was from Clint Dawson, sheriff of Eden.

RELEASE MY PRISONERS IMMEDIATELY STOP MISTAKEN IDENTITY STOP WILL SEND MORE INFO LATER STOP

CHAPTER FORTY-FOUR

The run-down building in font of Belle appeared more dilapidated than she'd remembered. *Mine? What to do?* At least those infernal odors she'd noticed on the breeze a few times before were absent. The building was long and narrow. A large rock on the boardwalk propped the door open, revealing a dark interior. No use putting her task off any longer. She needed to go in and meet Old Man Little, as Henry had so fondly called him. At least taking care of business would take her mind off that shocking telegram Clint had shared, and thoughts about who could be responsible.

Gathering her courage, she stepped into the small room sectioned off by a wall and a closed door. She'd imagined horror stories about the tannery, and she was about to face them firsthand. Warm air closed in around her.

"Hello?" She knocked on the counter. "Anyone here?"

A few leather products hung on the wall: reins, tanned hides of all sizes that hadn't been made into anything yet, floppy leather hats, leather chaps like Blake and the ranch hands wore. *I'd like a pair myself.* The inventory was next to nothing. She wondered how the place stayed in business.

"Hello?" she called again, knocking louder this time. Mr. Little was said to be nearing his ninetieth birthday. The man was hard of hearing and barely saw past the nose on his face.

The door to the back room opened to a gush of stinky smells. She resisted the urge to pinch her nose at the unpleasantness.

"Is someone out here?" a scratchy voice called. Mr. Little was half-way into the room before he saw her.

She had to step back to avoid a collision. "Hello."

Thick, round glasses magnified his eyes, making them appear much too large for his face. He pulled up. "I didn't see ya there, little missy. I hope ya haven't been waitin' long. What can I help ya with?"

She smiled and put out her hand. "I'm Belle Brinkman, John's daughter. I've inherited the tannery from my father."

"That's right. Blake was in earlier. Said you'd be stopping by some-time soon."

Blake? Already in town? She hadn't seen him yet that morning. An exciting flutter, one she'd gotten all too used to feeling since their kiss, made her stomach feel light and airy.

"My condolences about your pa dying the way he did." Mr. Little slowly shook his head. "He was a darned good fella. I liked him a lot."

"Thank you, Mr. Little," she said softly, looking into his too-large eyes. "That means more to me each time someone says it. I wish I'd gotten a chance to know him." Her father had gained the whole town's respect. "You sure have a nice collection of fine-looking items."

A craggy smile exposed only a few teeth. "Kind of you ta say. Will you be coming ta work here?"

Before she realized her actions, she pushed out her hands as if to keep the shiver-provoking thought back. Immediately, she dropped her arms and smiled. "Actually, no. I'll be spending most of my time at the ranch. I just wanted to meet you and have a look around."

"Fine, fine. I won't keep ya waitin'." He turned on his heel. "Follow me, if you dare."

There weren't as many hides as Belle had expected. A few were in the process of being worked, she guessed. Skins were stretched across large racks, both plain leather and others with colorful pelts. Mr. Little explained the process as he went, using a minimum of words. When it came to his business, he was as sharp as a tack.

They finally arrived at the back of the room, where a window was blessedly open. Here hung a rack of four jackets like the one Nicole owned. She hurried forward to feel their softness, lifting one sleeve to her cheek. "These are beautiful, Mr. Little. Why aren't you displaying any out front?"

He gave a good-hearted chuckle. "These are spoken for, that's why. I ain't as fast as I used ta be. At times I might have one or two for sale in the Toggery, but not often."

Dr. Dodge stuck his head in the back window. "Hello, Miss Brinkman." He smiled amiably, making his laugh lines double up on his cheeks. "I thought I heard your voice."

Belle felt a rush of affection for the middle-aged man who'd been so helpful with Katie. *He must have been very good-looking in his time.* His powerful build was quite impressive, even now, and his thick brown hair didn't have a hint of gray. He glanced at Mr. Little. "You doing all right today, Stinky? How's the rheumatism?"

Mr. Little frowned and shrank away from the window. "Not so bad, I guess," he replied haltingly, then glanced sheepishly at Belle. "My nickname on account of the smells my tanning creates. My real name's Marvin."

How mean! She'd like to let the doctor know, in no uncertain terms, that she thought him a bully. That he should apologize to Mr. Little. But he'd done so much for Katie, looking in on her several times a day, she felt indebted. Every time they'd met, his earnest smile held an element of protectiveness, and he'd been nothing but kind in the past. But all those good feelings flew out the window at Mr. Little's crestfallen expression. Calling an almost-ninety-year-old man Stinky was cruel, even if said in humor. *Especially if said in humor.* Particularly when it was apparent Mr. Little didn't care for the name.

"The tannery butts up to the back of my office." The doctor's eyes searched hers. "We're going to be neighbors. I've just come from checking on Katie a few minutes ago. She's making strides against her fears."

"Thank you, Doctor," she said curtly, unable to say anything else. She glanced at Mr. Little's clawlike fingers. Why hadn't anyone already alerted her to the man's poor health? "You'll both be happy to hear I intend to bring in an assistant for you, Mr. Little."

Shocked, the old man stepped back. "I can still do the work, missy. I wouldn't josh ya."

"Of course you can. I would never replace you. Not after seeing these beautiful coats. I'll have an apprentice do all the tanning, lifting, and preparations so you'll be able to go at a more leisurely pace. You're a craftsman of the highest order, Mr. Little. Men like you are few and far between."

The doctor frowned, clearly understanding he'd been put on notice. He straightened and pulled back from the windowsill he'd been leaning on. "I'll be on my way. But before I go, I'll pass on that your sisters are preparing to visit the sawmill, in case you'd like to stop over." He tipped his hat. "Good day."

She wondered how much Mr. Little had been able to hear. His face had brightened when she'd explained her intentions about hiring an apprentice. She smiled and moved closer.

"May I order a few of these coats for Christmas presents?"

His eyes widened. "How many would a few be?"

"One for each of my four sisters."

He ticked off the months on his fingers. "I might be able to get them done."

"And one for me," she added quickly. From the moment she'd seen Nicole's, she'd wanted one.

He gave her a wink and nodded.

A loud knock sounded on the front doorjamb. Startled, they both whipped around.

Blake.

She hadn't seen him since the kiss. Instantly, her heart rate kicked up, and she wondered what they would say to each other. He was too far away for her to see his eyes, but she had the distinct impression he was smiling.

He came forward, his Stetson dangling in his fingertips. When he was close, he halted and glanced around. "Well, what do you think, Miss Brinkman? Does your new endeavor suit you?"

She smiled sweetly, knowing full well he was teasing. "I'm intrigued, Mr. Harding. And I've so enjoyed the tour Mr. Little gave me. He certainly knows his business, and has graciously taken the time to explain the process for taking a hide to a finished product in depth. I can't thank him enough."

"Tweren't nothin', missy," he responded quietly. "Anytime you want another, you just let me know."

"Thank you, I will. I'll bring my sisters."

As if five of John's daughters at once were too much to think about, the shaping tool he held in his hands dropped to the floor with a clatter.

Blake bent to retrieve the utensil, and Belle took that opportunity to study his profile. It felt as if she hadn't seen him in years. She was parched for the sound of his voice. She hadn't dreamed she would get the chance to talk to him today.

"Mr. Harding, did you want to see me?"

"I do, if you have a moment. I have a little good news."

"That I could use. Shall we speak out front?"

"That's as good as place as any."

So polite. The conversation felt funny.

She bade Mr. Little goodbye and headed for the front door, with Blake following behind. Outside, she turned to face him. "What's the good news?"

"We'll be finished with the cattle sooner than expected. And the wrangler's outfit coming by to pick up the herd can come early. We'll be able to button this all up by Friday."

That's the good news? Funny he would search me out for that. But yes, she was happy they'd limped their way through and all had ended well. "That's wonderful." She was avoiding his gaze. Heat rose to her cheeks. *What else should I say?*

"And . . ."

"There's more?"

When he laughed, tingles danced up her back. *He certainly is in a good mood this morning.*

"We broke ground about an hour ago. A group of thirty builders showed up early and ready to work. If you get time later today, you should come out and watch. That is, if you have an escort. If you can't find one, I'm sure Clint will bring you out as soon as he's free. The house will go up fast with so many men on the job."

Having to be careful was cumbersome. "Can't I ride back with you?" Across the Old Spanish Trail and then the open lot, she could see movement at the mill on the other side of the river. She'd yet to go out there herself.

"I'm riding out in the next hour. I just came into town this morning . . ." His voice faded away.

That was curious. With all he had to do of late, she *was* surprised to see him. "For what?" She sucked in a breath when the truth dawned on her, and she searched out his gaze, unable to stay away a moment longer. "You came all this way to check on us?"

He slowly lifted a shoulder in a half-hearted shrug. "Guilty as charged. How's Katie? And everyone else? Were there any problems last night?"

"No problems, but there is alarming news."

His brow fell. "What?"

"The sheriff went to Dove Creek to question Katie's kidnappers—but they'd been released. The deputy there had received a fabricated telegram, supposedly from Sheriff Dawson, telling him to let them go."

Blake's jaw flexed several times as he studied the horizon. "Whoever's responsible is bold."

"Clint already spoke with the telegraph operator. Says the door was jimmied and a message sent while the office was closed."

"He believes him?"

She nodded.

"Then the sooner you're all out at the ranch, the better."

"I'm not sure all my sisters want to live out there. Seems they're beginning to enjoy the town. And there's more bad news . . ."

"More? What could be worse than that?"

"Henry got a lead on the Crowdaires. They're on a ship bound for the far reaches of the world. Finding them now is going to be tremendously difficult."

He gazed at her as if for the first time, studying her face.

He must have skipped shaving that morning because, once again, an intriguing dark shadow covered his sturdy jaw. The whiskers blended in with the beginning of his scar. She felt so close to him, having pondered what was going on between them all night—that is, if there *was* something between them. *Men don't just go around kissing women without a reason, do they?* She was mixed up, and he was the only one who could sort the puzzle pieces for her. If nothing else, he was a good friend—one she never wanted to lose.

"Your pain never seems to end, does it, Belle? I'm sorry about that, those scoundrels getting away—for now. But I won't let them go without a fight. You all deserve that, at least. Your pa used to say, 'Hurt makes you stronger, fear grows your courage, and heartache makes you smart.'" He grasped the post and gave her a smile. "It's not much comfort, but it's something."

"You're wrong. My father's words are much comfort, and you're so generous with them. Thank you, Blake." The sun had grown higher, casting them in the shade of the roof. Boldly, she grasped his hand and gave a small tug. "I want to ask a question, and I want you to answer honestly. Will you do that?" His brow arched stubbornly, so she pointed a finger in his face. "I mean it, Blake. Promise me."

CHAPTER FORTY-FIVE

B lake released a long sigh, mostly to make her smile. She did. "If I must."

"You must."

Belle looked feminine in a pretty yellow dress; he was glad it wasn't black. "Fine, but can we at least walk?"

"That would be lovely. I'd like to go to the mill. My sisters will be there soon, or they might already be there now. Is the lumberyard close enough that we can get there on foot?"

"Sure." He patted Banjo's hip as they left his gelding tied in front of the leather shop. "Just down the road and over the bridge." The breeze was brisk, but the sun helped to keep away a chill. "I see you're out of mourning?"

Her lips wobbled. "I'll never be finished mourning, but choosing our businesses last night felt like a new beginning. We took a vote and decided the time had come."

"I'm glad."

She pointed another finger. "And you're changing the subject."

He smiled and shrugged. "What do you want to know?"

"How you got your scar. I know Moses figures into the story somewhere. About your family too."

Kicking up a little dirt with his boot toe, he looked at her from a tipped-down head. Not fond of sharing his story, he'd known this day would eventually arrive. "I'd just turned ten years old when my brother set out for his first battle in the Civil War. He was fighting for the Union and was older than I was by seven years. We'd been on our own for a long time, but had been taken in by a kind, childless couple some six months before. Barton and me helped with the chores around the farm. They fed us and gave us a nice room with two beds. But Missouri was overrun with fighting. Barton felt strongly about signing up. I didn't want him to go, but he did anyway. Said a man wasn't much of a man if he didn't stand for the things he believed in. He'd been gone for three months' training and came back on leave to visit before his unit was sent into battle. When he left, I snuck away and followed." He glanced across the street for a moment, remembering. "I still feel bad about leaving that farm the way I did."

"What about your parents?"

"They'd been dead for years."

She reached over and touched his sleeve.

"I was small and fast. I didn't want to be left behind. Heard there was going to be fighting past Missouri's southern border, in Arkansas, which wasn't that many miles away. Barton would be furious if he knew I'd followed, so I stayed hidden, which wasn't that difficult in the sea of soldiers. Confederates were comin', and not a small number. Men were scared."

Blake felt his scar pulse. Belle was walking on his left side, so she was getting a vivid show of the mutilation, he was sure. *Nothing I can do about that now.* Talking about Barton made his heart trip in his chest.

"I surprised a young man with a bayonet as I tried to find Barton. We fought and he wounded me. When the shooting starts, you can hardly think with all the screaming and crying, smoke, and gun blasts. Men running here and there, dirt marring their uniforms. Blood everywhere." Remembering, he had to stop, collect his thoughts.

She reached over and grasped his arm. "Wait! You mean one of our own Union soldiers tried to kill you?"

"He was little more than a boy himself."

"Oh, Blake! That's terrible! I'm so sorry." Tears glistened in her eyes.

He gave a curt nod and began walking slowly. "After seeing so many dead soldiers, all I could think about was my brother. I needed to find him. Protect him if I could. In shock, and covered in my own blood, I struggled through a hedge of brambles and arrived just as he took a bullet in the chest. I would've died there by his side, but Moses came upon me. I was as still as a corpse. The battle had been over for hours, and everyone was gone. Moses had been thrown into a gully by an explosion and knocked out. He was eighteen, wore a ragged, blood-splattered uniform like my brother's, and was missing a boot. Disoriented and in pain from a gunshot wound in his arm, he plucked me off Barton's cold body and carried me like a baby until he found a deserted barn. Somehow, he cleaned me up, stitched my wound with a small sewing kit he carried, and cared for me for several days, maybe a week. He was sick with fever himself. Those days are difficult for me to remember. He told me later that he went looking for Barton's body, but by then it was gone, and most of the other dead soldiers' bodies had been collected too."

Belle had her handkerchief out and was wiping her tears. Blake had no more tears to shed. They passed Mrs. Gonzales, the Mexican woman who'd told him about the peddler's wagon, hard at work at her fire. She watched them with curiosity.

"What happened then?" Belle struggled to say.

"I got better, and Moses had to return to his unit. Since I was an orphan, he did my bidding by putting me on a westbound train, away from the fighting, and wished me luck. I told him I was going to ride until I got to Colorado. Barton always talked about the Rocky Mountains and how one day we would make our way west. Live in Colorado." He glanced at her and smiled. "I was weak. I stayed huddled in that train car with a handful of other bums until hunger forced me off—but I was in Colorado. Weeks came and went in a haze of hunger and fever. It's amazing I lived. Everyone I came upon was repulsed by the half-healed wound, still oozing pus in some places. When I could, I hitched rides farther west. I don't know how long after that I stumbled onto your ranch. The rest you know."

She cried into her handkerchief, her tears flowing freely. "I'm so, so sorry. To witness what you did, and be injured, and almost die is unthinkable. I can't even comprehend how much you must have suffered." She stopped to blow her nose.

People were looking, but he didn't care.

"I want you to know that the ranch is yours, Blake," she said, her tone filled with emotion. New tears bathed her face she'd just dried. "It's *your* ranch more than it's ours. *Always* remember that." She turned into his chest. He put his arms around her, holding her tight, letting her cry for several minutes. He hadn't meant to cause her such distress.

Struggling for breath, she looked up into his eyes. "B-but how did Moses find you after the war? It must have been years later."

"It was." He slipped the hankie from her quivering fingers and got to dabbing at her tears, which never seemed to stop. "That time in the barn, when I was hanging on to life and he was struggling too, he'd talk to fill the hours. He'd been a slave, but ran away and joined up to fight. He'd mentioned a town where his aunt lived, and where he intended to go after the war, if he survived. It was strange, but about ten years later, in a dream, I remembered the name of the town in South Carolina he'd spoken of. Your father helped me find him. By then, his only living relative had been dead for several years, so he jumped at the chance to start over."

She took the linen square from his hand and gave him what he was sure she thought was a very serious stare. "S-such a story. I don't know how you've kept that inside." More tears streamed down. "The Five

Sisters is your home, Blake Harding. Don't ever think different. And don't you ever leave."

He was touched by how Belle kept repeating that mantra, so he'd not feel excluded. *But will I ever really be part of the family? Belle is going back to Philadelphia to marry Lesley Atkins.* Blake didn't have any hold on her. Maybe Mavis or Lavinia would remain in Eden, he supposed, or perhaps all the rest of them. But Eden wouldn't be the same without Belle. He knew he'd better get used to that fact. With all the excitement ahead, there was going to be heartache too. And to that he was no stranger.

In the living quarters in the rear of the cantina, Santiago watched his father pull out a chair from the table and slowly lower his body into the seat. He looked old and decrepit, even though he was only forty-seven. His eyes weren't red from drinking. Today was Demetrio's birthday. What would turning twenty-seven in prison feel like while still facing ten more years? Santiago couldn't imagine. No words could cheer his father.

"Can I get you anything, Father? A cup of tea or breakfast from Mrs. Gonzales?"

"Gracias, my son, but no. I just want to be left alone."

Nodding, Santiago grasped the money pouch with its few coins of change and headed into the cantina, the scents of stale beer and whiskey still strong on the air. Chairs stood on top of tables. Their bartender had taken one chair down and sat at a table, drinking coffee while waiting for the bar to open. Santiago placed the money in a small strongbox, then picked up the broom. *Is this all I have to expect from life? This cantina, this town, this emptiness?* Feeling caged, he headed for the porch. He understood completely why Demetrio had run off in search of more.

"Santiago, my friend." Padre Francisco stood at the bottom of the steps.

"Padre," he replied respectfully, thinking back to the man's observant gaze the day Santiago had passed the message to the rider.

"A word?"

Santiago leaned the broom against the handrail and took the steps down. Padre Francisco smiled up into his face. The man never seemed to age. He always spoke in the same peaceful tone and never lost his patience—no matter what kind of mischief Santiago found himself in.

"What's on your mind, Padre?"

"I find myself thinking about you much these days. Whenever that happens, more often than not, something is amiss."

That was his way of saying, "Give up the goose. I saw you take it, break it, or start it." He was good at getting a confession without asking any questions at all.

"No, Padre. No trouble. You don't have to worry about me."

Padre Francisco studied him for so long that Santiago began to fidget.

"No? Well, good. I'm glad to hear that. How's your father? Today's Demetrio's birthday. I'm sure he's in need of a cheerful word."

"True. He's inside if you want to visit."

The priest gave a nod and then lifted his gaze one more time to Santiago's. He'd clearly seen the rider and somehow knew of the interaction. Santiago could fool himself all he wanted, but he knew he was going to spill his guts sooner or later.

"It's not what you think."

Padre Francisco pursed his lips. "I hope not. I know how much Demetrio means to you—to all of us. You can do nothing to help him now, except pray. He needs to walk a straight line. He is the only one who can help himself."

"I sent him a few things to make his life easier. A blanket, chocolate bars, a box of cigars. Things like that."

"No file, explosives, or weapons?"

Santiago shook his head, though the padre wasn't far from the truth about where his intentions had started. He'd arranged for a pack of mule freighters passing through to sell him dynamite so Demetrio could blow his way out and ride for California. But his good sense had returned, and he'd left it buried beneath the old barn. Instead, he'd sent a box filled with the exact things he'd just told the padre about.

"I'm happy to hear that. I know how much you desire to have Demetrio home."

"Not home. Just out of prison. He could never be happy here now."

A buggy approached. Four of the Brinkman sisters waved as they passed, the driver keeping the horse at a trot. The carriage turned at the rocks by the icehouse and crossed the bridge. They were on their way to the mill.

"A breath of springtime," the priest mumbled, still watching the buggy. "Let me know how I can be of assistance if you find yourself in need."

That was his way of saying, "Let me help you stay out of trouble." With that, the padre climbed the stairs to go in search of Santiago's father.

"This is quite impressive." Katie followed the lumberyard manager around the large steam-powered saws and equipment. Belle, with her other sisters and Blake, trailed at a respectable distance to give Katie a chance to affirm her place in the company.

When she and Blake had arrived, all four sisters had gaped at her red eyes and runny nose but kept their questions to themselves.

Katie glanced at them over her shoulder and then looked back at the manager, a twinkle in her eye. "It's much more advanced than I'd thought. I expected a waterwheel turning slowly down at the river's edge."

The river ran fast along an extended beach of white sand. Towering trees gave shade, and yet the sunshine that did get through the seemingly impenetrable leaves sparkled on the blue water like diamonds. A few logs were anchored to the shore by thick ropes.

What a beautiful spot to spend the day, Belle thought. *And a dangerous business to be in.*

"That's how we began, Miss Brinkman," the manager replied. "But your father liked to keep up with the times. He was always around, asking questions about how we could be more efficient and make more money and such."

"I can see that."

Blake leaned close and whispered into Belle's ear, "Katie seems quite interested. I'm surprised."

Belle couldn't get Blake's story out of her mind. Not only had he sustained a life-threatening wound, but he'd lost his only brother. Thinking of losing a single one of her sisters made her lose her breath. *How did he survive? And at such a tender age.* Her heart shuddered when she thought of him stumbling around each night, looking for food and shelter. She looked up into his eyes, and her heart melted.

"She really does," she whispered back, trying to hide her sentimentality. "I'm a bit surprised myself. I'm glad, though. She needs something to take her mind off her fears." She brushed away a layer of fine dust particles that had covered her chin. "The air is gritty, but I like the scent of the plentiful pine shavings. Much nicer than the tannery."

Blake laughed. Mavis, Lavinia, and Emma, who were admiring some newly milled boards stacked several feet high, turned to see what had transpired. They smiled and then looked away. Katie and the manager moved out of the pole building and headed for a small cabin that displayed a sign designating it as the office. The mountains loomed in the background, bringing a sense of peace to Belle's soul.

The Rocky Mountains that Blake's brother, Barton, had wanted to see. Is he up there now, watching over Blake?

"What do you think, Belle? Could you be a lumber baroness?" His eyes were filled with questions that looked to have nothing to do with the conversation at hand.

"Better than I can be a tannery baroness. I don't know what to do with that place. Was Mr. Little the owner before it passed to Father?"

"Indeed. He had a son who worked with him. He would be there now, but he was killed a few years ago by a band of out—" He snapped his mouth closed.

"You don't have to mince words with me, Blake. I already know the dangers. Anyplace in the world can be perilous. I could be run over by a wagon in Philadelphia just as easily as I could here. There're no guarantees in life."

He regarded her so long she felt her cheeks grow warm.

"True enough. After Mr. Little's son was gone, business fell off because inventory was so low. Mr. Little was starving, but didn't say anything to anyone. John went in one day, added two and two together, and made the man a handsome offer—"

KABOOM!

CHAPTER FORTY-SIX

At the thundering blast, Mavis, Emma, and Lavinia screamed. The ground under Belle's feet trembled. The buggy that had stood empty at the turnaround in front of the lumber office careened away as the horses bolted in fright. Belle jerked around to look at Eden.

"What the devil!" Blake shouted, and then grasped Mavis's arm. "Stay here with the lumber manager. Tell him to keep his eyes open."

He turned and sprinted away—not toward the road that led to the bridge, but into the trees on the far side of the clearing. Belle grasped the front of her skirt and followed, ignoring Mavis's demands that she stop.

Keeping up with Blake wasn't possible. Soon he was out of sight, but she could hear his footsteps pounding on ahead. "Blake, wait!" she called, fear over what could have happened pushing her onward.

At the edge of the river, she skidded to a halt. A bouncing rope bridge spanned the width of the rushing water, and Blake was already almost across.

"Blake!"

He turned. "Go back!" he shouted, jabbing a finger in the direction they'd come. "Stay at the sawmill until I know what we're dealing with!" The next moment, he was gone.

The bridge swung back and forth. Two thick upper ropes, which acted as handrails, extended the width of the river and were anchored to a large oak. Two lower ropes held wooden slats placed about a foot apart. By the looks of it, the wobbly thing had been here a hundred years. Her mouth went dry. She'd never been keen on heights. Five rotting steps led up to the platform, which would put her about ten feet above the rushing rapids.

Henry is over there! Karen and Mr. Little. Sheriff Dawson and the rest of Eden. Blake now too.

The blast had sounded deadly. She didn't have time to be frightened.

Taking a deep breath, she forced herself up the steps before she could think differently. Every cell in her body sprang to life. Clutching both sides of the prickly ropes, she tried the first slat with the toe of her shoe and then added a little weight. The board dipped dramatically and then swayed to the side. Her heart pitched forward as she jumped back to safety.

She glanced back the way she'd come. Should she return and use the other bridge, by the icehouse? That would take too long.

A rustle of wind through the leaves sounded like a man's whisper.

I love you. You're mine. Take a deep breath and go. Don't look down.

Unwilling to analyze what she'd just heard, she gripped the ropes loosely beneath her palms and directed her feet to step one after the other. When the bridge swayed, she set her weight in the other direction. Her skirt tangled, jerking her to a stop. With one shaking hand, she worked herself loose. Several times she gasped at the deep bounce, and another time her foot slipped on the slick wood. A cold mist sprang up, wetting her face and hands. If she fell into the river now, there would be no swimming out. In the middle she paused, breathing through her nose to calm her light-headedness.

KABOOM!

Another blast? What on earth was happening in Eden? She sucked in a deep breath and surged forward, counting the steps to the other side. Landing on the platform with a rush of joy, she bolted down the stairs. Emerging through the trees, she realized she was behind a smattering of small houses; one had been pointed out to her as the sheriff's. Kitty-corner was the tannery. There was not a soul in sight, and one side of the structure was now totally blown away. *Thank God Banjo is nowhere to be seen. Where's Blake? And the rest of the town? Did the first blast happen in a different location?* Fear for Mr. Little propelled her forward.

"Mr. Little!" she called, entering through the blown-away wall. "Marvin, where are you?" Boards and hides were strewn about. Smoke blocked her sight as she searched the room, stepping over a pail, a chair, broken glass. Finally, she spotted two legs extending from under a pile of boards. "Mr. Little," she cried, grasping the boards and pulling them off the groggy man.

"What happened?" he sputtered weakly, a large gash in his head bleeding profusely. His eyes blinked a few times and then closed.

She didn't know what to do. No one had arrived to help. She had nothing to stop the bleeding. "I'm going for bandages at the doctor's office!" His pallor had gone from bad to worse in just moments. She placed his hand over the cut. "Press down hard. I'll be right back."

Dashing through the room, Belle exited the back door and ran across the alley. Relieved the doctor's back door was unlocked, she rushed inside. She glanced about. Finding the infirmary, she grasped a bottle of iodine and a stack of clean dressings. She was almost to the door when she heard a scrape in the next room. *The doctor? Is it possible he's here?* She whirled and opened the door.

Dr. Dodge looked up from his position on his knees, reaching through a hatch in the floor. He scrambled to his feet. "What're you doing here?" he demanded.

"Didn't you hear the blasts?" she screeched. "Mr. Little is badly hurt. He's bleeding, and I'm afraid he might . . ."

Her words trailed away. Two sticks of what looked like dynamite were visible beneath the floorboards. Fear flooded her mind, and she inched back the way she'd come.

"Get back here!" He lunged forward, grasping her arm. She'd never heard him so angry. "You should have taken the payout and gone home!" His strangled tone sent a shiver down her spine. Eyes filled with confusion glared into hers. "No one was supposed to get hurt. You could have made this so easy, but you didn't! *You're* responsible!"

She clawed and struggled, but couldn't get free from his iron grasp. Panting, she realized these might be her last few moments of life. "*You're* responsible for all the trouble? The kidnapping? The snake? Who else would have such access? You did, every time you came to check on Katie."

Is that pride in his sneer?

"I even went out to the ranch. How did you like the bloody hatchet? I thought that especially entertaining."

I have to keep him talking! The alternative was too horrific to contemplate. "You were very clever to send the telegram to Dove Creek. *You* bandaged the kidnappers' cuts and bruises once Clint locked them up. It's all so clear to me now . . ."

In a moment of calm, she tried to jerk away, but he laughed and pinned her to the wall, both of them breathing hard.

Maybe someone will come. Keep talking. Keep talking.

"Please, Doctor! You're mixed up! You need help. Let us help you."

"I'll see this through, only in a different way." He glanced around.

Is he looking for something to kill me with?

"Please, Dr. Dodge. You were my father's friend. Why are you doing this? Why? I don't understand."

His deranged laughter made her want to cower, but she wouldn't.

"Your father was *never* my friend!" He flung the words at her so forcefully spittle covered her face. "*I* was the one who should have married Celeste. I treated her father the best I could, but he was destined to die. I had a flourishing practice, a nice place for her to live. I could have taken care of her, bought her pretty things. But no. *Your father* never gave me the chance before rushing her to the altar. I *loved* her! All those years, I *loved* your mother from afar, waiting, hoping. But like a rutting stag, he had her with child year after year. He was responsible for her unhappiness, for driving her away."

"Doctor, I'm sure you'll feel better later, once you lie down." His hold around her throat tightened. Her head felt light. Her vision grew dim. *Where is everyone?* As long as they were talking, he wasn't thinking about finishing her off.

"When I saw the will, I knew you'd come back to his beloved Eden," he went on as if it felt good to clear his conscience. "I'd finally have my revenge. Scare you away for good. You'd hate what he'd loved."

"And the money? Were you after that too?"

Another bark of malevolent laughter ripped from his throat. "That idea came to me later. How rich! I'd not only foil the mighty Brinkman's plan to bring you all back, but I'd end up with everything he'd worked so hard for." He sucked in a jerky breath. "With my brother as the mayor, getting access to that fortune won't be too difficult for me once Harding is dead. My brother has always been as dumb as a log. And then I found dynamite hidden behind the old barn. My plan was perfect . . . and I won't let you ruin it now."

His sweaty hand around her throat constricted ever so slowly. *No one is coming. No one will find me before it's too late.* She needed to save herself. In a move fueled with the thought that she might never see her sisters—or Blake—again, she jerked up her knee with all the force she could muster.

His breath swooshed out. He swung her around and slapped her with an open hand. "You shouldn't have come! Now I *have* to kill you."

Belle cried at the pain, but just then someone knocked them both over from behind. She fell. Blake and the doctor rolled one over the other until they hit the wall. They scrambled to their feet at the same time. Blake rammed his fist into the doctor's mouth, which sent him reeling through the doorway. Blake caught him in the infirmary. As they wrestled across the counter, medicine bottles and surgical implements crashed to the floor and against the wall. The doctor grasped a scalpel.

Holding the doorjamb to steady herself, Belle cried out, "Blake! Watch out!"

Too late! The doctor sliced open Blake's shirt, drawing blood. Blake hooked the large man with a foot around the back of his leg and drove his fist into his abdomen at the same time. Dr. Dodge doubled over with a cry of pain as he fell, but was back instantly with two punches to Blake's face. Stunned, Blake fell back against the wall.

The doctor dashed out the back door just as Clint rushed in the front.

The sheriff took one look at Blake and Belle. "Where is he?"

Blake hitched his head, and the two ran out after him.

Regaining her senses, Belle followed as best she could. She ran through the alley and found herself in front of the hotel. Frenzied people were everywhere. Nobody understood what was happening.

"Look!" someone shouted and pointed up at the sheer rock wall.

Belle glanced up in horror at the same time Henry appeared at her side. There was no time for words. They watched Blake and Clint closing in on the doctor as he scrambled up the sloped ridge that led to the top.

Blake stumbled, then regained his footing.

"Let him go!" Belle shouted, frightened of the steep drop-off only a few feet away.

At the sound of her voice, the doctor stopped and looked down. Then he turned back to see Blake and Clint closing in fast. Bending, he struggled to lift a large boulder over his head, bent his knees, and launched the weapon.

Blake and Clint darted out of the rock's path, and it careened past, clattering down the hill, and then off the edge, making people scream and jump back below.

Turning to run, the doctor's foot slipped. He cried out. With arms akimbo, he looked back the way he was falling, fright etched on his face.

Belle screamed.

Henry grasped her and spun her around to his chest so she wouldn't see.

A moment later, a deadly quiet settled over Eden—as well as Belle's heart.

CHAPTER FORTY-SEVEN

Two days later, Blake entered the Toggery, looking for Belle. The soft scents of new fabric, leather, and shoe polish wafted on the air. He'd been all over town, arriving at places just as she'd left a few moments before. At the café, Lavinia had not so slyly mentioned that Belle had recently received a telegram from Lesley, and then, as if she hadn't just dumped a fresh road apple in his pocket, asked if he'd like a piece of warm chokecherry pie fresh out of the oven. *Women.*

In the light of the side window, he spotted Belle in deep conversation with Emma and Mrs. Smith, the woman Henry was involved with. He'd met her a few times but still hadn't figured out what she meant to his friend. The women held several lengths of fabric between them. Laughter went up, causing him to smile. It felt darn good, having the threat to John's daughters removed.

"Blake," Emma called, giving him a quick, half-hearted wave. "Is Johnny over there? Seems he's hidden himself away."

Belle smiled, and Mrs. Smith shyly nodded.

"Let me have a look." He walked around the shop, nodding to Mr. Buns, who looked about as happy as a colicky horse. Wasn't difficult to guess he didn't like all the changes coming to the store. The boy wasn't behind a display of hats, or in the dressing room. At a rack of long dusters, Blake lifted one to find the child crouched underneath.

"Hello, Johnny," Blake said softly, not wanting to frighten him. "That's a good hiding spot."

"Hi," he whispered back with a slight lisp. He peered out along the floor, and a moment later up at Blake. "Want to hide wiff me?"

A little embarrassed warmth crept into Blake's face. The innocence in the boy's blue eyes was something Blake had lost at an early age. He saw caution there too, but not fear.

"Not today, but someday soon. How's that?"

Johnny nodded, climbed to his feet, and took hold of Blake's hand, surprising Blake again. He had little experience with children—except for the few months before the girls left the ranch. And then, he'd been a kid himself.

Now that Belle had a genuine reason to do so, she appeared at Blake's side. "There you are, you little scamp." She affectionately tweaked Johnny's nose. "Your mama's been looking for you."

Emma and Mrs. Smith walked over. His mother took Johnny's hand.

"Are you shopping for new clothes for the upcoming party?" Emma asked. "I'll be happy to help." She looked him up and down with a critical brow.

He chuckled and shook his head. "No. I have plenty to wear, thank you very much. Besides, we have time before that happens. I need to get the dance floor put in, close in some rooms, and have a few other areas at the building site to make safe. I wish you'd postpone this crazy idea until the house is completed. Wouldn't that be better? Then you can show it off."

"We'll have *another* party when it's finished, silly," Emma replied, undaunted. "A housewarming." The better he got to know each sister, the more mystifying layers he discovered. Emma was no exception.

He narrowed his eyes. "What has your color up? Are you plotting against your partner?" She snuck a quick look at Belle, who was smiling.

Emma went up on tiptoe and gave him a brotherly kiss on the cheek. "We'd never plot against you, Blake. You not only saved Katie, but Belle as well. And you're a good fellow." Her eyes sparkled with merriment. Apparently finished with the conversation, Emma put her hand on Mrs. Smith's back and directed the woman to the other side of the store. But only after giving Blake a surreptitious wink.

"How does your arm feel?" Belle asked now that they were alone. She gazed at his arm as if it was the most intriguing subject she'd seen all year. Since their kiss, and then her ordeal with Dr. Dodge, Belle had been friendly—but also wary. He'd seen the questions in her eyes.

Problem was, he didn't know how to get around the awkwardness without talking. And talking could make matters worse, since he was as confused as all get-out himself. He had to go nice and easy from this day forward.

He rolled up his sleeve so she could see the few stitches Moses had thrown in where the doctor's scalpel had sliced. "A mite tender, but I'll live."

"Good. Good that you'll live, I mean." She blushed scarlet. "Have you been by to see Mr. Little?"

"Nope, sure haven't. I planned to do just that when I went over to check on the livery, the madman doctor's *other* casualty of the first blast. Maverick and Mavis are darned lucky no one was hurt and that all that was affected was a small outbuilding. Why?"

"Because I have, early this morning. He's doing fine, and that's good, but even in that nice, large boardinghouse room, Mr. Little misses the stinky old tannery and his cramped quarters above. I don't know what I'm going to do. I had been thinking about tearing down what's left and building something completely different."

"Oh? Like what?"

She shook her head. "Not really sure. But I do know anything other than a tannery would break Mr. Little's heart. And I'd not want to do that to a man so old." She glanced over to her sister. "I'm leaving. Bye-bye."

Emma shot a hand in the air but didn't break her conversation with Mrs. Smith and Mr. Buns, who stood next to the drape that closed off the dressing room. Blake followed Belle to the door, not ready to let her slip away just yet. He'd been ranching for a couple of days and was in need of a little of her attention. *Why?* He tried not to ask himself.

He stepped out into the sunlight behind Belle and closed the door. The weather couldn't be nicer for the last day of September. People were coming and going as normal, and everyone had warmed up to Belle and her sisters considerably. Seemed after the doctor incident, everyone felt as close as family.

"Good morning, Miss Brinkman," Cash called as he led two horses down the middle of the street toward the livery. "Beautiful day."

"Yes, i-it's beautiful," Belle called back haltingly. Blake didn't miss her cheeks darkening.

Rogue! He may have only been fourteen, but with Clint's son's height and build, he didn't look a day younger than twenty-one. "Good to see you too, Cash," Blake called boldly. "I have several broken wagon wheels out at the ranch. You going that way soon?" Blake almost chuckled when the boy's shoulders slumped.

"You're incorrigible." Belle softly laughed and looked away.

"Somebody needs to keep that boy in his place."

"And that somebody should be you?"

"Why not?"

A smile appeared on her lips. She surprised him by taking his arm. "Oh, Blake, it feels so good not to be worried about somebody trying to scare us off—or kill you." She let go his arm and turned a full circle. "And the beauty of Eden has seeped into my soul."

But you received a telegram from Lesley. What did it say, Belle? And how did you respond?

"I can't believe at one time I thought of the ranch as a means to an end. Was I really that shallow?" A couple of cowboys riding down the street tipped their hats to her, and she smiled. "Look across the street. Mr. Little is waving to us from his room." She raised her arm and waved back, smiling broadly. "I need to bake him a dozen cookies." She captured his gaze with hers. "You think he'd like that?"

Who wouldn't? "I do, Belle. I think he'd like that very much."

They were heading for the hotel in the calm of the day, but Blake felt an edge to his mood. *What does that mean?* It was almost as if Belle had taken him at his word, saying the kiss didn't mean a thing. *She's gotten past it.* Too bad it was ever present in his mind.

CHAPTER FORTY-EIGHT

I n what would be her new bedroom when the house was finished, Belle fiddled with her hair in the reflection of a large mirror that was set on a temporary dresser. The party night had arrived. Decorations had been hung in the trees, the studded-but-open walls, and the barn below in the ranch yard.

Frustrated, she made a face. With shaky hands, she pinned the last of her hair into place. The second-story room was spacious and had a gorgeous view of the mountains. Her chest tightened, thinking how she'd been blessed—she and all her sisters. In this house, she felt almost as if their father was still alive. And their mother too. All of them together.

Wearing only her pantaloons and chemise, she refused to let any thought or feeling put a damper on their party. "I won't be sad tonight. Father intended this house as a gift. To be celebrated, not to be a reminder of things that could have been." She took a deep breath and lifted the photograph of her parents off the dresser. It had been taken after they'd married but before Mavis had been born. Blake had found several photographs right after her father had passed and surprised the sisters with the gifts. Belle fingered the image for a moment and then placed a kiss on each beloved face.

"My room will be perfect, Father," she said aloud, feeling a bit of comfort. "As will the rest of the house. Blake and the men have worked so hard, and Henry has practically burned up the telegraph apparatus with all the orders he's been putting out on our account. Furniture, wall coverings, hardware. As much as we've protested, he's not let us scrimp, and now I'm glad for it."

Heat pricked her eyes. "Mother, you'd love it here. You'd have all the necessities you didn't have before." She glanced around the bare upstairs room. Blankets enclosed the open walls. Blake had had the carpenters fashion a temporary-but-sturdy staircase so each of the sisters could prepare in her own bedroom.

Steps echoed on the bare wood outside her room. "Knock, knock. It's Mavis. May I come in?"

Belle quickly blinked away the moisture pooling behind her eyes as she set the picture back in its spot. "Yes. You're just in time to help me with my buttons."

Mavis floated in, looking beautiful in a lavender velvet gown perfect for her coloring. Tonight she wore elbow-length white gloves. She looked stunning. "Oh, Mavis. I've never seen you more beautiful."

Her face brightened. "Thank you, Belle. I do feel pretty tonight."

With the cool evenings, the girls had chosen to wear velvet, but in varying shades and styles. With the help of Mrs. Smith, Karen, and a few other townswomen, they'd been able to complete the dresses on time. Carefully lifting her periwinkle-pink gown off the bed, Belle lowered it, then lifted one petticoat-covered leg and prudently stepped inside. Shimmying the dress into place, she turned. Mavis began fastening the row of twenty-five fabric-covered buttons with practiced speed.

Finished, Mavis ran her hand over the fabric. "Turn around and let me have a look."

Feeling like a princess, Belle turned.

Mavis sucked in a breath. "Oh! Blake won't know what to do with himself when he sees you."

Belle, who was smoothing one sleeve, brought her gaze up. "Blake? What do you mean?"

Mavis smiled and tipped her head, tsking softly. "Seriously, Belle. You're not going to pretend there isn't something between you and Blake, are you? Your feelings are as plain as the nose on my face. Surely you're ready to give up the pretense of friendship."

"I have no idea what you're talking about," Belle sputtered, feeling muddled and a bit angry. Tonight was special. She didn't want to ruin the celebration with cross words with Mavis or confusing thoughts of Blake. He'd invaded her dreams for the last month, though, exciting and puzzling her. *He's made it perfectly clear we're friends and friends only! Why can't my sister leave me alone?* Tonight, all she wanted to do was relax and waltz a time or two. "Blake and I are friends. Just like the rest of you."

"You're being silly!" Mavis's voice had lost its softness. "If what you say is true, you'd better let *him* know. He's in love with you, Belle. There was a change around the time of your birthday, and I thought the two of you had an understanding but were keeping the surprise under wraps until now."

Remembering the kiss, she stood firm. "I can assure you that is *not* the case."

They stared at each other.

"Really?"

Unable to hold Mavis's stare a moment longer, Belle fluffed out her skirt and repositioned the yards of velvet around her petticoat. "Yes, really."

Lavinia pushed aside the blanket and slipped into the room. She stopped just inside the door. Her dark-blue dress was just as attractive as the others. "What's going on?" she asked, warily creeping closer. "I heard your voices. You're not fighting, are you?"

Belle and Mavis said nothing.

Lavinia smiled. "Well, good. The ranch hands have arrived. You should see them all spit shined and dressed to kill. They look so cute, you'll smile." She lowered her voice and came closer. "And Belle, wait until you see Blake. He's never looked more handsome. If I didn't know better, I would think he may have an important question to ask you tonight. He just has that sense about him."

Belle, facing the mirror, dabbed a tiny amount of eau de toilette behind her ear. Finished, she slowly turned. "What on earth are you going on about, Lavinia? Blake is no more special to me than the rest of the ranch hands." *Then why does my heart call me a liar?* "Except that he's our partner. I don't know where these silly accusations are coming from." She glanced at Mavis and then back to Lavinia. "Have you so quickly forgotten about Lesley?" *And then, there was the telegram . . .*

Already, he missed her. Said he wanted to come spend time.

What he's not saying is that he really wants to change my mind about the six months.

She was still deciding how to reply.

Lavinia's stunned gaze was frozen in shock. "W-what did I say? I only meant . . ."

"I'm sorry," Belle blurted. "I'm just nervous. The buildup for this night has had me on edge, and now that it's here, I'm a nervous wreck. First, let me say how gorgeous you look tonight, Lavinia. You'll outshine the stars." She went over and embraced her sister, feeling like a shrew.

She hadn't meant to bite everyone's heads off—especially not tonight. She was just so mixed up of late. Wrecking the party for her sisters was the last thing she wanted to do. "Has the quartet set up?" she asked a bit sheepishly.

"Yes, they have," Emma answered as she came through the opening where the door would someday be. "I saw to that myself." Dressed in ice-blue velvet, she looked like a royal queen. "Everything is set and ready. The food will be laid out on time, and we have absolutely nothing to worry about. The house, even though only halfway finished, looks gorgeous. I think Father would be delighted at how everything is turning out."

"And Mother too," Belle added softly. "Let's not forget her." She pretended not to see the worried, confused, perturbed looks flying around the room.

"Absolutely," Emma went on. "She's never far from my thoughts." She went to the window and looked out on the darkened landscape. "Blake and Henry have been unbelievable. Construction is whizzing along. I'm still amazed." She sauntered to the mirror, edging out Belle. Leaning close, she pinched each cheek several times and then smiled at her reflection, brushing a few hairs at her temple. "Belle, I can't wait until you see Bla—"

With composed restraint, Belle held out a hand, stopping Emma midsentence. "Let me say this *one last time*," she uttered softly, smiling, even though she didn't know what she was going to do about her irrational feelings. "Blake and I are friends and business partners. There isn't a thing more between us."

Emma stared in shocked silence in the mirror's reflection at Belle. Mavis came forward and laid a calming hand on Emma's arm before she had a chance to dig in any deeper, as the other two had.

"You look lovely tonight, Emma," she said, artfully changing the subject. Belle wished she could be as diplomatic. She could learn a lot from Mavis. "All the men will be speechless."

Belle nodded and bussed Emma's cheek with her own, thankful Katie hadn't shown up to add *her* two cents to the discussion. Having been rescued by him from the peddler's wagon, her baby sister was Blake's ardent devotee. Belle wouldn't want to cross her.

"You should be proud," Trevor said, handing Blake a glass of punch. "The place has gone up without a hitch." The other ranch hands wandered around the large room, anxious for the women to show up, he was sure. A long buffet table made of plywood and sawhorses and covered with several tablecloths held a punch bowl and glasses at one end, with plenty of room for the forthcoming food. The home would be finished in approximately two weeks, barring any complications. "To have the place this far along and roofed, all while completing a roundup. I'd say that's a record."

Blake took a sip of the sweet concoction and grinned. He did feel pleased. And a persistent other feeling also swirled inside. Whenever Belle walked into the room, his heart jumped with excitement. He couldn't get enough of her. He'd do anything to win her heart. But he didn't know how she felt about *him*. Lesley's telegram was ever present in the back of his mind. *Why hasn't she mentioned its arrival, unless it contained something I wouldn't want to know? Do I even have a chance?*

"We couldn't have done it without you, Trevor—and all the other men."

"And the thirty or so other carpenters?"

"Yeah, and them too. Everyone pulled their weight. I think their hard work was their final goodbye to John."

Trevor smiled in good humor. "And their hello to his daughters?"

Blake couldn't hold back a hearty laugh. "Absolutely." *As long as they don't have eyes for Belle, I'm happy to share.* "I think you're right about that."

He glanced around, the feel of the evening promising. Maybe the time had finally arrived to make his feelings known. One of them had to take that chance. It was pretty obvious Belle wasn't going to make the first move—and she shouldn't have to. Especially not after the way he'd acted after they'd kissed.

With his free hand, he grasped Trevor by the shoulder. "I'm thankful the conspiracy didn't turn out to be related to one of our men. Dr. Dodge must have read John's will when Henry brought it out to the ranch during the month John was dying." He shook his head. "A terrible thing."

"And you believe the mayor?"

"I do. What the doctor was trying was so far-fetched. Clint's posi-tive he had no knowledge of anything his brother was planning."

"Yeah, I think you're right."

"As strange as this sounds, I'm even glad Praig wasn't involved. As much as I detest the man for quitting and for what he did to Moses, he was once one of us, if you catch my meaning. We were comrades of sorts, at least for a while." He shook his head, letting out a deep sigh. "I'm sure you've heard that Clint received word from Denver. Praig's caused some trouble there and is locked up. As much as I'd like to give him a dose of his own medicine, I guess I won't get that chance."

"Blake. Look!" Trevor said, his voice filled with reverence.

The murmur of voices quieted. The Brinkman girls were descend-ing the stars in a talking, laughing group. They weren't in the least worried about making a grand entrance. Looking up to see all the men watching, they slowed and shyly glanced away. All dressed in varying shades of velvet, they looked a vision.

"Blake," Mavis said, heading his way, followed by the rest. The hands gathered around. The guests would arrive anytime. Practically everyone in Eden had been invited. Blake was surprised Henry hadn't yet arrived. "I speak for my sisters in saying thank you for all you've done on the house—and for indulging us with this party." He was all too aware of Belle's gaze.

To break the spell, Blake gestured to his loyal ranch hands. "Wasn't me, ladies, it was these fine men and the others. They're all happy you gave Eden a chance and stayed on." *And me, especially.*

Somehow, he'd wrangle a few private words with Belle to tell her how beautiful she looked, but that probably wouldn't happen until the dancing began and he had a chance to waltz her around the room. And maybe even out onto the slate patio.

Sounds came from the entry. Henry walked in, along with Elizabeth Smith and Johnny. The woman's eyes widened as she looked around. Behind them came Clint, his son, Cash, and Nicole—wearing a dress, of all things. Maverick entered, hat in hands, helping along Old Man Little. The room was filling. Someone must have driven a large wagon for so many to arrive at once. Or maybe even two.

Karen, and many of the clerks around town hired to help with the food, brought platters of hot, delicious-looking dishes. Soon, the long tablecloth-covered table was packed. Within a few minutes, a line formed, and ladies and gentlemen alike were filling their plates with the luscious concoctions. Guests kept arriving until the diners spilled out onto the patio, and others took their plates into the other rooms to find places to sit. Blake had lost Belle in the sea of people. His face hurt from smiling. Talking. Being congratulated.

As soon as the food is cleared and the music begins, I'll search Belle out.

He needed to feel her in his arms.

CHAPTER FORTY-NINE

E ven though Belle had talked until her throat felt hoarse, smiled until her cheeks hurt, and laughed until she cried, she felt empty, though she knew she shouldn't. This was *their* night. A time to celebrate. She'd just barely had a chance to say two words to Blake before everyone had descended. Now the quartet was warming up, and the ladies were taking their turns in the lovely outdoor area that had been set up for the women. At the end of a lantern-lighted path was a blanketed-off area that held an outhouse, a washstand, a large mirror hanging from a tree branch, a multitude of lights, and hairpins and combs.

Finished with freshening up, and making her way back down the path, Belle was relieved to see her sisters gathered close by. Katie was all smiles, Lavinia flush with happiness, Emma tapping her toe in anticipation of the dancing to come, and Mavis glancing around as if looking for a special someone. Belle couldn't imagine who.

"Belle, there you are," Emma gushed. "Isn't it wonderful? So many people. The night couldn't be better."

Belle returned her smile, but noticed from the corner of her eye that Blake stood a few steps away, speaking with Clint. "Very. The place is packed, and some guests have even gone down to tour the barn. That was a good idea." She gauged the dance floor. "I hope there will be ample room for dancing."

The musicians, tapping out a rhythm, began. Music lilted through the room. A hush fell, and all attention shifted to the quartet. Butterflies fluttered in Belle's stomach. *Will Blake ask me to dance?*

He'd let her know in no uncertain terms that there was nothing between them and the kiss was a silly mistake, a challenge answered.

Feeling self-conscious over what her sisters had said about Blake and her, she hadn't sought him out. She'd only seen glimpses of him from afar, among the crowd. *What would it feel like to be back in his arms?* Suddenly she wanted to be there—right now. So many emotions rushed to the surface at once that she failed to notice he'd already walked over and was standing by her side until he touched her arm.

She turned.

He smiled, his gaze reaching deep into her soul. Her heart trembled. "Miss Brinkman, may I have the honor of the first dance?"

Mavis was right. Lavinia and Emma too. He'd never looked as gorgeous as he did just then. Heat rushed to her face when he smiled, and she feared he'd know her thoughts. She'd never seen the set of tailored clothes that fit him like a glove. Everything about him awakened her senses, causing her breath to quicken. Mavis's smile was the last thing she saw before setting her hand in his outstretched one and struggling to answer. "Thank you, Mr. Harding," she replied, playing along. "I'd be delighted." They waltzed away, joining a few other couples. The cool night air, flowing through the open walls, felt good on her heated skin.

He gazed down into her eyes. "You look beautiful tonight."

"Thank you." *What's wrong with me? Surely I can think of something better to say.*

The feel of his hand on her back had her heart racing.

"Having fun?" he asked. "This is the first time we've had a chance to speak all night. I thought maybe you've been avoiding me."

She chanced a glance into his eyes, causing a ripple of new tingles. "I-I thought the same of you."

His eyes warmed. "I'd never sidestep you. You know that. Just busy answering questions and such. I didn't think so many people would make the trip out. It's gratifying, to say the least. They loved John, and already love you—*all*," he added quickly.

She hid a smile. They waltzed past Henry, who had Elizabeth in his arms. Looking around, she spotted Emma keeping Johnny entertained while his mother danced. "What do you think is going on with Henry and Elizabeth?"

"I'm sure I don't know. I've asked, but he's not saying. I guess he's not one to kiss and tell."

One song led to another, but Blake never gave her a chance to leave his side. She stayed in his arms dance after dance, and her heart soared with the eagles. She'd never felt such happiness. Or more beautiful, or cherished. One minute, Blake was gazing into her eyes, almost making her swoon, and the next he was making her laugh. She wished the night would never end. Then the music slowed, and the melody became soft and romantic. Blake tightened his hold, drawing her closer. Belle dared to lay her head on his shoulder and dream of lying in his arms all night. Dream of him trailing kisses down her neck . . .

With a small jerk in her breathing, she lifted her head.

He looked down, the handsome smile still on his attractive lips. "You okay?"

Not trusting her shaky voice, she held her breath and nodded.

Since when has just speaking with Blake caused this trembling? She'd ranched with him, for heaven's sake. *And kissed him too. Is that caress on the back of my hand intentional?*

"Belle," he began, his tone concerned, "would you like to rest? You're trembling."

"I, um . . . yes. I think that would be best."

The song was just ending, so Blake led her through the crowd and out the patio door. A few people sat in conversation, but no one was interested in talking to them.

"Have you gotten used to it yet?" he asked, his deep voice low.

"To . . . ?"

"The Colorado sky. It never gets boring. There's the Great Bear, Ursa Major, right there, low in the sky. Can you see it?"

Stepping close behind her, with his arm covering hers, Blake took her hand and extended her pointer finger slowly tracing the constellation. The rough warmth of his palm was all she could think about. And how close he stood, wrapping her in his protection, the side of his face pressed against hers.

"I thought that was the Big Dipper," she was finally able to say.

"You're partly right," he whispered, his breath warming the side of her face. "The handle of the dipper is the great bear's tail. The cup his flank. He has a head and four legs."

They stood like that much longer than they should. Surely somebody would take notice. When she hoped he was going to turn her in his arms and kiss her, he stepped back and led her to a bench.

"Sit here and wait for me. I'm going to fetch your shawl. Then we can take a walk in the starlight."

"But the guests?"

"Are having a great time. They won't miss us for a few minutes. Is it in your room?"

"Yes, on the dresser."

The lantern light made it possible to see his nod.

"Don't go away. I'll be right back."

Blake stepped inside and headed for the stairs. All he could think about was the feel of Belle in his arms. *And she was flustered.* His heart had been racing too. He'd wanted desperately to kiss her, but not where anyone would see.

Almost to the stairs, Trevor grasped his arm. "Where's the fire?" He held up his beer as if in a toast and grinned.

"Just making my rounds," Blake fibbed, glancing around the room. "You having a good time?"

"What do you think? This house is grand. And the scenery is pretty too."

Katie and Emma were speaking and laughing, with Tank and KT only a few feet away. One of the other carpenters who'd helped build the house was dancing with Lavinia. Few would forget this evening soon.

Trevor looked around as well. "Where's Belle? You two've been on the dance floor all night." He wiggled his eyebrows. "So . . . ?"

"So nothing," Blake replied. He needed to gracefully extract himself from Trevor and get up the stairs. He didn't want Belle to cool off too long. She was feeling what he was feeling, he was sure. *We're meant to be together. Making her forget about Lesley might take a bit of doing, but tonight was a perfect place to begin.*

Almost to the stairs, he heard Mavis call his name. He liked Mavis. Had a great respect for her, but right now he didn't want to talk, not even with her. He turned.

"Mavis." He tried not to sound rushed. "Having fun?" He was sounding like a one-phrase parrot.

"Of course."

In his urgency, he couldn't stop a longing glance up the stairs.

"She's not up there," Mavis said with a small laugh. "You two looked perfect dancing together."

That got his attention. "Thank you. I thought we might."

Her smile faded, and she looked away, causing a prick of concern.

"What? Do you have something to say?" He thought of the telegram.

"Be careful. I don't want to see you get hurt."

It was as if she'd slapped him across the face. All his breath pushed painfully in his lungs. "Has she said as much?"

"Not in so many words."

"I see." He couldn't even pretend to be happy. "I have to go."

With tunnel vision, he climbed the stairs, found her shawl, and hurried back to the bench on the outskirts of the patio, determined that Mavis must be wrong. Belle had responded to his touch, his gaze. She wielded a power over him he'd never before felt.

Still in the shadows, he skidded to a halt. Right there in front of his eyes, Lesley Atkins knelt before Belle on bended knee. Her hand was encased in his. It wasn't difficult to figure out that he was proposing. Belle gazed down at him, a rapt expression on her face.

I've been such a fool! Against my better judgment, I let my feelings run away with me. Now, if she stays in Eden after they marry, I'll have to work side by side with the woman I love but who doesn't love me. Can there be a hotter hell than that?

He'd just begun to turn when he stopped, as if by a hand to his arm.

She doesn't know you love her. You're giving up without a fight. That's not the man I raised. Blake glanced around, stunned.

Go fight for what you want.

Was this just his wishful thinking? By now, she would have already said yes. He couldn't hear the conversation, but Lesley was still on his knee.

I'll never know, and I'll always regret, he said to himself. *That is a hotter hell then the first!*

He strode forward. "You're in my spot, Atkins. Move aside."

Belle bolted to her feet, and Lesley scrambled up. Blake ignored the man and took Belle's trembling hand, unable to miss seeing the huge diamond ring Atkins clenched in his fingers. He swallowed hard, hoping he wasn't too late.

"Go away, Harding," Lesley barked. "This doesn't concern you. Do you have any brains at all?"

"Not many, but enough to know you could never love Belle the way I do. You could never make her as happy as I will. I may be a rancher without a college education, but Belle will *always* know how much she's loved."

He hadn't taken his gaze from hers since he'd picked up her hand. She was silent, and he prayed she wasn't about to break his heart. He lifted her hand to his lips and kissed the backs of her fingers. "I love you, Belle. Will you be my wife? At the moment, I don't have a ring or a head full of fancy words, but I do have a heart full of love. That'll never change, not even when I die."

He swallowed, bracing himself for the worst.

She doesn't want to hurt me, so doesn't know what to say. Dear God in heaven, Belle. Say something!

"Y-yes. I'll marry you."

Lesley crowded in, thinking she was speaking to him.

Blake knew different. Her gaze hadn't left his since he'd shown up. He swept her into his arms and twirled her around. Finding her lips, they kissed. His world came together in an earth-shattering burst of love. Such happiness was once in a lifetime!

"Belle!" Lesley screeched. He grabbed Blake's arm and tried to pull it away. "I've been patient. It's time you grew up and stopped acting like an imbecile. You were promised to *me*."

Blake halted and lowered Belle to the ground. They both stared at Lesley.

"Promised?" she said, confused.

The man straightened up, anger burning deep in his eyes. "I should have known better than to trust Velma Crowdaire. I wouldn't have spent a year on you, but her husband owed me gambling debts. You were their means of payment. A pretty wife whose monthly allowance would be mine—and then her inheritance too. I have no desire to own a ranch, and stay connected with your family, but fifteen thousand dollars would set us up for life, above and beyond what I already have." His eyes gleamed with desire. "Think of it. I never planned to let you stay two months, let alone six . . ."

Under his arm, Belle trembled. Blake's anger grew. *How could Atkins hurt her like that?*

"Don't listen to him, Belle. All he has are words. And words can't hurt you unless you let them. Who cares what his pathetic motives were." In a swift move, he grasped Lesley's shirtfront and pulled him close. "You're lucky I'm in a good mood tonight, Atkins. Get yourself off this ranch and out of town by tomorrow. I don't care where you go or how you do it. If not, all those mean words you just said are going to get crammed back down your throat so far you'll turn inside out. And I'll enjoy doing it. Do I make myself clear?" Blake shoved him away. "Now get! And don't set foot in Eden again."

"I won't go! Crowdaire owes me thousands. Harding, you don't—"

Blake landed a punch that sent him reeling backward. He hit the bench and fell to the ground. It was a moment before he climbed to his feet, one hand covering his bloodied mouth.

"Get the cotton out of your ears, Atkins. I gave you fair warning. That's how things are done around here."

Blake held Belle until he was sure Atkins was good and gone. "I hope you won't let that skunk ruin our night." He lifted her back into his arms and twirled her once more, her lips too tempting not to take another kiss.

"I love you so much, Blake," she whispered against his mouth as they turned slowly under the stars. "I don't care about Lesley. This giddy happiness feels so good. I'll never stop loving you, taking care of you, needing you. You're my everything. I'm going to cry . . ."

A sound made Blake glance over his shoulder to see Belle's sisters standing close, as well as Henry. Their eyes were shining with as much happiness as he felt in his heart.

"She said yes, everybody!" Blake called. "Imagine that." He stole one more kiss before setting his wife to be on her feet. "You've made me the happiest man in Colorado, Miss Brinkman. I hope you know that."

"I do," she whispered up into his face. "And I will."

CHAPTER FIFTY

H enry glanced at his calendar, marveling that Halloween was just two weeks away. He shuffled his papers together, put them neatly into the top drawer of his desk, and stood. He had a lunch appointment with Elizabeth. She'd been patient, but now he had a few answers for her. Taking his hat off the rack, he stepped outside to a clear, semi-sunny day. He was halfway down the stairs when Blake and Belle came galloping down the road at full tilt.

Blake saw him first and pulled up. Belle followed suit, having taken to a Western saddle like a drunk to whiskey.

Henry backtracked several steps to avoid the billowing cloud of dust they'd created. "You know better than that, Blake! I'm surprised at you," he chastised. "You could run someone over." Still, he couldn't stop a wide grin. *The two look so cute together now that they've finally stopped pretending they aren't head over heels for each other.* He glanced at Belle. "How do you like him?" he asked when Belle reached down to stroke Strider's neck. John's black gelding had never looked better.

She grinned at Blake, certainly unaware she had a streak of dirt across her cheek. "We're good friends already. He can run like the wind."

Henry narrowed his eyes at Blake. "You better not get her hurt."

Blake shrugged. "You try and stop her. It's a war all the time, and I've already lost. What will she be like *after* we're married?"

Belle laughed, her heart in her eyes. She sidestepped her horse closer to Blake and laid her hand on top of his, which was resting on his saddle horn. "Wouldn't you like to know?" she said in a sultry voice.

Blake actually blushed.

"Where're you off to, Henry?" she asked. "We came into Eden to have lunch at the café and see Lavinia. That sister of mine has jumped right in. She loves spending time there."

"Actually, that's where I'm going as well. I have a lunch appointment with Elizabeth. We have business to discuss."

"That's a likely story," Blake mumbled, then laughed when Belle wiggled her brows at Henry. "You two sure do a lot of 'business' together. I'll ask you again. Is there something we should know?"

If Henry wasn't such a coward, he'd admit to himself he had enjoyed dancing with Elizabeth at the party. She invoked in him something he'd never felt. Since that night, he hadn't been able to keep his mind on his work. He shook his head. "Nope, nothing at all."

"Well, we have several errands to take care of with the rebuilding of the leather shop before we head over. Maybe by the time we get there, you'll be finished talking business and we could join you."

"If we are, you're more than welcome. You know that."

Blake reined Banjo around. "Come on, my bonny Belle," he said good-naturedly, smiling at his wife-to-be. "We have things to accomplish so we can eat with a clear conscience."

Henry watched them ride away with a full heart. Both those young people deserved all the happiness they could find. Arriving at the café, Henry found Elizabeth already there, seated in one of the booths along the wall. He wasn't a man prone to feeling nervous, but he was at the moment.

"Elizabeth." He sat and got comfortable. The smile she gave was one he'd grown used to. One he would miss if she decided to leave.

"Henry."

There's affection in her voice, or is that just wishful thinking?

They made small talk until Karen came out, took their order, and returned with tea for Elizabeth and coffee for him. They couldn't avoid the topic any longer.

"Blake and Belle are in town today and may be in soon," he said quietly. There were a few other diners, and he didn't want to be over-heard. "They'd like to join us if we're through with business by the time they arrive."

The Brinkman sisters had gone out of their way to make Elizabeth welcome in town. And even more, it seemed they were friends. He couldn't imagine how things would play out. It might make this whole paternity business difficult when it came time to break the news.

She set her cup back in its saucer. "I'd like that."

He nodded, fiddling with the fork on the table. "Okay, then we better get talking. I've had a reply from Judge Wesley in Denver. As far as he could, he's corroborated your story about being in Denver at the time you stated by checking the hotel logs. Same with John. The waiter at the place you had supper had a local customer who recognized John Brinkman and a woman who fit your description. I'm prepared to go forward if you're ready to tell the family. I don't know what their reaction will be, but if I had to guess, I'd say they'll believe you and welcome Johnny as their brother. If that's what you want, I'll make an appointment to gather them together."

She stared at her teacup so long, Henry reached out and touched her hand.

She glanced up. "I'm sorry, Henry. I was just thinking."

"It looked like more than that. If you're too nervous to break the news, I'll do it for you. That is, if you still stand by *everything* you've told me."

Strange, it's as if she's avoiding my gaze.

"I can't go through with it. And I don't want you to either."

314

Stunned, Henry sat back as if he'd been shoved.

"I'm confused," he said slowly. "You can't now? Or ever? What's going on?"

Clearly rattled, Elizabeth took a sip of her tea, then resettled her cup in its saucer with a shaky hand. "Ever. I lied. Johnny isn't John Brinkman's son. As much as I wish he were, he's not. The Brinkmans have been so kind to me. Taken me in under their wings. I just can't go through with the deception."

He looked away, flabbergasted. Sometime during the weeks she'd been in town, he'd come to believe Elizabeth's story. As much as he wanted to be angry with her, he found that more than that, he wanted to *understand*.

"All right. How about you tell me what's really going on? Can you do that?"

"I'm not proud of myself, if that's what you're thinking."

"That's not what I'm thinking at all." Maybe he didn't have a right to know, but he felt like he did. He had been prepared to stand behind her and her story.

"I did meet John, just like I said. We had picnics in the park. All that was true. We were attracted to each other, but he was a gentleman. We had dinner, but that was all. I fell in love but knew we didn't have a future."

She looked down at her hands, her lips a tight, white line.

"You don't have to tell me any more."

"I do. You deserve to know. We left Denver that night in a panic because Mrs. Masters thought her husband had been caught in a compromising position, which later was proven false. Back in Virginia, once things were seemingly back to normal, one of Mr. Masters's business associates was over. They'd been drinking. Late that night, he found his way to my bedroom."

Alarmed, he reached over and covered her folded hands with his. "You *don't* have to go on, Elizabeth."

"I want to, Henry." Her voice wobbled. "Telling the story for the first time to someone other than Mrs. Masters feels good. He forced me. When I found myself with child, everything else played out the way I told you. Everything except for the fact I used to pretend in my mind that John *was* Johnny's father. I wished it true with all my heart. Wanting to avoid scandal, Mrs. Masters gave me the funds to move. I chose Denver, because that's where I had good memories. You know the rest, about me seeing the newspaper with John's image. I thought perhaps I could make a better life for Johnny by coming to Eden. We had so little, barely scraping by. I know what I did was wrong in every way. I feel so ashamed. I'm leaving town on Wednesday."

Henry was still trying to digest the turn of events. *Leaving?* "Where will you go?"

"I don't know yet. Anywhere. It doesn't matter. I kept back monies for the stage in case I needed to leave. And thanks to you, I haven't had to spend much. I can never thank you enough for all you've done. You're a special man."

In a daze, Henry felt himself shaking his head. "I haven't done a thing. But I can. I know a lot of people here. Why don't you stay in Eden, where you have friends? I can help you find work and housing." *And more.*

"I can't ask that of you."

"Then do it for Johnny. Don't go off into the unknown again." *Too many men waiting to take advantage.*

She shook her head. "Still, I just don't think I—"

He reached across the table and picked up her hand, intent on changing her mind. "Then stay because *I* want you to, Elizabeth. Right now we're friends, but I'd like there to be more." He held up one hand when she opened her mouth to speak. "You don't have to respond. Just know you'll always have a friend in me, if that's what you want."

Karen approached with their plates, arranged the food, and left. After his emotional speech, Henry had no idea what else to say. He finally dared a look to find her staring at him. He didn't know what to think.

"You're sure?" she whispered.

"With all my heart." Her face fell, and if he didn't take action quickly, he knew she would dissolve into tears. "Belle will be here soon and want to know why you're crying."

Her eyes opened wide. "You're right. We can't have that." Taking her napkin, she blotted the corner of each eye. A pretty smile blossomed. Without the strain of the unknown, she looked like a young girl.

Is Elizabeth my destiny? He didn't know, but looked forward to finding out.

CHAPTER FIFTY-ONE

B elle's hand nestled warmly in Blake's. They walked toward the hotel
in the crisp fall air, ready for a hearty lunch. *What will Eden be
like when it snows?* She could hardly wait to find out. Her mind—free
of the battle of what she should do with her life—felt happy, relaxed,
and in love.

She'd never felt this way with Lesley. Never once in all the times
they'd stepped out. She trusted Blake with her life . . . and more, with
those of her sisters. How wonderful to have such faith in a person.
Thank God I didn't let Mavis talk us out of making the journey to Colorado.
At the thought, she actually shuddered, making Blake glance down.

"You all right?"

The concern in his eyes over her small tremble made her smile. "I
am now."

His brow crinkled. Seemed that was happening a lot these days.
He wasn't used to a woman who teased. Ann had been sincere, calm,
and loving, according to what Blake had shared. Belle found herself so
giddy she wondered how Blake—or her sisters—could stand her. She
hoped that feeling never went away.

Her smile faded. *But it took Father's death to bring this happiness.*
That was the only aspect that pricked her heart. Without him, she'd

never have found Blake, and her future would be so different. *Life is so strange.* She sighed. *There's no explaining it.*

They stopped at the mercantile, where a bright display in the window caught Blake's eye. Facing it, he stepped behind her and wrapped his arms around her waist. He nuzzled her neck.

"Blake!" Chills cascaded deep inside. "Stop this. What will people think?"

"That we're looking at the display, sweetheart." He pulled her more tightly against him, making her breath come fast. "Isn't that the most interesting set of cookware you've ever seen?"

She elbowed him, but that only made him laugh.

"Relax, there's no one around." He nuzzled below the other ear, making her light-headed. "Mmm, you sure smell good. What is that?"

"Sweat."

"Really? That's good. I'll never have to buy you perfume."

"Yes, you will, Blake Harding. You're not getting off that easy."

He laughed and turned her around. "I'm glad you're so spunky. With you, life will never be boring."

They were on their way again.

"I should hope not."

Santiago and his father rode past. She smiled when they dipped their chins.

"What do you think about Santiago?"

"What about Santiago?"

"Surely you kid. He has eyes for Katie. I noticed it the first time they met."

Blake swiveled, glancing back at the riders. "I don't know. They're both young. I'm sure it's not what you think." He pulled her to his side and glanced down at her. "But if it is?"

That was a good question. She liked Santiago, but she couldn't picture Katie married to someone who owned a cantina. Then again, she'd never have pictured Katie owning a lumber mill either. Or herself a tannery. Life was a surprise.

Maybe it's best to let life happen as it will.

Crossing the street, they entered the hotel and stepped into the café.

"There they are." Belle gestured to Henry and Elizabeth sitting in a booth. "Looking like two little lovebirds, if I do say so myself. I wonder why he's being so secretive about his feelings. She's a beautiful woman, and you've seen how he's taken to Johnny. Why, I think he loves that boy as much as she does."

They made their way among the tables. Lavinia came through the kitchen door, a coffeepot in her hand. Her face lit up when she saw them.

"He'll tell us when he's ready," Blake whispered. They arrived at the table. "Did you save room for us, or are these for someone else?" He gestured to the two empty seats.

Elizabeth, her cheeks flush as a summer rose, looked like she had a wonderful secret. She was all smiles, as was Henry.

"Absolutely—for you," Henry stated, a grin chiseled to his face. "Slide in and get comfortable."

When they were seated, Karen came and took their order. As they waited, Belle couldn't keep her curiosity to herself any longer. Since Blake had proposed, there'd been a lingering question in her mind. One that was a bit troubling. She stole a fleeting glance at Blake, hoping the topic wouldn't upset him.

"Henry, I have a thought that keeps pestering me. How will the estate be handled when Blake and I get married? Do our shares go together as a couple, giving us a sixty percent stake? As much as I love Blake, I'd not want to do that to my sisters. I like that we're equal."

With a hearty nod, Henry wiped his mouth with his napkin. "I've been wondering when someone might get around to asking. Nope, everything stays the same. John didn't want to give any one of his children power over the rest. That's why he made the girls one entity at fifty percent and Blake the other. Everything stays the same. He was pretty certain one of his girls would fall in love with Blake, he just didn't know which one it would be."

Belle gasped, and Blake laughed and shook his head.

"You've known all along?" she asked. "You've been watching and hoping?"

Henry nodded. "And waiting! John talked about the possibility all the time, especially in the end. He was sure it would happen." He glanced over at Elizabeth with the most mystifying expression in his eyes. "I'm sure the two of you made him awfully happy the night of the party."

How wonderful. Our union will grant our father's last wish.

Now everything felt completely right. The sting of tears pricked Belle's eyes before she felt the warmth on her cheeks. "Really, Henry! What a blessing. I'm so happy . . ."

"You could cry?" Blake finished for her. He gently rubbed away her tears. "No more crying for you, sweetheart. You'll only shed happy tears from this day forward. You've earned them, and I'm dedicating my life to making sure that happens."

ACKNOWLEDGMENTS

I t's been several years since I've begun a "new" series. I won't mince words. Creating a fresh world filled with engaging characters, an interesting setting, villainous scoundrels, and an overall premise that tightly grips the interest of a reader is challenging. Not something for the faint of heart. Knowing this was my assignment, I tossed around ideas for a time, threw out a few I'd thought were jewels with a huff of disappointment, and ended up with a whole lot of nothing. Then, in a phone conversation with one of my sisters, she suggested I take on a story line with which I have firsthand experience. A handful of sisters! Thus, the Colorado Hearts series was born!

I'd like to thank all the fabulous people around me who helped me complete this first book.

Maria Gomez and Megan Mulder, my editors, and the fabulous support team at Montlake Romance. I feel so privileged to be one of your authors. Working for you over the years has been a joy. To Caitlin Alexander, my developmental editor, for never holding back. You always have the perfect prescription for any and all maladies my manuscript may suffer. Working with you is a delight. To Michael, my wonderful husband of thirty-five years, thank you for your love, support, ideas, help, and good times. I can't imagine this journey without you. My family: Matthew, Adam, Misti, Rachel, Evelyn . . . and new baby-to-be. You fuel my creativeness with your love. You hold me up with your support. You make me happy with your visits. I'm the most blessed wife, mother, and nammy in the world. To my four sisters—Shelly (reading this from heaven), Sherry, Jenny, Mary—and sis-in-law, Lauren, thank you for your part in my life. Being a sister is one of the most magnificent blessings a woman can have. Mary, singling you out for your plot idea—THANK YOU! It was a good one, and oh so fun to write. Thank you to my good friend Kendra Elliot and her husband, Dan Boucher, for the many enjoyable dinners. It's enlightening and fun to talk writing face-to-face. Thank you to my author friends for your friendship, advice, and support—you're as close as a phone call away. And, of course, thank you to my readers. I love and appreciate each and every one of you. Thank you for your continued interest in my books! And to our God! Thank You for all Your blessings. You've given me the most awesome life. I have to pinch myself to know I'm not dreaming.

ABOUT THE AUTHOR

Caroline Fyffe was born in Waco, Texas, the first of many towns she would call home during her father's career with the US Air Force. A horse aficionado from an early age, she earned a bachelor of arts in communications from California State University-Chico before launching what would become a twenty-year career as an equine photographer. She began writing fiction to pass the time during long days in the show arena, channeling her love of horses and the Old West into a series of Western historicals. Her debut novel, *Where the Wind Blows*, won the Romance Writers of America's prestigious Golden Heart Award as well as the Wisconsin RWA's Write Touch Readers' Award. She and her husband have two grown sons and live in the Pacific Northwest. For more information about her novels visit www.carolinefyffe.com.